AF421539

THEY'RE PLAYING OUR SONG

R. S. EGAN

Copyright © 2026 by R. S. Egan

All rights reserved.

Egan Books

Lafayette, Louisiana

www.rsegan.com

Paperback ISBN 979-8-9951787-0-5

Ebook ISBN 979-8-9951787-1-2

Original cover art and design by Annabelle Pavy

"Steal Away Girl" by R. David Egan. ©Jasben Music. Used by permission.

No part of this book may be reproduced in any form or by any electronic or mechanical means, including information storage and retrieval systems, without written permission from the author, except for the use of brief quotations in a book review.

 Formatted with Vellum

For the book boyfriends that get me through so many lonely nights,
and the authors who created them.
Thank you.
For the songwriters and musicians who help us all connect to
ourselves and one another with their work.
Thank you.

CHAPTER ONE

HOLLY

I TRACK the bead of sweat as it wobbles, freckle to freckle, beep bop boop, down the bald slope of the doctor's head. With the rise and fall of our coupling, I misjudge the little salty missile's speed and trajectory, and it drips into my eye before I can turn my face away.

"Ahh," I cry, squinting, shaking my head from side to side, which reads apparently as enthusiastic response, prompting said doctor to himself respond with a quickening of hip thrusts.

Mercifully, he drops his head into my neck, taking me out of the direct line of fire, and I use one hand to wipe at my eye with the pillowcase.

The bed, the room, the whole house, is a neutral, masculine bachelor catalog in shades of navy, grey, and black. All too new. Sparse. A clock on the bedside table would've been nice right about now. A glass of water. He has artwork, at least, some original paintings, the one here in the bedroom by my friend Oona.

Does she know it's here? Has Oona slept with him too? It's a small pool of men after a certain age, after all. Divorced doctor, nice man... *Stop thinking about Oona, for Pete's sake.*

I pat him on the back for encouragement, for lonely hearts solidarity, and close my eyes - well my eye that isn't already squinted closed - taking several deep breaths. *Must focus.*

I pull my heels closer to my hips and work to match his enthusiasm.

"Mmmm..." he murmurs.

"Mmmm..." I murmur.

A sharp sting of the doctor's cologne fills my nose. My husband never wore cologne.

Don't think about Ronnie right now, either. Jesus, Holly! Focus.

Breathing in this new man smell, it isn't unpleasant; I imagine a neat, clear bottle with small black type, lowercase, of course, *inoffensive*, somewhere in his sure to be neat and tidy bathroom. I pin my attention to the scent - *is it grass cuttings?* - and will the smell to keep me in the moment, to keep my mind from all the other thoughts I do not want to have.

Don't cry, don't cry, don't cry, I tell myself. *You can do this.*

Back to the doctor on top of me. I need to move this along.

"Yes, yes," I say, squeezing his butt with each thrust, hoping it does the trick.

How long has he been divorced now? This was our second date and, so far, talk of his ex-wife and my dead husband has been minimal. A year and a half, maybe that's what he said? Not the five years I've been a widow, after the two years of caregiving. I'm sure there have been others for him in that time, reserved as he is, a little rounded in the belly, that it hasn't been hard for him to find a date. Seems to be the way it is for men. It's also different when you fall out of love and are ready to move on instead of still in love with the one who was taken from you.

Until recently we only knew each other from a handful of social interactions; I recall seeing him at a few school functions over the years, saying hello, shaking hands. There was that time he made some funny joke about a kid's artwork we found ourselves standing in front of, considering our bids at a silent auction. I remember thinking he had a nice smile. He made me laugh, that nice man, Dr. Narula.

I had the same thought the night we met as single people out in the world, at my friend Mimi's deviled egg party. I was sitting alone on the brick hearth, plate balanced on my knees, sipping a glass of champagne and wondering how early I could politely excuse myself from the party and head home. I don't receive many invitations these days – so much socializing is about couples, and

I'm no longer part of one - so I wanted to make sure I stayed long enough to get credit for making the effort. Plus, my husband had been fifteen years older, and as we aged together, people seemed to place me more and more within his age bracket. I was in a weird no-man's land, literally, with no real age cohort of singles to easily hang with.

"Do they all think I'm eighty years old or something?" I said on the phone to my best friend Madeline after a wedding reception back in the summer where, as I looked for a place to sit, the only available spot was with a group of much, much older women. Lovely, all of them, but still, the grandma table?

"Does who think what, now?" she said.

"People. Men. That I'm an old lady?"

"Have you been meeting men?" She likes to get right to the point.

"No."

"I was going to say, alert the media."

"I'm just saying, there's no place for me. I thought there would be a lot more time between bride and widow."

"I know honey, I'm sorry."

When I tell her that Doctor Narula got my number from Mimi after the party and called to ask me out, she was emphatic. "Go out with him! Say yes and unless he's completely an ogre, I order you to sleep with him. Shave your legs and go have sex."

"Eww."

"Don't say 'eww.' Is he eighty? Is he Mitch McConnell?"

"That's the bar?"

"Putting this off is making it harder. You can't complain that you're lonely and you don't know what to do about it then not at least say yes when you get an actual invitation. He's not some young guy. It'll take, like, three minutes."

"Oh, god."

"Unless you're planning on celibacy for the rest of your life, humping that pool float forever..."

"I don't hump it! I hug it."

"I know it's scary, but just get it over with. Get the first one out of the way."

Date number one had been dinner. We talked about our children, moving in the typical conversational waltz to our jobs and bits of local news. My hands were shaking so much I tucked them under my thighs for most of the meal, barely able to touch my food. Separate cars, a hug as we parted. Not so horrible. I did not have a stroke, although I cried on the way home. For the millionth time, cried for me and cried for Ronnie, sick with ache from missing him, even now, even when I didn't want to.

"I can't believe you did this to me," I said out loud as I drove home.

The car is where I talk to him the most, Ronnie. I babble as I run errands, spilling out everything that's on my mind, telling him what's going on with our son Luke, all the milestones and triumphs and worries. All the things we would be talking about if he was here.

I called Madeline.

"I'm proud of you - you did it," she tells me.

"I hate this. Is dating now basically just sitting across the table from someone, deciding if and when you're going to sleep with them?"

"Yes. As it has always been and shall always be."

"I don't know. Who wants to take their clothes off in front of a new man at this age? How in the hell do you do it?"

"A lot of people think it's fun," she chuckled. "Plus, if I had your boobs, I'd whip my top off before dessert, if I liked the guy."

Madeline is a committed singleton, with a roster of lovers that should be printed out into the hottest smoke-show of a calendar ever imagined. We met in college, auditioning for a play the first semester of our freshman year. She complimented my eye make-up, and I knew we were meant to be friends. I cackled at one of her bullseye one-liners she thought no one else heard, and she knew we were meant to be friends. From Florida, she had grown up on a citrus farm in the middle of the state and was prone to dress more like a redneck than a debutante, despite all her beauty, or maybe because of it. Every frat boy and basically every professor fell in love with her. It might've made me jealous except for the fact that she never tried to make any of the attention happen, never flaunted anything about herself. Friends for more than thirty years now, teenagers to fully grown, experienced women, we have lived through some shit together.

Wait. I should correct this description of her to be more accurate. She has *grown* into a committed singleton. We both dreamed of finding the one; of trips together with our future husbands and having kids that would be friends. Timing, luck, whatever it is, fate can be fickle and random and heartless. She says she's made peace with it although I'm not sure I buy it. In the years since Ronnie died, as I learned to make every decision in my life again on my own, without a partner, I've been wondering how she does it. Was she ever exhausted with the endless decisions? Has she been lonelier than she let on? It was shameful to think I hadn't considered this before, for someone I loved so much. I hadn't been in her shoes until now.

"You say that because you're... you. Miss Florida. And I'm more like... well, serving wench. Or lady mud-wrestler."

"If anyone's a lady mud wrestler in this scenario it's me. You have those teeny tiny girlie hands. And any man would be lucky, fall on his knees and thank the lord, halle-fucking-lujah and praise Jesus lucky, to see you naked."

"Well, that's true," I wiped at my nose. "Oh, thank God, you make me laugh."

"Listen to me. There's a lot of beautiful life still ahead for you, but sometimes you have to walk towards it, invite it into your life."

"And invite it into my pants."

"Sometimes, yes."

"I haven't seen a new one in a long time. Like, since the nineties," I sighed.

"There have been no design upgrades," she laughed. "You'll know what to do. Think of it as a present to yourself. Start a new decade by setting your intentions."

"My intentions for dick? I think I'd rather get a massage and a bottle of champagne."

"Yes, all that and lots and lots of dick."

DATE NUMBER two with the doctor started with the symphony in Lafayette. I told him I couldn't make dinner before because, frankly, I couldn't imagine coming up with anything else we could talk about for another hour unless I really, really wanted to learn more about hip replacement surgery, and also, I had a plan best implemented without a full stomach, and without having to stare at him over a table, looking him in the eye and losing my nerve.

The music was relaxing, as was the half an edible I popped in the ladies' room before the program started. Back at his place he invited me inside for wine, and after sitting close together on the sofa, he leaned over and kissed me.

The first kiss from a new man since I was twenty-five years old.

Stunning, really, now that it's happened. Lips pressed to lips, so quietly, and the roller coaster that's been my life over the past seven years crests another major peak and I'm careening again into new territory. Farther away from Ronnie.

Don't think of Ronnie right now. Suck it up, Holly. Well, don't suck anything, let's keep this simple, but you know what to do. Stop thinking.

I leaned away from him, took a deep breath, and blurted out, "Would you like to have sex with me, Doctor Narula?"

One might say, perhaps unkindly but nonetheless accurately, I barked out the words in a near shout. In my defense, I did add, in a much less poltergeist-y, drill-sergeant-y voice, "Please."

He stared at me, eyes wide and unblinking.

Had he lost consciousness, with his eyes open? If I poked him, would he fall straight over? Maybe he's calculating in his head the distance between us and the sharp knives in his kitchen.

I took a sip of wine, willing my hand not to shake, hoping to project an air of insouciance. I am cool. I am worldly. I'm a French film star.

Credit to his gender, he finally, calmly replied, "You should call me Amir."

And now, after assurances that no, I was not too intoxicated to know what I was asking, and yes, this was what I wanted, and again, yes, I consent, please just do the merciful thing and take pity on me with your penis, here I am having sex with Doctor Narula.

I have to stop calling him that. I know it's weird; he's not my doctor, he's just a dad from school, Amir. His name is Amir and he's inside me right now. The first man after my husband. The first man in seven years. Surely a first name basis situation.

Imagining how I'm going to tell Madeline about it all, I unintentionally mumble "Doctor Narula" out loud. He laughs and rises onto one arm. I hope he won't hold all this against me later or take it personally, because I already know I'm not going to see him again, will have to avoid him now for the rest of my life.

He looks at me, a question on his face.

"What is it?" I ask. He bobs his head twice, in a *come on, you know* kind of way.

Oh my god, what does he want me to do? I panic, until it dawns on me. Ha-ha, funny guy.

"Amir," I say.

"Thank you," he smiles, and goes back to the task at hand.

The condom almost ended this whole thing before it even started, a detail I hadn't thought about, hadn't had to think about in a long time. So foolish. But after kissing a little more in his bedroom, we each undressed, matter-of-factly, certainly not sexily - the words *doctor's office* flashing on and off in my head. I turned back the blankets and climbed in while he opened the top drawer of the bedside table and, angled away from me, his more-hair-than-on-his-head bare bottom my full view, opened the wrapper and rolled the condom onto himself.

The sound – the foil tearing and the lisping slide of it across his skin (*has THAT ever been anyone's ASMR??*) – listening to him prepare himself, like I was about to be worked on or examined, like something was about to be *done to me*, nearly caused me to leap, screaming out of the bed.

The speed of his thrusting increases, I can hear the squish, squish, squish of the condom and I desperately wish for some music to mask the sound. To not be here, to not have this be my life, in this perfectly nice house, in this nice bed, with this perfectly nice man.

I want *my* life, my old life, back.

He shudders and collapses, sweat dripping, onto my torso. I burst into tears.

CHAPTER TWO

I'm so tired of crying.

You'd think I'd have more control over it by now, but it's like there's a string on my back and anyone, anything, can pull it and surprise, there goes the waterworks. Sometimes a lot, sometimes a little, but they keep coming. And I don't want them.

There should be a special eye cream, extra soothing, for all this crying. Dolly Parton should bring it to your door. "Here, sugar, hush those tears now, you're gonna be okay," she'd say, and hug you. Tell you a dirty joke to make you laugh.

Tonight, this ambush of tears make sense, though they sure add an extra layer of awkwardness to the situation. Dr. Narula - I think we can forget about Amir - is catching his breath while I'm staring at his ceiling, weeping.

"Can I get you anything?" he asks.

"No thank you," I sniffle. "That was great." I slide off his bed, dragging the duvet with me, swipe up my things from the floor and struggle into the bathroom. After some time, he knocks on the door.

"Be right out," I say, making my voice sound what I hope is chipper and sane, and not, *let me just finish looking for any valuables in here.* When I do emerge, the bedroom is empty. I make my way to the front of his house and he's in the kitchen, fully dressed, with all the lights on. This nice man is dying for me to get out.

"Something happened to your eye," he says, not stepping close to get a look.

Ignoring this, I say something about the symphony, and his

lovely house, and he says something about seeing me around town sometime. Stilted and awful and I wish the overhead lights weren't so bright. Each of us wants this to be over.

"My car will be pulling up any second," I say.

For some reason he gives me a granola bar and a bottle of water, and I shake his hand. Then I'm out on the sidewalk, standing in the dark, his door closed firmly behind me. I hear the lock turn, the latch clicking emphatically. Aggressively, even.

I mean, really, that's not necessary.

I picture the doctor with his back pressed against the door, wishing he had asked me to sign some sort of release form. Pulling my glasses from my bag I see the car isn't set to arrive for another eight minutes, so, what the hell, I open the granola bar. There's a missed call and message from Mike, the studio manager, but I don't listen to it. It's late, I'll call him tomorrow.

The ride out to my place is far, and I swing from crying to laughing, a lunatic metronome, playing back the night in my head. The driver, Marcy, is worried I'm going to throw up in her car. "It's a hundred fifty extra, so you better have me pull over if you need to."

"That won't happen," I assure her. "I wish I'd had that much to drink."

She rolls down all the windows, turns up the music, an old school country station, and we roll through the night with the wind and road roaring through the car. When we get to my property, I direct her hard to the right, through the sprawling oaks dripping with Spanish moss, down the long driveway to my house. It's very dark out here at night, away from town.

"This could make a gal nervous," she chuckles, eyeing me in the rear-view mirror. When she comes to a stop at my front porch, she turns to the backseat before I climb out.

"Isn't there a recording studio out here somewhere?"

I tilt my head left. "Over there, other side of the property. Riverside Studio."

"Pretty in the middle of nowhere for that sort of thing, ain't it?"

"Yep, no distractions. People seem to like it."

She nods, studying me. "Honey, it's none of my business, but I hope this ain't all over some man, that some man ain't treated you right, makin' you cry like this. You don't have to put up with that. Life's too short."

"That's the truth," I agree.

"Don't ever let a man put you down or set you back," she says, emphasizing her point with quick chops of her hand on the seat, big silver rings on every finger. "I had to learn that the hard way. But you know what I say now? I say, if you don't have a man to be sweet to you, just go be sweet to yourself."

I don't have the heart to tell her I had the best man. Until I didn't. That it might've all been a lie. I don't tell her because I haven't said it to anyone. Not even Madeline.

"Thanks, that's good advice."

In my house, my reflection in the mirror by the front door gives me a great guffaw of laughter. The streaked mascara; one angry, bloodshot eye; my hair standing on end, a tangled mess courtesy of the windows-down car ride. No wonder she had to say something.

In the shower I scrub my skin to a bright pink and comb conditioner through my knotted hair before standing, shoulders curved, under the hot water. Those stages of grief, seems like I found a heretofore underreported one best described as lonely women/one-night stands and the doctors who should be afraid of them. I don't know what I was thinking, what sleeping with this man was going to do for me. Take charge of my destiny? Prove something? Hurt Ronnie?

I slip on a caftan and pad through the house to the kitchen. The clock on the stove reads eleven fifty-three. Seven minutes until my birthday. I turn on the range hood light and grab the notebook on the counter – my love songs notebook - and write down the George Strait song that played in the car, before I forget. "You Look So Good In Love."

"Not tonight, George," I snort, grabbing a bottle of champagne out of the refrigerator, then spend several minutes looking for my phone before finding it exactly where logic should immediately have led me, on the table by the front door. I also fish in my purse for my tin of Altoids, to pop the second half of that edible. Why the hell not?

Out by the pool I pull up a playlist, the one named EVERYTHING RONNIE HATES, and hit shuffle, dropping my phone onto a chaise. It links with the outdoor speakers and REO Speedwagon blasts away.

The playlist started as a running joke between us after one typical, hyperbolic rant at a party about how much he hated Jimmy Buffett before launching into an elaborate argument about how the Eagles ruined radio. Ronnie was a sweetheart, a big friendly bear of a man. Gentle and very funny – gifted with wit, but also a healthy dose of bombast. He could really get his dander up. Most especially when it came to music. Politics and music. Lord, he had a whole thing about "The Star-Spangled Banner." He'd yell at singers on the television, "Just sing the goddamn melody!"

My tastes are a lot more, he would say, common, I would say eclectic, but after a while, a lot of stuff made the list that he really didn't hate – only make him roll his eyes and kiss me. Like, *okay, settle down there. I get the picture.* It made him laugh. I loved to make him laugh.

I open the champagne, strip off the caftan, and walk to the edge of the pool. Taking a swig, I grab Eric, my big white swan pool float, and drag him to the ladder. In a move I invented and perfected since Luke went off to college and it occurred to me I could do anything I wanted, basically, at any time, in my now empty house, I throw one leg across the swan and push off from the side, all in one, sort of smooth, move.

"Happy birthday to me," I raise the bottle to the night sky.

After a few songs I turn onto my back, drifting and drinking, the house dark, the underwater pool lights shimmering. It's peaceful. I can think out here. The stars are out, and I like the way the hot night air feels on my skin. The night blurs around the edges until "The Wreck of the Edmund Fitzgerald" comes on and it, you know, wrecks me. I sing and chug champagne, a drunken sailor adrift on the keening of the melody, my playlist massaging every lingering bruise in my apparently still fragile little soul.

"Fuck you, Ronnie," I whisper. Drunk now, head fuzzy, I'm so mad at him. So mad. And there they are, the tears.

I shake them off, flipping again on the float, nearly toppling over but staying upright – I am a professional - and with a grip on the bottle, I squeeze my arms and legs tight around Eric's neck, bobbing up and down in the water.

I know I'm lonely. Madeline, as usual, got that right. I'm really, really lonely. It caught up to me. It was easy to run from it in the years after Ronnie died, putting my focus on Luke, our wiped-out-by-a-health-crisis-atomic-bomb finances, the studio, the hurricane that put the studio out of business for a year, keeping my own business afloat - anything and everything else. Exhaustion from simply trying to survive kept me occupied. But now that I've made my way through so much of that, or at least wrestled it down to a level or two below panic, and with the past few weeks alone since Luke went back to school, I finally felt it. Let myself start to face it, anyway.

I'm lonely. So goddamned lonely.

"And fuck me, too," I toast myself, because after tonight, I don't see how the hell I'm going to ever try that again. What a fiasco.

I need to get out of this pool while I can still move my limbs, but I stay, holding onto Eric, lulled by the hypnotic lapping of the water, my face pressed into his vinyl neck.

It's the song "Emotions" that revives me and I shout a thank you to the music shuffle goddesses and the one and only MC. I sing at the top of my lungs, laughing, finally laughing, swigging more champagne and bouncing on Eric like a bronco.

Which is why I don't hear the latch open on the gate to the wood privacy fence at the corner of the house or see the man in black clothing advancing through the darkness, until I twist on the swan and he's standing right at the edge of the pool.

I blink, slack jawed, for the count of three while Mariah hits the high notes, then scream bloody murder.

CHAPTER THREE

HOLLY

"GET OUT, GET OUT, GET OUT!"

I kick furiously, beating at the water to back myself as far to the other side of the pool as possible. "Jessie's Girl" comes up on the playlist, the guitar intro and low register suddenly, weirdly menacing.

"Get out!" I scream again, "I have a gun!"

The man is mouthing words I can't hear over the music and my screams, his arms reaching out over the water. In my complete terror, when the float hits the opposite pool wall, I twist, thinking I can leap off and run (like a magic gymnast?) but I lose my balance, the float flipping me over like a kayak in a class five rapid. My grip on the champagne never fails me, however, and the bottle slams against the wall as I flail, breaking off the bottom half of the glass. I hit my head too, the pain a thunderclap to my skull, and I find myself under the water, under the float, disoriented.

My knees touch the bottom of the pool, the pain in my head the center of all my awareness. Then this man is in the water grabbing for me. My instincts are immediate. I kick and swing wildly, screaming underwater, lungs burning, and ribbons of blood appear in the water.

I'm gonna kill this mother fucker.

A strong hand squeezes my forearm. I try to pull away, my hand with the bottle raised over my head, when the broken glass punctures Eric and he melts into the water on top of me. My face breaks the surface, the float lifting with me, and I gasp for air.

"Drop the glass!" the man barks, his knees churning into my

back as he rises behind me. He reaches across my chest to flip the float out of the way and clamp down on my wrist, and I release the bottle. I'm manhandled, dragged across the pool, sputtering and shrieking.

"No! Let me go!" I shout, thinking of Luke. I'm not going to let this happen to him.

But the man's arm is locked across my chest, one hand gripped on my boob like it's a luggage handle, hauling us through the water to the ladder. My head is throbbing, my heart hammering out of my chest, my mind racing to think of what might be on the patio I can use as a weapon. I tear at his shirt and sink my teeth into his shoulder.

"Stop! Holly, listen to me, stop!" He pivots, pinning me between the ladder and the side of the pool. The sound of my name reaches some still functioning part of my brain, and I freeze. We're both panting.

"Holly," he says again. "I'm Adam, I'm here for the studio. I'm Adam."

Adam. What should that mean to me?

"Adam?" I repeat.

The words, the logic or meaning I'm supposed to make of them, are all too blurry. His body though - that is coming through loud and clear. The rough feel of his jeans, his knee braced between my thighs, the palm of his hand flat against my sternum. He's holding me upright and when I clasp his arm he braces as if I might bite him again. We stay like that, pressed together, eyes locked, letting our adrenaline calm down.

"Are you able to get out?"

I nod, and he places my hand on the ladder before climbing out and turning back to me. As I rise, he grips one hand firmly into my armpit, the other taking my hand, never letting go of me until I'm completely out of the pool. Hand still in his, he walks me to a chair, grabbing a towel and wrapping it around me. I sit and he kneels in front of me.

The playlist goes to Echo & the Bunnymen. He spots my phone on the chair beside me and reaches for it.

"May I?" he asks, stopping the music before I respond. "I'm sorry I scared you. God, no wonder, coming out of the dark like that. Mike was supposed to call you."

"Oh," is all I say, as if I understand.

"He said it was alright if I came tonight, he'd tell you to expect me. Everything was dark out front, no one answered the door, but then I heard the music, voices, in the back."

"Adam? With the band?" In my head, lurking somewhere important information is stored, a light is flashing, a signal for something I should find important here, but it's like trying to read without glasses. I can't make it out.

He studies me, pushing his wet hair back from his forehead. "You hit your head. I thought you might have knocked yourself out."

"I think I'm good," I say, reaching to feel the back of my head, wincing when my fingers meet the large lump. "My head's not so hot though."

He smiles indulgently. "Do you mind if I check?"

After I give permission, he leans forward and reaches into my hair to match his fingers to mine, gently prodding my scalp. His face is close, and I watch his eyes focus above my head in concentration, then let my gaze trace the lines that curve parenthetically around his wide mouth, lips set tightly together. I scan down the rope of muscle in his neck, watch as he swallows. He rocks back onto his heels, placing his hands on my knees.

"I don't think you have a cut, but you might have a concussion."

That's when I notice the cut across his forearm and the open, bloody gash in his tee shirt, right above his heart. The sight punches through my haze. I gasp. "You're bleeding, you're really bleeding! I could have killed you!"

"Come on now," he scoffs, "There's no way the last thing I

hear on this earth would be Rick Springfield." He looks down at his chest, then his arm, eyes widening. "Well, damn, you did get me, didn't you?" He flinches as he stands, pulling the shirt away from his skin.

"Let's go inside," I say, standing. He holds out both arms to catch me from falling. "I'm fine." I swat his hands away as I lean about thirty degrees to the left.

"Just take my hand, and you can lead the way," he insists.

His outstretched hand gives me pause. A strong déjà vu. He waits, watching me, while I try to pin down the familiar feeling flitting through my mind like a moth, tap tapping away at a window. I can't grasp what it is, so I blow air out of my mouth as if I'm indulging his insufferable attitude while he bleeds in front of me. I grab my caftan, take his hand, and lead us through the door and into the kitchen. I turn on a light, squinting at the brightness.

"Oh, your eye is really red," he says.

"I'm aware. Can you pull that over your head, or should I get scissors and cut it off?"

"No more sharp objects for you tonight," he responds dryly, carefully pulling the tee over his head, sucking in air through his teeth.

The cut on his chest is bad. About four inches long, with a jagged crescent shaped flap of skin sliced open. I pull open a drawer and take out a clean kitchen towel, pressing it on top of the bleeding wound. He winces, bringing his hand to cover mine.

"It's going to need stitches. I'm so sorry; I can't believe I did this to you."

"God help whoever tries to come after you," he snorts.

"Can you keep this pressed there like this?" I slide my hand from under his, leaving him to hold the towel in place, and slip my caftan down over my head, letting the large pool towel wrapped around me fall away from my body. "This is not going to feel great," I warn. "Raise your arms."

Once I pass the pool towel behind his back he understands

and lifts his elbows away from his torso. I bring the ends together in front of his chest, across the smaller towel over his wound, knotting it tightly to keep the pressure. He makes a grunt of pain.

"I'm sorry, I'm sorry, I'm sorry," I push the words out in a rush.

"I'm okay, good job. I can tell you're a mom."

"Why do you say that?" I frown, pulling another kitchen towel from the drawer and wrapping it around the cut on his forearm, the one dripping blood onto the floor. This man gets a look at me naked, and his first thought is mom? Fucking hell. Champagne and a little THC might dull my reflexes and my rational mind but not my nearest and dearest negative intrusive thoughts.

"Because you went into full mom mode. Drunk, wet, knocked on the head by a murderer…"

"Ah, so you are here to kill me."

He ignores this with a smirk. Or a scowl. He has a scowly face, I'm seeing now. He could be a murderer. A very good-looking murderer. I'm seeing that now too.

"And still, you went right into action. It's a beautiful thing."

"You think you can drive?" I ask, "Or should I call an Uber?"

"I can drive but you're coming with me," he says, digging in the front pocket of his still soaking wet jeans for his keys.

WITH A HOODIE from Luke's room for Adam, my purse, and dry towels from the laundry room because he insists, we climb into his swanky black SUV. After, of course, we cover the leather seats with the towels, because someone is particular about his car, stab wounds or no.

"If you're going to be sick, let me know," he says.

"I know, I know, a hundred and fifty extra. It's not gonna happen. Everyone needs to relax," I tell him, head listing heavily as I buckle my seatbelt. I'm rewarded with that scowl again. That sexy scowl.

"That does not have the effect you think it does," I say, a little slurred, and he tilts his head quizzically. "Never mind."

We get to the road at the end of the driveway and after giving him directions to the walk-in clinic, the commotion of the crisis behind us, we fall into silence. Headlights cut across the blacktop, tracing the steep shoulder that falls away to the drainage coulees lining the sugar cane fields. The cane is nearly at its highest, soon to be harvested, the narrow road tunneling through dark shifting walls of stalks swaying shoulder to shoulder.

With the late hour, the events of the night - *all* the events of my night - and the hushed interior of the car, I'm overcome with sleepiness and close my eyes, letting my head rest on the window.

"Holly." I hear from afar. "Holly... I think you should stay awake."

I stay as I am, eyes closed, holding on to the sleep.

"You should stay awake. You might have a concussion."

I don't respond. Maybe he'll leave me alone. But then comes the hand, firm on my upper arm. "Holly, come on."

"You know they found out that's not true," I murmur, unmoved, desperate to keep my eyes closed.

"What's not true?"

"You don't have to keep people awake with a concussion. You can let them sleep. Sleep is what the brain needs. Concussed people and drunk people. High people. Need sleep."

He laughs, a low rumble from his chest like the wheels of the car on this country blacktop. "Maybe the man with the open wounds, the bleeding man driving the car, would appreciate an awake person next to him."

Oh alright, if you have to put it that way, is my exact petulant body language as I turn in my seat towards him. His hand, the one on my arm, slides across my shoulder, his fingers curving around the base of my head.

"Thank you," he says, with a soft massage of my neck, his eyes looking straight into mine before he turns his attention back to the road.

My response is automatic, outside of thought. As if it was the most natural thing in the world, I turn my cheek into the warm palm of his hand. My voice is a caress. My voice is smiling. "I'm right here, Adam."

Then I can't help it, my eyes drop closed once again. And he lets me sleep.

CHAPTER FOUR

HOLLY

IN THE CLINIC's empty waiting area my body feels about five feet ahead of my brain; I'm straining to catch up with myself and bring the world into focus. When I woke up in the car, I needed a minute to understand the situation, the oddly intimate feeling as confusing as the drowsiness. All very awkward.

And now, Adam, bandaged in towels, wet jeans, hoodie unzipped, sits across from me filling out a form on a clipboard. Mine is in my lap, ignored. I'm too aware of my nakedness under this thin cotton, the places where it's sticking to my body. The cowboy boots I randomly pulled on over my bare feet, my wet hair, the sunglasses I'm wearing, fished out of my purse as we sat down because of the harsh lighting. I can't help myself. We look ridiculous, and I laugh.

"Look at us, we look like a country song."

We size up the state of one another, smirking at our mutual conditions. "Next time I'll know to knock real loud," he quips, raising his towel wrapped forearm aloft as exhibit A.

"I'm so sorry," I say, shaking my head.

"At least you didn't actually have a gun."

"Where would it have been?"

We laugh, and he brings a hand to his chest wound, wincing. But I swear I can see him conjuring an image of me in his mind; he's not trying to hide it, not one little bit. Maybe he thinks I can't see through my sunglasses, but something playful dances in his eyes and instead of looking away, with some good sense of modesty or mortification, I let him show me just what he's seeing, and enjoying, making no move to avert my gaze. Warmth blooms under my skin and my nipples harden against the damp fabric of my caftan. Blame it on the champagne. Or the knock on the head. I shift in my chair and shiver, crossing my arms over my chest.

"Come on, give it to me, at least I still have all ten fingers." He reaches a hand across to me and I pass my clipboard to him. He asks me for the usual information as he fills out my form.

"Date of birth?" he asks. When I don't answer, he repeats the question, tapping the pen on top of the clipboard officiously.

"Today," I admit.

"Your birthday is today?"

I nod.

"Today?"

"Every year."

"Speaking of year..." he says, and I glare over the top of my sunglasses. "Want me to guess?"

"I'm fifty, alright," I say, defiantly. "I'm someone's mom and I'm fifty."

Grinning, he says, "Well, happy birthday, Holly. You threw yourself quite the party."

"You have no idea. And how old are you? Want me to guess?"

"I think I do, yes." He crosses an ankle over one knee, enjoying himself more than a man should, given the situation. I take my time, looking him up and down.

"One hundred and three." This gets a big laugh.

"Ow," he says, clutching his chest again, "You know how to count in musician years."

A door swings open into the waiting area. A nurse, holding the door ajar with her body, looks from me to Adam and shakes her head at the sight of us.

"Alright then, come on," she waves us through, passing silent judgment with one dramatic sigh. A *Lord give me patience* sort of sigh. At her assumption that we're together, I look to him, but he shrugs, standing and reaching down to help me.

"Let's go Bonanza Jelly Bean. Easy does it."

"Who are you talking to old man? I'm fine," I retort, standing, arms out to my sides to test my balance, before I lift the front hem of my caftan as if it's a ballgown and pass through the door with as much dignity as I can muster. The nurse directs us into an exam room.

He follows, mumbling, "Woman, I'm forty-five. Officially a different decade than you."

"What's that saying, it's not the years, it's the mileage?" I climb up on the exam table, booted feet dangling from the side, sunglasses pushed to the top of my head.

He takes a seat in a nearby chair. "You do have some good tread left on the tires there, honey, I'll give you that."

And for the first time in I can't even say how long, a blush rises up my neck and across my face. He has one eyebrow cocked rakishly and, God help me, because I can't help myself, I'm grinning.

The nurse intervenes, pulling a rolling cart into the room with her. "Who's gonna tell me what all this fuss is about tonight?" she asks, stopping in front of me and wrapping a blood pressure cuff around my upper arm.

"I was minding my own business in the pool with Eric..." I begin.

"You Eric?" the nurse asks over her shoulder, but I answer before he can.

"No, Eric is my swan. Was my swan. He..." I nod over at Adam. "He killed him."

"Like a *swan*, swan? You killed a swan? Did it attack you, is that how you got all cut up?"

He shakes his head. "She's talking about her pool float."

"You know, big white swan," I add, as if this should be obvious. "I was in the pool with Eric—"

"—Drunk in the pool," Adam interjects. I purse my lips, giving him a narrow-eyed look. What a total snitch.

"And he," I point, "Came into my backyard, creeping through the dark—"

"—There was no creeping. I was walking."

"I thought he was a murderer! I fell off Eric and the glass broke."

"She hit her head on the side of the pool," he explains, with the nurse looking back and forth between us.

"He jumped in and cut himself on the broken bottle."

"Cut *myself*?" he scoffs, rather ungentlemanly, if I do say so.

She removes the blood pressure cuff and sticks a thermometer in my mouth. Looking in my eyes, she asks – to Adam, not to me, "Did she lose consciousness at all?"

"No, I think it only stunned her."

"Any vomiting? Bleeding?" I shake my head in the negative. "Your pupils are dilated. Anything else tonight besides the alcohol?" she asks, removing the thermometer from my mouth, and I chance a glance at Adam. He raises both eyebrows in an expression of *you're on your own now* incredulity. The nurse frowns.

"Okay, an edible, but a little one. For my birthday."

The nurse frowns again. Like a double rainbow. Which makes me want to giggle, but I choke it back, and the sound I make is a weird, strangled cough. This is all suddenly quite absurd. And I really, really want to lie down.

"That explains some things, but this eye is really irritated. Did some glass get into it?"

"Um, no." Might as well just put it all out there. "That was from earlier, before the pool. Sex with a bald guy. You know…sweaty head."

She looks from me to Adam's full head of dark hair, then back to me. I can only shrug.

The nurse checks his vitals. She examines the cuts on his arm and chest, agreeing he'll need stitches. "The doctor will be right in. Think you two can behave for a few minutes?" she says as she turns to leave. "Try not to break anything."

When the door closes behind her, I lay back on the exam

table, turning onto my side and drawing my knees up inside the caftan.

"You cold?" he asks quietly.

I nod my head and let my eyes drift closed. I hear him move then feel his hoodie drape across my shoulders. It's damp, but warm from his body. I open my eyes and he's close, tucking it gently around me. "You're the one who's injured; you don't need to take care of me."

"Just holding on to a little bit of my manhood. Let me be old fashioned for a minute."

"Thank you," I murmur, as he sits back in the chair. "Good thing your manhood didn't meet my champagne bottle."

"Prayers were answered."

As we wait, he rests his head on the wall, face lifted towards the ceiling. I take the moment to look him over. He's not as tall as Ronnie; I'd say right at six feet or so, and slim. Ronnie was a big man, heavier than Adam, with broader shoulders. Adam is more fit, with lean, compact muscles and visible abs. No muscled gym rat, but attention has been paid. *Strong enough to drag me out of the pool.*

There's some softness of middle age around the edges, but I like it. Gray around the temples, wrinkles around his eyes, dark hair across his chest and down his belly, disappearing into the waistband of his jeans. A tattoo circles his left bicep, with a long, elegant feather also inked from his wrist to his elbow. A Texas flag tattoo sits inside the opposite forearm.

Where were you earlier tonight? The thought makes me smile just as he drops his head and catches me staring. His expression is open, amusement lifting the corners of his mouth, as if he's allowing me to get the full picture. Which of course he is, his eyes saying take your time. Fair play it is.

I don't look away immediately. I can't help it, there's something about him, some bit of humor, a stillness too, that dilutes his cockiness just enough to invite my gaze rather than repulse. I keep smiling, and staring, my substance influenced brain giving me permission to return his frankness in kind before I again let my eyes close.

It could be two minutes or twenty before the doctor comes into the room, I have no idea. The nurse follows, carrying a metal tray draped with surgical cloth and all the paraphernalia required for stitches. I drag myself to an upright position, recognizing her from previous visits over the years.

"Luke's mom, right?" she asks, looking at the first of two charts in her hands. "Mrs. Theriot?" She recognizes me, too. Great. Just great.

"Good to see you, Doctor Viator."

"Well, this is certainly a—" she looks from me to Adam, "situation." She clears her throat, shifting the charts in her hands. "And you are Mr...."

"Sexton," he supplies.

Sexton. Holy shit. That's who this is? I injured *Adam Sexton*? Am I that out of it? And why was Adam Sexton at my house? My expression, the surprise and recognition, elicits an arched eyebrow from him.

"Pleasure to meet you," she nods, then turns her attention back to me. "Would you prefer to be seen one-on-one, Mrs. Theriot?"

"Umm," I drag my eyes from his. "No, it's alright, he pulled me out of my pool naked, so, privacy is.... pffttt." I wave my hand. Dr. Viator looks at Adam. "I was naked, not him," I add, as if that was her question.

She shines a light in each of my eyes, checks my pulse, listens to my heart and lungs. "Everything been all right at home? Luke must be in college by now."

"Yes, he's in Savannah. He's a sophomore."

"That's a transition, I know. An empty nest. Especially since... well, do you feel you might need some extra mental health support these days?"

"No." It comes out of my mouth in two juvenile syllables, and she takes a once over of my appearance with silent *are you seeing what I'm seeing* skepticism.

"Are you frequently drunk and high in your swimming pool, alone? Do you think that's safe behavior?"

Dear Lord. I take a deep breath, schooling myself to not get defensive or make a smart-ass remark, and to definitely not look over at Adam, whose eyes I can feel on me. I muster as much sobriety as my brain cells can find scattered amidst the remnants of my dignity.

"I appreciate you asking, but this was just a night... my *birthday*, that went a little bit sideways in the road. That's all, really. I'm fine. And more frequently boring than not."

She holds eye contact for a moment, weighing my truthfulness, then inspects the back of my head. "It's abraded. It'll be tender for a few days, but you don't look to have a concussion. You were very lucky. Take some acetaminophen in the morning and take it easy for the next few days. Missy will give you a printout of symptoms to watch for, but you should be fine. Avoid alcohol, and whatever else, for the next few days as well.

"Alright then, switch," she says, and Adam holds out his hand to help me down, but I don't take it, nor do I look him in the eye. "Mr. Sexton, would you prefer to be seen one-on-one?" she asks him.

He declines, tilting his head with a small smirk in my direction. Which I don't return. This back and forth, the familiarity, the flirting, whatever it is, I don't feel like it anymore. I shiver and he notices, and I wish he wouldn't, wish he wasn't so attentive. I don't want him looking at me, *seeing* me, and I avoid eye contact as Dr. Viator goes through the same routine checks with him.

The nurse raises the head of the exam table, propping him in a semi-reclined position. When the doctor begins to numb the injured areas, he flinches with the first injection and reflexively, idiotically, I flinch too.

"You okay there, Holly?" he asks.

When I don't respond, all three of them – Adam, Dr. Viator,

nurse Missy – they all pause, turning their heads to look at me in unison.

"I'm good," I say, and they turn back to their work, the doctor softly asking Adam questions as she sutures his cuts. I tune them out, staring at the floor, sending my mind out of the room.

Especially since, she said to me. *Especially since your husband died* is that full sentence, the asterisk that will forever be a tender spot in my biography, the spot marking the end of one part of my life and the beginning of another. The notation, the fine print of my story, the landmine people can't seem to avoid and the quicksand I can't seem to escape. The permanent excuse for any and every fuck up.

A cold, heavy lump settles high in my chest, at the base of my throat, and I swallow to try and press it down into my gut. A momentous thing happened tonight, when I threw myself at that doctor and tore a page out of the book of my life and ripped it to shreds. Launched myself even further from Ronnie, leaving him on the other side of a great void.

That happened. Tonight.

Did he ever feel like this when he slept with someone else? Did it make him so nuts he acted out and was asked if he needed help, as if he was mentally ill? Did he have sex with someone who wasn't his wife then hours later flirt with someone else who also wasn't his wife? Did he ever do that? Did he lock it away when he walked up our front steps, forget about it when he crawled into our bed? Was it nothing to him, screwing someone new, or was it ever this sick feeling of disaster and shame?

It's this tug of war inside, whenever I feel Ronnie slipping away. The urge to reach for him, to stretch out my arm in the dark until his hand takes mine and I can pull him back to me, fighting with the equally strong urge to find him and punch him in the face.

And this, this *man*, barged in and killed Eric *and* my great buzz, and everything did go sideways and now *I'm* having to explain myself? You know, maybe I should be frequently drunk and high in my pool, or any other place in my house that I damn well want to be. Maybe that's my problem, I haven't done it enough.

And, oh yeah, I turned fucking fifty. There's that.

"Holly?" Adam softly calls my name.

Will you just let me be! I want to yell, snapping to attention, only to see they've finished and he's standing, ready to leave, arm extended for me to pass through the door ahead of him.

CHAPTER FIVE

ADAM

Those tits.

I mean, goddamn, the image will be burned into my brain for the rest of my life. I hope if my life flashes before me when I die, I can hit pause for a minute on that one snapshot. Because it was fucking glorious. She was fucking glorious.

I know what that sounds like, and I'm not some asshole—well, I'm no angel, alright, but fuck me, those tits. I'm a man who's only telling the truth here. A man does not forget a sight like that.

I do feel terrible for scaring her. The terror on her face, I'll never forget that either, and don't want to think about how badly she might have been hurt, but to just back up for a minute, before all hell broke loose, to when I opened the gate and walked the first few steps across the patio. Can you picture in your head what I saw?

This woman, this voluptuous, naked woman straddling that pool float, singing with abandon at the top of her lungs. Golden hair curling across her shoulders, belly curving down to a flash of dark hair between pale thighs as she ground herself against that swan. Arms above her head, lifting those full breasts, the way they bounced. The way they fucking bounced. God. Line up the armies and let's go to war - those kind of tits. It turned me into a fucking Frankenstein idiot, just walking towards her, mouth agape.

It was like there was a spotlight on her, or light coming from within her. She was radiating, I don't know, *life*. That's the only way I can describe it. She was naked and glorious and uninhibited and shining, and I wanted her. Felt like I climbed a mountain in Tibet and found her. I wanted her, felt greedy for her, a taste in my mouth like pennies rotting on my back teeth causing me to swallow all the saliva in my mouth. A primal part of my brain wanted to lock that gate behind me and keep the world away, growling out *mine, my woman*, to any other caveman who came lurking.

Yep, I'm hearing it. It's fucked up, right? I agree with you. I've seen naked women before, obviously. Lots and lots of naked women. Beautiful women. All the varieties.

But are you really hearing me, are you getting the full measure of the first time I laid eyes on her? Well, technically, the second time. On Holly. That's her name. I finally know this woman's name. After twenty years.

The way she fought me, she would've killed me if she could have. That woman was not going down without a fight. I don't believe in heaven but damn, maybe I'll change my mind, 'cause dear God what a fucking way to go. Let me bury my face in those tits and walk with the angels.

I need to stop saying tits.

She fell asleep in my car. It was so quiet, driving to the clinic after all the chaos. Not even thirty minutes earlier I was talking to my sister about our mom and then stepped out of the car from one life, was thrown into a tilt-a-whirl of literal bloody chaos, then stepped back into my car with this woman and was living someone else's life.

When she rested her head in my hand, the way she looked at me, said my name, it was like we'd been in this car together all our lives. Like she already knew everything about me, and I knew everything about her. She said my name and an anchor dropped down through my chest to settle deep in my gut. I didn't move my hand; I couldn't let her go. I would've driven to the ends of the earth with her.

Must've been the blood loss. Because I have no business reading anything into anything from this night. Drunk woman has boyfriend. Acts out on birthday. That's it. A lot of adrenaline on an eventful night. And she owns the fucking studio, let's not forget that.

But.

There was a moment.

In the exam room, when we were alone, she looked so vulnerable there on the table, and I covered her with that hoodie when what I wanted to do was drape my whole body over her. Tell her I was going to take care of her. Every impulse told me to. I know it's ludicrous, but she was, for a minute, sweet and unguarded. Like she was in the car. And in that unguarded moment, I swear she gave me a full body once-over with those blue eyes of hers, an appraisal as frank and full of lust as I've maybe ever received in my life. And I let her. I caught her staring and I let her have me.

It was like being appraised by a lioness; she weighed up what I had to offer, smacked her lips with a yawn, and drifted off to sleep knowing she could have me whenever she wanted.

Then it was over. The doctor came in and somewhere in the conversation she disappeared into herself. Whatever it was, the night effectively ended. She was not in the room anymore. The lioness had become a doe, one we all got too close to and, thinking to reach out and touch her, with a snap of a branch underfoot, spooked, she leapt away.

CHAPTER SIX

HOLLY

I REALLY NEED to pee but can't bring myself to get out of bed with this headache. Rolling over, facing the wall of windows, the sunlight outlining the blinds doesn't look like gentle early morning light. It looks like mid-day, Louisiana high beams from the sun. I forgot to close the black-out curtains last night. I carefully reach for the silk eye mask I keep in a pretty cloisonné bowl on my nightstand, with lip balm and nail polish and matches, and slip it over my head, sighing at the relief of my soft pillow and darkness.

When I wake again my bladder is screaming, which finally gets me to throw back the covers and place my feet on the floor. I'm in the caftan I had on last night.

Last night. Ooof.

I shake my head, which does not feel great, but I stand without too much trouble and make my way into the bathroom. My reflection in the mirror is what you'd expect. Haggard would be accurate. Comically haggard would be more accurate. After a pee that feels like it lasts for forty-five minutes, I pull the caftan over my head, thinking I might need to burn it, and step into the shower, letting the hot water do its work. As I slowly come around to wakefulness, I think about Adam.

Adam Sexton. Here. At Riverside Studio. Guitar prodigy, guitar *god* to many fanboys – and many, many women I assume – axe for hire, touring the world, that Adam Sexton. Not pop star famous, but for those in the know in a specific part of the music world, a big damn deal. I would've known if he was with the young New Orleans singer booked for the next six weeks.

No one booked that much studio time anymore, at least not up front and paid in full. But Chip Walker was THE hot new star in country music, riding a rocket of fame from his sexy social media videos and years of touring relentlessly. Even I knew who he was. It was a shock when his father, "Big Dollar Bill" Walker, the personal injury lawyer known state-wide for his ubiquitous billboards and tv commercials, called us himself. Chip had signed to a major Nashville label, and he'd have access to all the session musicians and writers of his dreams there, but clearly his dad was calling some shots, insisting his son make this record close to home.

When I dropped a hefty quote on him, he didn't even negotiate. He said yes and we had the wire two days later. It was huge, giving me the tiniest bit of breathing room, financially, for the first time in years. The night the wire cleared, I sat at the kitchen table, whiskey in hand, stunned with relief.

Now Adam Sexton is here with them. It's unexpected, and... odd.

Out of the shower, I throw on an old, loose-fitting chambray dress from my closet. I take a minute to smooth some glowy primer onto my face, a little cream blush on my cheeks and lips, and a swipe of mascara on my top lashes. It makes me feel awake, I tell myself, and it's still my birthday. Everything is perfectly normal.

Finding my phone outside, on the chaise where I left it last night, I mark the blood on the flagstone pavers, making a mental note to hose it all down later and call the pool people Monday morning to ask how to clean out the glass. *That shouldn't be an expensive hassle at all,* I chide myself. Eric lies in a crumpled heap on the opposite side of the pool.

There's no sign of Adam in the pool house but the blinds are closed, so I go back inside, not knowing if he's asleep or over in the studio. Or if he's here at all – maybe he bolted. We were silent on the drive home from the clinic. When I did steal a glance in his direction his face was drawn and tired, the lines around his mouth and between his brows etched into deeper, darker creases, like they had been traced with a fine point marker. Maybe he couldn't wait to get the hell out of here.

My phone is lit up with text messages and missed phone calls. I also see the time, twelve fifteen. Who's the rock star now?

The first voice mail I listen to is from Mike, our engineer and studio manager, the one I ignored last night. I grab acetaminophen from a cabinet, listening to him tell me of the last-minute hiring of Adam as producer for the project, replacing the label's chosen Nashville guy, at the special request of Bill Walker. That Adam would be driving in late from Shreveport and would I please make sure he was able to get the key to the pool house.

"This is major for us," he says excitedly, "We need to make it perfect for them."

"Sorry, Mike," I mutter guiltily as I open the refrigerator to grab a can of Diet Coke.

There's a voice mail with birthday wishes from my parents and really sweet ones from Luke and Madeline. There's also a courtesy message from the clinic, checking in and letting me know to call if I had any additional questions.

Then I start scrolling through my text messages.

MIKE

What the hell did you do????

Hello??

Hello? Really??

I type out a question, praying for good news.

Is he over there with you?

Yes. DON'T COME OVER HERE

I'm definitely coming over there

BTW I'm fine

Holly ⬤

See you in 10

Mike's wife, Jackie, has also texted me.

JACKIE

Happy birthday! 🎉🎂

I hear this 🎸 dude is 🔥 I invited him to your
birthday dinner – see you at 7! 🩶

Did you make the 🥕🎂?

Fuck me. She invited Adam to my birthday dinner? Great. That's just super, super great.

Great.

And thank you! Yes, I did 🥕🎂 see you at 7
🩶

I fold over and rest my cheek on the cool stone of the island countertop. At least Adam's still here. Maybe if I act like last night wasn't that weird, he will too, and we can all swim in happy amnesia and forget it ever happened. It can't be that big a deal, can it? If you leave out the needing stitches part. He's a famous musician, for heaven's sake, he's probably hauled naked women out of swimming pools four at a time. My little scene likely didn't even register on his radar.

I have to show my face, I know, because to hide out today would give the impression I was embarrassed about last night – which I am – but I need to stroll in there and pretend I'm not. I slip on flip flops, grab sunglasses, and begin the walk down the long driveway to the barn that holds the studio.

Adam's car is backed up to the main door. Another good sign, I hope, so I go to the far-right side extension of the barn and pass through a screened porch that opens into a kitchen and lounge area. This is the part of the studio closest to the river, the part that flooded last summer in the hurricane, so it's all newly redone. A long cypress dining table divides the kitchen from the seating area, where there's a big comfy sofa and chairs.

There's no one in here but someone - Mike, I'm sure - has left donuts on the counter. I'm taking the first bite of my second donut when he walks in. He gives me a hug.

"Happy birthday, and what the hell, Holly?"

"I didn't get your message! I don't know what he told you, but I was minding my own business and he crept into the back-yard while I was in the pool. It was after midnight, I thought he was a murderer, what else was I supposed to think?"

"You were supposed to listen to your messages and not kill the golden goose! Not maim one of the great American guitar players."

"What if he would've strangled me and left me floating face down naked in my pool? One of the great American.... persons?"

"You were naked?"

"Don't lose the plot here."

"What if he calls Bill Walker and has them pull the whole project? You better be kissing that man's ass."

A low drawl glides into the room as if on rails, causing Mike and I to turn in unison. "Mike, it's all good man. I have no desire to tell anyone the lady of the house here kicked my ass. Let's keep that between us, if you don't mind."

Mike laughs nervously while Adam walks straight to me at the counter, reaching for the coffee pot to refill his cup. He's wearing faded jeans and a white t-shirt, the gauze bandage around his arm on full display, the outline of the one on his chest visible through his shirt. His thick, dark hair is raked back from his forehead, his stubble on the heavier side of shadow.

With side-eye to me and an upturned corner of his mouth, he adds, "But I'll let you do some of that ass kissing on me if you want to." Leaning against the counter, he keeps looking at me, kind of smiling with his eyes over his mug as he sips.

Is he waiting for me to say something?

Maybe it's because the word naked was just batted around in conversation, but it's flashing through my mind now, heat blooming across my cheeks. *Naked naked naked. Naked naked naked naked naked.* For the second time, this man has made me blush.

Hoping to sound unflustered, I say to Mike, "See there, clearly, he's fine. The golden goose is just fine."

"I prefer golden swan."

This does make me laugh, even though I don't want to. I don't want to give any more airtime to last night.

"How's your head feeling? Any nausea or anything?"

"I feel great," I lie. "What about you? Were you able to get any sleep?"

He nods, taking another sip of coffee.

"How's the pain with the stitches?" I ask.

"This pain in my heart caused by you?"

"Could have been your face."

"I'd look pretty sexy with a scar," he says, reaching around me instead of walking around me to grab a donut. His body is so close I can smell his soap, his skin warm where his arm grazes mine.

Maybe I do have a concussion, because I don't quite understand what's happening here. Why is he lingering? He's making me sweat. Or I'm having a hot flash.

Oh wait, it's last night. I have a flash of memory. The quiet gloom of the parking lot, when we left the clinic and he rifled through a duffle bag in his trunk, pulling out a soft black tee. Standing close just like this, wordlessly touching him, lifting the shirt away from the bandage covering his stitches, sliding it down his torso. My hands lingering on his skin. I think I did that.

I stand my ground, pretending to be cool while he's so close. I hope he can't hear me swallow. He chuckles next to my ear, like we shared a private joke, then steps across the kitchen to pull out a chair at the table.

The second his back is turned I glance at Mike, who mouths, "What the fuck?"

I mouth back, "I don't know!"

"Be nice," he silently admonishes me, hands raised in the classic calm down gesture.

Adam sits, leaning back in his chair to cross an ankle over one knee, taking a bite of donut. All three of us are silent until Mike can't stand it any longer. "Good thing there's no behind the music documentary crew here, am I right?"

"They're coming tomorrow with the band," Adam deadpans.

Mike laughs, relief crossing his face, and he joins Adam at the table.

"Bill Walker hired you? How did he manage that with the label?" I ask.

"Money," Mike interjects, and Adam nods his head to acknowledge the obvious. "He's not completely crazy, I love that last Jennifer Carson record you produced. I think it's her best. And your fifth Grammy, right?"

"Thanks," Adam says warmly. "She's a real sweetheart."

I bet they all are, says the sarcastic little devil on my shoulder. *Why would you care?* I silently rebuke myself.

I catch him watching me again, with a sense of unease that he can read my mind, see this conversation in my head like it's closed captioned across my forehead. I purse my lips and reach for my Diet Coke, tipping it in his direction before I take a drink. Before I'm tempted to stick out my tongue at him.

"I bought a place in New Orleans last year, I guess it wasn't too hard to find my number."

"Mike's message said you were driving in from Shreveport," I say.

"I was visiting my mom," he answers, clearing his throat.

"So old Big Bill turned on the money hose and bumped the label's producer to get you?" Mike presses. "They let him do that?" Adam raises his shoulders, one hand lifting off the table, meaning either *I have no clue* or *that's all I'm going to say about it.*

He's discreet, I think to myself, gratefully. Maybe he won't tell every person he knows in the music business about what happened last night. But I do wonder now what the full story is with Chip Walker. "Why did he want so much time?" I ask. "And why out here with us?"

He weighs his answer before responding. "From what I've gathered from Chip, the songs aren't all where they should be, so he needs the writing time. And from Bill, he implied there are some... distractions he'd like to get Chip away from." Mike and I nod over this, because it's one of our major selling points - our remote, for the music business, that is – location. "I've wanted to work here for years. That Neve console is a dream, and I believe your Grammy count here is..."

"Seven," Mike and I say in unison.

"Right," he says. "I've heard wonderful things, so I said yes."

Mike lets out a low whistle. "Nice work if you can get it."

Sensing it's time to wrap this up, I push myself away from the counter. "Well, I'll leave you two to get on with it. Adam, nice to meet you. Please let us know if we can do anything for you all while you're here."

"Appreciate that," he replies, getting to his feet. "There is one thing. Mike said I could take a look at the vintage mics you have up at the house. You have a couple U47's up there?"

"Ronnie's office," I nod. "Just let me know when."

"If I could do that now, it would be good, if it's alright with you. I'd like to get one vocal booth set up this afternoon."

"Yep, of course." I move around the table, back towards the way I came in. "I'll see you tonight," I say to Mike as I walk past.

"Jackie invited Adam, so maybe you can give him a ride."

"Or did you plan to ride with your boyfriend?" Adam asks, with a meant to be innocent look pasted on his face. My feet stutter to a stop.

"Boyfriend?" Mike guffaws. "Yeah, right."

Adam, circling one eye with his finger, adds, "That looks much better, by the way."

"What's he talking about?" Mike asks, seeing the *shut up right now* look I shoot Adam.

"Nothing," I say at the same time Adam says, "Her date last night." So much for his discretion.

"Her what?!" Mike exclaims.

Instead of stabbing both of them I turn and stalk through the back porch. Adam catches up to me at the screen door leading outside, and I let it slam shut behind me. I hear him yelp, which I'm going to count as a birthday present to myself.

"Watch the money-makers, will ya?" he gripes, jogging up to my side, holding his hands out to check for all his fingers.

CHAPTER SEVEN

HOLLY

I LEAD Adam to the small back bedroom that was Ronnie's office, practically untouched from the last time he set foot in here. I don't have much of an excuse for not dealing with it. I've moved a few things over the years, tossed a few things, but it's one of those tasks that grows in scope and dread until it overwhelms and then becomes very, very easy to avoid. The more time passes, the worse you feel, which makes you put it off all the more.

I didn't have much of an excuse, that is, until this summer when I did finally decide to tackle it. My plan was for Luke to help me while he was home from college, pack up what we were keeping, then turn the room into my own office. I set aside a weekend for the job and gave myself a pep talk. It was time.

That's when I found the journal. The first hour, practically the first desk drawer I opened, there it was, stashed at the bottom of a stack of notebooks. I wish I'd never found it and I definitely wish I'd never read it. That was months ago.

Opening the door now for Adam, I'm acutely aware of how obvious it is the room has been left untouched. I haven't intentionally left it as a shrine, but being in here with another person, I'm embarrassed at how much it looks like one.

His eyes rove over the bookcases, the memorabilia, the Grammy's lined up along one shelf. There's a pair of Ronnie's reading glasses on the desk, with a shiny round pitch pipe and some loose change, like he just emptied his pockets. I reflexively hug my arms around myself, wishing now I'd not let him in here. It's as if I'm letting someone examine my most painful secret with a magnifying glass. I should've told Mike to bring him whatever he wanted.

Adam scratches his chin as he looks around, not sure what to say. Eventually, motioning to a photo, he says, "Fats Domino, that's pretty cool."

"They're in here," I say, stepping forward to open the closet.

There's a tall black safe inside, with old Mardi Gras costumes and Ronnie's heavy overcoat hanging to the right. A pair of worn leather boots rests on the floor. I type in the combination then stand back to give him access.

"No fucking way," he whispers reverently.

I know it's blowing his mind, would blow any professional musician or producer's mind, to get a look into Ronnie's collection. It was part of his passion, his obsession, with vintage equipment. He scoured online for treasures, dug through pawn shops and small-town music stores. Scooped them up when other studios went out of business. It's another significant reason so many artists have been willing to trek all the way out here to record.

I stare out the window as Adam kneels on the floor. He's in awe, a supplicant at the altar of Neumann and AKG and RCA.

While he looks, I feel the location of Ronnie's journal in the house lighting up inside me, a painful pin in the map of my heart. It's under our bed, exactly where I threw it after staying up all night to read it, the same day I found it. To me, right now, it's pulsing hot, throbbing like a heartbeat, like an ancient relic in an adventure movie calling for attention.

"Holly?" Adam's voice brings me back into the room. "Can I also bring this 84, would you mind?"

"No, I don't mind, use any of them you want." He hands the microphone to me carefully, then turns back for the 47's, which are in individual, velvet lined boxes. Standing, he closes the safe. "That'll be one million dollars, please."

"The greed must be written all over my face," he says sheepishly. "What a collection. I'll make sure they make it back to you."

"Mike will if you don't," I say, walking to the door.

I want to get out of this room, away from the recrimination and reproach each and every untouched surface represents. But Adam, still floating from the choirs of angels in his head, stops when something on a shelf catches his attention. He reaches to pick up an eight by ten black and white movie still, shrink-wrapped on a piece of cardboard.

He holds it out to show me, unabashed. "Look, 'The African Queen.'"

"Uh-huh," is all I can say, nodding my head. I do not offer to explain. His gaze then passes over the desk, and I watch as the thought occurs to him, as it appears in his eyes, the awareness again of his surroundings and the state of this untouched room.

"Sorry, I shouldn't have..." He tucks the picture back into place on the shelf. When he looks in my direction, I'm already in the hallway.

After agreeing on a time to depart for dinner, he leaves, and I do a quick scan of my house, noting the many chores that need my attention, then decide the best thing to do is flop down on the sofa with a book.

Unable to escape into the story, my mind intent on its own agenda, I only get through one chapter. Dropping the book to the floor, I stretch and yawn, turning onto my side.

Fifty. How in the hell did this happen?

Wasn't I twenty-five, like, yesterday? Wanting my "real" life to begin, yearning for love, to be loved and in love, wondering what my future would be. Who I would be. Now here I am, all this history unspooled behind me, in a future that in no way I could have predicted.

"Fifty," I say out loud to the room. "Here I am in my real life."

So many goals I wanted for myself, I've accomplished. And I feel proud, I do. By any standard, it's a full measure of life, with a full measure of blessings and sorrows. But when I was that young woman, with her hopes and dreams, trying to see into my future,

I'm certain I didn't see this, didn't imagine that where I was headed was here, alone. So soon.

No, I imagined a constant, steady rise, this upward path of improvements and gains, and didn't give much thought at all about life's apex, about when you begin the slow slide down into oblivion. Or if I did, I imagined it at ninety.

Oblivion? Good grief, that's harsh.

But what I must have looked like to Adam last night. The thought makes me cringe. And again, just now in the office. A lot of unpleasant adjectives are knocking on my brain right now, begging to be let in and wag their judgmental fingers in my face.

I grab the blanket from the back of the sofa. All that brain garbage will have to wait because I think the best thing I can do right now is take a nap.

IT'S A GREAT NAP. A Saturday afternoon, hung over, sleep as long as you feel like it, deep dive into darkness nap. It's a huge check mark in the pro column of being an empty nester. The only thing that could possibly have made it any better was if there was a thunderstorm.

But wait, *is it raining?* I hear water, a whir and slap against the house. Staring at the ceiling, slowly coming back to the here and now, I recognize that no, I don't hear rain on the roof and no, I don't see rain through the windows.

Untangling myself from the blanket, I stand and pad over to the kitchen just as an arc of water sprays right to left across the French doors. When I look outside, there's Adam, shirtless, hosing down the back of my house. The spray slurps against the siding as he fans the water back and forth, eyes shaded with black sunglasses. The flagstone decking surrounding the pool glistens wet in the sun; clearly, he's hosed that down too.

He's cleaning?

I let that sink in. Someone has cleaned something at my house, someone I didn't have to pay or specifically ask, someone handsome and shirtless with that muscle flexing in his forearm as he squeezes the water hose nozzle.

Holy hell.

Maybe I'm still sleeping. I'm definitely ogling. Water streaks across the door in front of me and, startled, I see Adam grinning, having caught me staring. I pretend that he hasn't, that I wasn't, and open the door.

"My goodness, look at this," I say, holding one hand over my eyes to shield them from the sun as I walk over to him. "There's a pressure washer in the garage if you want it."

"I love pressure washing, it's very satisfying."

"You didn't have to take this on..."

"I was only going to wash the blood away; then thought I might as well hit the rest of the patio. And I watered those plants," he waves his hand in the direction of the clay pots of flowers grouped at one end of the pool. "They looked thirsty. Then I saw a few cobwebs up there," he motions towards the house, "And decided to get those. This kind of thing, something sort of mindless; it helps organize my thoughts."

We stand in silence, side by side, as he sprays water back and forth across the house. It is soothing. When he reaches whatever standard of a job well finished exists in his mind, be it for my house or his thoughts, he stops and smiles at me, his eyes still masked by the dark glasses. Shirtless. Hand on his hip. Jeans riding low.

"Well, thank you. Aren't you sweet." I leave it at that, holding back any other flippant or, God forbid, flirtatious remark that might want to pass my lips. Because I'm irritated. He's irritating. He's so... so I don't know what, and it's pissing me off with this peevish sort of anger, and an urge to bite him.

I met this man less than twenty-four hours ago and he has seen me naked, hell, he's held me naked; I've been drunk and stoned and asleep in his car; we've been to an urgent care together like a pair of brawling bar flies. Stitched up and bandaged where I cut him, he's now, for some completely unfathomable reason, taking care of things around my house. He's a stranger! Adam is a stranger, and an important client for the studio when we desperately need one. Yet, everything about him seems to provoke me, beg for a reaction.

Look at him, standing there, sweaty.

I wish I brought sunglasses out here because can he see what I'm thinking? Is that why he's still smiling? Can he take one look at me and know I'm wondering what that hair on his chest would feel like rubbed against my breasts, pressed on top of me and—

God bless America, Holly, get a grip before you embarrass yourself!

He probably believes that's what every woman he meets is thinking. So full of himself. This is really his problem, not mine, clearly. I'm not going to be another woman in what I guarantee is a long line of women falling all over themselves for Adam Sexton. I've met too many musicians in my time to be that cliché. And I don't want the reputation as some sort of lagniappe for booking the studio, offering myself up like a welcome basket of muffins. Fuck that.

I will politely say no thank you to being the desperate widow throwing herself at men.

And yeah, *I know*, technically I'm a woman who actually did throw herself at a man last night; made a fool of herself, had a little pity party, then landed Mr. Sexton's cute butt in the ER. But a man like this looks at twenty-five-year-olds. Uncomplicated, unmessy, not going to drown him, trim and perky twenty-five-year-olds.

"You okay there, Holly? Maybe you shouldn't be out here in the sun." His words interrupt my internal diatribe. Like he's sooo innocent, standing there, half-dressed.

"Let me put this away," I say sharply, snatching the hose from his hand and dragging it to the cradle attached to the house. "Thanks again, but you should be mindful of those stitches."

"If you have a broom handy, I'll sweep up that glass."

"Adam, you're a guest here. I've got it," I call over my shoulder, winding the hose around the bracket. My voice sounds angrier than I mean for it to, but I don't really care. What's he doing out here, anyway? Running up my water bill for his own therapy?

"Oh, and I shut down the filters—"

"I've got it." Straightening, I turn to face him. "You're off duty. Go relax, get cleaned up, I'll see you out front in an hour."

"Okay," he says, backing away towards the pool house. He points to the white, melted lump that was Eric. "Should I—"

"Adam!" I exclaim. Does this man not get the message?

"Okay, you've got it from here," he concedes, opening his door. "See you in a bit."

"Jesus," I mutter under my breath, turning away.

That's when he calls out, "Put some shoes on so you don't cut your feet," disappearing as I spin in his direction. A firm, fast close of the door says he's had the last word.

"Thank you! I was going to!" I yell at his closed door.

After waiting to make sure he's really and truly inside, I stalk into my house, going straight to the laundry room for the broom. I have a feeling if I don't do this right now, he's going to come out here in the middle of the night and do it himself.

Rolling my eyes, I go over to the sofa to slip on the flip flops I kicked off when I took my nap.

"Happy now?" I grumble. "I hope you're putting a shirt on."

CHAPTER EIGHT

HOLLY

I'M BACK INSIDE, in my closet, trying to figure out what to wear.

Just pick something comfortable. You're not trying to impress anyone, I tell myself, shifting through hangers aggressively one after the other. *No, but it wouldn't hurt to feel pretty on my birthday, would it? Instead of the drowned rat someone pulled out of the pool.*

Someone? This voice in my head asks, one eyebrow raised. *Shut up* I tell that voice.

My hand stops on a dress wedged in the very back of the closet, in the land of things saved for a "maybe one day when I have a life, I'll wear this" occasion, an off the shoulder black linen dress I found on sale a few years ago on a visit to Madeline in Florida, never worn.

Should I? It's just a few people in Mike and Jackie's back yard. I don't want to look like I'm trying too hard. I hold it up in front of myself, looking in the mirror. The dress is an easy drape, almost Grecian. I remember joking with Madeline that I should plan a trip somewhere Mediterranean and eat gelato. Of course, I've never been on a trip like that, and the dress still has its tags.

What am I waiting for? My sixtieth birthday? It's not a ball gown; it's just a pretty dress. *Wear the damn dress, Holly.*

So, I do. After spending twenty minutes looking for my strapless bra.

Miraculously, when I survey myself one last time in the bathroom mirror, I don't feel like calling and cancelling, hiding away at home. I don't say harsh things to myself about my belly or my arms, or my hair or my face or the whole long list of flaws I typically run through. Tonight, I see a version of myself in the mirror that makes me happy, and I smile at my reflection.

I am running late, however, and hustle to the kitchen to retrieve the cake from the refrigerator. In the garage, Adam is there, leaning against the outer door frame, reading something on his phone. He pushes himself upright but keeps his eyes on his screen.

"Sorry to keep you waiting," I say.

It's then that he raises his eyes to me, his reaction stopping me in my tracks. He lifts a hand to his heart, a huge smile lighting up his face.

"You," he says. "You look beautiful. You make me feel like it's *my* birthday."

"Is it me, or is it because I'm carrying a cake?"

Chuckling, looking right into my eyes, he drawls, "You, darling, definitely you."

And maybe because I do feel good, I don't question his sincerity. Or it could be because he looks so handsome – soft, white linen button down, dark jeans, black loafers, that hair swept back off his forehead – I'm distracted. Possibly it's something in the timbre of his voice when he said *darling*, and my belly button tingled. Whatever the reason, my own smile can't be withheld.

"You are very skilled with a compliment, and I like it. Feel free to keep 'em coming."

Still standing by the garage door, hand over his heart, still staring, he grins. "Happy to."

"Ready?" I ask. His stare is making the tingle spread.

"Yeah, I brought my car over from the studio," he motions to the driveway behind him, lifting one hand to show me his keys.

"I'll drive," I say, crossing to the passenger door of my car to open it for him.

He shakes his head. "Let's take my car, I prefer to drive."

"Uh, uh," I wave my free hand at the open door. I literally need to be in the driver's seat with this man before some of this energy, whatever it is, gets out of control. "You. Important, paying guest. You. Big chest wound. You. Don't know where we're going. Please get in sir."

Standing his ground, he negotiates, "Come on, I'll drive, and you can drink all you want for your birthday. I'll get you home, and it'll help me learn my way around a little bit."

"The doctor said I shouldn't drink for a few days, remember? I'm confident you won't burst into flames if you sit in the passenger seat of a Honda this one time. Get in." Seeing he's about to offer another protest, I quickly add, "And the seatbelt from this side won't cut across your stitches." Sugar-sweetly, I finish him off. "I would also like to say you look quite handsome, and it's my birthday. Please get in the damn car."

Giving in, his lips pressed firmly together, he walks towards me.

"Thank you," I say, with an unusual degree of pleasure in my small victory. I act the gracious winner and refrain from rolling my eyes.

"Hold this for a sec." I pass the cake to him then grab file folders, lose receipts, reusable tote bags, a hair clip I've been looking for all week – "there you are!" I exclaim - out of the passenger seat and toss them all into the back. I wave my arm once more to invite him in. "That should meet your standards." He grumbles under his breath something too quiet for me to hear.

As I back out of the garage, he says, "Something smells good."

"Again, is it me or is it the cake?"

He leans over, bringing his nose close to my neck for a deep inhale. His face barely an inch from mine, he says, "It's you." He inhales deeply again then shifts back into his seat. My face must give me away, my flustered surprise, plus I've stopped the car, because he adds, "You did request compliments."

He's got me there.

"So I did," I acknowledge. My upper hand sure didn't last long. After pulling forward into the driveway, I say, stupidly, as if it matters, but it's the only thing I can think of, "It's fig."

"The cake?"

"No, me. My perfume, I mean. The cake is carrot."

"Delicious," he murmurs, and I steal a glance at him. He gives me full squinty eyed sparkles with, if I'm not imagining things, a suggestive smirk.

It works. I'm about to say, "You smell good too," because he does, and why is that some sort of straight line to my vagina? I've smelled soap before. Is this where I am now, is this the standard? A man just takes a shower and I'm horny?

I trap the words behind my teeth. He said something about me drinking all I wanted, and he didn't want me to drive because, after last night, why would he? He thinks I'm a total lush. I need to remember that horrible first impression and turn the temperature down on all of this. Be professional. We really need this booking to go well. He can do this sexy thing he does. I don't have to respond.

"All set for tomorrow?" I ask brightly, in my best *let's change the subject* voice. "You seemed pretty serious with your phone, back at the house. Everything alright?" He shakes his head, and I exhale, anticipating banal chit chat for the rest of the ride. Which lasts for all of two seconds.

"Last night you told me I had a very "scowly" face," he says.

"I did?"

"I don't doubt you're right, it's just I don't think anyone's ever said it to my... scowly... face before."

"I'm so sorry," I grimace. I don't remember saying any such thing to him. What else did I say, or do, last night that I don't remember?

"I'm just teasing you."

"Oh, then, I didn't say it? Because it sounds kind of mean..."

"No, you said it," he confirms.

"I must have meant it as a serious face, like a compliment, like a Tommy Lee Jones sort of good Texas scowly face."

"Now you're just calling me old," he laughs.

"No," I laugh, despite myself. "Like from 'The Fugitive'. You know, a taking care of business, serious—"

"Manly..."

I answer mock-seriously. "Yes, *manly*, definitely manly, sexy scowly face."

"Sexy, huh?"

What is coming out of my mouth? Every conversation with this man ends up being a fencing match. Thrust and parry. Thrust and parry. And stop thinking about thrusting!

I must still have drugs in my system. I make a frustrated *arrrgh* kind of noise. "Okay, okay, I'm sorry. I won't mention your scowly face anymore."

"But now that it's a *sexy* scowly face, I'm going to have to insist that you do."

"Stop," I groan.

"Hey, you said it. Me. Big important guest. Me. Knife wounds."

"Stop," I jokingly plead again. "I didn't knife you, and if you didn't want to answer my question you could've just said so."

"You mean about the studio?"

"Yes, everything ready for tomorrow? Is there anything you need out there?"

"I don't think Mike misses anything, that guy's an ace." He makes a vague gesture with the hand that's on top of the cake carrier in his lap. "As far as what we can do, yes, we're ready. I've met Chip only once, out in L.A. We've never worked together before, and I've never met his band."

We ride for several miles in silence, until he says, quietly, "I was texting with one of my sisters. We have this thing going on with my mom." He's staring out the window. I don't even know if he realizes he spoke out loud. I'm wondering if it's best to say something or leave him be when we reach the turn off to Mike and Jackie's.

I FUMBLE THE CAKE, nearly dropping it in the driveway, so Adam insists on carrying it inside. "Why are you bringing the cake to your own birthday dinner?" he asks.

"Because I wanted carrot cake and I make it better than anybody," I reply, just before the door opens. "And to try and keep Jackie from overdoing it."

"Happy Birthday!" the woman in question cries, waving me inside and pulling me into a hug.

Everything about Jackie is warm, from her glossy brown hair, to her glow-from-within, olive Cajun skin, down to the bright pink polish on her toes. Petite, curvy, and full of laughter, she always makes me smile because she meets everyone, meets the whole world, with a smile.

"And Adam, I'm so pleased to meet you. Welcome, come on in y'all."

"Thanks for having me," he says, and we follow her down a short hallway to the kitchen.

"I've been dreaming of this cake all week. You think anyone would notice if I snuck off with a fork and had my way with it?" she grins, checking Adam out as he puts it on the counter.

"I think you get to do whatever you want," I motion to her swollen belly, ignoring her blatant top to bottom scan of him.

"This your first?" Adam asks, turning to us, oblivious.

"Third!" she exclaims. "Mike says it's the last, but we'll see. I'm very persuasive."

"Where are those little angel babies, anyway? I'm ready for some birthday hugs."

"My parents took them, so mommy and daddy get to have a little lie-in tomorrow," she does a wiggle of her eyebrows. To Adam, she says, "The guys are playing it cool, waiting out by the grill so they wouldn't be standing at the door like a fan club when you got here. Would you mind taking that tray there out to them please? There's drinks outside, too."

She tracks him with her eyes and a lewd smile as he heads out the door. The minute it closes behind him she whips her head around to me, her eyes comically huge. "Oooohhh, hooooo, hoooo, this is going to be good," she whoops, fanning a hand in front of her face.

"You mean the guitar world bromance about to start out there?" I ask, picking up a cube of cheese from the wooden board on the counter.

"Oh no, with you. He's perfect for you!"

"What?" I sputter, hand to my mouth to keep from spitting out the cheese. "What in the world are you talking about?"

"Are you blind? He's so hot, and you already look like you're a couple."

"No, we don't."

"Uh, yeah you do. You look like you coordinated your outfits and everything." She leans in and nudges my shoulder, waggling her eyebrows again. "Mike said something already happened last night, something *naked*."

I really shouldn't kill Mike since he has all these babies, right?

I shake my head at her. "Not in the way your filthy knocked-up mind is thinking, nothing like that. It involved stitches and the walk-in clinic. And a tetanus shot. Not romance."

"I don't know, you guys gave me the tingles when you walked in. And my tingles are pretty accurate."

"I know you have all the love hormones right now, but I'm not looking for anyone—"

"Uh-huh, Mike also said you had a date last night with a different guy, so sounds to me like you are. Finally."

Those kids wouldn't really miss Mike all that much, would they? After a while?

"Well, I'm not," I counter, puffing air out through my lips. I dart my eyes to the door, paranoid someone is going to hear us.

"And I'm not about to start chasing the paying customers. I love you, but cool it, don't make this weird tonight, please. Alright?"

"Alright," she sighs. "You know we love you, and we worry about you."

And here it comes. The windows should rattle now, the pity train is passing, right on schedule. The we-feel-so-sorry-for-you sincere moment.

"We just want you to find someone, and Ronnie would want you to be happy," she says earnestly, hugging me. "You're too wonderful to be languishing, alone."

Languishing? Is that what this has come to now, I'm languishing?

I pat her on the back and mumble a thank you. She means well. Everyone always does. But how much do I have to handle, to manage and *survive*, how many years before the pity ends? Dammit, maybe my legs shake and I stumble sometimes, and it hasn't always been pretty, but I have not, ever, quit. And I haven't asked for anyone to feel sorry for me. I feel sorry for myself sometimes, that's allowed, but I do not want it from other people.

Why just not say anything? Or, I don't know, what about, *wow, Holly, you are amazing.* For that to be the full sentence for once would be refreshing. Yes, for fuck's sake, I'm lonely, but would everyone please stop talking about it.

And I'm not fucking languishing!

Gently lifting her arms from around my neck, I say, "I'm fine, really. Look at me, I think I look fabulous, don't you think I look fabulous?"

"Gorgeous."

"I'm enjoying my life and don't need anyone to worry about me. I promise." Once I'm sure I've made her feel better, I lead us outside to join the others.

In the backyard, two tables have been pushed together, layered with mis-matched vintage tablecloths, flowers and candles, creating one long tableau under strings of lights scalloped between the house and an enormous live oak tree. It's lovely, the evening is warm, and I take in a few deep breaths of fresh night air. Aside from our hosts, there are three other couples plus Adam and me. Everyone except Jackie, who's an accountant with a large firm in Lafayette, and D'Shawn's wife Michelle, a nurse, are musicians or artists.

For a while we're divided into men at the grill, women at the table, and my attention wanders occasionally to the laughs I hear from the guys. From my seat I can see Adam, his back to me, sipping a beer and from what I can tell mostly listening as the others carry on around him. Once, he looks over his shoulder and our eyes meet. He raises his beer to me in a small salute before turning back to answer a question from Mike.

When the men declare their work at the grill complete, everyone arranges themselves around the table to eat family style, and Adam and I end up seated next to one another. I worry he's going to think this is all a set-up, that he's being nudged in my direction, and I find myself oddly nervous. At the few dinners like this I've been to in the years since Ronnie died, I've been the only single at the table, biting the inside of my cheek when I see some quiet word or touch exchanged between a couple, their affectionate intimacy causing the cleft in my heart to burn with pain. Recognizing this is not that, reminding myself I'm many exits down the road from those days, I coax myself to relax and appreciate the company. I even manage a few words of small talk with Adam.

Jackie snaps photos with her phone, including one of Adam and me, calling for us to smile at her from her seat across the table. He raised his arm across the back of my chair, grazing my shoulder with his hand, and my skin prickled with awareness of the parts of him that were close to the parts of me. As he shifted in his seat, his knee pressed into my thigh and it was like flashing arrows, all pointing at the spot where our bodies touched. *Right there! Right there! Right there!*

Stories about gigs gone wrong and tales from the road bounce around the table, to my ears exaggerated in their details even more than usual, likely due to the guest sitting to my right. There's extra effort to engage or impress him, to get a laugh from him, and it's interesting to watch him handle it. He's warm and attentive to everyone, looks to be relaxed despite the obvious attention, but he never tries to become the center of conversation. He's a master at deflecting attention away from himself.

Ronnie, on the other hand, would've been holding court tonight, leading the laughs and the stories like a conductor swaying a baton over an orchestra. I always appreciated it about him, that I could ride his extroverted coattails. He walked into a room ready to be the center of it. I would hold his hand and go along for the ride.

My cake is brought out, adorned with only five candles, thank goodness, and Mike rises from his spot at the head of the table. All eyes turn to him, and he pauses nervously. Jackie gives him a nod of encouragement.

"Thank y'all for coming tonight, and um, for bringing all this food. How does leftovers sound for the Saints game tomorrow?"

Jackie makes an exaggerated "no way" gesture with her arms in mock horror, and everyone around the table laughs, with D'Shawn calling out a "Who dat!"

"Holly, you and Ronnie saved my life." I shake my head at this, but he continues. "And I have this life..." he looks at Jackie with adoration, then back to me, "All this, because of you. You and Luke are family, and I just want you to know... to know how we feel about you. All of us. And we couldn't be here tonight without thinking about the big guy, our brother, and how much he'd want to be here. How much he's missed."

He raises his drink, and everyone around the table follows suit.

"Somewhere he's toasting you, and I know he'd be real proud of you. That man knew how lucky he was. He always said his best songs were about you."

Jackie chimes in here, "He also said smart chicks turned him on!" which gets another hearty round of laughter.

He rushes to finish the rest. "To Holly. Our lady of Riverside Studio, we love you. Happy birthday and here's to many more. Cheers!"

My eyes sting with tears, my throat tightens, and I place my hands over my heart, mouthing "thank you" to everyone at the table before I blow out the candles.

CHAPTER NINE

IN THE CAR on the ride home, I'm lost in thought, mulling over my conflicting emotions.

I'm lonely, I'm not lonely. I'm lonely, but I don't want anyone telling me I'm lonely. I want sympathy one minute; I don't want anyone's pity the next.

I miss Ronnie, but I'm furious at him. I miss Ronnie, but I wish everyone would stop bringing him up all the time, reminding me again and again of what's been lost. I want his friends to remember him affectionately, and I want to shout at them that he wasn't this saint. I want to remember him with only love, but I can't stop litigating all the mistakes we made with one another over and over in my head. Picking at every little scab.

Shouldn't all this be easier by now? I wish there was a way to flip a switch or punch a button to make it all stop. Quiet this argument inside my head.

"Everything okay?" I jump at Adam's voice when he speaks. He's staring at me from the passenger seat - I might have been pounding my fist on the steering wheel. My right hand is clenched above the horn, and I straighten my fingers, lowering them to run my palm down my thigh. "You went a million miles away."

"Oh. Sorry. I'm good."

"Did you enjoy the night?"

"I did. It was nice." Clearing my throat, I add, "How about you?"

He nods. "It was nice to be invited. Nice people, great food. Nice to meet Mike's wife."

"Really good food," I agree. I guess we've established every-thing was nice.

Then it's silence. Not entirely comfortable, not entirely awkward. I can tell he's unsure of my mood, simply being polite, so I lob an easy conversational volley.

"Good manly talk around the grill?"

He chuckles. "Yeah. You know, D'Shawn, we figured out that I met his granddad, maybe fifteen years ago. Tokyo, of all places."

"No kidding? That's cool. That whole family is ridiculously talented."

"I got his number."

"Any of those guys would love to get a call from you."

"I don't know about that, but for sure from Chip Walker. And come on, all those guys would jump at any call from Holly..." He motions a hand in my direction, and it takes me a minute to realize he's waiting for my help.

"Theriot."

"Thank you - sorry, I drew a blank. They'd all come running for Holly Theriot."

"That's just the studio."

"I don't think so. It's not just about the studio. Clearly, they adore you."

"Thanks, that's a ... kind thing to say."

More silence, the passing landscape growing darker as we get farther out of town. Past the strip malls and gas stations and car dealerships.

Out of the blue he says, "Mike has *three* kids?"

"Yep, about to. Poppy, Grace, and whatever this new one will be."

Adam shakes his head. "God bless 'em."

"Do you have any kids?" I glance over at him.

"No. No kids."

"Not yet anyway."

"Never wanted any kids. I'm nobody's daddy, and I don't wanna be a daddy."

Oh, you're a daddy, a snarky voice whispers in my head, and I tell it to mind its own business.

"You've got time. Ronnie was about your age when we had Luke. You guys can just change your mind whenever you want, marry some young girl and pop a few out."

"Not for me. I had a vasectomy. No kids."

I hold a hand up in peace. "Okay, I got it, no kids. You don't mess around, do you?"

"Not with that, I don't. And I'm not looking for some young girl."

Ah, yes, there's that scowly face. Clearly a sore subject. But wait - he's *looking*? This man is single?

"You have just the one?" he asks.

"Luke. He's twenty and a sophomore in college, in Savannah."

I've given Adam a quick run-down of Luke's studies – recording engineering and film scoring – and his plans to work with Mike to expand the business, when we reach the property, and I guide the car down the driveway, under the canopy of oaks. Likely obnoxiously boring to the younger single man with no kids. We pull into the garage, and I turn off the car.

"I hope to keep this all together for him until he's ready. That's the goal, and way more than you needed, or wanted, to hear. Sorry for the over-sharing."

"Don't apologize. What a lucky young man," he says, smiling warmly. He seems to mean it and I think again that he is kind.

"We'll see. Plenty of time to still screw it all up." With that, I climb out of the car and meet him at the passenger side just as he's standing, arching his back in a stretch.

What would it be like to take three more steps and wrap my arms around him? Hug him like we were a couple, home at the end of the night and ready for bed. I can remember what that was like, and I miss it.

Closing his door, he hands me the cake plate, with the one large piece Jackie insisted I bring home. Impulsively, I say,

"There's no use pretending I'm not going to eat this the minute I get inside. Wanna help?"

"You sure? I've got sisters and I know better than to get between a woman and the last piece of cake."

"You'd be doing me a favor," I say, heading to the door of the house. "Come on."

"Yes, ma'am," he answers, following me inside.

In the kitchen I flip on a few lights and wave him to a seat at the island while I pull plates from the cabinet and grab two forks. I also get us each a glass of water. When I pull a knife from the block on the counter, he holds out his arm in my direction.

"Absolutely not, hand that over."

"You gonna be touchy about that forever?" I say, hand on one hip.

"Yes. At least until the stitches are gone. Hand it over."

I huff and turn the handle so it's facing him then offer it up. He slices the one large piece into two while I come around the island and pull out the stool next to his. Sliding a plate in front of me, he says, "Happy birthday. Did you make a wish tonight?"

I shrug, reaching for my fork. "Didn't really occur to me."

His hand moves to my wrist, stopping my fork mid-lift. "Well then, make a wish."

"Eh, I'm alright," I mumble.

"Aw, come on," he says, rubbing his finger in a slow circle on top of my hand, doing some cajoling, amused thing with his eyes. Eyes that I'm now seeing are dark brown and gold, like melted chocolate, like pools of caramel and Hershey kisses.

I need to be careful. Although he might be kind, he's a musician. A good looking very successful musician, which means odds are he's a highly tuned, slow burning come-on machine. I've seen it many times over the years, even with the ones who seem shy and awkward. A gear many of these men have whenever a woman is near – any woman - this need to flirt and charm and *win*. Prove they could have you even if they don't want you. It's a dance they love, plumage they have to display. The cocks of the walk crowing at every sunrise.

I need to remember Adam is one of these men. Maybe, to him, he's doing me a favor, flirting with me to make me feel good, like he's doing community service at the retirement home. Maybe he's trying to charm me as the owner of the studio, or maybe this is just fun practice. Regardless, whatever sparks or flutters or unusual electricity I might be feeling, it's all manufactured. It's not real. It's not a genuine, reciprocated situation, so don't be lulled into thinking that it is and do anything stupid.

Do not humiliate yourself, Holly. You're just lonely.

Besides, I don't even know what I'd wish for. I'm out of practice. Except for Luke. I wish for everything for him.

"Okay." I pull my hand from under his and lift the fork, pressing it against my lips, closing my eyes like I'm thinking deeply about something special.

"And it can't be about your son, or someone else, not for your birthday - that's cheating. It needs to be about you. Make a wish for you, Holly," he says, annoyingly reading my mind. I open my eyes so I can roll them at him, then tap the fork against my lips three times, making a show again of giving this wish serious thought.

Finally, letting my smile bloom slowly, I lean in to nudge my knee against his, batting my eyelashes shamelessly. "This might be too much to ask, but now that I know *you*, my wish is that for my birthday next year I'll get a private performance from my favorite guitar player."

Pushing his knee back into mine, his voice unfurling into a low, smooth drawl, he grins. "I believe I can make that wish come true."

Gulp. Ignore that.

"Awww, really? You are so sweet. So, you do know Mike McCready?"

He's stunned like Bigfoot caught in one of those gotcha

photos before he slaps my knee and leans back with a hoot of laughter. I take my first bite of cake with satisfaction.

"You are a painful woman to get to know," he laughs, holding a hand to his chest, placing pressure on his bandage while his shoulders shake. "At least you have good taste."

After a few bites, he puts down his fork. "That really is good fucking cake."

"I know!"

"If you do say so..." he says, taking a drink of water.

"That's right. I want credit."

Returning to the final bits of cake left on his plate, he spots my open notebook on the counter and pulls it towards him. "Are these song titles?" he asks after scanning the first page.

"Yes, that's my never-ending-song-of-love notebook."

"Your what?" he flips a few pages. How do I explain this? I've not shared this weird obsession with anyone. "These all have love in the title," he stops at a page, drawing his finger over the columns of my scribbled handwriting. "Love or lover. Loved."

Although I feel a little self-conscious, there's a part of me that's excited to talk about this.

"I got so mad at being ambushed by love songs all the time. You know... "All You Need Is Love," "Love Is All You Need," "Love Is Everything," "You're Nothing Without Love"... when *my* love was gone. I mean, if love is everything and you don't have it, you've got nothing? You're just fucked?

"It kept happening, these constant, perfectly targeted darts at my heart. In the grocery store, the salon, the gas station, every restaurant. When I didn't want to hear it, when it was the last thing I needed, they were everywhere. Everywhere. Making me cry."

I run my hands through my hair then drop them to the counter. "One day, Pure Prairie League pushed me over the edge."

He wrinkles his nose. "Pure Prairie League?"

I agree with his skepticism with a shake of my head. "I know. But that song came on, with that line, something about finding love only once in your life, and I fell apart. Sat in the garage, sobbing in my car. It broke me."

"I'm sorry," he says, his hand flat on the notebook as if trying to absorb the songs through his palm.

"It's weird, I know."

He's quiet for a moment, eyes on his hand, emotions I can't decipher crossing his face like shadows. "I don't think so. It's the whole point of music, isn't it? Songs are feelings, and our most important feeling is love. Makes sense to me. If music can give us the most joy it should be able to give us the most pain, too. Like love."

"Yeah," I say, gratified and moved by his words. It's as if he used my notebook like a bible, telling a truth about music and songs that I've been trying to articulate. That I've lived.

"There must be hundreds here."

"Uh, try several thousand."

"No fucking way," he's astonished, lifting his eyes to look at me.

"I started writing them down at first because I wanted to know how many were out there waiting to get me. Then it changed. It became more of a hunt, a little thrill every time I heard one or found one that wasn't on my list yet. It started to feel fun. I created a word document, and about once a week I spend time inputting them, arranging them to tell a story. I'm considering, eventually, turning it into a very strange book."

"How will you know when you're done? Because never-ending is right."

"I know, that's the issue now, when to stop. Knowing I'll never get them all."

"You know it's—"

"Insane? Epic avoidant behavior?"

"Every songwriter's wet dream. A shrine to songs. A shrine to love. It's powerful and beautiful."

Laughing, enlivened by his compliment, and his sincerity, without thinking I lean across the counter to run my finger across the cake plate, gathering up some of the left behind frosting. Sucking it from my finger, I joke, "I think 'every songwriter's wet dream' should be my first tattoo. Written right across my ass."

I look to Adam, and he's staring at my mouth. I freeze, my laughter fading away. His reaction is small but unmistakable – he licks his lips then compresses them into a line, swallowing slowly. His gaze moves from my lips to lock onto my eyes with a focus that generates heat across my face and neck, my scalp tingling. It's a moment of absolute stillness.

Desire.

It's been so long, but I still know it when I see it. Know it when I feel it. *Shit, what do I do?* Take my stupid finger out of my mouth, for starters.

I'm the one to look away first, placing both hands in my lap to wipe them on a napkin.

He looks over his shoulder to the door as if he heard someone outside. If I was a different person, a bolder, braver woman, I would swipe my finger through that frosting again and lift it to his lips. But I'm not, so I clear my throat and stand, reaching for the plates.

"Finished?" I ask, my voice about an octave higher. It would help if Adam wasn't watching me again. It's unnerving. I feel like shouting at him- *careful there, cowboy, I might jump you and see if you can deliver. Don't you fucking dare me.*

Part of me also feels like a rabbit, heart racing, pinned down by the stare of a wolf.

Coward. Tramp. Coward. Tramp. I could go either way.

After placing the dishes in the sink, I turn to lean against it, crossing my arms, keeping myself on the other side of the island from him.

"Can I ask you..." he begins, quietly, "You don't have to tell me, but... what was last night about?"

"Last night? My birthday?" My questions are a stall, as if I don't know what he's talking about. He waits, studying me with the smallest tilt of his head to one side.

What do I tell him? I don't have to answer, I don't know this man. I should tell him I'm fine, make a joke. I should open the back door and let him walk out. But he got my list of love songs, the feelings behind it. The pain. He understood, or at least I don't think he judged.

His hand is on the notebook again and I'm reminded of his palm on my chest last night, the firm way he held me as we caught our breath together in the pool. Maybe if I can explain it to him, it will help me understand it myself. Truthfulness with a passing, sympathetic stranger. He's so still, waiting, while my thoughts settle on the two sides of this scale until I'm resolved to an answer.

Sighing, I push away from the sink and step to the island, swiping at non-existent crumbs on the counter. This is not some sultry Tennessee Williams play.

"It was only a little howling at the moon."

TUCKED INTO BED, I've just turned off the light when I get a text.

JACKIE

Wanted you to see what I'm talking about.
Tingles!

She's sent a photo of me and Adam, the one she took at the table tonight. I enlarge it, studying his face. It's etched and almost stern, despite his smile. Masculine and darkly handsome.

She's delusional and I don't want to fall into the same trap.

Haha. I've done the musician thing. It's only plumbers and mechanics from here on. Useful men. If you know any wine merchants or chefs send them on over.

Thanks for a wonderful night. Love y'all

I put my phone and glasses away and turn on my side,

hugging a pillow to my stomach. I'm almost asleep when I hear another message ping, then another. I'm about to ignore it, thinking it must be Jackie again, but there's that maternal part of my brain that always, always wants to make sure it's not Luke. When I check, it's an unknown number.

The texts are links to songs. Bob Marley's "Is This Love" and "Could You Be Loved."

I stare at my screen and go from vowing to stop this fantasy nonsense to giddy. Dammit. Am I that easy? He needs to stop flirting so that I can stop flirting. I know he's just playing, but it is fun. Nothing wrong with fun. I shimmy down in the covers, smiling.

> Who is this? Richard? Tommy? Pedro?

UNKNOWN NUMBER
Like I said, painful.

> Ah, Giovanni! Ciao lover, are you in town?

> Don't pretend you don't like it that way.

Too many to keep straight?

I send him a video, Kylie Minogue's "All the Lovers." And wait. And wait.

He finally sends a song back to me. JJ Cale. "New Lover." I snort, typing back in a flash.

> Darn. Not Giovanni?

He sends a video. "Love Hurts."

> ...

> ...

Did I lose you?

Apologies – I needed some alone time with
that Nazareth drummer

Not the fucking hairy drummer

Oh yeah

In fact – hold on – watching it again – gonna
need another minute

I'm gouging my eyes out

Oh my goodness, sorry again!

Where were we? Philippe? Johann? Come on
then, give us a hint

And do you happen to own a denim vest?

In a flurry, more links land all at once. "Loverman" by Charlie
Parker. "Whole Lotta Love" by Led Zeppelin. "Love Machine" by
the Miracles.

So much bragging. Is this that guy in my pool
house?

Just the facts ma'am.

How'd you get my number?

Stole your checkbook

I send him "Lovefool" by The Cardigans. I'm trying to
picture him right now. Is he in bed while he's texting me? Shirt
off, pants off.

Oh, stop it.

But there's no more texts. I guess he got tired of the game. I'm
about to put my phone away when I see that he's typing again.

He sends "You're Only Lonely" by J.D. Souther, a song I love.
I listen as if Adam is listening with me, a brightly visible current

of electricity connecting us through the walls of my house, the shift away from the banter unexpected. It's so direct I don't know how to take it other than at face value. He might as well be here holding me close. The music is melancholy and full of longing, with lyrics that offer shelter to a lover.

?? No love in the title

Not for your list

From me to you

I know a little about howling at the moon

Happy birthday Holly

CHAPTER TEN

ADAM

I'VE SKIRTED the line with some women before, women with boyfriends or situations with exes that probably should've warned me off, especially when I was younger. I wasn't hiding in bathrooms or ducking down in cars, fuck that, but I did some whispering and tiptoeing around. Back room, private room, hotel room. If your girl wanted me and I wanted her, well then, fair game. But not with anyone married; I had that standard at least.

There was that whole hellish mess with Gina. She wasn't married but it was bad enough to blow up a lot of people's lives. No gold stars for me.

Tonight, I had that shiver across your back feeling when someone's watching you. Holly did that thing with the frosting and I'm staring at her mouth, her pretty, wet mouth. God help me I want to fuck that mouth. And I had to look behind me, like Ronnie was about to bust in and punch me in the face. Catch me in his kitchen with his wife.

He's everywhere, that guy.

That office, Jesus, it's a shrine. Like the man's gone out for milk and will be right back. I clocked the glasses on his desk because there's a pair on the console in the studio, too. I've known engineers with all kinds of superstitions, with good luck charms and mementos around, but I never felt it like this. It made me think of those giant eyes on the billboard in the 'Great Gatsby,' telling me, *I'm watching you. I see what you're doing.*

He loomed large at dinner tonight, still heavily in their thoughts. It's like they're all back in time and I'm visiting from the future. Mike said he's been gone five years. *Five years* and it's like he's gonna walk in the door any minute. I've been here one day and can feel that, see it everywhere. Does it feel that way to her?

At the end of the night, she did that thing, that disappearing thing again. Like a fish that flips its tail at you on the surface and dives straight down into the deepest water, out of sight. She just goes away inside of herself.

I like her – she's funny and playful, and warm. Yeah, there's something about her that's warm. That's the best way I can describe it. She wakes something up inside me, like a pilot light coming back on. It's been a long time since I've found a woman this interesting. Since my dick showed much enthusiasm for anyone. Isn't that some shit? If you would've told my twenty-year-old self, that kid with a Fender and a hard on every twenty minutes, that one day he'd get bored to death with the endless supply of available pussy, he would've laughed in your face.

I was in L.A. too long, in the same circles too long. It's easy to get isolated there, the people around you winnowed down to a few stereotypes. Plastic faces, plastic tits, same lips, same noses, same haircut, same clothes, same conversations, same demands – demands for more. More shiny shit to show off to the people who have the same shiny shit, more access, more excess, more anything and everything that keeps you one step ahead of the poor fucker next door. Fawning all over me for what I do then resenting the hell out of me for what I do.

That younger me would not believe a lot of things. If you showed him a movie trailer of all the coming attractions of his life – the music, the awards, the parties, the heroes he would meet, the places he would go, the women he would bed, the money – if you showed him all of it, told him it would one day all amount to nothing, that he'd get all of his dreams and more but it wouldn't make him happy, that he'd look around at his life and feel empty and lonely, wondering if there was a point to any of it, he wouldn't believe a fucking word.

Ronnie probably had similar dreams. He did alright for

himself, built the studio, wrote some great songs, had a family. But he never got that big fame. He never got that brass ring.

You know I saw them together once – I almost mentioned it but decided to let it go. She must not remember, or I think she would have said something. It was in Shreveport, for some Louisiana Hayride anniversary show. My first record had come out, with that one hit. I was invited as the new hot kid gone big.

I remember a moment in the green room when I saw him sitting back in a corner with this pretty young woman on his lap. A woman I'd been watching all night. He had his arms around her, one hand gripped on her thigh, fingers just under the hem of her skirt, whispering in her ear. She was laughing. She had a drink in a plastic cup, and I watched her sip, then he kissed her. Two people totally into one another, as if no one else was in the room.

And that was her. I didn't know her name, didn't meet her, but I know now it was her. That was Holly on his lap.

I wanted her even then.

I also remember what dumb ass, arrogant thoughts went through my immature head back then, too. I remember thinking that even the old musicians pull the hot girls. Even the small-town low-level ones. If this old dude was scoring someone like that, then I was going to have it made. I'd have a lot of women like that.

He was about the age then that I am right now. Damn.

Now that same man, dead five years, is haunting this whole place. His life was so full, so many people miss him, he's practically still fucking here. His wife is cataloging love songs. And I can't stop thinking about her.

So, I was wrong. He did get that brass ring, didn't he?

I hope to hell he knew it.

CHAPTER ELEVEN

HOLLY

ALRIGHT, time to shake off this mess and get back down to earth.

"You had quite the little crack up, didn't you," I scold myself in the mirror as I brush my teeth Sunday morning, pointing my toothbrush at my reflection. "Something in there just had to get out. Are we good now? You good?"

I'm not going to worry too much about my episode with the doctor and whatever this was with the guy over in my pool house. There's no need for any obsessive navel gazing about this weekend. I was in a bit of a state over my birthday, I've been in a state over Ronnie's journal – let's not think about that today – and grief saw the opportunity and pounced. It's sneaky that way. Sometimes grief is just going to tap me on the shoulder or knock the wind out of me, pull a string attached to the back of my head and open me up like a puppet. I can give it its due, let it all pour through me, then put some ice on the bruises and get on with my life.

Pulling on yoga clothes, I keep this pep talk going. "You had bad sex, so what? You and every other woman who has ever walked the planet earth."

I barely dated before I met Ronnie; why did I think it would be easy for me to figure out how to date now? All there is to do now is laugh at my own ridiculousness.

The yoga is wonderful today, and I don't really care for yoga all that much. It stresses me out when the teacher walks around telling me to relax and breathe. But this class, which is every other Sunday, is basically a series of deep stretches and then a good nap.

All on the floor with pillows. Technically, you're not supposed to nap, but who are they kidding? I have my lavender eye pillow and I zone out for ninety blissful minutes.

My friends and I go for brunch afterwards, and it's especially fun and festive for my birthday. I feel terrific as I turn onto my property late in the afternoon. Driving in I see several cars and a huge tour bus parked down at the studio. They're all at it now, it's begun, so I probably won't have to worry too much about running into Adam from here on out. He'll be occupied.

I call Madeline and we talk for nearly two hours.

"You released the kraken!" she laughs, when I tell her how it went down with the doctor.

"My vagina prefers to be addressed as her ladyship, if you please."

"That's way too Downton Abbey, lace doily between your legs, to be sexy."

"It wasn't sexy, at all."

"It's kind of sweet he gave you a granola bar. Like you had low blood sugar and he wanted to help."

"He wanted me out of his house."

"Well, it's done, cobwebs are cleared. Who's next?"

"Besides the Pelicans starting lineup I have booked in for tomorrow night?"

"Look at you, so ambitious now. Cancel your reservation for the nunnery."

I tell her about Adam finding me in the pool, the trip to the clinic, the birthday dinner. I don't tell the rest - about the conversation in my kitchen, the flirting, and the texting last night. I'm not sure how to describe that, what to say about it.

"Hold on," she says, "I'm looking him up."

"Tell me what's been going on with you. Is it as bad as you thought?" I ask, knowing how worried she's been about the farm, and wanting to change the conversation.

"Worse. Let's not talk about it." I can tell in her voice that she's scrolling. "Oh, I know who he is! I've seen him play before. You were naked in the pool with this guy?"

"I was."

"He's gorgeous."

"People seem to think so."

"People are right. You're telling me you've got this hot-ass man living in your pool house right now? Mere yards away."

"He's here to work. I doubt we'll cross paths again."

"For how long? Is he single?"

"I object to this line of inquiry, your honor. The prosecution is leading the witness."

She cackles. "This is going to be sooooo good, I can tell. What's he like?"

"I don't know, scowly. Nice enough I guess."

"He doesn't look so nice in these pictures. He looks like a bad, bad boy who could show a woman a very dirty good time."

"I nearly killed the poor man already," I laugh. "I think I'll spare us both."

"You'd be doing him a favor! He'd be another man to write a song about you."

"I'm just happy he didn't have me arrested."

I'm barely off the phone with her when Luke calls. That happens a lot – his "Auntie Madeline" sends him nudging texts telling him to call his mother. I love it. This school year, he's been calling me less and less, taking longer to respond to my texts. I try to not make a big deal about it, hoping it's a reflection of all the time he's spending on his class work and his friends. Building a life that he enjoys, becoming independent – it's what a parent hopes for. But it's hard. Sometimes I almost chew my fingers off to keep from calling him. Tonight, he's talkative and funny, and we laugh together so much that by the time we hang up my cheeks are hurting.

After a shower, warm and happy, and the good kind of tired, I crawl into bed to read.

What a great way to wrap up the weekend, a weekend that

feels like it lasted a month. Tomorrow, I'll get back to my routines, this bachelor style of living, as I like to think of it, settling around me once more. Everything back to normal.

When I turn off the light and settle cozily down into the pillows in the dark, Adam slips into my thoughts like he's been waiting at my door, like he was my date, quietly gliding down the aisle and taking a seat right next to me as the lights go down in a movie theater. I wonder how the first day was in the studio, if they're still out there even now. I could text Mike and ask, that wouldn't be so unusual.

I take my phone and glasses from the bedside table but instead of pulling up Mike's name, I pull up Adam's. I look through our texts from last night, finding the link he sent for "You're Only Lonely" and press play. I listen in the dark, eyes closed. It doesn't sound as sad as before. Tonight, it's comforting.

WITH THIS GETTING BACK to normal business, I am. Really, I am.

I get up and call the pool company straight away before diving into the appraisals I have this week, starting with six paintings for a collector in New Orleans. Mondays are tuna salad, so I make that and have lunch at my kitchen island, reading, just like I usually do.

The pool guys show up at one. They tell me the recommended course of action is to completely drain the pool of water so it can be vacuumed thoroughly, which isn't all that surprising. Idiots who bring glass in the pool pay handsomely for their mistakes. It's going to take a painful bite out of my portion of the proceeds from this Chip Walker booking, money I had planned to put towards the debt for the studio repairs after the hurricane last year.

They also commend me for turning off the filters, saving myself the expense from glass damaging those mechanicals. Yes, thank goodness *someone* around here had the sense to do that. I can picture that someone's self-satisfied face right now.

And it's here the first signs of my problem appeared. When something decidedly not a typical part of my normal began.

It's these two pool guys.

Probably late twenties, in their uniforms of navy shorts and white t-shirts, I watch them work and all I'm able to think about is that shorter one's thighs. They're thick and well defined. Why haven't I ever paid attention to any of these guys before? And how are they like that, those thighs? They're huge. His shorts are almost too tight for them, and the way they pull across his muscular backside, *mmm, mmm, mmmm.* His shoulders and biceps are huge too. Meaty. He might be able to pick me up, that one. The taller one, the quiet one who hasn't said a word to me, he's not so muscular but he's smooth and fluid in his movements, long dark hair up in a knot, and very, very tan, with tattoos and an earring. He'd like it slow, I bet. Slow and sensual.

It doesn't stop there.

Tuesday, I drive into Lafayette to pick up a catalog I'm borrowing from a curator at the University Art Museum, then stop at an oil change place to get my car serviced. While the two men in coveralls move around my car, I'm imagining the one with the short dreads and dimples, gold cross around his neck, asking if I'm up for a quick fuck in the back seat. On the house.

On Wednesday, grocery day, I find myself checking out men as they step out of their trucks in the parking lot, push carts down the aisles with their big hands and oversized watches on hairy forearms.

I'm trying my best to get back to my routines, but I am H.O.R.N.Y. When have I ever been this humping-the-doorknobs-level horny? My head might've been telling me all was back to normal, that I had everything I needed here in this cushy solo life, but my vagina has raised her hand and said, *hold on there a minute.* She's saying she absolutely does not have everything she needs, and someone better serve it up pronto. Now.

NOW!

I'm possessed. Maybe when I hit my head an alternate personality was triggered, an insatiable let-me-sit-on-your-face sex demon. Madeline was right, I have released something. My vagina was the tin man who got a little grease in those joints and now is ready to dance. Dance on some dicks. A match was lit, and my house is on fire.

I'm getting all my work done, grinding out these appraisals late into the evening, then climbing into bed with The General, my favorite vibrator, diddling myself into oblivion every night. My vulva is on constant, high alert, and I've had to treat it with coconut oil every morning. Wednesday night The General sputtered off mid-wank and I wailed, tossing him across my bed.

And these damn pool guys are in and out of the back yard all week. At one point, when they were both in the empty pool, shirtless, I had to lock the door and go into my room to masturbate in the middle of the afternoon because I was about to proposition them both.

If people could read my thoughts, they'd be appalled. Maybe it's a brain injury. Some nympho sex spot was damaged, and I need an MRI. Well, I know what I need, dammit, and it's not to see another doctor. What I need is a good railing, but there's no relief in sight.

By Friday afternoon, pool cleaned, filled, and shimmering in the late afternoon sun, I've finished my work and two Jameson and gingers, laughing at myself as I face plant onto a lounger under an umbrella. The pool guys have escaped safely, and I have not one, not two, but three vibrators charging in my bathroom. I'm exhausted.

When I wake, still sprawled on my stomach, it's nearly dark and I'm covered with a towel. I raise myself to my elbows and see Adam in the chair beside me, a book open on his stomach, one arm crossed over his head covering his eyes, the other hanging loosely off the chair at his side. I watch him breathe in and out, deeply asleep.

We haven't talked or texted all week. I was tempted but too scared of saying something cringeworthy in my current over-heated state, plus, he's here to work and he would've texted if he wanted to talk to me. I saw him leave the pool house one morning around eleven, while I was standing at the kitchen sink, but he didn't look my way.

I go inside to use the bathroom, but it seems weird to just leave him there alone like that, so I go back outside and when I cross to the chair, he says a quiet "hey" to me as I sit.

"Hey," I say back, wrapping the towel around my shoulders. "Thanks for the towel."

He moves his arm from his eyes, turning his head in my direction. "You were really knocked out."

"I'm not the only one."

"I hope you don't mind."

"Not at all, I'm happy to see you." I'm rewarded with a slow smile.

"You too," he says, pushing himself upright, swinging his knees to face my chair. He runs his hands through his dark hair, then down over his face, waking himself up. "But you didn't know it was me, didn't wake up. It could've been anyone walking back here."

"Like creepers late at night when I'm in my pool?"

"I'm not joking, Holly. You're by yourself out here and two times in a week I've caught you completely unprotected."

"You 'caught' me because you have a reason to be here. This isn't the city; this is barely the suburbs. I don't feel afraid out here." That last bit hasn't always been true, but I don't want to explain that to him.

"I don't want you to feel afraid, but if you were my.... if you were my wife or sister or mom, I'd not want you to be so vulnerable."

"Well, I do live alone, and I love it out here, so..."

"One easy thing would be to put a lock on that gate and add motion lights to that side of the house."

I tilt my head, considering this. Admittedly, it's a practical solution. "That's two things, but not a bad idea. I'll think about it."

He gestures with his chin towards the pool. "Glad to see it's all done."

"They said turning off the filters saved them from being damaged, so thank you for that."

"I'll let you cook me dinner as a thank you, how's that?" he grins, clasping his hands together on top of his knees.

"You'll *let* me?" I scoff. "Sorry, you're out of luck. I don't really cook anymore." *Or take care of men.*

"What were you going to have for dinner?"

"Um, peanut butter and jelly, then a bath."

"I guess," he sighs, "I'll have to settle for that. Let's go you." He stands, grabbing my hands and attempting to pull me out of the chair. "Tell me you love a lot of bubbles."

I pull my hands away, laughing. My vagina is clapping her hands and jumping up and down, shouting, *yes, yes, yes!* But we know she's lost her mind this week. "I don't think you're supposed to soak those stitches," I say.

Hands on hips, he bends at the waist to lean over me. "That didn't sound like a no to me."

"Oh, then, no. No thank you." I smile at his frown.

"We still need to eat. Can we get anything delivered out here?"

"In the boonies, on a Friday night, it'll take two hours. You're all done for the night?"

"For the weekend. Chip has a show in Dallas tomorrow night." He holds out a hand to me again. "Come on, let's go get something."

TWENTY MINUTES later we're in a small strip mall at my favorite Thai place. It's decidedly un-fancy and delicious. Adam insisted on driving because, as he put it, he needed a win after the whole "bath rejection incident."

"You're saying you're not a sharer?" he asks, looking over the menu.

"Correct. I want to eat what I order, and you eat what you order."

"Not even a bite?"

Awww, look at him. So used to getting his way.

"That's a slippery slope. If you are one of those people who wants to order a lot of things to try, then order a lot of things to try, *for yourself*. Go crazy. My treat. But I don't like it when I know what I want to eat, and I have to fight to get two bites of it. I don't want to feel bad about it so I'm just telling you up front."

He sucks in his cheek, sizing me up, eyes bright and calculating. "Alright, I accept your terms. Tonight, no fork will cross this," he waves his menu across the middle of the table between us, "official no-go zone, unless expressly invited."

"Thank you, maybe there's some masking tape around here," I say, as our waitress arrives to take our order. She collects our menus and heads back in the direction of the kitchen.

"For the record, you can have whatever you want from mine." He's sitting with one hand on his thigh, the other on the tabletop, drumming his long fingers as he says it, all masculine energy and focus on me. Something inside me stands on tip toe because he's about to serve.

"Is the gentleman from the west side of the table—"

"Texas," he coughs.

"...attempting to offer a preemptive quid pro quo to the lady from the east side of the table?" I bring my own hands to the tabletop, clasping them together in a prim authority pose.

"I respect what you said. I'm not trying to maneuver for your dinner," he laughs.

"Good."

"However, I wanted you to know that when you want what I've got, which you will..." he leans back in his chair, so confidently, "I'm going to give it to you."

"I don't think so," I say, crossing my arms.

He shrugs, as if he's stating the inevitable. "You might even beg for it."

I don't want to like this, don't want to smile, because, really, the nerve of this man, but I'm incorrigible. And there's this nympho currently living in my pants.

"*For the record*, we both know, out of the two of us, who will do the begging." I lean back in my chair, mirroring his pose, picking up my water glass and narrowing my eyes at him over the rim. This man needs a little tit for tat. And yes, pun very much intended.

His eyes do not leave mine. We allow each other seconds of uninhibited view into the other, counted off like heartbeats. *One, two, three.*

He lifts his glass to me. "I can't wait to find out."

He might be playing with me, his pick-up skills on auto pilot, but my ego is lapping it up. I'm not dressed up, I don't have on any makeup, but he looks at me as if I'm interesting to him, with his full attention. It's powerful and I'm sure not specific to me, but Adam is making me feel great about myself.

Horny with no available outlet aside from silicone devices, so horny I might need a shock collar to safely move about in society, but great about myself.

We talk through dinner about the week in the studio. He's more open about it than I thought he'd be, with what went well and what he sees as the challenges. He asks a lot about my work and though it shouldn't come as a surprise to me, since he's travelled all over the world, his genuine curiosity about some of the artists I mention is not what I would have anticipated.

I excuse myself to the ladies' room and when I return to our table, he's signing the check.

"Wait," I say, dropping into my chair. "This was supposed to be my treat."

"I took care of it."

"But—"

"Holly, I took care of it." He picks up the fortune cookies that came with the check, and after passing them back and forth between his hands, he holds them out to me, palms down. I tap the top of his right hand and he gives me that one, opening the one from his left hand for himself.

As we're leaving, when he opens the car door for me, he says, "That's the best first date I've had in a long, long, time."

I bark out a sharp laugh in disbelief. "That was not a date."

"It certainly was. Why do you think I paid?" He shuts the door, walking around to the driver's side, smiling at me through the windshield.

"I was going to pay!" I shout, repeating it when he opens his door.

"Not when you're going out with me."

That stupid smile. This man is picking a fight with me.

"Okay, first of all, this was not a date. This was a business dinner."

"It was a date," he says, backing the car out of the parking spot.

"Both parties have to know it's a date for it to be a date. Secondly, this is the twenty-first century. I'm a grown woman with a job and I can pay for a date if I damn well want to, when I'm actually on a date."

"If you want to pay, you can cook me dinner."

"I'm not cooking for you!"

"You don't have to shout."

"I'm not shouting. I'm trying to be heard over the chest thumping."

"I asked you out to dinner, I drove, there was flirting, I picked up the check, and now I'm taking you home." I stare at him open-mouthed, flustered. He reaches over with his right hand, using one finger to gently lift my chin and shut my mouth. "Maybe you're out of practice."

Swatting at his hand, I sputter, "This was definitely not a date because if it was, I'd be wearing much nicer underwear."

His laugh bursts from deep in his chest, filling the car, and I feel like I've won a prize.

"Well, sweetheart, that's something else to look forward to."

Back at my house, after he's made a show of kissing me on the cheek and I've made a show of rolling my eyes, I'm in my bathtub when my phone dings with a text.

ADAM

You in the bathtub?

No, I'm washing my wigs and waxing my mustache

Already prepping for date #2

And your mustache is adorable

Hey! Mean

Are you in the bathtub?

I lift one foot out of the water so that my painted toes are visible and text him a photo.

Need help reaching any dirty places?

Too late

Next time...

Then he sends a link for a song I'm unfamiliar with. "Dreams of Love," by Bert Jansch. Just a man and a guitar. It's... well, it's a little odd. An old-fashioned, coffee house sounding folk song. Lost love sort of thing, which makes me laugh. As I listen, the spareness of it, the beauty of the playing, quiets me though, and it becomes unabashedly beautiful.

CHAPTER TWELVE

HOLLY

SATURDAY THE GG's come to clean. Technically the business is named All Clean Acadiana, but I dubbed them the GG's because of Teddy and Jim, the older, married owners. The gray gays. Teddy is here today, and we chat as I re-stock the kitchen in the studio while his crew is upstairs. Pulling beers from a case at my feet and loading them into the refrigerator, I mention Chip Walker and he swoons.

"Lord, I could eat up that boy from head to toe, but bless his heart what is with that hair?"

"I haven't met him. What's your problem with his hair?" Teddy has been dusting the sitting area behind me. He pulls his phone from his pocket, scrolls for a few seconds then walks over to me, turning the screen in my direction and pressing play on a video.

"He has a mullet. A red neck mullet."

"I think the kids do it ironically."

"I can't stand it," he turns the phone back to himself. "But damn, that ass though."

I crane my neck to see his screen again. "I should try to see that in person."

Adam is on his way to Chip's show in Dallas, leaving before I woke up at the crack of ten am. He didn't go up with the band because he wanted to stop in Shreveport to see his mom on the way there, then spend the night after the show with his sister, who lives in Dallas. I learned all this on our non-date last night.

I had a look around the pool house before the GG crew went in there. The bed was made, nothing personal in the bathroom except for some bandages and first aid supplies, presumably for his stitches. I lifted the lid of a suitcase inside the closet. Jeans, tees, black boxer briefs, all folded neatly. A tub of protein powder and one of those small bullet blenders was on the counter of the kitchenette, the refrigerator empty except for a container of spinach and plain Greek yogurt, two bags of mixed frozen berries in the freezer.

"California," I mutter.

I struggled to pick up a kettlebell tucked along one side of the sofa, grunting, needing both hands to curl it up to my chest. It says twenty pounds on the side, and I can't believe how wimpy I am but then realize it's kilograms and feel better.

Some of the messes left behind by musicians over the years have been horrendous. I once found an open mayonnaise jar, spoon inside, on the bedside table. Used condoms in the kitchen sink. But not this time. Neat as can be. I admire it, which gives me a pang of guilt. Not for my nosiness – I'm human! Who wouldn't have snooped??!! - but for the disloyalty of comparing him to Ronnie.

Ronnie was handsome but more the rumpled mad-genius type, and it stressed me out to a degree that he could never understand. The debris, the wrappers and empty containers that never seemed to find a trash can. The endless stacks of notebooks and papers on every available flat surface, in every room, even though he had an office in the house and out in the studio. When people talk about their loved ones sending them signs after they died, coins or playing cards or faces in clouds, I imagine Ronnie leaving me crumpled up saltine wrappers on the kitchen island.

I close the door of the pool house, guilt diluted with affection for one of Ronnie's foibles that seems so unimportant now. I can almost feel him winking at me, and I shake my shoulders. *I'm mad at you*, I say to him in my head. *Don't be cute right now.*

I work late into the night Saturday on one of my freelance auction catalog jobs. I do mainly artist bios and lot descriptions for the bigger sales when the staff need the extra help. The pay is decent for what it is.

Adam texts me around nine-thirty. My chest goes fizzy like a shaken can of soda.

How's your Saturday night?

My first instinct is to search for an image online of a club rave, full of shirtless men. But I decide to be real and send a photo of my dining table; laptop, reference books, papers scattered around me.

Exciting

Adam sends a photo, obviously taken from the backstage wings over the top of a large speaker, showing Chip and the band from behind, with lights and the crowd beyond.

Did Hank really do it that way?

And here I am lookin' at the backside of Chip Walker

Not having fun?

I can think of much nicer backsides

I can't wait to tell Mike how much you miss him

You have me all figured out

Have fun

See you soon

See you soon. That brings a small smile to my lips and the fizz changes to tennis balls knocking against my ribs.

. . .

I TAKE it easy on Sunday, which means a little laundry and a lot of television, with a short swim in the evening. This is the gentle, solitary routine of my life that I love but Adam strays into my thoughts throughout the afternoon. I find myself hoping he'll knock on my door.

A few minutes of witty banter, some of those tingles I get when he aims that suggestive stare at me – that's all I need. Just a little bit of that. A transfusion of fun and vitality straight into my veins. There's no real harm in it. He's only here for a few weeks, so why not let him flirt and why not flirt back? He'll be a sexy B-12 shot for my soul.

I can handle that, keep it from going too far. No problem.

MONDAY MORNING, I look out the window over my kitchen sink to a sight that makes me burst out laughing. I rush outside to stand by the edge of the pool. Delighted beyond belief, I hold my arms out, looking around as if to say, *is anyone seeing this?*

There's a brand new white swan pool float bobbing in the water. There's also a companion swan, a shiny black one, floating nose to nose with the white one. That fool.

Still laughing, I text him immediately.

> THANK YOU!

> I love it. Now I've got an Eric and a Bill

About ten minutes later I get a reply.

> We'll work on the name

> He's Bill

> I'm not going to ride a Bill

> Fair enough

> For you he'll be William

I don't receive any other texts from him Monday. The fancy tour bus is over there. I saw it when I took a walk to stretch my legs, along with Adam's SUV and a sleek silver Maserati sedan - *who in the world could that be?* – but I haven't been invited to stop in. I don't hear from him Tuesday either, nor do I manage to see him coming or going from the pool house.

Great. Just when I've decided to let myself flirt with him in small doses – I know I've been doing it already, okay, a teeny tiny bit - but now that I've decided to *enjoy it,* like some sexy version of a cheat day, a rationed, hunky Texas sugar cookie treat, he's not around.

Wednesday, my doorbell rings early, which can never be a good thing, because anyone who knows me would never, ever show up to my house at eight in the morning. I throw on a robe and stagger through the house, my sleep mask pushed high up on my forehead. When I yank open the front door there's a middle-aged man on my porch in faded khaki carpenter pants, blue t-shirt, and baseball cap. There's a van over his shoulder in the driveway but I'm not awake enough to read the logo printed on the side. I don't have a pulse yet.

He takes one look at me and says sheepishly, "Oh, sorry ma'am."

"How can I help you?" I say, squinting.

"Yes ma'am, uh, I'm Keith with Cajun Contractors. I have a work order to install a gate lock and some outdoor lights for you."

"Say that again please?"

He refers to the clipboard in his left hand. "New lock on outdoor privacy fence. New motion sensor security lights."

"I didn't schedule any work like that."

"Maybe your husband?" After checking the clipboard again, he looks back to me. "Adam is the contact name."

Fury rises in me like a comic book dragon.

"I'm sorry. I didn't know to expect you. If you go around to the back, please, I'll meet you out there."

"Yes, ma'am," he says, retreating down the steps, and I stomp through the house to meet him on the patio. After he looks over the gate and advises me of the best locations for the lights, I march directly to the pool house, banging loudly on the door. There's no answer but I don't believe for a second they've started out in the studio this early. I knock again, louder.

The door swings open and Adam shields his eyes from the sun with one hand, the other raised over his head, clasping the door frame. Wearing only black boxer briefs, like the ones I saw in his suitcase, his tousled dark hair falls over his forehead. Sleep clings to him, I can practically feel the warmth from his bed coming off his skin, and a picture of him tangled in sheets, smiling that lazy grin, fills my mind.

I take a sharp inhale of breath. I sure have a pulse now, and it has conveniently started right in my vagina.

"You..." I stammer, but my eyes don't care that my brain needs all hands on deck to form words at this moment. No, they tell me to fuck off because they, my eyes, take a deliberately slow walk all the way down his body. As I conduct an inventory down to his toes and back up again, my eyes slow at his crotch, at the erection lifting the pouch of his briefs.

Fingering the neckline of my silk robe I swallow hard, praying for the strength to not let this man see me lick my lips. I drag my eyes back to his face. His eyes are narrowed, watching me, one of those slow, cocky smiles spreading across his face. He's not self-conscious at all, standing here with his morning wood greeting the neighborhood. He's proud as hell.

"What do you need, Holly?" he asks in a husky voice, his expression suggesting he's fully aware of every single one of my needs as he takes his own slow look up and down me. My robe suddenly feels like it's made of tissue, that's it's going to fall away in pieces under the heat of his gaze, and my stupid nipples harden to attention. It infuriates me.

"Someone was banging on my door to do work on my house that I did not order. It's presumptuous... overbearing... high-handed of you. I do not care for it."

He moves from his dream lover pose to peer across the patio. "He's here?"

"Yes, he's here." Fuming, I step back to keep a healthy distance between us. Between me and his dick, which is like a radio tower sending out signals to all my nerve endings. My nerve endings that are dancing a conga line throughout my body like they've just won the lottery.

"They were going to let me know when they were coming. Sorry he woke you."

"Yeah, well, you deal with it now," I snap, turning on my heel to stride back to my house.

Inside, I throw myself into bed, pulling my mask down over my eyes, but I can't fall back to sleep. I toss and turn, kicking at the blankets. *Who does he think he is?!*

I get up and go to the shower, bringing The General with me. I'm so angry. That man makes me so angry. Yes, alright, I told myself I liked the flirting, but this arrogant way he has of just assuming I'll fall all over myself for him, it's too much. Like I'm any other woman on a constantly moving assembly line, smiling and ready to screw Adam fucking Sexton.

And I played right into it, didn't I? One nearly naked man in my backyard and I lose my head, drooling over him like I'm leaning over a case of French pastries.

Mouth-watering, lickable, warm, arrogant guilty pleasures.

Growling under the hot water I use the vibrator roughly, banging an orgasm out of myself in waves so intense I double over the tiled bench onto my forearms to keep my shaking legs from collapsing.

CHAPTER THIRTEEN

HOLLY

"He's pursuing you," Madeline pronounces.

"The swans, that was cute," I concede. "But don't you think it's pretty nervy to assume I would want his help?"

"I don't think it's about that. He's wooing you, showing his interest in you."

Scoffing, I say, "Showing off is more like it. I think he's just another musician who chases women like it's a competitive sport, and I happen to be the only woman out here."

"I'd guess he's never really had to chase many women before, that they usually chase him," she says.

She's right, and it irritates me.

"Well then it's presumptuous to assume I'd just fall into bed with him."

"Why don't you?" she laughs. "You don't like him?"

I don't answer.

"You do like him?" she presses. Again, I don't answer, which to Madeline, is an answer. "Is that so terrible?"

"Yes," I mumble.

"Are you still freaked out by what happened with that doctor?"

"No, this isn't like that."

"How's it different?" Her tone makes clear she knows the answer and just wants to lead me there, hear me say it out loud. Which I am not going to do. "It's different because something about Adam scares you," she says.

"A person who nearly drowns is not crazy for avoiding the water," I blurt, wincing at my own melodrama. She bites her tongue, I know she does, because she loves me, and she takes a deep breath before answering.

"You're not crazy, honey."

"Uh, I love you, but we both know it's embroidered on pillows for people like me."

"The stakes feel so high, and they don't have to, you know. A little fun, letting someone woo you, maybe you could let yourself enjoy it."

"Maybe." She's making the same pitch I made to myself. To have some fun.

"Look, pick your poison. You could suffer hiding yourself away forever, and you know that already because you're lonely and mauling doctors and about to Mrs. Robinson the pool boys. Or you could suffer if you open the door to this man who's knocking so loudly. It might not go well; he might turn out to be a jerk or lousy in bed..."

"Oh no," I hadn't even thought of that. Frankly, it seems impossible.

"Maybe you'll decide that being single is what makes you the happiest, and trust me, it can be marvelous, but it's not always perfect. Nothing is. So, decide which imperfect is best for you right now. You can always change your mind, but don't be the cause of your own suffering because you were too afraid to make a choice, that you covered your head and just let things happen around you."

AROUND SEVEN O'CLOCK that evening there's a knock on my front door again.

"Jesus, this day is a pain in my ass," I huff, getting up stiffly from my laptop at the dining table.

After my call with Madeline, I was too tired and honestly, too knotted up, to do anything else, so I've been sitting here scrolling and fantasy shopping. Opening the door, I'm surprised to see Mike and Adam, then remember the new lock installed on the gate today. They'd need the code to come to the back door.

"Gentlemen," I say, standing back in invitation. The fact they're both here, and their gloomy faces, tells me this is not good. They take up positions at my kitchen island and I walk around to the sink to stand opposite. I address my question to Mike.

"You look like someone shit in your boots. What's going on?"

"We need a sweeper," he declares, without preamble.

"Oh, come on, you're joking."

"I wish we were joking," he says, hands on hips in frustration, "But this ship is about to go down if we don't do something."

"You're barely two weeks in!"

This is bad.

You see, Ronnie had a system, deploying me strategically in certain situations. We had code words.

Cat Toy. This was when Ronnie wanted me to drop in to say hello, be a bright and shiny distraction. He said even fifteen minutes of something new to focus on gave most people time to calm down, let some harsh words dissolve. Also, people might be goofing off, wasting time, but when someone else came in and held things up, they felt the time lost more acutely and would be ready to get back down to work. They might get annoyed with me, the wife stopping by, but who really cared about that. I could be a re-set for the room.

Woodshed. This one was fun. I'd pretend to be furious, barging in as if I was there to murder my husband, demanding, "May I speak to you privately? Now, please!" And he'd make a show, behind my back of course, as he was leaving – a roll of his eyes, a pretend loosening of his collar - the poor husband in trouble. Outside, we'd just talk for a few minutes or make out. This was useful when the artist was struggling, either with some part of their performance or their overall self-confidence, or perhaps he had given some feedback that landed badly, accidentally pissed them off or struck a tender nerve. He said almost every time he came back in, looking like I had ripped him a new one, it shifted the power dynamic in the room. People felt bad for him and forgave him for whatever he said, or, seeing him brought low buoyed them up. I don't know how he figured that one out, but he said it was highly successful.

Sweeper. This is the one I didn't like, when someone in the studio needed to be removed. Sometimes it was a friend of the band who couldn't read the room and see their presence was no longer welcome. Too drunk, too opinionated, supplying too many drugs. Too something that was getting in the way of the work and too uncomfortable or inconvenient for the (mostly) men to deal with. I've ushered wives out of the studio and plied them with wine by the pool. Invited them to the movies or lunch and shopping in town. I've taken girlfriends to dinner so they wouldn't cross paths with the wives. I've lured people to my house under multiple pretenses, then given them a quick bouncer heave ho, foisting them into a cab before they realized what was happening. Most people are too stunned to protest in the moment, but I've been cursed out several times.

"Who's the problem?" I sigh.

Before Mike can answer Adam speaks, and I look at him for the first time since they came in. "Bill Walker."

"That fancy car, that's his? He's been here all week?" I ask, incredulously. "Why on earth would he need to be here?"

"Yes!" they say in unison, practically shouting.

"And why do I have to come out there and deal with it? You can't figure something out between the two of you?"

"Because it's a damn cage match about to happen, they've already taken a few swings at each other..." Mike says, waving one hand in the air.

I glare over at Adam. "You punched someone?"

"No," he fires back at me.

Mike says, "No, it's Bill and Chip going at it. Adam's had to get in the middle of them a few times to break it up. We're not able to get much done and I don't know what's going to keep Chip from just walking out at this point."

"Damn," I say softly. We've already been paid for the studio time, so that's not the worry. The concern is having no record to show for it, no record from someone on the rise like Chip Walker to hold up as a billboard to attract other acts of similar stature, similar deep pockets. The concern is damaging or distorted rumors getting around of trouble out here.

"He's rich and mean, and a fucking personal injury lawyer. I'd lay him out on his ass right now, if I thought he wouldn't sue me and you, and hell, everyone we've ever met, for everything we have," he says.

And, okay, there's that concern too.

"So, sweeper. I don't know what the hell you can do, but why don't you two talk about it because I'm going home. I'm over this bullshit. I'm going to go put my kids to bed."

When Adam and I are alone in my kitchen we stare at one another, waiting for someone to speak first. His body is stiff with tension, fatigue etching his face. My irritation subsides seeing him like this. I grab two beers from the refrigerator then take a seat at the island, opening one and setting it down in front of the empty stool beside me, opening the second one for myself. He walks over, dropping onto the seat, and we sit side by side and sip in silence.

"Thank you," I finally say. "That's what I should have said this morning. You didn't have to do that, but it was very kind of you, and I appreciate it."

He inclines his head in my direction. "You're welcome. I'm sorry I didn't let you know he was coming, or if I over-stepped." We drink a little more before he says, "You really are not a morning person."

"No. No I am not." Twisting on the stool so that I'm facing him, I say. "Alright, tell me, what's going on down there?"

"I had it so wrong," he sighs. "I thought Bill Walker strong-armed this whole thing to help Chip out somehow. You know, a drug problem, or girl problem. Keep it private."

"And that's not it?"

"Not that I've seen. No, it's clear Bill just wants to control everything. He wanted Chip closer to home, somewhere isolated. He's trying to write songs for fuck's sake, he was elbowing Mike out of the way at the board—"

"Oh, and Mike loves that," I interject.

"He's going to need blood pressure medication to come back tomorrow."

"Chip's a grown man, he's what, twenty-seven or something?"

Nodding in the affirmative, he says, "And talented. We got two good songs last week, but Bill listened to them, like he's the head of the label or something, and started rattling off how he thought we could fix them."

"He's been doing this in front of everyone, in front of Chip's band? In front of you?"

"Yep." He arches his back for a stretch, scraping back his hair in frustration. "And Chip just takes it and takes it until he explodes, then they go at it."

"Why hasn't Chip made him leave? It's his father, yeah, but it's his band, his record contract, his career."

He scrubs at his face. "It's not so easy when your dad's a son of a bitch like that. They are locked in a battle that's been going on for a long time."

"Then why in the world would Bill want *you* here? Seems like you'd be the last person he'd want around if his plan was to be some sort of top dog shadow producer."

"Good fucking question."

"You're in charge. You kick him out," I say, taking another drink of beer.

"It's about to come to that, but then he'll fire me, and I know I can make this record something special. I'm the right producer for Chip."

"Then he'll fire the studio. Or worse, like Mike said."

"It's a real concern." He exhales a deep breath, looking directly at me. "The code words are clever; I could've used any one of them over the years. Ronnie Theriot was not only a saint, but he was smart, too."

He shakes his head, raising his beer in a small salute, something in his tone that isn't entirely pleasant. There's a sour note and that scowl is forming around his mouth. Whatever it is, I have no desire to sit here with him and talk about Ronnie tonight.

I stand up and cross the kitchen to drop my empty bottle in the trash.

"No one's a saint, and unless you two are expecting me to bring Bill Walker poison in a cup, I don't know how I can help."

"If you have poison, I'll give him the cup."

"Come on," I say. "Let's go get some dinner."

He shakes his head. "I need to go by that clinic and get these stitches removed tonight."

"We'll do that. You can distract the nurse with your shirt off and I'll steal some drugs or something. Problem solved. Then we'll get dinner."

NURSE MISSY TAKES one look at us and snorts, "Look who it is," before waving us inside.

She's the one to remove his stitches, and in a replay from our last time here, he stares at the ceiling, semi-reclined on the exam table, and I admire his torso. The bunched muscles in his shoulders, the way they curve down across his pecs, with the scattering of dark hair spreading across them. The points of his nipples. The definition still visible in his abs, the concave scoop of his belly as he rests in this position, that same dark hair stretching from his navel to the button of his jeans. I thank the stars he's not any younger because I wouldn't be able to take it; he's aged to my comfort zone now.

I lower my head to study my hands in my lap, thinking over my conversation with Madeline. And I tell myself the truth.

I want him.

I'm attracted to him, drawn to him like a cartoon bear to

honey. I want him and it scares me. I've been dancing around it, bobbing up and down with the feelings like I'm on a merry go round. Flirting, not flirting; telling myself he's charming then telling myself he's some sort of middle-aged fuck boy.

I want him and I'm in knots about it, knots made out of electrified barbed wire. This is nothing like my mortifying escapade with the doctor. I had no attraction to him, we had very little in common. He was safe. I could prove a point to myself, take a swipe at Ronnie, with little emotional risk other than embarrassment.

But Adam.

I wasn't prepared for him, haven't sorted out my feelings about letting another man into my life. I crushed those feelings into a tight little ball of pain and shoved them into a deep dark corner of my soul, to be excavated at a later date, a date I expected would never arrive. Now here he is, waltzing in with that sexy come fuck me smile, saying, hey, let's me and you get all into it, dig up this pretty ball of pain and take a look. And I'm practically hyperventilating. When I'm not masturbating.

Madeline is right. I've got a decision to make.

After the clinic we pick up Greek salads and soon we're back at my kitchen island, eating. It's easy, companionable, but I'm distracted, this question of what to do about him, whatever this is between us, breaking into my thoughts like the low hum of a television in the next room. I've pushed my salad away, been rolling my water glass between my hands.

"Holly?" I lift my gaze to his when he speaks. "If you're worried about this sweeper thing... it's not on you to solve this. We'll throw the guy into the river and be done with it."

"I thought I'd have dinner brought in for everyone tomorrow night so I can at least meet him, see the situation for myself. If that's okay with you?"

"Yeah, of course, thank you. I'm sorry we laid it at your feet, but we didn't want it to come as a surprise if everything went sideways."

He goes back to eating while I gulp down the rest of my water, studying his profile. He notices that I'm watching him. Whatever my face is doing, it's enough to cause him to put down his fork and slowly wipe his mouth with his napkin.

I speak before I lose my nerve.

"What do you want from me, Adam?"

"I'll deal with Bill Walker, don't worry about it," he frowns.

"That's not what I'm talking about." My voice is steady, somehow, even though my heart is racing. "The attention, the flirting, what are you doing? What do you want from me?"

I have not looked away, will not let myself look away, and his eyes probe mine.

"I want to get to know you," he offers, but that's not enough, which is immediately clear to him when I stay silent, waiting for more.

He looks around the room, his shoulders rising and falling with a deep inhale and exhale of breath, then reaches out to me, taking one of my hands in his, and begins to rub slow circles in my palm with his thumb. His touch is a spur in my flank, I could jump out of my skin into his. I pull my hand away and let the words rush out.

"I found one of Ronnie's journals this summer. I know what you were thinking when you saw his office... I know what it looks like. I just... I just can't stand being in there."

"You don't have to explain anything to me," he says, confused.

"The journal talked about..." My face grows hot, tears fill my eyes, and I hate it. I am not going to fucking cry right now. "About other women. Women he loved, women he couldn't forget, women he invited to his gigs. I never knew. Never had a clue." The bitterness in my voice, the pain, is beyond my control.

He reaches for my hands again, taking them in his, coaxing me to unclench my fists.

"I was mourning this life we lost, and it might have all been a lie." I can't handle Adam touching me while I'm saying this, it's too humiliating. I lift my hands back into my lap. "Maybe he thought none of it mattered if I didn't know about it, and he's not here for me to slap his face and tell him what I think of him. I'm so furious, but all these people love him..." I can't say more. Not if I want to do what I'm about to do.

"I'm so sorry, Holly." Adam's face is stricken, his voice strained.

I sit up straight, squaring my shoulders, refusing any pity that might be tempted to show itself in his eyes.

"I don't know what you want from me but let me tell you what I want from you. I want to have an affair with you. I want to fuck you until I can't remember that man's name, until I don't feel like his wife anymore. I'm not looking to fall in love, I don't need anything from you except respect and kindness. I'm not looking for a boyfriend, but I am looking for someone who can show me a good time. And I think you might be the right man for the job."

This is the poison I choose.

CHAPTER FOURTEEN

ADAM

WHAT DO you want from me?

I've been preoccupied with exactly that, all the things I want from her. Holly in my arms, in my bed, riding my dick with those beautiful breasts bouncing above me. On her knees, sucking me off, blue eyes staring up into mine. My name on her lips when I make her come. I've been preoccupied by all of her, wanting to talk to her, text her, find ways to make her laugh. Looking for love songs like I'm waving a sign under her window - *pay attention to me!*

But when she straight up asked me, I couldn't find the words. I went fucking mute. Her pain wrecked me. It was so raw I could barely stand it. It was her defiance that made me take it, kept me from looking away. It was like taking a punch.

And not just from her hurt and anger but from knowing, fuck me, *seeing* in this beautiful woman the pain I've caused a few women in my own life. I wasn't married to any of them, hadn't made that kind of vow, but I'd be a liar if I said they wouldn't have had some expectation of fidelity that I didn't uphold. The same "what they don't know won't hurt 'em" mentality she named, not knowing it was an arrow right at my black heart.

Or maybe she did know.

Maybe that's why she sees me as someone to fuck this man out of her with no risk of any attachment. I'm the perfect, low life asshole to get the job done, as she put it. I don't know if I've ever felt so called out in my life. What she thinks when she sees me, well, she made it crystal clear. She took my breath away and not in the way I've wanted.

The irony that I left Los Angeles to change my life, to extricate myself from the circle of shallow people that had come to be my life, my lonely fucking life, and that I haven't been with a woman in over a year - the *miserable irony* that I would literally stumble out of the dark into this person, this incredible, singular woman - of course she would only see me for the man I've been.

And that's it. The man I no longer want to be is exactly what she saw, what she named, and who she wants.

It's poetic, really. As predictable as fire rhymes with desire. The collective prayers and curses from a long list of women from my past, all answered here and now by the one woman I'm interested in, coming back to bite me like the karma that it is.

Fucking bullseye.

Why in the hell didn't he burn that damn journal?

CHAPTER FIFTEEN

HOLLY

HE DIDN'T SAY YES. He didn't say no, either, but he didn't exactly throw me over his shoulder and haul me off to bed.

What he did was slow blink for a full five seconds, that scowl pulling his lips into thin lines as he studied my face, eyes inscrutable under his dark brows, before standing up and pulling me into his body for a hug. A long, tight hug, one that I was about to file in the *bless your heart* category of pity hugs, until he placed his lips at my ear and whispered gruffly, "I'll think about it, sweetheart," and ran one hand down my back to tap me lightly on my butt. Then he walked out of my house.

Kind of a mixed signal.

Maybe he wants to keep some semblance of the upper hand here. We'll see. Men generally say yes to available sex, right? Does that go away with certain significant birthdays? I know I didn't imagine his attraction for me, I know it, but maybe I overestimated it. Confused it with mine for him.

Anyway, the deed is done, I've made my offer. We'll either get it on or avoid each other for the next few weeks.

And note to self: if I'm going to keep propositioning men like this, maybe I need to work on my messaging.

That hug, though.

I felt him pressed against me long after he left; my chest, the inside of my arms, my thighs, like heat from the sun that remains on the skin, slowly fading as a hot day turns to dusk.

It's another unexpected part of grief, one I didn't realize I'd feel so acutely.

The first few years after Ronnie died, I'd fall asleep on a stack of his pillows, as if resting my cheek on his chest. I've cried silent tears during a massage, the touch almost too much to bear, the longing it brought forth the worst, painful kind of craving.

I hug my son, I hug my friends, but it's not the same as being *held.* Having someone take you in their arms, being caressed and soothed and offering the same in return. Oh, how I've missed it. I wrapped my arms around myself when Adam closed the door to hold on to the sensation.

I want him to say yes. I want to text him but forced myself to put my phone away. And I don't let myself bring a vibrator into bed, even though the craving is pulsing through my sex. I'm going to go to sleep unsatisfied, letting that need build in my core until it radiates down my legs and up my spine, spreading through me like a current. An energy maybe he'll feel, a call of longing he'll not be able to ignore.

Sometime after midnight I'm pulled from sleep by the ping of a text alert. Adam has sent a song. Leonard Cohen's "I'm Your Man."

My smile is immediate, and I roll under the covers like a cat, listening to the low timber of Cohen's voice stroke my skin with words of declaration, all the ways he'll be who I want him to be, luxuriating in the delightful smut that floods my imagination as I drift into dreams of imminent pleasure.

Hallelujah.

CHAPTER SIXTEEN

HOLLY

I BLOW off most of my own work the next day and set out for the grocery store. Thankfully, Mr. Tony was free when I called him this morning about making one of his big black pots of jambalaya, so in addition to picking up what I need to supplement dinner, I've decided to make a cake. I feel like celebrating.

As I'm walking out of the house, Adam texts me. Seeing his name on my phone now gives me a big, double *zing zing* of excitement.

Good morning

Forgot to get the code for the gate

0420

Are you kidding?

What???

Let's go out this weekend

Are you free?

Like a date?

Yes a date

Saturday night – me, you, that better
underwear you mentioned

We don't have to do that

I'm not looking for anything from him other than sex, but what's the harm if I let Adam woo me a little bit more? Could be fun, which is the point after all.

AFTER AN IMPULSIVE DETOUR TO buy firewood because maybe a night around the fire pit is just what everyone needs, by the time I get home I'm behind schedule. While I'm waiting for the cake to be done, I eat a sandwich and check email until it's time to take it out to cool on the counter, then drive myself down to the studio.

The fire pit is behind the screen porch at the back of the studio. I smooth out the gravel, raking away leaves and twigs to neaten the area, and prep the pit before stacking what's left of the firewood in the metal rack inside the porch. The doors to the seating area are open to let in some of the rare cool fall air. I've just carried my last armload inside when shouting from the kitchen behind me causes me to jump.

Turning, I see Bill Walker charging into the room, hot on the heels of Chip. Bill, around sixty, is broad and stocky, like a man who used to be muscular before the years behind a desk got the better of him, with a remarkably full head of silver hair and heavily tanned skin. He's in jeans and a faded LSU polo shirt.

"What the hell's the problem now?" he's shouting at his son's back.

Chip, taller than his father, heads straight to the refrigerator. Throwing open the door, he pulls out a beer and twists off the cap, bringing it to his mouth for a long drink. My first thought is how young he looks in person, not much older than Luke.

"You're gonna fucking listen when I talk, you ungrateful piece of shit," Bill's pointing a finger in Chip's face. Chip stands his ground, the outline of his jaw severe as he lifts his chin defiantly.

"Get back in there," Bill says, jerking his thumb over his shoulder.

"You're not in charge here; you're making an ass of yourself," Chip says.

"Son, I'm in charge everywhere."

"You're a joke here," Chip snarls, while I remain in place on the porch, wishing I wasn't a witness to this scene. But then Bill lunges for his son, grabbing his shirt. Chip's beer falls to the floor as he pushes against his father, his right hand squeezing around Bill's throat.

Yelping, I run through the open doors, shouting, "Hey, hey, HEY!" as I round the dining table to where the two men grapple. "Get your hands off him! Let him go!"

Adam, Mike, and a young man I don't know burst in from the studio but freeze at the scene. I'm holding a piece of firewood over my head, ready to strike.

"Let him go!" I shout again, the threat in my voice causing Bill to look up.

In that second of distraction, Chip pulls his hand from Bill's throat, rearing back in a flash to leverage a punch that lands right across his father's jaw. Bill staggers to his left, folding over the counter, and Chip, not waiting or gloating or making eye contact with anyone in the room as we all stare in shock, stalks away, out through the porch, letting the screen door slam behind him.

Bill rights himself, turning slowly to face me as he wipes a trail of blood away from the corner of his mouth. I gotta hand it to the man, he can take a punch. Probably had a lot of practice.

He looks at the log I'm holding above my head, sneering derisively, and I lower my arms. Smoothing his hair, he takes a step towards me, his mouth twisted with words I don't get to hear because Adam and Mike position themselves at my sides.

Faced with the three of us, he draws back his shoulders to gather in a posture of authority. Keeping his eyes only on me, he says, voice dripping with curdled cream, "You must be Mrs. Theriot. Pleasure to meet you." He doesn't wait for a response. He leaves the room, brushing past the young man who's been watching from the doorway.

"Can I throw him out now?" Mike asks.

"I want to talk to Adam about that. Go make sure he doesn't do any damage to equipment." I call a "thank you" after him as he leaves with the other musician. When he's out of the room, I turn to Adam.

Reaching to take the log from my hands, he says, "Alright killer, you sure are creative when you need a weapon." I see admiration in his eyes, his lips forming a grim smile. "I almost wish you would've clobbered him."

"What an asshole. Bully and an asshole," I grumble. Adrenaline is flooding my body, I'm ready for a fight. "I'm glad Chip landed that punch."

"He's out. I don't care anymore; I'm kicking him out."

"No, don't," I touch his arm. "That's what I want to talk to you about."

Exasperated, he balks, "I'm not spending another second with that prick."

"Listen, Chip is trying to stand up to him, and he needs to be the one to make him leave. He needs to win this, not you or me or Mike. It needs to be him."

"He's had all week, what's he waiting for?"

"He's trying. He punched his own dad, for Christ's sake. But if it's one of us that kicks him out it's just that much more humiliating; another parent handling his business, like he's still a boy, and that won't help him. I want to help him, Adam."

"You think I'm old enough to be Chip's dad?"

My deliberately loud inhale and exhale at his vanity helps me gather the last of my patience.

Shaking his head, biting his lip to keep from smiling, he says, "Okay sweeper, any ideas for how exactly we do that?"

"I'm forming one, yes. Here's what I want you to do."

I TAKE my time getting ready, keeping it all minimal, the kind of minimal that takes effort to look effortless, because I want to feel confident. Armed. Dressing in slim black joggers and a matching long-sleeved tee, I look in the mirror.

Be an assassin, I tell myself. *Be cool*.

I asked Adam to speak to Chip alone, outside, man to man. Tell him it was time to ask Bill to leave and that he needed to be the one to do it. To let him know the reason no one had done it already was out of respect for him, not his dad, and if it turned into a brawl it didn't matter, everyone would have his back, including me and the studio. We agreed one of us would find a way to provoke Bill tonight, which shouldn't be that difficult, to give Chip an on-ramp for a confrontation in front of everyone. I wanted him to have this moment in front of his band, to step into his leadership, his own authority.

Adam and I also agreed that if this didn't work tonight, he was free to handle Bill Walker in any way he chose, which he made clear would likely involve a baseball bat.

At the studio, I'm relieved to see Mr. Tony is early. As I unload food from my car, he brings a cooler of ice inside for me, then begins setting up his table and cooking rig outside. Soon enough I hear, then smell, meat browning. Pulling a bottle of Johnnie Walker Black from my bag - seemed like the night might call for a nip - I pour two fingers in coffee mugs and head outside. Tony spoons browned sausage out of the big black pot, into an aluminum pan, then adds cut up chicken from another pan in its place. I pass him one of the mugs and we chat and sip while he stirs, the sky growing dark around us. Texting Adam that we're about thirty minutes away from dinner, I light the fire pit.

It's a lovely fall evening, the jambalaya smells delicious, the aroma released every time Tony turns his spoon through the rice. If it wasn't for this business with Chip and Bill, I'd be excited about the night, but I'm jumpy with nerves, even after the whiskey.

When the guys start filing into the kitchen I go inside and place two loaves of garlic bread into the oven as they grab drinks from the cooler. Adam steps across the room to me. Hand lightly at my hip, he speaks quietly into my ear, "You look ready for business."

"How did it go with Chip?"

"Good." His fingers give me a small squeeze. I want to lean into him, my body reacting with a mind of its own, but thankfully I'm saved from myself when the band member who was part of the earlier scene here in the kitchen approaches.

"Holly," Adam says, stepping back from me, his voice rising to a more public volume, "This is Ewan, Chip's drummer. Ewan meet Holly Theriot, the owner of Riverside Studio."

Adam introduces me to two other band members and also, officially, to Chip himself. He shows no outward signs of nervousness but as he shakes my hand and offers a few very kind compliments about the place, I mentally note that Bill hasn't shown himself yet. However, right as the timer on the stove begins to beep and I excuse myself to tend to the bread, the man himself walks in. The pungent smell of hot bread and garlic fills the room when I open the oven door. It's the perfect distraction.

"Serve yourselves, guys. Salad and bread in here, and Mr. Tony has jambalaya outside for you." I stand back as they circle the table, murmuring and filling their plates. The atmosphere is subdued, not jocular or celebratory, which is sad because all the guys in the band are quite young, in their twenties, and I'd usually expect them to be horsing around out here, blowing off steam like over-grown puppies.

Mike comes to me, plate in hand, and kisses me on the cheek. "Thank you," he says, before heading outside. Mike, the man with two young children at home, a pregnant wife, and an asshole making trouble in his studio, is definitely not a kid and definitely not pleased. He looks positively depressed.

When everyone has a plate, I make one for myself and one for Tony, tuck two sodas under my arm, and go outside. Loaded up with a generous helping of jambalaya - Tony knows I'm going to eat like a starving linebacker - I turn to the guys eating around the fire. Adam stands and waves me over to his chair, which I take, and he goes inside, returning with one of the chairs from the dining table, settling himself beside me.

As we eat, things start to loosen up, the small talk less stilted. The fire snaps and crackles, the guys have seconds and another round of beers. I'm asked about some of the people who've recorded here, artists they've no doubt seen in the photos lining the walls, and I offer up a few of the more entertaining anecdotes I have at the ready for situations like this. With the laughter and ease taking over, as pleasant as it is, I begin to worry I might not find an opportunity to provoke Bill, who has been conspicuously quiet, as has Chip.

I steal a glance at Adam, raising my eyebrows in a silent *I don't know why they're all suddenly being so nice* expression of consternation. After the guys have cake, however, and compliment me and Tony for our efforts, the guitars come out, and I know the egos will follow.

Rob, Chip's guitar player, begins with a lighthearted nod to our evening with the Hank Williams classic "Jambalaya." Even Tony cracks up at this, singing along as he's cleaning up his gear. Rob sings my name instead of Yvonne in one verse, earning a laugh from me.

When the song ends, he looks to Adam. "Time to hear something from you, man."

Adam brings his guitar to his knee, thinking for a moment,

then calls out to Chip, "See if you know this," before launching into Jimmy Reed's "Baby What You Want Me to Do."

And it is *sexy*. Rough voiced, kind of growly, it's all I can do to stay in my chair because what I want to do is wantonly sway my hips in his face. I drop my chin to my chest, closing my eyes to let his deep, drawling voice caress my skin. Chip joins in for a verse, and I open my eyes, tapping my hands on my thighs.

When they finish, Chip keeps playing, slipping from that shuffle into an almost rumba beat, slapping his palm on the face of his guitar between strums. My heart drops into a low gear when I recognize the piano intro he's interpreting, one I'd know if someone wheezed it out on a kazoo or tapped it on the soles of my feet. He speaks quietly, commanding the attention of our small circle as sure as he would a sold-out arena.

"I learned this song when I was sixteen years old. Got first place in the talent show... got the girl." At that he looks up at me, smiling. "I never imagined I'd get to play it for *the* girl, the one who inspired it. This one's for you. Thank you for tonight."

There are echoes of *thank you Holly*, drinks raised in my direction, but it all fades to a whisper in my peripheral vision when Chip sings the opening words of Ronnie's song, "Hallelujah, I'm a Dreamer." He sings with such simplicity, his smooth tenor following the melody without embellishment, that it heightens the intimacy of the words, drawing us all into a moment together here in our circle around the fire, and I'm genuinely moved. When the final notes have drifted up into the night sky, we all applaud and I'm wiping a tear from my cheek.

"Has anyone ever told you that maybe you ought to be in the music business?" I feebly joke. I hold my hands to my heart and mouth thank you to him, and he returns the gesture, smiling over his guitar. He has completely won me over.

Before the star dust has had a chance to settle, while we're all still floating on the echo of Chip's voice, Bill clears his throat and brings his own guitar across his lap. I would bet good money that every person here inwardly groaned.

Here we go.

"Not a bad song," he says, strumming with his right hand, adjusting the tuning pegs with his left. My eyes instinctively search for the fire iron I brought outside earlier. I steal a glance at Mike, and I swear he's making a fist. "My son knows hundreds of songs, but it's funny, he won't accept a song, a hit song, when it comes from inside his own family." And he begins to play.

He's a serviceable guitar player but not much of a singer, making up for what he lacks in range and tone with heavy emoting and volume. It's fine for a guy hanging out with friends, a weekend enthusiast. Based on the chorus, I assume the song is called "I Admire You Forever," and it's an over-wrought, patronizing mess.

This is going to be rough. I better be careful and not enjoy myself too much.

He looks around when he's finished, waiting for a reaction, but everyone is silent. I take it as my cue.

"Did you mean that as a love song?"

"It is a love song," he says.

"Who wants to be *admired* in a love song? Loved, desired... I love you so much, I want you so much, I need you, adore you, miss you, got to have you. You don't tell a woman you admire her in a love song, that's terrible. That's a breakup song, like saying it's me, not you. I admire you so much is code for let's be friends."

No one speaks, which makes the sounds of the fire and the croaking frogs down by the bayou, louder.

"I disagree," he says flatly. This man wants to smash his guitar over my head.

"And if you do admire her, the *art* would be to *show* it, poetically, metaphorically..."

"I guess it's not for you then." He laughs this off, putting his guitar to the side. Everyone else is transfixed. I steel myself against any instinct to ease up; I know what needs to be done.

"Who's it for then, him?" I say, raising my hand in Chip's direction. "You think it's for him, when he can pick any song from any writer on the planet, when he already writes his own hit songs, you're saying he should pick *that* song? Because it's his daddy's song?"

Big Dollar Bill does not like this, not at all, his jaw working like he's chewing through leather. But trial lawyer that he is, he holds onto his cool with a lethally calm voice. "How is this your business?"

"This," I wave my arm to signal everything around us, "is literally my business. You think because I like to argue that I could put on a suit in the morning and join you in court? I wouldn't disrespect you like that. Have some respect for these guys who are all professionals. And when you're here on my property you will show some respect for my husband. But, you know, good job, keep trying."

I watch his expression go black, his sneer, and know that I've done my job.

He snaps, rising from his chair. "Listen, bitch, you forget who you're talking to. Blowing some cut rate writer out here in the middle of the woods doesn't exactly make you an expert."

Adam and Mike are both on their feet as soon as the word bitch leaves Bill's lips, but Chip is also standing, and he turns on his father. "That's enough, I've had enough!"

"Don't start with me now, son," Bill warns.

"Enough!" Chip shouts. "You're out! You've cost me this whole week, fucking around, and I'm not having it. I've got too much on the line to prop up your ego anymore. Get your shit and get out."

Bill is practically pawing at the ground. "I paid for this—"

"About that," Chip advances on his dad, shoulders back to benefit from his full height advantage. "I called Ross at the label to set it all straight. This is my band and my time. *I've* paid for this now and Riverside Studio has kindly agreed to reimburse you, minus, of course, the costs you incurred wasting our time this week."

Bill looks in my direction and I nod, once.

"Now, get the fuck out." Chip stares him down as Bill's face contorts with anger and the urge to lash out. Mike takes a step forward, crossing his arms over his chest, followed by Adam, then the rest of the band, each one in turn standing in solidarity. Looking around the circle at the men who've chosen his son, he walks away without another word.

Mike and I exchange a look and he follows Bill, while Adam reaches down to offer me his hand, helping me stand. I can't look at Chip because all I want to do is hug him and tell him how proud I am, which would be all wrong in this moment. Chip's bandmates surround him, and they go back inside, speaking in low voices.

"Holly," Adam says, keeping his voice down. "Can I just say that I admire you so much."

I swat at his chest, groaning. "I was so mean; I can't believe it."

"He had it coming, and he got off easy. Don't think I didn't see you eyeballing that fire poker."

We walk together through the screened porch into the kitchen and the band is there milling about, cracking a few jokes, eating more cake. And by some sort of unspoken agreement, they help me clean up. Loading the dishwasher, putting the remaining food in the refrigerator, wiping down the table and countertop.

Adam murmurs to me, "Look what happens when mom gets pissed off."

The guys kiss me on the cheek one by one before leaving. It's funny, and sweet, given what's happened.

Chip has lingered, the last of the band to approach me, and when he leans in to peck my cheek, he says thank you into my ear. He then swipes the bottle of Johnnie Walker from the counter, giving me a wink, and walks to the door.

Over his shoulder he calls out to Adam, "Come on old man, let's get to work."

Adam shakes his head in mock horror.

"You heard him," I say, laughing. "I did my part, now get to work."

CHAPTER SEVENTEEN

HOLLY

I SLEEP until nearly eleven the next morning, artless provocation of a bully clearly being exhausting work. When I wake and check my phone there's a text from Adam, sent at three fifteen am. It's just one photo of Mike, smiling into the camera from his position at the board. A smiling Mike is all I need to see, and I feel a little better about the ugliness of last night.

My fingers twitch to text him, but I resist. He hasn't said anything else about our date this weekend and, sensing it likely won't happen now that the situation with Chip has improved, I push away my disappointment, resigned to reality. Making headway on the record will be his priority now.

On Saturday, early in the afternoon, I'm unloading bales of pine straw from the back of my car next to the screened porch at the studio, with some azaleas in three-gallon pots positioned in the bed where I want them planted. I'm digging the hole for one of them when I hear voices behind me. Turning, I see both Mike and Adam on the porch.

"Y'all done for the day?" I ask, speaking to them through the screen, pushing my sun hat back on my head to wipe my brow. "I wondered where the tour bus was."

"Til Monday," Mike confirms. "They're in New Orleans for a gig tonight." He locks up and they walk down the steps. "Do you have a number for Cassie Touchet? They're looking for a fiddle player next week, thought I'd see if she was available."

"Oh, that's a great idea. Yeah, you know she used to babysit Luke sometimes."

"I remember. Ask her to give me a call, will you?"

"Yep," I nod, directing my eyes to Adam. "She's a good singer too."

Mike looks over at the plants, keys spinning on one finger. "Need help with any of that?"

I shake my head, knowing how ready he is to get home. "No thanks, I'm about to get it all knocked out. Go enjoy your weekend." He smiles gratefully, and the dust is following his car down the driveway in under a minute.

Adam doesn't ask. He just lifts his bag and guitar case into the cargo area of my CRV and walks up to me, taking the shovel from my hands. He goes to work on the hole I'd been digging, and I fetch my water bottle from the ground nearby.

After taking a long drink, admiring the muscles in his back and arms as he works, I say, "I have another pair of gloves if you want them."

"Yeah, sure," he says, and I retrieve them from my car.

"How's it been going?" I ask, handing them over, wishing he had to take his shirt off to put them on.

"So much better."

"Are you worried this might backfire onto Chip down the line somehow?"

"Are you?" he moves down to where I have the next plant waiting.

"Yes."

"I don't think we solved years of father son dysfunctional history, but I think Chip might be better prepared for the next go-round."

"You say that like someone with some personal experience," I venture.

He strikes the shovel into the dirt with force, his features flattening into a hard, expressionless surface. He turns out the dirt to the side of the hole and stabs at the ground again. When he answers, his words carry a gruff finality, but his eyes are not angry when they meet mine. "My experience is that men like Bill Walker don't really change and the sooner you accept it, the better."

I nod, acknowledging that I understand he's said all he wants to.

"Do you like working with Mike?" I ask, removing the azalea from its pot where he just finished, getting it into the ground and scooping the displaced dirt back into the hole.

"I love working with Mike. We never lose time because he's not ready; he's always ready, and intuitive about it. And he keeps his mouth shut."

"Doesn't try to be a back seat producer, you mean?"

"Exactly. No offering unsolicited opinions, which can be hard for some engineers, but it makes me crazy and can really undermine artists."

Trained by Ronnie, I say to myself. "And I know he definitely has opinions."

He laughs, "Oh yeah. But only shares them when asked, and now that I think about it, usually only when it's just the two of us. Really sharp cat."

"The studio wouldn't have survived without him, after..." I don't let myself finish that sentence, although it's obvious what I was going to say.

"He's very loyal," Adam agrees. "I talked to him about engineering my next record and he said he'd only do it at Riverside, not in New Orleans, or anywhere else."

Aghast, I stare at him until he stops digging. "You tried to poach my engineer?"

He shakes his head, bewildered. "No, I assumed he'd not want to travel anywhere, he's got a house full of kids, although for some guys that might be a good reason to travel..."

"And the run of a world class studio, that's not nothing."

"Absolutely. I'm only saying, he made it clear before I barely had the words out."

"And what would you have done if he said yes, for you, Adam Sexton, I'll say screw Holly and follow you anywhere?"

He takes a deep breath, leaning on the shovel, and replies extra calmly, "I never asked him to travel anywhere and never expected him to. But I don't see how it could be much of a surprise to you that someone might ask him to work on a project somewhere else, if it hasn't happened already. He's that good."

"They can't have him," I huff.

"That wouldn't be up to you, it would be up to Mike. It's business."

He's right, and I've never let the thought enter my mind before, which now seems quite foolish. And scary. Naturally, I'm peeved at him for making me think about it.

Gently, he says, "Did you miss the part where I said I'd like to make my next record at your place? Do you think that's just about Mike?"

He offers me his hand, and after a long look into his eyes, willing myself to calm down, I give him my hand, which he squeezes. Then he releases me and goes back to digging.

"I'll give you a good rate," I offer, checking out his butt as he bends to shift the next pot.

"Sweetheart, charge me what you want. It's the perks I'm after." He winks wolfishly at me over his shoulder and in an instant my body lights up with warmth from the inside, like a gas oven set to pre-heat.

We continue working in silence and I like it, the not talking. It's companionable and easy, which I haven't had in a long time. Adam spreads the last of the pine straw while I water the plants. When he's finished, he straightens, taking off the work gloves.

"Looks good," he says, surveying our work. "It's so satisfying."

"Until the next hurricane, but thanks for your help, that went so much faster."

"Well, we don't want you worn out before our date now, do we?"

Laughing, I can't look at him, and instead keep my focus on my watering. "Is that still happening? Tonight?"

"Yes, ma'am it is," he declares, walking past me to carry the shovel to my car. "Or did you forget and double book yourself with that doctor, what's his name?"

I shoot a quick spurt of water in his direction as a reward for his comment. "What are we doing on this date?"

"I made dinner reservations for eight, then I thought we'd go see D'Shawn's band. He said they were playing tonight at a place called Feed & Seed. You know it?"

"I do," I say, turning off the hose at the spigot. "That'll be fun. They draw a big crowd there." I say it confidently, as if I've been out anywhere like that in ages.

CHAPTER EIGHTEEN

IT's like there's a thousand bees under my skin; a type of high, breathless excitement that makes me almost lightheaded. Adam takes my hand as we walk through the gravel parking lot, and it might be the only thing keeping my feet from lifting off the ground.

On the ride from the restaurant we didn't speak, this attraction between us, the anticipation, stifling, and I asked him to turn up the air conditioning. It was a monumental effort to not order him to turn the car around and take me home. And take his pants off. But I command this monster currently typing out crazed directions inside my vagina to hang on a little longer.

The sounds of an accordion and rub board immediately grab me, an impulse to shimmy impossible to resist. It's the magic and joy and full body experience that is zydeco. Perfect for working out these nerves.

The club is a long rectangle with wide wood floors and industrial ceiling fans, a stage running along the left wall, the bar on the right. Garage doors at the far end are wide open. It's crowded, with a circle of dancers in the middle of the floor. We make our way around them, along the bar, to a spot not far from the open doors.

Adam is taking in the scene with keen interest. "This is incredible."

I give him a huge smile, feeling a moment of pride in this town. It is incredible.

We get beers and watch the action, and I'm grooving in place, the music loud and syncopated. For possibly the one hundredth time in my years living here, I marvel at how diverse the dancers are at these shows, in age and race and appearance. It's about as inviting a crowd as one could imagine, and I absolutely love it. How have I stayed away so long?

He leans over, speaking loudly enough to be heard over the music. "You wanna dance?"

I'm amazed. "You dance?"

"Not *that* good," he says with a lopsided grin, head motioning to the dancers. "But yeah, three sisters. I didn't have a choice."

I put my hand on his shoulder and pull a face. "I'm not really that good either..."

"I bet we can manage," he says, as a rare slow song begins, and takes me in his arms right where we stand, still holding our beers. We rock gently from side to side, his chin grazing the top of my head. His chest is strong and solid – I could do this, just this, for hours. But he sets our bottles on a nearby table.

"Come on," he grabs my hand and leads us forward.

The music shifts into high gear again, and we muddle through, dancing and laughing. He's much less self-conscious than I am, and it's contagious. Pulling me in and out of his embrace, twirling me under his arm, we touch each other more and more freely with each song. On one of our turns in front of the stage, D'Shawn spots us, lifting his cowboy hat in a salute.

Hot and sweaty, we return to the bar to catch our breaths. When I excuse myself to go to the ladies' room, he walks with me, ducking into the men's room.

I'm dabbing my face with a paper towel at the sink when my friend Simone walks in. When we make eye contact in the mirror, I swear she winces before catching herself, plastering a smile on her beautiful face. Lithe and graceful, she's probably the best dancer in the building. Her dress is long and loose, swirling around her ankles. It would be a potato sack on me, but on her it's effortlessly cool. The thin straps would last about thirty seconds against my boobs.

"Hey," she says, taking me in a quick hug. "It's so good to see you."

"Hey yourself, I didn't see you out there."

"Just got here. How are you? It's been a while. You look gorgeous."

"Thanks, you too."

This is so awkward. We've had a good friendship over the years – she teaches at the local university, and we have friends in common there, and Luke went to one of her summer Shakespeare camps when he was a kid. She's witty and fun, always great to spend time with.

But last spring she called me one evening to see if I was home. She wanted to surprise her boyfriend Stan, who was recording out in the studio, by bringing him dinner, and she was in route, wondering if I knew what sort of schedule they were on. An instinct rang loudly in my head, and I told her to stop at the house and say hi before she went down there.

I immediately texted Mike and my suspicions were confirmed. Stan had a guest with him.

So, I had the thankless job of keeping her away, pulling a sweeper on my own friend. I made up some pitiful excuse. *I just received word they already ordered dinner in, planning to work late into the night, interruptions would not be welcome... blah blah blah,* while in my head I was planning to staple gun Stan's dick to a poison ivy covered tree stump.

She eyed me closely then just flat out asked me, "He's got someone out there with him, doesn't he?"

It killed me, but I wasn't going to lie to her, tell her that what she already knew wasn't true. My loyalty was with her. "I'm sorry."

The look on her face would've broken anyone's heart. It wasn't surprise; it wasn't even anger, really. It was embarrassment and hurt. A deep, shitty hurt. She left and I haven't seen her since.

"Well," she says, ducking into one of the stalls. "Have fun

tonight. The band's on fire." She latches the door, and that's it, conversation over.

It feels rotten, and unnecessary, over some stupid guy. I want to talk to her, but I stop myself. It's not the time or place.

"Have a good night," I say, and walk away.

When I leave the restroom, looking for Adam, who is he talking to? Stan! Of course he's talking to Stan. Does Simone know he's here, I wonder, or is she here with him and that's why she looked like she'd rather run into a masked chainsaw murderer in the ladies' room than me?

The last person I want to chit chat with right now is Stan, and I absolutely don't want to be standing here with him when Simone walks out, so I veer right and go back to the end of the bar, where straight away a man walks up to me and asks me to dance. I can't think of a reason not to, so I say yes, and he leads me by the elbow into the fray.

He's a much better dancer than I am despite being easily twenty years older. Better than Adam too, but sweet about it, and when the song ends, he takes my hands for a two-step, keeping me on the floor for another turn with waves of couples doing the same. As we move, I spot Adam on the periphery of the crowd, smiling at me. No Stan or Simone.

I'm winded when I make it back to him, and he throws an arm around my shoulder. "You ready to get out of here?" I nod my head. "Good, let's go before someone else grabs you."

Outside, the night is wonderfully cool after the heat of the club. When we get to the car, I walk to the passenger door, standing aside for him to reach the handle, but instead of opening the door he gently pushes me against the car, taking my hands, unfurling my fingers until he's lightly holding them against his chest.

"I'm going to have to keep my eye on you," he says, voice low and amused, bringing my left hand to his mouth and kissing my knuckles before guiding it behind my back.

"It's my..." licking my lips, I'm having trouble speaking. "It's my... incredible dancing."

"Is that what it is?" He brings my right hand to his lips, holding it to his mouth for a few seconds, his touch lighting up cells all the way down to my toes. He tucks this hand behind me.

My arms now pinned, he steps closer, fitting one leg between my thighs, taking my hips in his hands. Through the fabric of my skirt, his fingers flex against me, and I arch my back to lift my body into his, the pleasure of my response curling one corner of his mouth into a sexy half smile. He presses me into the car, holding me in place with his hips, moving one hand slowly up my side until it stops at my breast, cupping it in his hand, the other curving behind my neck to fist in my hair.

I've seen flirting Adam before, suggestive, naughty Adam, but when I lift my gaze from his mouth to his eyes, I'm staring into the smoldering brown eyes of a different man. A man who has me under his hands, pinned by his body, and knows just what he wants to do with me.

Holding my head firmly, squeezing my breast, his thumb passes across my nipple. His eyes never leave mine, watching as I inhale sharply at the sensation. He swallows hard and I shift against his knee, craving every inch of contact, longing for him to kiss me.

Please kiss me. Kiss me now, my body begs.

He pulls away a few inches, shifting his stance, then rocks forward, his bulge pressing into me. He moves against me again, then again, the smallest of movements, his hand never leaving my breast, studying my face as I react. It's hypnotic, this pace; his gaze, his touch, lulling me into a state of total, melting submission. Pulling my head to one side his lips nuzzle the skin of my throat, just under my ear, and when I hum softly, he kisses down my neck, nudging aside the neckline of my shirt with his face to kiss the top of my breast. All the while slowly shifting back and forth against me, my body on fire in all these places where we connect.

Using his thumb as a guide, he bites my nipple through my clothing, and I jerk with a jolt of surprise and arousal. Chuckling, he lifts his mouth to plant another kiss on my neck. When his teeth graze my earlobe, I might weep if he doesn't kiss me.

"Adam," I whisper.

He tilts my face, his thumb now stroking the spot where his lips were moments ago, staring into my eyes again, searching deeply. If I knew what he wanted, what he needed, I'd give it to him. Anything so that he'd kiss me.

"*Adam.*"

Like an archer who has their target in sight, has pulled their bow as tightly as it will go, the string creaking with tension, when I say his name something inside him is released and he lowers his mouth to mine.

I DON'T REMEMBER my first kiss with Ronnie. Isn't that strange? I think I remember when it happened, where we were, more or less, but I don't remember the actual kiss. Not how it felt, what he did, what I did. I do remember our first kiss as husband and wife, when Ronnie went for it before the minister said the go-ahead words and everyone laughed. That's a sweet memory.

I know people who can tell you in detail about their very first kiss – little Jimmy somebody in the cloak room in sixth grade or whatever. I couldn't tell you that either, I have absolutely no clue.

I will remember this first kiss with Adam for the rest of my life.

It's as if he slowed down time, every touch deliberate and purposeful, recording all of it. Telling me to pay attention, *remember this*. Hands and heat and breath, heart fluttering, nothing but his lips and mine, his body and mine, everything around us still and quiet.

It sounds ridiculous, I know. Overwrought. I know. I imagine anyone walking by wouldn't find us all that remarkable, other than thinking, *oh, look at those middle-aged people, making out like that.* Because you think of barn burning first kisses as a rite of passage for the young, those tender shiny souls with a long future stretched out in front of them, one of many first kisses inevitably leading they feel sure to a one true love and a happily ever after. Not for the older, battle scarred among us.

Not for people with wrinkles and hot flashes, sore knees and indigestion. Not for those of us who've loved and lost. Not for those who have kissed and kissed and kissed and never found the one but instead found that the fairy tale is sometimes out of reach for no other reason than plain bad luck.

But I challenge anyone, twenty-five or fifty or eighty-two, to close their eyes and simply, lightly massage the inside of their own wrist. Make slow, soft circles on the skin. Imagine it's a lover. The sensation transcends time and age and appearance.

First kisses, making out in a parking lot like a meteor is heading to earth and it's your last hour alive, can still happen.

And dear Lord, I know I've had some very judgmental thoughts about the body count that must be in the wake of this man. I apologize. Sincerely, I do. I was intimidated and maybe a little jealous but now, if I could I'd hug each and every one of those women from his past. Bake them a cake. They raised him up, trained him up. He worked his way up through them all to the major leagues. Whatever cringe metaphor works best, you know what I'm saying. These women were the soldiers who got him here. Because holy fucking hell, can this man kiss.

Taking his time, he presses his lips again and again to mine until he breaks away, leaving me reaching for him with my chin. I make a small noise of displeasure and he dips his mouth immediately, sucking my bottom lip into his then releasing it, teasing it several times, coaxing my lips apart. As I open my mouth to him, he's gentle with his tongue at first, not rushing to invade but stroking lightly, gaging my response, letting me invite him in. But the pace, the rhythm, are all him. As his stroking becomes stronger, his tongue more urgent, he moves one hand down my side, lifting me away from the car to slip his arm around my waist and squeeze my body to his. I free my arms, raking my hands up his back and onto his shoulders. Wanting more, to be closer, I clutch at his shirt, raising a leg along his thigh, and he groans softly, pushing his hips into me.

I don't know how long we kiss like this; it wouldn't have surprised me to open my eyes and have it be another season, another year. But when he finally steps back, I'm dazed. He caresses my cheek, placing one last soft kiss on my lips before shifting me away from the car to open the door.

I'm soft and shaky, like a wobbly bowl of pudding. If he kisses like that, well... Jesus, what will the rest be like? I want to know, and I want to know now. I'm dying for him to drive faster, but don't say a word. I don't want to highlight the fact that this might be just another normal Saturday night in his life, whereas for me, this is a fucking sexual Halley's Comet.

He parks in my driveway and holds my hand again, walking me around to the back, punching in the code to unlock the gate. At my door he wraps both arms around my waist, pulling me slightly onto my toes, and we kiss for several minutes, his tongue so strong in my mouth that my clit starts throbbing.

I drag my lips from his. "Let's go inside."

"Uh-uh," he says, backing out of my arms.

"Oh," I laugh, stepping with him and putting an arm around his neck, "Your place then."

He disentangles me from his neck, setting me at arm's length. "No, sweetheart, I'm saying goodnight."

All the hormones in my body do a collective groan, like a full stadium of fans when a pass is dropped in the end zone. At first, I think he's joking, a quick flash of admiration crossing my mind at how he's able to keep such a straight face. But just as quickly I see the look of regret in his eyes and the set of his mouth. And the fact he's rooted in place, several feet from my door.

"I don't understand," I stammer. He's rejecting me, after the way he's kissed me? My face flushes at the humiliating thought.

"There's no rush, let's take our time," he says, putting his hands in his pockets. Something casual in his tone sets me off and I can't help myself. I stomp my foot in frustration. This is not the rock star treatment I signed up for.

"For what? We're not virgins at church camp. I told you what I wanted from you. We did your date, let's do this."

"I know exactly what you told me. And I told you I wanted to get to know you."

"Get to know me naked!"

"Believe me," he says, suppressing a laugh. "I plan to."

Offended, outraged, my vagina starts sending my brain a telegram. *Push. Man. In. Pool.*

He steps to me, wrapping his arms around my waist again. Lips to my ear, he drawls, "Trust me, I'm going to give you everything you want." With a kiss on my cheek, he says, "Let's talk about it tomorrow," before leaving me for the pool house and closing his door.

Inconceivable.

Even after a shower, I'm still aroused and frustrated. I grab The General and climb into bed, arguing with Adam in my head. I text him Jeff Buckley's "Lover, You Should've Come Over." Then, for good measure, a photo of the vibrator.

He responds straight away.

Don't you use that thing, not tonight

> Could have been you

It will be - I'm telling you no, you're not to come with that thing

You're saving for me

> Repeat chorus

> Could have been you

I'll make it worth it

> That's very bossy for someone not currently in my bed

> The next time you come will be on my face

> The next time I'll come will be on those gorgeous tits

> Deal?

Holy hell. Yes, please.

I'm trying to figure out how to respond, wondering how I'm going to get any sleep after reading those words. Then he sends a song which makes me throw myself back into my pillows and laugh. Guns N' Roses. "Patience."

So full of himself.

> Don't make me wait too long.

CHAPTER NINETEEN

ADAM

SHE STOMPED her foot at me.

I didn't know how I was going to keep myself from her, had to keep from reaching for her in the car on the drive home. She's so responsive, so soft and pliant in my arms, I was ready to say to hell with my plan and have her right there on one of the patio chairs, tell her to keep those boots on.

But then she stomped her foot, and it was so damn cute it made me laugh, must've allowed a little bit of oxygen to reach my brain, and I said goodnight.

I went straight into a cold shower, hoping to mute these *more, more, more* demands pulsing inside my head, trying to numb all this out of my system. Dammit. I do want more. I want to fuck her, could break down her door right now, but the thing that stopped me, the last bit of reason that hasn't abandoned ship for my dick, is that I don't think her little tantrum had that much to do with me.

Holly made up her mind to get some payback for what she read in Ronnie's journal, and she had to find someone she deemed morally compromised, or at least emotionally uninvested, to get what she wanted. Beautiful, independent woman seeks available male, a breathing warm-blooded dildo, for no strings attached affair. I just happened to come along at the right time.

Hell, it's fucking humbling.

Without a doubt, if I give her exactly what she says she wants from the man she thinks I am, that's exactly and *only* who I'll ever be for her. With no going back. I've been that for so many women, and it's not what I want anymore. I want her to see beyond this superficial version of me. I want a chance to be more.

If all these women have taught me anything, it's how rare it is to cross paths with someone who feels special. Who you want to make feel special. If I don't want to be that disposable guy, forever attached to and tainted by this transaction, I need to lead her away from the whole scenario. She'll have to choose me.

Tonight, before we kissed, I had the thought - how many more first kisses am I going to have in my life? How many more awkward dates and stilted getting to know you conversations, pretending to be interested, groping someone in the dark just because they're willing and available. Am I going to be doing this when I'm fifty-five? Sixty-five?

I wanted to slow it all down, remember every detail, in case our first kiss was my last, first kiss.

Don't get me wrong. I'm gonna fuck her silly, but if I can control this situation a little bit, it won't be about some other man. At least not entirely. It has the possibility of becoming something new. Something real.

It makes complete sense in my head, but I am the man taking the cold shower. This trying to change my ways business is some real blue ball bullshit.

CHAPTER TWENTY

HOLLY

Let's talk about it tomorrow.

Did he mean let's have sex tomorrow?

I want to get to know you.

What's that about? What more could he possibly need to know about me before he can put his penis into my vagina? My credit score?

I really don't get it. It seemed like as good a time as any to start this thing. Dinner, dancing, all that kissing.

And time out for a second – *Come on his face? Come on my tits?* I like it. Really like it. As in, please sir, I'm a lady but, take my panties.

What in the hell is his problem? What does he need to talk to me about before we can get on with it?

Oh my god. There's someone else.

But he implied he was single, so that doesn't really make sense. Why would he do that if he had a girlfriend? He's a stinking musician, that's why, for fuck's sake, you idiot. Do you need to watch a Ted Talk about it?

I don't know, maybe I'm just destined to be naïve about these philandering men, but I really don't think that's it.

Oh my god. *Oh. My. God.*

"Use your blanket for support," the instructor, Stacey, says gently and I realize I've not kept up with the class. I've got my forehead on my mat, butt in the air, having this conversation with myself while everyone else is flat in a half frog. Also, I've groaned those last words out loud.

I move into their pose and this time I groan as the deep stretch radiates though my hip and lower back, breathing through the pain until my muscles relax.

He's got some problem... *down there.* Could that be it? He's got a problem and needed to get to know me so that he would be comfortable talking about it?

But I felt his erection through his jeans. It felt *significant.* Like, call your friends and brag about it significant. Maybe he can get it up but can't keep it up - he is in his forties. That would be a real shame.

Oh wait.

Oh no. *No, no, no, no, no.*

Good looking guitar player, decades of groupies and touring and fucking around in his never married life. It's the only thing that makes sense. He must have some sort of STD. A flare up.

Shit.

This thought stays with me through the rest of the class and I'm in a sour mood as I sit down to brunch afterwards with my friends. I hit the mimosas hard.

WHEN I COME in through the garage and look out the kitchen window, I see the top of Adam's head above one of the lounge chairs, under the large umbrella. If I was completely sober, I'd avoid him today, but since I'm a good too many glasses of cheap champagne and sugar deep into my feelings, I march straight outside and plop down onto the chair next to his.

He has an iPad in his lap, phone to his ear, wearing lose black sweatpants, a dark green tee, his feet bare. He's pulled a chair to the left side of his lounger, upon which rests an acoustic guitar, a moleskin notebook, and a pen. When I sit, he smiles at me, reaching one hand out to touch my knee.

Looking back at his screen, he moves the image with his finger. "I understand what you're saying, but I don't want to do it," he says into his phone. The iPad is big enough that I can see he's looking at a color-coded calendar. He listens to the voice, a woman's voice, before responding, "Just tell him no, not this time."

It's warmer out here than I expected. I pull my over-sized, off the shoulder sweater over my head, but it catches on my earring, and I'm stuck, struggling with it, the fabric covering my face. It's way harder than it should be. Think raccoon trapped in a garbage bag.

"Gretchen, I understand, but no, I want to be home those weeks, it's the only time I'll have to record before the summer tour." I hear him sit up, facing me. "I don't know about next fall... look, I need to call you back. Yes, I'll call you back."

"Stop fussing with it," he chides, standing above me and taking the fabric in his hands.

"Don't pull it. It's caught on my earring and I don't want to tear a hole," I direct him, tugging one arm out of a sleeve and lifting the sweater over my head, except for where it's attached to the small gold hoop. "Just hold this up for me."

He holds the sweater and I carefully take out my earring, fully freeing myself.

"Thank you," I sigh, sitting back on the lounger. "That's better."

He sits down on my chair, his hips pushing against my legs to make room, a hand on either side of my shoulders. Leaning in to kiss me, warmly he says, "Hello."

"Hello," I repeat as his lips touch mine.

Running a finger under one of the straps of my yoga tank, he says, "I wondered where you were this morning." He trails his finger across the tops of my breasts, to the opposite strap. "Have you eaten?"

My nipples harden at his touch, traitors, and I know they're visible through my tank because Adam's eyes drop to my chest. Jesus, this man has a thing for boobs. One corner of his mouth lifting in a flirtatious smile, he moves his finger down my breast, tracing a small circle around one erect nub.

"Yes, I went to brunch after my yoga class." I pluck his hand away, but he entwines his fingers with mine, lowering his face to kiss me again.

Why is he being so affectionate? I'm in no mood to be all revved up again only to be left hanging. We need to talk, but I'm getting a headache.

"It's so nice out here today," he hums, lifting his lips a few inches from mine. Noticing that I'm not kissing him back, he leans away to study my face. "Everything okay?" He narrows his eyes. "Are you drunk?"

"No, not drunk. Not sober, but not drunk. And right now, I'm having a sugar crash, so I'm sleepy."

"You didn't drive yourself home, did you?"

"No, Adam, I didn't drive myself home." Annoyed, I shift to one hip, pulling my knees up to create a bit of a wall between us. He has to let go of my hand and sit up straight to accommodate my change in position. "I took an Uber. I'll go get my car tomorrow."

"Why didn't you call me?" he asks, puzzled, as if it should have been my first thought.

I shrug. "Didn't occur to me."

Frowning, he starts to say something then stops himself. He considers and discards whatever it was and instead, in a neutral tone, offers up, "That's too bad." He moves back to his own chair, picking up his phone and iPad.

"You weren't waiting for me to eat, were you?"

"I'm good," he says, tapping his iPad.

Surprised, and more than a little confused, I press, "Tell me you've not been waiting for me."

"I've not been waiting for you," he dismisses the idea.

Now I feel bad although I know I shouldn't. How was I supposed to guess he'd be waiting for me today? And why would he? I can't figure this man out. I wouldn't say he's exactly pouting or anything, but I believe I've been accidentally hurtful.

Standing up, I say, "I need some water, can I bring some to you?"

"Sure, I'll take some water, thanks," he says, eyes still on his screen.

"Will it disturb whatever you're working on if I hang out here? I'd really love to close my eyes for a while... like you said, it's so nice."

I'm relieved when this time he looks at me again, smiling. "Of course you can, I'd like it." As I walk to the door, he calls to me. "Unless you snore, are you a snorer Holly?"

"You would know if you'd come to bed with me last night," I retort.

"If I had come to bed with you last night there would've been no sleeping, sweetheart."

"Yeah, big talk there big Tex."

Maybe because I've had so much to drink, or maybe because he slipped so easily back into good humor, I put together a plate for him, gathering the little nibbles I keep around for my own no-cook dinners. Grapes, cheese, Italian salami, mini cucumbers, pâté, crackers. Small ramekins of cherry tomatoes and almonds. I load this onto a tray with two tall ice waters in large blue plastic cups and carry it outside.

Shifting his feet as I place the tray at the end of his chair, he exclaims, "This is for me?" He's beaming, reaching already for a tomato, thanking me, and I know I did the right thing.

"It's purely self-interest. There's a little-known part of Louisiana law, in the fine, fine print, a law that declares she who feeds the songwriter is due a part of the copyright."

"Is that so? Josephine's contribution to your Napoleonic Code?"

"That's right," I nod, impressed with his quick comeback.

Setting my water on the ground in the narrow space between our chairs, I make the lounger flat and stretch out facing him, tucking my sweater under my head. Sleep is already pulling me under. "Music won't keep me awake, so do your thing. But I want that talk you promised later."

Closing my eyes, I sigh with the surrender of a Sunday afternoon, seventy-five degrees in October, mimosas with brunch nap. Occasionally the strum of a guitar or Adam's soft singing filters through my consciousness, but it barely registers, so deeply do I sleep.

It's his phone that wakes me, and judging by the shadows around the pool, I'd guess I've been asleep for two hours or so. Adam looks over at me, mouthing the word *sorry*. Sitting up, I wave my hand to let him know it's alright. My head is cloudy, like it's full of cotton balls, and I blink slowly, reaching for my water.

"Yes, Gretchen," he answers the call, "I know. I'm sorry, I got distracted." He winks at me. The voice on the other end says something and he laughs, giving me an appreciative look.

"Hmm, I think she would be your type. Blonde hair, big blue eyes, beautiful—" he doesn't finish the sentence because the voice starts speaking animatedly and he laughs harder. Eyeing me, he says, "You might meet her this weekend but hands off, I will fight you."

Scrunching up my face at this, I stand, slipping my sweater back over my head. I do a pantomime, indicating I'm going inside. He gives me a thumbs up, his phone perched between his ear and shoulder as he wakes up his iPad. I pick up the tray, pleased that he ate every bite.

Adam comes into my house about fifteen minutes later while I'm finishing the last of a kitchen clean-up, placing dishes into the dishwasher. He walks straight to me and wraps his arms around my waist from behind, pressing his lips into the side of my neck.

The feel of him pressed against me, his hips against my ass and his breath in my ear, cranks the dial up on my pulse. I turn in his arms, and he hinges at the waist, placing his hands on the edge of the sink on either side of me, leaning away so that his face is level with mine. He smells like laundry that's been on the line in the sun all day.

"Can I help with anything?" he asks.

"Nope, all done." I swallow hard at his closeness and his smell and the eye contact. I don't know where to put my hands, so I bring them together in front of my stomach. Standing upright, he takes them into his and places them, one at a time, around his waist.

"Adam, I want to—"

"I know," he says, sidling closer. "I know, we're gonna talk, but I've been waiting all day." Running his hands from my lower back up the full length of my spine, his eyes drop to my lips just as his hands reach the base of my skull, and he pulls my face to his. "All day," he repeats against my lips.

I can't help myself; I curl into him like a ribbon stroked by scissors, and when he drops a hand to cup my ass my mouth opens to his, our kiss deepening.

Who needs conversation?

When we break apart, he caresses my shoulder, rubbing my sweater between his fingers. "I like this," he says, "it's very soft." With another kiss, he adds, "Very sexy."

He's tactile and touchy and my body loves it, having someone take me in their arms, kiss me, caress me. My life has been an affection desert far too long. Is this just what you get when you hook up with Adam Sexton? Or is something else going on?

"Adam..." I say, but it's muffled as he kisses me. "Adam..."

"Holly..."

I bring my hands to his chest, but he drops his mouth to my neck, a deep "mmmm" coming from his throat as his lips tease my skin, his hands slipping under my sweater. The sensation is so distracting and wonderful I feel my knees sinking. I'm about to get lost to this sexy fog, without any guarantee of actual sex, and I need to remember my goal here. I'm trying to fuck him, not date him.

"Adam," I say again, more insistently. "Is there something wrong with your penis?"

This gets his attention.

His hands freeze and his kisses stop. Head cocked to one side, he says, "What?"

I bite my lip. How to put this? "I thought, after last night..."

"You thought my dick is broken?"

"I thought several things…"

"Does that feel broken?" He pulls my hand to the crotch of his sweatpants, giving me the full measure of his growing erection.

Flustered, I blurt it all out in a rush, my whole list. He starts laughing, dropping his forehead onto mine.

"Don't laugh at me, I need to know. You're the one who put on the brakes and said we had to talk about it tomorrow. It's tomorrow and I want to talk about it."

"We can talk all you want," he says, still laughing, brushing a kiss on my temple. He looks pointedly down between our bodies where, without realizing it, I've been stroking him. "But you're gonna have to turn me loose, baby. Let go of my dick."

CHAPTER TWENTY-ONE

HOLLY

ADAM COUNTS off on his fingers.

"You need to know if there's something wrong with my dick, if I have any diseases, a girlfriend… essentially if I'm a broken geezer dirty cheating whore, or am I forgetting anything else? Let's get it all out there." He's sitting in one corner of my sofa. I'm in the other, turned to face him with one foot tucked under my body.

"And who's Gretchen?" I add, raising a finger to mirror him.

"Gretchen is my sister, the youngest of the sisters. She's your age, lives in Pensacola, she was a nurse in the Air Force for twenty years. She works for me, has for a long time. She keeps my calendar, manages my website, handles booking for North American dates and coordinates with my European agent, handles merch, …"

"Sounds like maybe you work for her."

"God, please don't ever say that in front of her," he grimaces.

"What was with the 'I'll fight you' remark?"

"We've been known to have similar… preferences."

"Blondes with big boobs?"

A bark of laughter escapes him. "Given what you seem to think about me, you may find this hard to believe, but she's got way more of a conquering all the vaginas she meets mentality."

"Says her musician little brother," I snort sarcastically. "Sounds like I propositioned the wrong person in your family."

He lifts his hands in front of himself, in a gesture of *who knows* resignation, shaking his head with a hint of aggravation. Looks like I hit a nerve.

"Have I offended you?"

"You've made a few assumptions."

"You're right, I'm sorry." He acknowledges my apology with a dip of his head. "What did you mean, I might meet her this weekend? Is she coming here?"

"We'll get to that. After these questions you have for me and the ones I have for you."

That makes me nervous. "Ones you have for me?"

"Yep." Adam pats his lap. "Give me your feet."

"What?"

"Let me rub your feet," he says, patting his lap again. "Come on."

"Why?" I ask, mystified and yes, suspicious.

"You don't like a foot massage?"

"I'm a breathing human being, of course I love a foot massage, but why are you wanting to do that right now?"

"I like touching you, but we can't talk if I'm kissing you, and you're sitting all the way over there." He half-heartedly reaches an arm across the sofa, pretending he can't reach me.

"I've noticed that you're very touchy-feely."

"I've been told that before. Does it bother you?" This isn't easy for me to answer, and I hesitate. "It does?" he asks, disappointment causing his brows to knit together.

"I wouldn't say that, not exactly." *I like it. I really like it. Touch me everywhere.* That's what my body is saying. But my charred, shriveled heart knows it's a dangerous gateway drug I should keep in check. "It's a little confusing, or... well... concerning."

This earns me a textbook Adam scowl. I might've killed this conversation before it got far at all. But then he speaks in a soft, careful voice.

"The touching helps me feel less anxious. I've found in the past, with other... people, conversations go better if we're connected and relaxed. But I'd never what to make you uncomfortable, so if it's too much, just tell me."

I thought we were going to get this job interview portion of our hook up taken care of, make out some more, then get naked. What in the hell kind of conversation does *he* think we're having, that he needs to feel less anxious for? He's defensive about being seen as a horn dog musician and now, if I'm not mistaken, wants to talk about *feelings*.

Have I picked the one guitar player in America that has suddenly, right now, decided not to be slutty? For fuck's sake.

Alarms go off in my head and security gates slowly drop around my heart. The man simply wants to be connected and affectionate. Naturally, I can't stand for that, so I have to be an asshole. "It's not really some fetish thing you're tricking me into?"

He sighs, and I do feel like an asshole.

"No, Holly, and if it was, I'd just say so and not feel the least bit bad about it."

Swiveling my body to lift my feet into his lap, I make a face that I hope is genuinely contrite. Because I do feel bad - he seems sincere. But I'm also wary.

He takes one foot into his hands, running a thumb firmly down the center, and I practically purr like a cat, my torso relaxing into the sofa. So much for my resistance.

When he begins massaging the ball of my foot I groan, "Oh my God, thank you Jesus."

"Thank you, Adam, you mean."

"Yes, thank you Adam." I'll tell him whatever he wants. This feels so good. "If you like touching so much, why did you stop things last night?"

"A few days won't kill you. Anticipation is a great thing."

"A few days!" I bang one fist on the back of the sofa. "What? Why?"

"It'll make the sex better," he says, shaking his head in amusement.

"Are you telling me you've gotten to know every woman you've screwed on the road like this? How have you had the time?"

His hands stop. "Are you seriously making a crack like that again to me?"

I blow air out of my cheeks. "Sorry."

"I'm not the man you're mad at, but I am the man you asked to help you. You said you needed respect and kindness; I expect the same."

Way to hit me where it hurts, man, with the brutal truth, in my own words.

"You're right. I am sorry, and I'll do better."

He takes a deep breath. "How's the sex with your doctor?"

This throws me for a loop. "My doctor? What are you talking about?"

"The night we met, your birthday, that guy. How's the sex?"

"Oh," I cringe, remembering how he locked the door behind me, kicking me to the literal curb. "Terrible. The reason alcohol and many pharmaceuticals were invented."

"And how well do you know each other?" he presses.

"Barely at all," I admit.

"If we do this, it'll be better if we get to know each other," he starts to massage my foot again. "And I'm in charge."

"Excuse me? Of what?"

"The sex," he says matter-of-factly, a dip of his head, a lift of an eyebrow, punctuating the statement.

I laugh.

"I'm not joking."

"Maybe you're not, but—"

"No buts, Holly." He presses into the arch of my foot with his thumb and my shoulders lift off the sofa.

"Okay, okay," I say, squirming, and he smiles with satisfaction. "I'll let you think you're in charge."

He presses again and I buck a little, but he holds my foot firmly. "Say it," he says, eyes locking with mine. "If you want me, you have to say it."

I drop back onto the sofa, assessing his expression. He's serious. And smoldering. My vagina starts doing cartwheels in my pants. I do have a goal here to consider.

I give him what he wants.

"You're in charge," I purr, which sounds both sweet and sarcastic. That pleased, sexy smile spreads across his face.

"Good girl," he drawls, matching sarcasm with sarcasm, patting my foot and cocking an eyebrow at me again, daring me to sass him.

And boy, do I want to. Good girl my ass. *Who do you think you're talking to?*

But I keep my mouth shut, opting instead to arch my own eyebrow, smirking, letting him know I see his game. He takes the win and moves on immediately.

"Are you really worried my dick is broken?"

I shake my head from side to side.

"Good. Are you really worried I have herpes or something?"

"It's not an unreasonable question."

He puffs out his bottom lip, acknowledging this. "You're right. I've been lucky, and careful about condoms. Aside from a few brushes with chlamydia in my twenties and some crabs, I've been clean, but I haven't been tested in a while. What about you?"

"What about me?"

"When did you last get tested?"

I bring a hand to my neck, pulling my sweater up into my fist. Me? What in the world is he thinking?

"It's part of the blood work you get when you're pregnant, but other than that, never. Why would I?" He gives me a skeptical stare, tilting his head. Indignantly, I sputter, "I only had one boyfriend before Ronnie!"

He pulls on my foot to calm me down. "And the doctor. Are you still dating him?"

"No," I guffaw, shuddering. "Oh my god, definitely not." The corners of his lips turn up in the barest of smiles. "That was just the one time, and we used a condom,"

"Well, if Ronnie was having other women..." *Don't make me*

say it but you know what I mean the unspoken words hanging there in his unfinished sentence.

Fuck. I hadn't thought of that. I throw one arm over my eyes and say it out loud.

"Fuuuuuuck."

He gives me a minute, taking his time to massage each individual toe, rubbing in between, before he resumes.

"You asked me about a girlfriend."

I lift my arm to the top of my head so that I can see his face.

"I've had four what I'd consider girlfriends in my life. The first was in high school, Katie. She went off to SMU and I moved to Nashville. When she finished, she moved to Nashville too and expected us to be a couple, but I was traveling all the time, hustling my ass off. Girls were everywhere, parties, and well... other life shit going on. I was immature and dishonest about all of it. Exactly all the worst things you've thought of me. I moved to Austin so that I could end it."

"You moved to another state to break up with her?"

"Not entirely, but also... yes." He shakes his head at himself. I find it endearing.

"PJ - Patricia Jean - in Austin, we dated for about four years. She's a tattoo artist, that's how we met, she did this." He holds out his right arm to show me the tattoo on the inside of his forearm. A guitar, inked with the colors of the Texas flag, sits within the outline of the state, with roses vining up one side and three small stars floating just outside the western edge.

"It's beautiful," I say. "I'm glad I didn't ruin it."

Running his finger over the raised, red scar just above the tattoo, he agrees with a nod.

"She did this one, too," he indicates his left arm, showing off the large feather inked there, starting a few inches from his wrist, stretching to his elbow. It's monochromatic, all black and grey, and somehow, incredibly delicate.

"We lived together for a while, but same story. I was touring all the time, I mean all the time, and it takes a toll. It was lonely for her, but truth be told," he pauses to rub his jaw, ruefully. "I didn't want to change. I wanted to be on the road, doing what I loved. It's what I'd dreamed of my whole life. I'd come home, sometimes only for two or three days in a month, sometimes not for weeks, and I'd dread opening my own front door. She would just be furious. And I had been very clear about not wanting to get married, not wanting kids, because of this life, and she said she felt the same way, but then she started bringing it up all the time."

He sighs with resignation. "One day I came home, and she had moved out."

"Can you imagine the days when people could make a living selling records? Before recorded music was just free?" I murmur.

"Yeah, that's a black hole, those kinds of thoughts. Imagining record sales in the seventies and eighties." We take a moment of silence, reflecting on our own slices of this fucked up business.

"At least you didn't have to move out of state," I tease, to break up our individual reveries. He purses his lips, dropping his head to one side. "You didn't. Wait, you did?"

"Didn't have to, no, but I did move out to L.A. not long after." His eyes go distant, as if he's watching a short film of that time, a specific memory.

"I'm not gonna have to do this for you, am I?" I press a foot playfully into his stomach.

"Move?" he asks, confused, his attention coming back to me here in the present.

"No, massage your feet."

Smirking, he leans over and kisses my toes. "Not today." Clearing his throat, he keeps going. "Girlfriend number three was Gina. She, well... I should say we... we..." he stops, searching for his words.

"You don't have to tell me," I offer.

"Maybe that's best," he agrees, eyes lowered.

"You loved her," I state, rather than ask. "She left?"

Quiet for a beat, he lifts his gaze back to me and offers a

crooked, totally relatable, *yep, that one hurt* grimace. Naturally, I blurt out the worst thing that pops into my head.

"Man, you've been left a lot."

Momentarily stunned, he makes a small head shake - he can't believe I said it. Then he bursts into laugher. Relieved, I laugh too. It turns almost goofy, staring at each other, until we settle down and he remembers what he was saying.

"Oh, and Emily, she was the last one. I mean, I've dated a few women since her, but she was the last one I'd call a relationship."

"How long ago was that?"

"Couple years," he shrugs.

"Any of these women as old as me?"

"You're basically my age," he says dismissively.

"That doesn't answer my question," I press. "And I'm older than you. Have you dated anyone older before?"

"I've mostly only ever dated women my age or older. Younger women aren't as honest, in my experience, and they—"

"Want kids."

"Exactly."

"Ever dated anyone who had kids?"

He thinks about this. "Ummm, yeah, I guess I have. Not very seriously though."

"But you think you've seen stretch marks."

He shakes his head. "I know you had a baby, Holly, if that's what this is about. I'm not a child for fuck's sake."

"Knowing it and seeing the evidence are two different things."

"I've already seen you naked."

I forgot about that. Of course he has.

He seizes on my expression, eyes blazing. "And don't pretend you don't know what you do to me. There's no way you would've made your proposition if you didn't."

And what do I say to that? I swallow, hard, working to keep my expression neutral even though I know I'm flushed from my chest to my forehead. "You're single now?"

"Yep."

"That really surprises me."

"I don't know why, weren't you just listening? It's a hard life for most people, being apart so much. Women think they can do it but so far, they can't. Not with me anyway, even when I've been completely faithful and walking the line."

"Is that still something you want, a relationship?"

"Yes, I want a partner, someone to be devoted to, someone devoted to me. Be each other's soft place to fall. I want all of that."

How does he say these things?

My hand goes to my throat involuntarily. Is something wrong with my air conditioning? It's very warm in here. Am I breaking out in hives?

Injecting lightness into my voice, I say, "It's not that you're ugly or anything, and you do know how to kiss. You do things around the house, you can do this," I wave at my feet. "If I was looking for a boyfriend, I'd be throwing myself in front of your car, so I'd imagine there are literally thousands of women out there who'd feel the same."

His face changes, like the sun rising over the horizon, his mouth shifting into a sexy grin. Oh man, how easily was I led into the trap, and all it took was a few minutes of rubbing my feet and male vulnerability. This better get me laid.

"Aww, you think I'm not ugly?" he asks, eyes sparking like flint.

I meet his gaze full on, thinking of my goal. Close this deal. "Not all that ugly."

Sliding one hand along my foot and up my leg, he caresses my calf. My eyes are drawn to his tongue darting across his bottom lip, like he's parched and I'm a cold glass of lemonade. I'm practically sweating like one, that's for sure.

His attention drops to my mouth. "I love kissing you."

"I'm right here."

"You're single..." he says, and I nod. "And I'm single," he continues that slow glide up and down my leg with his palm. Putting the idea out there so easily.

I draw in a deep breath, counting to four in my head, then exhale slowly. I do it again, aware that he's watching me, my face hot, eyes stinging like I've stepped too close to a furnace.

Breathe, I tell myself. *Breathe.*

What would it be like, to hear his words and be thrilled with the possibility behind them? This is why he wanted this kind of conversation, and why he stopped us from having sex last night. The pursuing and flirting and touching. He's looking for a partner. I swallow hard against the burn in my throat. It can't be me.

"You'll find someone," I say, pulling my feet from his lap, knowing my words are a knife, knowing I have to throw it. I see it land, see him blink from the sting of what I'm saying, and coward that I am, I look away. But I will be very clear here. Set a firm guardrail.

He leans away from me, running his hands through his hair. I speak as if I'm patting him on the back, like a buddy, looking up at the ceiling to blink away my tears before they fall. "You will, you're great. And she'll be a very lucky woman."

One tear escapes, rolling down my cheek. I turn my face into my shoulder, wiping it away before he can see. When I look back to him, he's studying me, his lips pressed tightly together, expression inscrutable, and I force myself to smile.

In a flash, he rises, crawling over me, pressing himself between my knees, holding his torso over mine as I fall back into the sofa. His arms squeeze against my sides, his hips shifting to fit between my thighs. Carnal, dominant, caging me aggressively with his body. My heart begins to race.

"So," he says, pressing his face into my neck and breathing deeply. "While we're here..."

"If we're on the same page," I shudder at his teeth grazing my skin, using every ounce of willpower to stop myself from lifting my legs around his waist and locking him onto me. But I need to make my point.

I grip his head in my hands, lifting his face to look at me. "Adam, I want an affair. I'm not available for anything else."

He smiles seductively but it doesn't reach his eyes. They're dark and clouded, nearly black. I should see it as a warning, a big flashing caution sign, but the strength of his arms, the weight of his body, the feel of him between my legs... it could make a woman beg. And tell a man he's in charge.

"Can you give me that?" I plead in a ragged whisper.

He drops his mouth onto mine, crushing me with a kiss.

CHAPTER TWENTY-TWO

HOLLY

"Ooh, how fun," Madeline coos naughtily, "I love hotel sex."

After our conversation last night, and a lot more brain-cell-obliterating kissing, Adam asked me to go away with him for the weekend, for a two-show run with Jennifer Carson, booked before the project with Chip Walker came up. Friday night at the Saenger Theatre in Mobile, Saturday night at the Alabama Theatre in Birmingham. The plan is to leave Thursday afternoon, coming back here to Lafayette Monday morning.

I'm thankful to laugh with her about it because he's driving me bonkers with all the making out, then holding out on me like I gotta buy the bull before I get the balls. Or the horn. Whatever. See, he's scrambled my brain.

"I better come home not being able to walk," I say, and we both cackle.

"I'll light a candle for you."

For the first time in a long time, I'm excited about something. Something just for me. I get to be selfish and go away for a weekend with this gorgeous man. I want to have fun and not think about anything else.

"And you got the STD conversation out of the way," she says.

"Can you believe this guy?"

After the weekend question was asked and answered, Adam suggested we retrieve my car, which I took to be a perfectly innocuous offer until we were on the road, and I realized something else was happening. He pulled into the walk-in clinic parking lot, announcing that we should both get tested. How could I argue, given we had just talked about it?

I would, however, have chosen a clinic that was the farthest one in town from my house instead of the closest.

Of course, our favorite, charming nurse was there. When she saw it was us in the waiting room, she dropped her clipboard down to her thigh. "Lord Jesus, you sure you two should be spending this much time together?"

"No, I am not," I agreed, and Adam smacked my butt as we followed her to the back. We peed in cups and gave blood, then he drove me to my car. By the time we got home, I'd had enough of Adam Sexton for the day.

"He's so bossy," I complain. "You know, he tried to tell me not to use The General this week."

"Yeah, that's an overreach there." She says between bites of popcorn. I take a sip of my Diet Coke and pick at some fluff on my sweatshirt. Madeline narrows her eyes. "Wait. You're not..." she lowers her voice. "You aren't getting off this week because he told you not to?"

I drop my forehead to my hand.

In mock horror, she gasps. "Nooooo..." pretending to faint, falling to her side out of the camera view

"I can't believe it either," I groan. "But he said..."

She pops back into view. "He said what?"

Looking at her through my fingers, I wince as I confess, "He said the next time I come it would be on his face."

She lifts her glass of wine in a toast. "I like this man. He takes care of business."

We laugh and talk for a long while. As we're winding down, she says, "Have a great weekend, you deserve it. If you're not in a sex coma, text me and let me know how it's going."

"Shoot, I hope I'm in a sex coma this weekend."

"I feel I have to say this... men this age can fall really fast. Hard and fast. It's their own kind of biological clock, they want to be settled."

"Okay," I say, wondering what her point is. I already explained the situation to her.

"I mean, it's what Ronnie did with you."

This pains me, talking about Ronnie in the same conversation as Adam. My revenge affair. But she doesn't know about that. That secret, a rare something I haven't shared with her, is part of the stab I feel.

"That was different. I was much younger than him, his chance to have a family, and Adam isn't looking for that." *But he was clear about wanting a partner.* I don't share this with her either.

"I know," she waves a hand in front of her face. "Go! Have this fling, live it up. Just be mindful of what I said. I like what I've heard about Adam so far, so... be careful with his heart."

AFTER WE SAY GOODNIGHT, I cue up my playlist, then start a load of laundry and send another text to Luke. He's been sparse with his communication and it's frustrating. He's lucky his school is so far away because I'd be knocking on his door right about now if I could.

Madeline's warning has left me a bit unsettled. I'm not ready for bed, not eager to toss and turn, so I bring my laptop to the kitchen island and work on transcribing more of the love song titles from my notebook. Ironic, yes. Distracting, absorbing, also, yes.

When a soft knock on the door pulls me out of this rabbit hole, I check the time. One-forty-five a.m. I've been at it for hours. I look over and see Adam; we make eye contact, and he lets himself in.

"I saw the light on." Voice frayed, he's squinting from fatigue. "What are you doing up?" He puts a hand in the middle of my back, gently massaging between my shoulder blades.

"Working on this love song book. You look beat, how did it go today?"

"Good," is all he says, too tired to talk about it. He looks over my shoulder to my notebook. ""Love Is Like a Boomerang," "Love is a Boomerang," "Boomerang Love," "Love Boomerang." I really missed the boat with the boomerang songs I guess." Rubbing his chin, he smiles, and the wrinkles around his eyes look so sweet to me. I wonder why I don't think that about my own wrinkles. I never see mine as sweet.

"Well, you know, give it a while, one might come to you."

Too tired to make small talk, we sort of stare at nothing. But it's comforting, his hand warm on my back. I'm usually up late all alone.

"It Serves You Right to Suffer," the John Lee Hooker song, comes up on my playlist and he begins to softly tap his fingers on my shoulder.

"So good," I murmur.

"So fucking good," he echoes.

The late hour, the way he's standing so close, how we're intently listening together, whatever it is I feel inspired. Emboldened to share an idea. When the song ends, I reach for my phone and pull up my song library. "Do you mind if I throw something out there? Or do you prefer to generate your own ideas? I completely understand if you do."

"No, go for it," he says, easing himself down onto the stool beside me.

Scrolling, I find what I'm looking for, watching his face as "Cry, Cry, Cry" by Bobby Bland begins to play. "Every time I hear this, I think it would be a great cover for someone. It's so cool and menacing. Lose the horns, add a pedal steel, or fiddle..." I stop talking. He should hear it his way.

Leaning forward to rest both forearms on the counter, his head bobs with the music. "I haven't heard this in a long time," he muses.

"I love how angry it is, it really gets to a fuck you level of pain, but so beautiful too."

"A fuck you level of pain," he repeats, eyeing me with appreciation and understanding.

"It's just a thought," I shrug, when the song ends. The hour now seems very late when the kitchen goes quiet.

He stands, yawning deeply, which causes me to also immediately yawn, earning me another one of his wrinkled-eyed smiles. "Thank you," he says, "I'm gonna turn in."

He studies me, just standing there looking at my face, and I start to wonder if I have something in my nose. Also, I really, really want him to kiss me. So, I babble.

"Ask Mike to pull the Lil' Bob & the Lollipops version for you, we have the CD in the office out there. It's not online, not on any streaming platforms. It was recorded here in Lafayette in the sixties, over at La Louisianne. Or wait, look up Pacific Gas & Electric on YouTube."

"Yes, ma'am," he drawls, walking to my door. No kissing, no hugging for me tonight apparently. "You sure are some secret weapon, you know that?"

"Of course I do." I grin. A compliment like that might be the next best thing.

With a chuckle, he opens the door. "Goodnight sweetheart. Lock this door please."

Staring at the door after he's gone, I remind myself.

Just a fling, Holly. He's just a fling.

CHAPTER TWENTY-THREE

ADAM and I haven't seen much of each other this week.

He's been in the studio for long days, and I've been pushing to get my own work done before our road trip. He came over here yesterday, sweeping in and out like a hurricane, telling me to check my email then taking me in his arms, hands tangling in my hair before running down my body, kissing me deeply. Then back out the door with barely a hello or goodbye.

In my email, I found a message from the clinic with my test results, and an email forwarded to me from him with his results. Both in the clear. I reciprocated by sending mine. Who says romance is dead?

Today, he knocks and opens the patio door all in one motion, calling out, "Ready?" as he strides inside. "Why is this door never locked?" he begins to lecture, but falters, stopped so abruptly in his tracks, one foot hanging in mid-air, that he has to swing his left arm out in front of himself to keep his balance. He opens and closes his mouth, gaping, working to say something. Or, my guess is, working to not say something.

"Ready!" I call cheerfully, waving two aluminum water bottles in his direction. "Why don't you take the bags and I'll do this and lock up."

"Umm..." he stammers, one hand going to his forehead, staring at the row of four suitcases lined up in front of him. Crossing to the refrigerator to fill the water bottles, I peek over my shoulder. He's rooted in place, still searching for words.

"You alright?" I ask innocently.

"Yep, fine." He puts on a stiff smile, reaching for the two suitcases closest to him. Jerking roughly on the handles they both lift effortlessly into the air.

I burst out laughing. "Your face! Oh my god, the panic."

He's laughing too, a hand to his chest. "I *was* panicking. I was thinking I had to re-write in my head who this woman is."

"And how can I get out of this," I add, wiping at my eyes with the back of one hand, happy he's a good sport about my prank.

"You have no idea, this has literally happened before," he says.

The man was going to take those suitcases and not say a word to me. It's rather sweet. I walk over and give him a kiss.

"Just the small one there, and the garment bag please."

In the car, making our way to the interstate, my phone chimes with a text.

JACKIE

I heard someone is going away for the weekend

Did I call it or what? 😁

How does she know I'm going with Adam to his gigs? I didn't tell anyone but Madeline.

"Did you say something to Mike about me coming with you this weekend?"

He glances over at me, eyes hidden behind black sunglasses. "Is it a secret?"

"Not anymore." I hold up my phone. "Jackie is texting me."

"I guess I assumed you and Mike would talk about that kind of thing."

"Why would you think that?"

"I don't know, you seem like friends," he shrugs.

"We are friends, but he also works for me, and you're working with him, so I thought it best to be discreet."

"I'm excited you're coming. I'm sorry, have I made it weird?"

There he is being sweet again, and it's only the first half hour of the weekend. I sigh, giving him a smile that's meant to reassure myself as much as him. "It's alright, I'm the one probably making it weird. Don't worry about it."

I type out a quick text.

> Just looking to drum up business for the studio

Right 😊😋

Have fun! Do everything I would do!

"I need to do a little listening homework, if you don't mind," he says, once we're cruising on the highway.

"Sure," I say, rooting around in my bag, pulling out my Kindle and a package of Twizzlers. "Do you play with Jennifer very often?"

"A fair amount. We've known each other since way back when we were coming up in Austin. We find ourselves at a lot of the same festivals, there's crossover with our fans."

"Did you ever date?" I offer him a Twizzler, but he shakes his head, so I eat it myself.

"No, um, that would be my sister."

"Gretchen?"

"Yep, they've had an on and off kind of thing for years. I'm glad you'll meet her; I've told her about the studio."

"You have?"

"Of course. She'll be looking to record again next year, so it's a good time for her to be introduced to you."

"Thank you so much. That's the excuse I just texted to Jackie, actually."

He cues up his playlist, the songs he's reviewing for these shows, and I open the cover to my Kindle.

. . .

HIS PLACE in New Orleans is in the warehouse district, a condo with high ceilings, wood beams, and wide plank pine floors. It's an open layout, with a modern kitchen overlooking a window-lined living area decked out in leather and velvet furniture and layers of vintage rugs. It's plush and decadent, and very inviting.

"Adam, this is gorgeous," I say, and he smiles with pride.

"You like it?"

"I love it. Did you do all this yourself?"

"I found the place, but I can't take credit for the furniture. That's all Audrey and Gretchen, they swoop in and do that."

"Audrey?" I ask.

"Middle sister. The one in Dallas." He takes my hand and leads me down a hallway. I'm liking these sisters.

He points out two bedrooms, one a small, cozy guest room, and one that's secured by a high-tech keypad lock because it's a full-on guitar shrine, a custom cabinet dominating one wall. Adam flips a switch and LED lights illuminate the guitars inside.

"Whoa," I say, turning a slow circle to take in the whole set up. There are four more guitars hanging from hooks on the wall, plus five in cases in the closet. There's a soft shag rug under foot and a worn leather sofa, two chairs, a vintage floor lamp and an old trunk for a coffee table, plus a small bar cart and an amp. A bookcase with - hello, Grammys - framed photos, and a pair of speakers takes up the wall opposite the door.

"This is the bat cave," I whisper, while he pulls a guitar from the closet. "How many guitars do you own?" I can't believe I was ever annoyed at Ronnie for owning three Hammond organs. Just three.

"Between the ones I play and the ones I collect, hmm... maybe thirty-five, forty? I have some in Dallas, in a fine art storage place there."

"Forty?"

"Maybe."

I narrow my eyes at him. "Is it more than forty?"

"Not telling," he shakes his head.

"What's that song? "Nobody Understands Me But My Guitar?" You must feel tremendously understood in here."

He gives a small snort of a laugh.

The primary suite is minimalist, with a king-sized bed against a distressed brick wall, its four cypress posts reaching nearly to the ceiling.

"I'll just be a minute," he says, dropping his leather travel bag onto the bench at the end of the bed and crossing to the door that leads to the bathroom and closet.

I walk to his dresser. There's not much on top; a lamp, a large wood tray with a candle and matches, and a small leather dish with loose change. There's also a framed photo with Adam and who I assume to be his mother and three sisters. They're outside, Christmas lights visible over their shoulders. He looks very young, late teens maybe early twenties, skinny with longer hair, his arms around his mother, hugging her from the side, both smiling broadly. All the sisters are in some state of laughter, mugging for the camera, all of them touching, linked together as one big mass of dark-haired happiness. They radiate love for one another.

I'm not sure what I was expecting but his private space is normal. Quietly luxurious, layered with textures, edited down to a specific, masculine warmth. It's him. It's a home.

I set the picture down just as he walks back into the room, tossing a garment bag onto his bed, along with a few pieces of clothing. "Do you want to use the bathroom while we're here?"

"Good idea."

The bathroom makes me want to weep, I'm so jealous. It's all white marble, with a huge walk-in shower, a soaking tub, and double sinks. The closet is twice the size of mine at home. I yell to him while I'm sitting on the toilet, "This bathroom is a palace!"

When I've washed up, inspected the few toiletries on the counter and sniffed his yummy cologne, I open the door and he's zipping up his travel bag. "Seriously, how did they get that bathtub in there?"

"I'm thinking more about when I'm going to get you in

there," he pulls me to him. Hand on my ass, those melted chocolate eyes pouring into mine, making me warm all over, he speaks gruffly. "I'm glad you're here, thanks for coming with me this weekend."

Melted is right. This man turns my bones to syrup. "Thanks for inviting me."

He kisses me, his tongue sweeping into my mouth, and everything between my navel and knees starts to pulse. His lips are demanding, pressing and pulling mine to follow where he leads. One hand gripped tightly to my backside, he brings his other between my legs to stroke me through the thin fabric of my leggings. I groan into his mouth while his fingers move back and forth along the outline of my folds, firm and slow, pressing into me with each long stroke, the strength and sureness of his touch a promise for a damn fine time ahead.

I moan again and he stops, bringing his hands to my shoulders, separating us.

"We should go," he says hoarsely, but nothing about him looks like he means it and his palpable desire fills me with a sense of power.

If I wanted to, I could have us in that bed in ten seconds. I want to howl - I want to bite him on the neck, branding him with my mark. I'm fucking falling apart, delusional with lust.

He reads it on my face, shaking his head. "Nope, not yet, baby."

Tonight, tonight, tonight, I remind myself, taking one step back from him.

We take the elevator and the walk to his car in silence, the air between us arcing and humming with electricity. My heart rate struggles to return to normal, my breathing shallow, still way up high under my collar bone.

This sure has been one long stretch of foreplay.

CHAPTER TWENTY-FOUR

HOLLY

I FALL ASLEEP NOT long after we clear New Orleans, waking at the changing sound of the highway when we enter the tunnel under the Mobile River.

I watch Adam as he drives, studying his profile, the set of his jaw. His right wrist hangs at the top of the steering wheel, ropes of muscle along his forearm, left hand on his thigh, an energy to his body even in repose. Classic black wayfarer sunglasses, tee shirt and jeans, he's solid male, self-contained, unfussy. Confident and competent. It's been years since I've been a passenger like this, relaxed enough to let someone else take the wheel. He could drive for hours, and I'd never have to worry about a thing.

Just a fling, Holly. He's just a fling. I should've printed it on flash cards.

He turns his head in my direction and his smile is instant - it feels like a caress. He does not make this easy.

The traffic moves slowly, the road rising at an incline, sunshine the literal bright light at the end of the tunnel. It doesn't make sense we're here and my eyes go to the navigation screen on the dashboard. "Why are we taking the tunnel? The hotel isn't downtown, near the venue?"

"Worried you're being kidnapped?"

"Taken away and held for ransom?" I joke.

"We're headed to Point Clear."

I jump up in my seat. "We're going to The Grand?!" His satisfied grin, starting in one corner of his mouth and spreading across his face, is all I need for confirmation. "No! Really?"

"I thought it would be nicer to be separate from everyone else. It's another thirty minutes, I hope you don't mind."

"Do I mind? Are you kidding me?" I look out my window, across the waters of Mobile Bay, the late afternoon sun blinking along the top of the waves. I'm elated, my own smile stretching from ear to ear. "I've always wanted to stay there. Have you been before?"

"No, I hadn't even heard of it until I found it online."

New to both of us. He's made an effort to do this, when I'm the one who propositioned him. I'm moved by how it makes me feel. Moved in the horny kind of way. Effort is hot.

I'm enchanted when we drive into the resort - oak trees dripping in Spanish moss, boats in the marina, the promenade along the bay. I've seen photos of the two-story lobby, with the stone fireplace reaching all the way to the wood beamed ceiling, rafters surrounding it like rays of sunshine, the open balconies, but to see it all in person is wonderful.

Our room is a lovely big suite, done in ocean shades of blue and cream with a balcony overlooking the marina. Double doors across from the king-sized bed open to a sitting area and a second balcony.

When the door closes behind the bellman I throw my arms around Adam's neck. "I love this, thank you."

He squeezes my waist. "You know I write all this off, don't you?"

"All business, are you?" I lean back, pursing my lips at him playfully.

"I was given a job to do, ma'am."

He showers first and as much as we've been kissing and touching, this sort of intimacy begins to make me nervous. Getting ready for the night, in a hotel room, makes it feel like we're a real couple - I feel a little like I'm acting in a play about someone else's life. When he comes out of the bathroom in a cloud of steam like some movie stud with only a towel around his hips, I can't help myself. I let out a hoot of laughter.

"Jesus, do we really need to go to dinner? Let's order up some whip cream and let me rub it all over you."

"Sweetheart, I'm starving, but we can make dinner a quick one." Hands on hips, that cocky smirk.

After my shower, when I come into the room in a bathrobe, Adam is out on the balcony talking on his phone. By the time he comes inside, I'm dressed and primped, sitting in a chair, slipping on one of my heels. He's wearing slim black slacks and loafers, with a white button down, hair still damp and brushed back off his forehead. He's just as at ease as he is in jeans. And just as sexy.

When I stand, he whistles. "Maybe we should skip dinner."

My dress is dark teal blue silk, flowy and soft, an easy wrap style with long sleeves and a low v-neckline. It's pretty, and it feels like pajamas. "No way, I've done all this work, you've gotta take me downstairs and show me off."

Sauntering to me, he rests his hands on my hips, dropping his mouth to my collarbone. "I don't know if I want anyone else looking at you tonight. My God, you smell delicious."

THE RESORT'S main restaurant glows gold from the lingering sunset outside the curved wall of windows and the enormous chandelier in the middle of the room made of floating gilded leaves. We're seated at an intimate banquette with a view of the shimmering watercolor bay.

"This is beautiful," I say as Adam slides in next to me.

"You're beautiful," he says, leaning towards me, one arm on the table. Faces close, we simply look at one another, smiling, holding the connection.

Our meal is a blur to me. I didn't care about the food, I can't recall what we talked about. We have wine and touch each other the entire time we're seated - knees pressed together, his hand on my thigh, mine on his; my hand on his arm, his arm around my shoulder; his lips on my neck, at my ear. It's a miracle we don't sweep the dishes off the table and go at it right there. Declining dessert, he settles the bill and with his hand firmly at the small of my back, we make our way through the restaurant, through the hotel, my skin electrified with tension.

The second the door of our room closes behind us, with the snap of the lock, we fall into one another. Melded chest to chest and hip to hip. I toss my clutch into the room, uncaring, taking his face into my hands, pulling his mouth into mine.

"So beautiful," he says huskily, sliding his hands down my body. "So damn beautiful."

His mouth falls to my neck, his kisses feverish against my skin, and I shiver, aching with need to end this longing. I move a hand between us, taking a slow inventory up and down the length of his cock and he groans, the sound causing me to arch into him, my spine on a string. He turns us together, walking me backwards until I feel the bed against the back of my legs. I look down to the belt of my wrap dress and start to undo the knot.

"I want to do it," he says, shooing my hands away. Head lowered, he squints with focus, and I run my fingers through the thick strands of his hair.

I'm here. This is happening. I'm doing this, no turning back.

That feeling I had with the doctor, of crossing some gaping chasm leading me further away from Ronnie, telegraphs a chill through my chest like a cold blast of air from an open freezer. It burns into my heart, and I take a sharp intake of breath against the pain. I don't want it. I don't want that feeling. Not now, not with Adam.

I'm not doing anything wrong. This is all good. More than good. I need it.

He's undone the knot, slipping the thin fabric belt away from my body. His eyes lift to mine and he pauses, scanning my face, his lips turning down at the corners from concern.

"You okay?"

Reaching for the buttons on his shirt, I shake my head. I

mean, look at this man. We'll have none of this sweetness right now. "I will be when you're naked."

"Not yet," he says, stopping my hands.

With a long hiss of silk, my dress falls open as he tugs the belt free. He lifts one side of the dress, then the other, parting it open like curtains for a full view of my body. His eyes, luminous, fiercely intent, rake me up and down. He trails a hand across my collarbones to where my breasts swell over the top of my black bra. It's mesh and sheer, my nipples hard against the fabric.

"I've thought about this every day, from that first night we met." His knuckles brush across one nipple, then the other. "Thinking of this."

He moves lower, gently stroking my stomach, before he slides his hand between my legs, eyes on the sight of me through the sheer mesh. He stops over my swelling clit, starting a slow circle. "Touching you here. Burying my face here."

I clutch his arm to steady myself, inhaling and exhaling raggedly. He looks in my eyes, his hand continuing to stroke me over my panties. "You want my mouth here?" he asks, increasing the pressure of his finger.

"Yes, God, yes," I groan, and his lips drop to mine, his tongue plunging into my mouth matching the drive of his finger, working like the opposite ends of a spring, torquing a knot of tension in my core. When I start rocking myself into his hand he pulls away, skimming up my body to slip my dress from my shoulders, letting it fall to the floor, then he reaches behind me to unclasp my bra.

"Baby," he says hoarsely, sliding the straps ever so slowly down my arms, and it turns me inside out, makes me want to purr, that gruff *baby*. He lifts my breasts with both hands, cupping the weight of them, squeezing them together. "Baby," he repeats, sinking his face in them. "Oh my god, look at you."

Lavishing me with attention, his mouth explores each nipple, licking and nipping, his tongue rubbing across the textured nubs until they are wildly sensitive. I'm whimpering, mewling, dragging my hands through his hair, and when he settles his lips around me, drawing one nipple fully into his mouth and sucking, hard, I wobble in my shoes, off balance. I grab his forearms, my head lolling backwards, trying to remain on my feet, this coil of need he keeps turning and turning now begging for release. He doesn't understand how long I've waited.

Years. I've waited *years* to touch and be touched in this way again. I reach for his cock, and he puts his hand on top of mine, pressing me into him, guiding my touch.

"Adam... please."

With a small, wet smacking sound he releases my breast, easing me down onto the edge of the bed. "Lie back," he tells me, "Raise your arms over your head."

He stands above me, rolling up his shirt sleeves, kicking off his shoes, and the sight of him takes what little breath I have left away. The almost black hair against the white shirt; his eyes, lids lowered, full of desire and purpose as he looks me over; the hard-on in his pants like the crest of a ridge on a map.

I arch my back, lifting my breasts together, displaying myself for him, and his mouth twists into a sexy, smoldering smile. Reaching for my foot, he slips off my shoe, letting it drop to the carpet with a thump, then does the same with the other one, tossing it over his shoulder. This makes me laugh but he's having none of that.

"Open those legs, sweetheart," he orders, and I lift my knees, biting back a smile at his bossiness, resting my feet on the edge of the mattress. He fits himself between my thighs, his hand back to my panties, palming me, his expression nearly a dare. I hold his gaze, my laughter quieting but my heartbeat erratic.

Seconds tick by. He doesn't move. It's as if he's waiting, listening for a message, his hand gripping me, and we're suspended like this, a stillness between us at this last moment of no return.

Has he changed his mind? Is he waiting for me to change my mind?

His palm grows hotter, my pussy ready to pucker up and suck him in like slurping down the last bit of a milkshake. I can hear the sound in my head. Want floods my entire body.

"Adam..." I move first, squeezing my legs around his waist, my voice a plea hanging on every letter of his name. Lightning strikes in his dark eyes.

"You need me, baby?" His hand begins to move, the wet fabric clinging now into my folds. "You feel like you need me."

"Yes," I whisper, writhing, arching into him. "Please, yes, I need you. I have not been playing hard to get."

With a low, amused chuckle, he reaches for my panties, and I lift my bottom. In one smooth motion he slips them down my legs and sets my thighs open before him again, my feet back on the mattress. Eyes to my exposed sex, he speaks adoringly, "There's the pussy I've been dreaming about. Look how beautiful you are." The walls of my vagina pulse in response and I think my breasts sit up and salute.

Stepping away, he walks around the edge of the bed, trailing one hand along my torso. He takes a cushion from each of the chairs in the corner, returning to stack them on the floor at my feet, dropping to his knees like a supplicant. I guess even rock stars have middle-aged knees.

I lift my hips off the bed, shamelessly begging for his attention. He loves it, his hands smoothing down my legs, kissing the inside of my thighs with parted lips, nibbling with his teeth. He forms a smile against my skin when I shiver, his hand going straight to my wetness, swiping up and down my sex.

Rising onto my elbows, I watch his face as he slips two fingers inside me. I exhale in pleasure, holding his gaze, biting my bottom lip. Looking into his eyes as he's inside me this way for the first time, it's intoxicating. And warm. So warm.

Why can't vibrators be warm? Wouldn't that be perfect. Maybe they are and I haven't found one yet. God, if The General was warm, warm and wet and silky, I'd maybe never leave my house ever again.

Moving slowly, his fingers curl in and out of me, his hand beckoning every blood cell in my body to rush to this one spot, the sound of my wetness an erotic echo in the room. Lifting his fingers to his mouth, he sucks away the slickness. "Every part of you is delicious."

My mouth forms a silent O at this sight, my brain processing on a delay when he pushes my thighs further apart, drops his head, and flattens his tongue into me.

"Oh God..." I breathe, "Yes..." as he gives me exactly what I need. "Yes," I moan again, sinking back into the bed.

I close my eyes, brain going offline to the feel of his tongue insistent against my clit, strong and sure. He reaches a hand up my body, squeezing my breast, and I cry out at the sharpness of the pleasure, my vagina clenching, hips bucking. He gives a low, approving hum in response. He rolls my nipple between his fingers as he plunges his tongue inside me, and I lift off the bed like I've been jolted with a taser. I'm not gonna last long like this.

Moving his hands under my thighs, he lifts my hips and I grind myself into him. He squeezes my ass while I fuck his face, tension building until I'm right on the edge. "Your fingers," I pant, "I want your fingers and your mouth."

"Fuck yes, baby, give it to me," he hisses, kissing the inside of my thigh, then attaching his mouth right back onto my clit as his fingers push inside me. When my thighs begin to shake, my skin prickling from my scalp to my toes, I clutch at his hair, arching my back into a wave of pleasure lifting me up and out of myself.

"Don't stop, please don't stop," I beg, his stroking and sucking and licking twisting me as tightly as a woman can go until everything inside me unfurls, a beautiful spiraling release that has me bucking with the spasms. Too breathless now to make a sound, my sex pulses as he continues to attend me, his skilled tongue keeping my orgasm afloat for as long as it will go.

I start to laugh, joy pouring out of me as my body comes back down to earth, settling through several more tremors and jolts. I needed that so badly.

Laughing because I'm laughing, he drags his wet face along the inside of one thigh then the other and I shudder, the sensation almost too much. Bones liquid, skin humming, I bathe in the dopamine flooding my body, yet I want more, still need more.

I let my legs drop over the side of the bed and reach out to him. He pulls me up to sitting and wraps his arms around my hips. Sex-stoned, smiling stupidly at each other in a shared second of holy-shit-that-was-fun mutual appreciation, our mouths devour one another, tongues urgent.

"Baby," he says against my lips, "I want to be inside you; I need to fuck you."

After another long, heady kiss, I fall back on the bed while he stands. Bringing one foot onto the mattress, I hook my other foot behind his thighs, tugging him towards me.

"Take these off," I command softly.

He reaches for the buttons on his shirt, undoing each one slowly as I watch, writhing before him, massaging my breasts, putting on a show because I feel like a goddess. A glowing, ready to fuck him into next week goddess.

Shirt off, he walks over to his bag, coming back with a strip of condoms and a bottle of lube, dropping them onto the bed.

"Just you," I say. "I just want you."

"You sure?" he asks, and I shake my head. His hands go straight to the button on his pants, the sweet metallic *zzzffftt* of his zipper my new favorite sound. I say a silent prayer, heart rate climbing as he slips his pants and underwear down to give me my first look.

I can't help it; I smile like a fool. He's magnificent. I should be applauding. Veined, a prominent head, and thick; big enough to make me wet my lips, not so big that I snap my knees together. And I swear, it looks muscular. Is that even possible? The absolute raw maleness of him, standing in front of me, erect and proud, seconds away from filling me up, has my vagina singing the hallelujah chorus.

I am so happy to be here.

Standing at my open thighs, he takes the bottle of lube and squirts some in his hand. I hook my foot around his leg again, staring as he begins to stroke himself, his expression scorching my skin.

"Adam?"

"Yeah, baby." His slow, even strokes are hypnotic, I can't take my eyes off his cock.

"Remember when you told me to make a wish for my birthday?"

"Mm-hmm." He moves his hand down my thigh to the bend of my knee, lifting my leg so that it rests flat against his chest, foot by his ear, giving the inside of my ankle a kiss when he has me where he wants me.

"This..." I begin but inhale sharply when he teases his tip along my folds, when I feel his first push. "This is what I really wanted. You are what I wanted."

Something heated flashes across his face at those words, his eyes drilling into mine as my body yields and he slides all the way inside. He fills me as far as he can go, balls hanging heavy against my skin, and I give him a welcoming pussy squeeze. He rotates his hips from side to side, making room, stretching me.

"Welcome big Tex," I whisper, and he grins the sexiest grin I've ever seen in my life.

One hand wrapped around my raised leg, the other down around my ankle, holding it close to his hip, he pulls himself nearly all the way out then pushes inch by slow inch back inside. Groaning, I close my eyes as he finds his rhythm, giving me the full length of his cock stroke by stroke. He keeps it slow, fucking me with deliberate, long thrusts, until it begins to drive me wild, and I pull at him with my foot, my heel digging into his ass.

He lifts my other leg to his chest to get both feet by his head, scooping his hands under my hips, and really begins to give it to me. His tempo quickens, his stroke shorter, we're breathing hard, grunting, skin slapping skin, his fingers digging into me. I reach between my legs and as soon as I'm on my clit, I'm close to coming again.

I slam my free hand onto the bed, calling out one long, low, guttural moan.

As I'm about to detonate, he lowers my legs, letting my knees fall open. Cock buried to the hilt, he leans over me, sliding one hand under my neck, the other going to my breast. Squeezing it hard, he drops his mouth onto mine and begins thrusting again, long deep thrusts so that I feel every hard inch of him, out of my head with pleasure.

My orgasm slams through me and I'm bucking under his weight, pulsing around his dick, sucking his tongue into my mouth. He's everywhere in me, over me, and I cry out with each spasm.

"Yes, baby, yes," he growls into my mouth, his hips driving into me urgently, pushing as far into me as he can go.

"Fuck," he moans, "Fuuuuuck... can I—" he rasps between breathes but I cut his words off with a tilt of my bottom, gliding myself along his shaft. He groans, dropping his forehead onto mine. When I lift my legs around him, my ankles in the small of his back, and give him another wicked move of my pelvis, he responds with a very hard thrust, like he's trying to nail my spine with his dick.

"Can I come here?" he asks, pressing his hand flat to my chest.

"You promised you would."

He kisses me roughly then slides out, leveraging himself into position. With three rough pumps he spills himself onto me. Breathing hard, twitching with his final spasms, he runs his hand through the slickness, rubbing it across my chest, caressing it into my breasts.

"Thank you," he murmurs, crawling onto the bed beside me, pulling me into his arms, face to face, his leg thrown over mine. We lie together, entwined, kissing, floating back down into the room, until the chill on my bare skin is too much and I shiver.

"Hold on," he says, climbing off the bed and walking into the bathroom. I hear water running then he comes back to me with a warm washcloth and cleans me up, dropping light kisses on each breast, circling my neck with his hand and pulling our faces together for another long, lingering kiss.

I'm complete mush, melted into this lovely hotel cloud of a bed, so you'd think all the crazy nympho cells in my vagina would've hung out the do not disturb sign for the night. But that kiss. Adam Sexton, naked beside me, lips on mine, and those girls are answering the door, saying come on in, let's keep this party going. My vagina starts twitching and tingling, my breasts tightening, all because he's kissing me.

Maybe his penis has an early warning detection system for greedy, Venus flytrap vaginas, because he stands up, hauling me up onto my feet. Hugging me to him, he pats me on the bottom and sends me into the bathroom. I wash up, laughing at myself in the mirror. Hair tangled, eye make-up blurred, skin flushed and red from his scruff, I'm disheveled and feeling terrifically fucked and sexy as hell. This is what I wanted, this feeling.

When I open the door, Adam gestures to the bed. "Pick your side," he says, before walking back into the bathroom.

I gather our clothes up off the floor, tossing them across the arm of one of the chairs. *What are we going to do now?* I wonder. I don't exactly feel sleepy. I climb into bed, skipping pajamas, because, well, he's still naked and I don't want to seem like I'm silently saying let's not fuck again tonight. I want to be loudly saying let's please fuck again as soon as you are able.

Adam switches off the bathroom light, checks the lock on the door, then comes to bed, twisting off the cap of a water bottle and taking several large swallows. Even this is a beautiful sight, this blast of full frontal, his chest moving up and down as he drinks, stomach contracting, his dick hanging freely between his legs.

"I knew you were perfect," he drawls, climbing in beside me. "This is the side I like."

"You left it to chance? What if that would've been my side?"

"I'm a gentleman." Kissing me, he drops down onto his back, head nestling into a pillow.

"I think you would've just scooched me on over if I'd been on that side."

Reaching to switch off his lamp, he grins at me. "We'll never know, will we?" Then he hauls me over until I'm lying on top of him. Stroking my hips, he asks, "Can I get you anything?"

Staring down at him, I nearly make a joke, asking if he has any granola bars, but I keep it to myself. Although I can't keep myself from smiling.

"I think I'm good, thanks."

"I know you're good," he exhales with satisfaction, shifting my thighs around him. "Now, let's see what else we can get up to."

A CHILL WAKES ME. Squinting at the lamp on my side of the bed, I look over my shoulder and Adam is on his side of the bed, flat on his back, one arm draped over his eyes, snoring softly. I pull the covers over both of us and switch off the light, hugging a pillow to my stomach, falling right back to sleep. Only to find, sometime later when I try to roll over, his leg draped over me. I carefully free myself, trying not to wake him, and close my eyes.

Then it happens again. He throws his knee and his arm across me, like a lion trapping his kill to save for later. He mumbled "sorry" when I less gently shoved his limbs off me, but that was it. I don't think he even opened his eyes. He's still breathing deeply, rest undisturbed.

Fluffing my pillow, flipping it to the cooler side, I roll away from him, but just as I feel sleep descending, he scoots over, his arm snaking around my waist to spoon me. Knees tucked behind me, his face in my hair, he pulls me into his body, sighing out a large breath.

I freeze, this porno vagina I'm packing saying, *hold on there a minute, maybe he's ready for more action. I'd gladly wake up for that.*

I press my ass into his crotch and wiggle. When he doesn't respond, I wiggle again. He's not waking up. He sighs, giving me a little squeeze.

I climb out of his embrace and out of bed, fighting an urge to snatch one of the pillows and swat him on the head with it. But he looks so contented, so deeply asleep, and he's been completely lovely this whole day, not to mention the multiple, spectacular orgasms, that I just can't. The man has been too darn thoughtful.

Wrapping up in the hotel bathrobe and finding the spare blanket in the closet, I slip into the sitting room, then let myself outside, taking a seat in one of the rocking chairs, the blanket tucked around my shoulders. The balcony overlooks the marina, and although it's the middle of the night, the lights along the walkways and dock give me a view. The sounds are wonderful, the low thump and slap of boats moving against their moorings, of water against hulls, the creak of my chair as I push myself back and forth. It's peaceful and meditative to be alone here on this secluded perch when the world is sleeping. The cool black mass of the water relaxes me like a firm hand pressed onto my chest. Before I know it, I'm wiping at my eyes.

Why does this still happen and when in the world will it ever end? It's still in me, this tangled mess, these knotted threads of grief and anger and pain. I wish I could pull them all apart, once and for all, fill these boats with them, and launch them across the bay. Fire flaming arrows across the sky to set them alight, stand here on this balcony, and wave goodbye.

Staring out at the water I feel pulled by the heaviness of its depths, the endless, ancient shape of it forming the curve of the earth before me, and a sob chokes from my throat, something elemental within me reaching out to be received. My tears fall like they're racing over a cliff to find home, the inevitability of them almost a relief. I cry until I'm spent, until I've given some part of this burden to the depths of Mobile Bay.

A sound reaches me.

I stop rocking, waiting to hear it again. It's a soft, irregular clink; a metal on metal, *clink... clink*, stirred by the wind. Likely from a rigging or flag on one of these boats. It's soothing, this call, as it rises to me. *Clink.... clink*. And in its way, beautiful, as if the whole world has quieted itself so I might hear this one specific sound. I listen deeply into the night. I sit very still and listen until a fully formed truth speaks to me.

A measure of this sorrow is part of me now, and always will be. It is mine. I can't outrun it or wish it away. If I could hold it in my hands, it would have a shape and weight and color much like a crystal, and I would marvel at its beauty.

On this night I learn that it will call to me, my sorrow, and I will honor it, my tears an offering to the pain through which it was earned. I've been waiting so long to feel like myself again. But I will never be that woman again, I can stop waiting for her to come back. Let her go.

I did not choose any of this, but it's who I am now. I'm altered, transformed, infused with this elemental change that must be accommodated. When I accept that, maybe I won't be so afraid. Make peace with the sadness, let it have its place instead of waiting for the day it's no longer there, and then perhaps I can accept this woman I am now, welcome her to her new life.

Did that man just fuck me into an epiphany?

CHAPTER TWENTY-FIVE

ADAM

Where is she?

What does it say about this situation when that's my first thought? When the coldness of the bed wakes me, and I realize she's not here and immediately worry she's left me. That's my first thought - she's gone.

I check my phone. Four-fifty a.m. No message from her.

Sitting up, I look around the room and see her dress draped over the chair. I throw back the covers and shuffle to the bathroom. Her makeup bag is on the counter, her hairbrush, a little bottle of perfume. She wouldn't have left without these things.

Calm the fuck down.

Leaving the bathroom light on I go back into the room and walk over to the balcony door, lifting the curtains aside. She's not out there. I pull open one of the doors to the sitting room and there she is, on her side, blonde hair curling around her cheek, asleep on the sofa.

My heart contracts. That's not a metaphor; there's an actual goddamn squeeze of pain and relief through my chest and I know right then I'm already in way deeper than I've admitted to myself.

Part of me wants to laugh because who am I kidding? I fell for this woman when I was twenty-five years old and saw her with another man and thought, one day I'll be that guy and have a woman like that, sitting on my lap, looking at me the way she's looking at him. I fell for this woman when I jumped into her pool, and she nearly cut my heart out of my chest like she knew she already owned it.

Another part of me wants to pat myself on the back, say sorry buddy, you are completely fucked. Because this woman is clearly not falling for you. All your moves and plans got you here to this fancy hotel, this expensive room, and she climbed out of your bed to sleep in another room on this stupid couch.

I don't know what to do. I'm frozen in the doorway, standing in the dark watching her sleep, and I don't know what to do. I do know grief. I thought I could handle it because of Heather, but this is some other sort of beast.

And is it also something about me? Some tarnished part of me she sees right into and can't, or won't, move beyond despite my efforts. She's been clear about how she sees me and what she wants from me. Only a fool would think this could be more.

Then again, only a fool would meet a woman who makes him feel gutted when he wakes in the night and she's not beside him, a woman he so cravenly desires he has to practically mark his territory on her like a grunting half-wit caveman the first chance he gets; a woman whose world, for once in his life, aligns with his own; a woman he wants to show off for like a schoolboy; a woman who makes him long for future conversations still to be had; a woman whose pain should scare him but instead makes him want to cover her with his own body – well, only a fool would turn away from her.

I step over to the sofa and touch her leg, speaking softly. "Holly."

She wakes with a start, looking up at me.

"Hi," she breathes.

"Is something wrong? Why are you out here?" She looks around the small room and up and down my body, rubbing at one eye before pushing herself upright. Taking it as an invitation, I sit down. "What's wrong?" I repeat, bracing for words I don't want to hear. Her regrets, that this was for her, a mistake.

I should've put pants on. I don't really want to get punched in the gut with my dick hanging out.

Squirming, pulling the blanket out from underneath herself, she pushes it away from her legs then adjusts the thick collar of the bathrobe, tugging her hair away from her neck. She's stalling, and I just want her to talk. Let's get this over with.

"You can tell me."

Reluctant, she studies my face before confessing. "It's all the touching."

"What?"

She rubs at her eyes again, sighing. "I haven't shared a bed with someone in a long time, and... you kept touching me."

"Touching you."

"Yes, in your sleep. Your leg over me, your arm over me. It's too much touching."

"Why didn't you wake me up?"

"This isn't so bad."

I shouldn't say it, but I do. "You'd rather sleep out here than have me touch you?"

Cursing myself, I'm about to make that into a joke so I don't sound so hurt, but before I can think of something clever, she's shushing me, climbing on top of me.

"Can I touch you now?" I ask.

"Yes," she answers with a soft, low chuckle, and I throw my arms around her, holding her tightly to my chest. Her body is so warm. "I just like space when I sleep, it's nothing more than that. I thought I'd sneak back in before you woke up and talk to you about it tomorrow."

"That's really it?"

"Yes," she says, brushing my hair off my forehead. She strokes my face, smoothing her fingers slowly around my eyes and then my mouth, mapping my features. There's not enough light in the room for the beautiful blue of her eyes to be visible but I've memorized the color, can feel them bright and warm on my skin. She leans in to lightly kiss my lips then goes back to studying me, running both hands through my hair, sinking lower into my lap.

"I like your face." She traces her fingers down my temples and along my jaw. "I like your lips."

When she passes one finger along my bottom lip I suck it into my mouth, biting it gently, touching it with my tongue. She tugs her finger along my lips and back across the tip of my tongue, testing out the sensation, teasing my mouth.

"You like my tongue," I say.

"I love your tongue." She bows her head to kiss me. Slow, lingering kisses, my face in her hands.

I'm willing my twitching cock to have patience when she shifts in my lap, continuing her exploration by dropping her hands to my shoulders, running them down my arms. I don't want to rush her or break this spell.

Tilting her head, she studies the tattooed lyrics around my bicep, trying to make them out in the near dark of the room. ""Little Wing,"right?"

I nod as she strokes her palms down my chest, lifting her right hand off my body as she goes, avoiding the area over my heart, the place with the new scar. "Is it sensitive?" I shake my head, even though it is. "May I touch you there?"

"Yes."

She skims the arched line of skin lightly with her fingertips and I shiver.

"I hurt you," she whispers, brushing her lips against the scar. "I don't want to hurt you."

Her mouth closes around my nipple, grazing me with her teeth and I drop my head back onto the sofa. This woman. She makes me want to cry, fucking cry – she doesn't want to hurt me – and want to rail her until she's unconscious.

When her lips move across my chest, her tongue touching my skin with each kiss until she takes my other nipple into her mouth, I raise my head and bring my hands between us, fumbling at the belt of her robe. As I toss the ends of the belt aside, she stills my hands with hers.

"I don't want to hurt you Adam," she says again, voice thick with emotion.

Then don't hurt me. Give yourself to me, I'll give myself to you.

That's what I want to say.

"I know," is all I manage, barely able to get the words out.

It must be enough because she lets go of my hands, dropping her lips onto mine hungrily. When I have the robe apart, I run my hands up her waist. Craving the weight of her tits in my hands, I lift them together, squeezing, my thumbs meeting at her sternum. I caress her, circling her nipples in tandem, raking across their peaks. She breaks our kiss, lifting onto her knees to offer them to my mouth.

"Baby," I murmur against her, sucking, licking, loving how she jerks when I bite down. I bite again, tugging, and she's gasping, hands pulling against my hair, grinding on top of me, whimpering and cooing these pretty sounds of pleasure that are all hers.

When she takes my hand, lowering it between her legs, I growl into her neck, "Is this not too much touching for you?"

"Is it too much touching for you?" she huffs, guiding my hand shamelessly back and forth, exhaling a long sigh when I slip two fingers inside.

Soaking wet and warm, she drops her head to my shoulder, holding on tight, rolling her pelvis into me. Taking hold of her hips, I slide lower down the couch, my ass now at the edge of the cushion, and kick roughly at the coffee table to push it away. Spreading my knees wide, opening her thighs fully across my lap, she moves before I can, grabbing my cock and lowering herself assertively onto me.

Her first stroke is perfection, her arch and roll a smooth glide along the full length of my dick. I let her set her own rhythm; I just tangle my hands in her hair and watch her face as she rides me, as she bites her lip and closes her eyes, dragging her pussy along my cock again and again and again, those tits swinging above me. Holly, above me, taking her pleasure.

"Touch me," she commands breathlessly, and I do, watching her mouth fall open when I fondle her sex. Pressing the side of her face into mine, digging her fingers into my shoulders, she moans, "That's it, that's it," over and over like a chant. The quick snaps of her pelvis, the clenching heat of her pussy, have me there too, my thighs beginning to shake.

"Fuck baby, just like that," I hiss into her ear. "Give me a few more of those."

Arching then pushing herself along my cock, she doesn't neglect an inch. I grip her ass, my feet driving into the floor as I lift my hips into her, going deep.

Breathing raggedly, I have no more words. It's just a hard thrust, then another, while she's panting, crying out above me, the slick glide of her juices dripping down my dick, launching me out of my head. My cum, my heart, my sanity, everything pulsing into her.

CHAPTER TWENTY-SIX

HOLLY

ADAM IS IN THE SHOWER, having gotten up earlier to work out. I'm yawning and stretching, enjoying waking up slowly tangled in the sheets. He came in with chocolate croissants in a bag, a coffee for himself, a Diet Coke with a cup of ice for me. The man pays attention.

I slip into the robe and open the curtains, flooding the room with sunlight, then step outside to the rocking chairs on the balcony. Tearing off a piece of croissant, I watch the marina. It's a different view from last night, when I was alone in the dark, the water black and endless, without a horizon.

I don't know if what happened was a meaningful break-through or simply a release of a lot of built-up emotion. I guess what I felt last night was *possibility*. A small loosening of the tangled scraps of anger and hurt in my chest, the possibility of a new version of myself.

It's more uncomfortable to consider it here in the light of day. Cracking open that door – allowing the idea of a different future to open its files in front of me and display some options - is monumental. Astounding and terrifying and fragile. Do I take a peek at these options, or do I slam the door?

Closing my eyes, I listen for that sound, that metal on metal sound that caught my attention last night. I listen for that voice of clarity.

Adam walks onto the balcony in jeans and a black tee, hair wet, smelling like soap and sex, dropping a light touch of his hand on my shoulder and a kiss on my head before taking the chair beside me, coffee in hand. Smiling, I pass him the pastry bag with his croissant.

"How are you this morning?" he says, reaching inside.

"Well and thoroughly plundered, thank you very much." He coughs around his bite of croissant, recovers, and wipes at his mouth. "I'm just telling it like it is. And how are you this morning, sir?"

"I'm good." He grins, eyes crinkling. "Very, very good."

We rock in our chairs, eating, sipping at our drinks, staring out over the view. After a while, I ask, "Are you bored, sitting here like this?"

"God no, I love it. Are you?"

"No, I could do this all day. I just assume other people don't like it." Ronnie and I had this in common, too. This shared, unapologetic desire for idleness.

I want to say something but don't know if I should, or even how to get the words organized enough to speak out loud. But I'm me, so I decide to wade in and figure it out.

"Adam," I say softly, looking out across the water.

"Hmm?"

"I want to talk to you about Ronnie. I can't exactly say why, but if you think you could deal with it, I'd like to."

"Of course, say whatever you want to say. I'm here." I glance over and he nods encouragingly, so I look away, squinting to see as far across the bay as I can, picking at the belt of my robe.

"I was fairly sheltered growing up, and a hopeless romantic. I wanted to be like a heroine from one of the novels I loved, you know, some guy would spot me in a crowd and see how special I was and spout poetry or Shakespeare and fall instantly in love." I laugh ruefully. "In college, this cute bartender I'd been flirting with followed me home. I hadn't invited him; I just answered a knock on my door and there he was. I thought it was a little weird, but also flattering. All the girls flirted with him, and I thought, oh, he picked me. He likes me. I let him in, stupidly, and well, it went bad and scary very quickly."

Adam shifts in his chair, bringing his arms to rest on his thighs.

"Don't worry, it was a tiny apartment. I got to my kitchen and pulled a butcher knife on him. He ran out before he even got his dick back in his pants and I never saw him again."

"Fuck, Holly, what an asshole."

"Yes, he was," I agree. "And that innocent, naïve part of me that thought she was going to be Lucy Honeychurch and live out some romantic eighteenth-century novel, I let her go that night. What I'd dreamed up in my head did not exist. It made me afraid, and I didn't trust my judgment."

Adam is nodding his head, his hands steepled together in his lap.

"This is getting somewhere, I promise," I say, uncrossing my legs, then re-crossing them to the opposite side, loosening the belt of the robe because it's digging into my waist.

"From the first night I met Ronnie, he was different. It was at this small club, and when the band took a break, he's somehow stuck holding open the door as people are going outside for air, and I'm stopped in front of him. He looks me over and says, 'You're not leaving, are you?'"

"Good for him," Adam chuckles.

"He took my hand and led me through the crowd until we were out on the sidewalk." I lift my hand here, remembering the feel of Ronnie's huge hand in mine. "We started talking and we never stopped, for twenty years. He took my hand and never let go. He was my safe place, my best friend, my whole heart. I had my epic romantic story after all.

"Anyway," I sigh, rubbing my forehead. "When he died, to say I was shattered is an understatement." Adam's no longer looking at me but staring out across the water. "I'm sorry, this is too much isn't it?"

He turns his face to mine. "No, I want to hear it all." I regard him skeptically. "Holly, I want to know. You can always tell me anything, no matter what."

He waits for me to acknowledge this, his features earnest. I scrape my hands through my hair. How much of this do I really want to say out loud? After searching his eyes, after he doesn't look away, I plunge back into the deep end.

"I got to a point where I thought, okay, I've reached some flat ground here, I can do this. I've adjusted to this baseline of sadness, I can coast like this now, keep my expectations low for what my life is gonna look like from here on out, and I'll survive. I can make this work, be happy enough."

"Baby," Adam murmurs, and I want him to say it a hundred times, want to beg him to call me baby and smooth it over my skin in a warm, healing balm, but I lift my hand to stop him from saying more.

"And then I found the journal. Like a land mine. I know he never would've wanted me to find it, much less read it, he'd be horrified, but it was brutal. I could've brushed it off, the petty, normal stuff... everyone complains in journals..." I take a deep breath here. "But the women, that was the poison; the women he loved, you know he named them, described them. His pet name for me, the one he had engraved on a locket when we got married, it was a hand me down from one of these other women."

Adam can't help himself here, his shock shows on his face.

"I know! Unbelievable, right? It was from early in our marriage, so I don't know if there are more of them, journals or women – I've been too afraid to go back in there, you saw that office. Maybe that was it or maybe he kept at it, I have no idea."

I get emotional here, I can't help the burning in my chest and in my eyes, the catch in my voice. "I never, ever had a clue. Not one. It was humiliating. I felt safe and loved, I believed that man *adored* me." I scoff bitterly. "I was missing him every hour of every day and then... the story changed, overnight. I was that naïve, stupid girl again. I mean, what was real?"

I can't say the rest out loud. That I don't know how to reconcile my love for Ronnie, how much I miss him, with how hurt I am, how angry and betrayed I feel. That I don't know if I'll ever trust my own judgment again, or ever let myself be that vulnerable.

I drop my hands into my lap, sighing heavily. "That's the story, basically. Aren't you lucky today's the day I decide to let it all out."

"Holly—" he begins, but I reach my hand over to touch the arm of his chair.

"I don't need you to say anything, and don't feel sorry for me. Please don't, I don't think I could take it." He nods, frowning. "I wanted you to know why... why I'm like this. And if this is a bad idea for you, I completely understand if you want to change your mind."

This poor guy, he should jump over the railing right now and run.

Adam stands, squaring himself in front of me. He takes my hands, lifting me to my feet, pulling me into his body and pressing my head to his chest, my ear right above his heart. I burrow into him, absorbing all the comfort he's offering, letting it infuse through my skin like whiskey in my bloodstream.

"Thank you for telling me," he says gruffly, stroking my hair. "I want to know everything about you. I can take it and I'm here, okay. I'm here for as long as you'll have me." I shake my head against his chest, watching the boats rise and fall in the marina as he speaks.

"For what it's worth, I have no doubt Ronnie loved you. How could he not? You felt safe and loved because I think he worked hard to protect you from his mistakes. I bet he'd hate himself to see you like this. I'd also bet those mistakes were so far in his past, it's why he forgot about the journal. He wasn't that man anymore. I'd say he spent a lot of his life proving to himself he wasn't that man and loving you as hard as he could."

This shouldn't be Adam's job, to reassure me that some other man loved me, but selfishly, I can't make myself let go of him. We stay in this embrace, our breathing in synch.

"You can set yourself free, you know, when you're ready. If you focus on all the love, choose those memories, it would be less suffering. Life does a great job all on its own, giving us pain, we don't need to do it to ourselves."

"Where'd you learn to say things like that?" I sniffle.

He squeezes me. "Lots and lots of therapy. And Instagram."

I take a quick swipe at my eyes. This is not how I pictured my sex coma weekend going, it's not exactly light and flirty banter. "This has been very sexy, hasn't it? Do you end up doing therapy with all your dates?"

He kisses the top of my head then releases me, taking a seat in his chair. "Don't underestimate what I can find sexy."

"Is that right?" I sit, shifting on one hip in the chair, leaning in his direction.

"Oh yeah, I'm thinking filthy things about you right now."

"You have some sort of vulnerability kink?"

He smirks. "Um, I have a, your robe is open, and I can see your boobs kink."

"Adam!" I snort with laughter, adjusting the robe that yes, has slipped open. "You never stop, do you?"

"Do you want me to?" Those dark brown eyes of his, they are dancing with a challenge. I stare right back and shake my head at his self-assured, randy smile.

I didn't think so is the exact translation of the look he gives me in reply.

I WALK into one of the resort cafés about two hours later. Adam has been meeting with his sister, Gretchen, who texted him when she arrived, while I showered and relaxed, waiting for him to summon me. They aren't hard to spot in this lunch crowd of pastel polo shirts and tennis whites.

Gretchen has thick, almost black hair like Adam's, down to her shoulders, cut into a cool, long layered shag. God, I've always wanted hair like that. Same as her brother, she's in a black tee and faded jeans. Her tee is a sleeveless, fitted ribbed tank, her arms decorated with tattoos.

He stands as I approach the table, kissing me on the cheek. "Holly, this is my sister Gretchen," he says, pulling out my chair. "Gretchen, this is Holly Theriot."

"Holly," she says, neutrally, giving me a quick up and down. So neutrally, in fact, I catch a small twinge of unease.

"Pleasure to meet you. Are you sure I'm not interrupting your business? I don't want to cut your time short."

"You're perfect and I'm starving," Adam says, craning his neck to look for a waiter.

Gretchen reaches into a tote bag at her feet, then drops four folded t-shirts onto the table in front of me. "Which one do you like best?" No preamble or explanation.

"What are you doing?" Adam raises his eyebrows at her, dropping his upturned hands onto the table.

"She's a neutral third party, I wanna hear what she thinks," she says to him, then back to me she says, "Go on, have a look."

Is this some sort of test? It's a funny little sibling thing, that's clear, even when said siblings are middle aged. However, the minute I walked in here and smelled food, my stomach started growling. Like Adam, I'm ready to find a waiter and order. I'm going to cut this off right now. I flip through the tees one by one.

"New merch for the website and the summer tour," he offers.

"Easy," I say. "Adam, which one did you choose?"

"Come on...." Gretchen protests while he reaches across the table to pull the bottom one from the stack, dropping it onto the top and giving her an exaggerated side-eye. It's deep blood red with his Texas tattoo big and bold on the front.

"This is the one I like, too," I declare, and both siblings lean back in their chairs. Adam full on smiling, arms up in victory, and Gretchen scowling, so it runs in the family. "This one," I continue, flipping to a gray tee underneath. "This one, I'd make it in white, and change the font."

Adam holds out his hands in my direction, grinning at his sister, as if to say, *exactly, isn't she wonderful.* Or something like that. I need food. And more caffeine.

She leans forward in her chair, lowering her voice to a gossip loud whisper. "He's really not *that* good in bed, is he?"

"Gretchen..." he warns.

"Oh, he one hundred percent is." I'm looking not at her but right at her brother. He stands, taking my face in both hands, and kisses me square on the lips with flourish.

After we've ordered, I'm reaching for my Diet Coke when she speaks. "At least you didn't try to suck up to me the first chance you got, and you ordered a pizza for yourself that apparently, you're not going to share—" Adam snort laughs here.

"The menu said it was an *individual* pizza," I protest.

She ignores us. "So, you're not another one of these California gluten-free skeletons." She lifts her glass in a toast. "You've got potential, I think I might like you."

"Gee, thanks," I say, touching her glass with mine. "I don't know if I like you yet, I'll have to get back to you." They both let out sharp belly laughs, which makes me laugh too.

They're obviously close, the way they talk is easy and familiar, with some light sibling jabs here and there. And they look a lot alike; she's lean like Adam, with the wide mouth, a sort of stern face that completely changes when they smile, and dark brown eyes. I'm jealous of her arms. They're firm and muscled, and her tattoos are really sexy.

I wonder if I could pull off a tattoo? Even if I could stand the pain, which is unlikely, I wouldn't look tough and hot like her. I've never been able to look tough; I'm too soft, too round and squishy.

Just as our food arrives, a young man approaches our table, dressed in crisp navy pants and a white button down with the resort logo. Gretchen immediately stiffens, hands hovering over her plate. Attention fully on Adam, he says, nervously, "Forgive me Adam... uh, Mr. Sexton, sorry to bother you—"

"Yes?" Gretchen interrupts impatiently.

"I'm Jason, a manager here, um, are you all enjoying your meal with us today?"

"Not yet," she grumbles.

"Good. Good, good..." he stammers. "Please let me know if you need anything. Anything, just say the word."

"Thank you, Jason," Adam says, leaning heavily on his Texas drawl, and I watch the guy's face light up. "Everything has been wonderful so far."

Then Jason bursts.

"You're my favorite guitar player! I'm a guitar player, and I've watched every video of you online, I've seen you play live, like, three times. Man you are a legend. A living goddamn legend and when I heard you were staying here, I couldn't believe it. I wanted to shake your hand and if I could ask some questions, like how are you tuning that—"

"We're in the middle of lunch," Gretchen points out.

"Oh yeah, so sorry, of course, I won't keep you," he says, "It's just I have a band... Dream Away, that's our band, you can check us out on YouTube..."

"Cool name," Adam says, and this kid looks like he might fall over. "I tell you what, let me enjoy my time here with my family and then I'll give you fifteen minutes, you can ask me anything you like. Musician to musician, sound good?"

"Are you kidding me, thank you! That's so fire!" Jason exclaims, leaving our table after several more effusive thank you's and offers of assistance. I look around, wondering if there are more people ready to approach.

"Does that happen to you a lot?" I ask.

"I wouldn't say a lot, no..."

"Enough," Gretchen says, picking up a French fry from her plate. "It happens enough."

"Don't listen to her," he says to me. "It really doesn't. Fans keep me working, so it's part of the deal, but it's not like I'm

Keith Richards or anything. And why wouldn't I want to talk to a young musician who's curious about an old guy like me?"

"Oh, are we old now?" she laughs.

"Sorry to break it to you," he says, stealing one of her fries.

"He's about the same age as Luke. I hope there are people in the world who'd show him that same kindness, that some stranger would be helpful to him, to my son, if he asked. It's really sweet, Adam." I reach for his hand, and he takes it, lifting it to his lips.

"Gawd..." Gretchen moans, rolling her eyes. "Just for that—" she sneaks a hand towards my plate. Normally this would be dangerous for anyone, with a high probability of getting stabbed with my fork, but I let it go this time and she slides a slice her way. Adam has made me benevolent today.

After lunch, I browsed the gift shop while Adam visited with Jason, then we walked a few turns around the resort. Back in the room, he called for a bellman and for the car to be brought around. Since we're not close to the theater, and there's a VIP meet and greet after his sound check, we agreed I would catch a ride with Gretchen.

As he brushes his teeth, I stand in the doorway of the bathroom.

"Do you have any pre-show preferences I should know about, like do you prefer not to talk to people? Just let me know if you'd rather me not come backstage until after the show, or not at all. Whatever works best for you, I'll be good. I can look after myself."

Spitting into the sink, he looks over to me. "I don't think anyone's ever asked me that before."

"I don't know why; pre-show rituals are important to people."

He rinses with water cupped in his hands, then dries his mouth and hands with a towel. "I like quiet before, to clear my head and rest my voice."

"Okay then, you got it."

"But that doesn't go for you. I want you wherever I am."

Something in my chest, could be my rumored-to-be-dead heart, thumps. He's six feet away from me but I feel heat from his skin, could close my eyes and detect his pulse. He tells me he wants me, and my body reacts immediately. No doubt, this must be an extreme form of skin hunger, a sign of how deprived of affection I've been, starved for touch.

"You do?" I raise an eyebrow, hoping to sound playful.

"In fact, come here," he commands, voice edged with something not so playful.

I shift against the doorway, crossing my arms over my chest. "Over there?"

"Yes, come here."

For a second I think to object, turn this into a game, but my body has other ideas and I step forward, pulled to him like he's the source of all gravity. I stop when I'm standing inches away and he reaches out to caress my cheek, his dark eyes possessive as he drags his thumb across my lips. I'm motionless under his gaze, breathless at how much I want him. A chill rumbles down my spine, a warning shiver. I'm getting infatuated with this man.

I don't need to worry about it, right? We're in this lust bubble because it's new, and it's easy when the stakes are low. We're having fun. *Keep it about the lust, Holly.*

It's not hard. He makes lust very easy.

Dear whomever controls the universe, please give me time to lick him all over before this ends.

I move until my hips meet his, arms at my sides, offering myself to him. Hand still on my face, he lowers his mouth onto mine.

Knock. Knock. Knock.

Continuing the kiss, he lifts his free hand behind me to palm one side of my ass, pressing me into him.

Knock. Knock. Knock.

He pulls his face away, scowling, and I can't help myself, it makes me smile.

"Time to go to work," he sighs, giving me one more deep kiss before letting me go and walking out of the bathroom to open the door.

Never mind me.

I'm just waiting for my ovaries, and best laid plans, to get back up off the floor.

CHAPTER TWENTY-SEVEN

HOLLY

IN A NOD to Adam's standard color palette, I'm wearing all black, all pieces pulled from the back in my former life part of my closet. A short faux leather skirt, quilted bustier, and a fitted velvet jacket, with opaque tights and boots.

I was worried I might have over-dressed, even though this is my habitat, so to speak. It's been a while, you know. But when I meet Gretchen in the lobby, she gives me what can only be described as a completely inappropriate, completely ego flattering, panty-dropping smile. I believe she mentally undressed me and I'm not mad about it.

I know it's wrong, but I don't want to be right. Not right now. Right now, I want to feel good, and she has made me feel great.

"Holy shit," she says appreciatively. "Tits on the half shell, flaunt 'em if you got 'em."

"I was worried it was too much."

"Fuck no. But Adam might need a defibrillator."

"They oughta be good for something, give 'em a few more laps around the block before they're down to my knees."

She's wearing what she had on at lunch, having only added a whisper thin, expensively supple, tight black leather jacket – the nicest I've ever seen – and black cat-eye liner. Outside, her car is waiting, and she walks around to open my door.

The manners on these Sexton siblings, I tell you what. I hope I've done this well with Luke.

"You look like the queen of all the rock-n-roll vampires," I tell her.

Speaking confidentially, she whispers, "Maybe because I am," then shuts my door with a firm hand after I'm settled in the passenger seat.

We're not far out of the resort property when she asks, "Adam said you do something with art?" Surprised, I look over to her, but her eyes are on the road.

"Tangentially, yes," I reply. "I do estate and insurance appraisals, mostly contemporary art, but some Southern folk artists too, and freelance projects for some regional auction houses and museums. Artist bios, exhibition catalogs. That's actually the work I like best."

"The studio's not your business?"

"No, well, yes, it is. I guess I still think of it as Ronnie's business I try to keep afloat. And I got the impression you are basically chief operating officer for all things Adam Sexton."

She snorts. "Some might say that, but I doubt my little brother did."

"I wasn't supposed to let on about it."

"I can imagine he made that very clear." Affection colors her voice. "I love that I've been able to be on this ride with him, that I get to look out for him."

"Sounds good for both of you."

"Yeah, it is."

I take in the view as she steers us west onto I-10, and the bridge that spans Mobile Bay.

"Ronnie, your husband, he had cancer?" she asks carefully.

"Lung cancer," I reply, nodding my head.

"That's a bad way to go."

People usually have no idea, the horror of it, the suffering, but in this case, I believe I'm wrong. Nurses have generally seen it all. "It is."

"Adam said you took care of him at home?"

They really did talk about me. I exhale, smoothing my skirt with the palms of my hands. I don't want to get into it, not tonight, but I don't want to be rude. I glance over, meeting her penetrating gaze, and understanding passes between us, respect, like two soldiers sharing a moment of solidarity.

Looking back to the road she says, "I know how hard it must have been."

Nothing else needs to be said.

GRETCHEN KNOWS JUST where to go, navigating to a secure parking area, giving her ID to the security guard, who checks it against his list and waves us in. Out of the car, I do a quick readjustment of my boobs, bending at the waist and scooping them up one at a time.

"Nope, you didn't get it," she says, and I shimmy, pulling the top, and my boobs, higher. "Do it again and I'll help."

I laugh, hard, and she does too. "Okay, I've decided. I do like you."

"Lucky me. And stop being nervous, he's already a total goner over you."

Say what now?

I follow her to the stage door, glad she can't see the flush I'm sure is reddening my chest and neck. *Stop being nervous*, she says, then makes a comment like that. I wasn't *that* nervous, just wanting to look good, but now I am. Now I'm completely flustered. Flustered like I've just seen that shower scene from 'Sex/Life' for the first time, that kind of jump off the couch and shout "Oh my god! Rewind! Rewind!" kind of flustered.

We follow a narrow hallway to the green room, pausing behind a bottleneck of people lined up along the wall in front of the open double doors, the last of the meet and greet. Gretchen flashes her pass, so they don't think we're cutting.

"Wait." I tug on the back of her jacket, and she looks over her shoulder. "Oh, this jacket feels like butter."

She scowls. How very much like her brother.

"Put your arm around my shoulder," I say.

"What?"

"You don't wanna have a little fun?" I give her the double eyebrow raise, because it wouldn't be a terrible thing to mess with Mr. Sexy Bossy Pants. Let him be the flustered one. It all registers in her eyes, which she then narrows at me.

"You little devil."

"Yep, so put your arm around me." She does, and I link my hand through hers where it rests on my shoulder, wrapping my other arm around her waist. We fit together well. This Sexton pheromone/sexual chemistry thing is powerful.

She gives me a, "Tits up baby doll," and we make our entrance.

I don't have to bother looking for Adam because Gretchen steers us to a spot directly opposite the band, where they stand shaking hands and taking photos with fans. My eyes go straight to him. He's already watching me, scowling, a small shake of his head at our antics. The line keeps moving, autographs are signed, and Adam makes eye contact with me repeatedly through it all, keeping us connected across the room.

This band is all middle-aged. It's not a raucous scene. I do notice the fans who want photos with Adam alone are not equally divided between men and women. The guitar loving guys are there, for sure, but it's mostly women who line up to put an arm around him. Some kiss his cheek or link an arm through his, some have cards or gifts. There are whispers in his ear, hands that linger a little too long for my liking – and yes, I'm feeling possessive when I have no right to be – but really, it's a lot of touching.

Meanwhile, I've been checking out Jennifer Carson, who is a beauty. Petite, with short, thick, dark blonde hair that swoops dramatically over to one side, stupidly high cheekbones, and eyes highlighted, also dramatically, in smoky, sparkly shades. She's in black pants and a bright pink blouse, frilly bow tied at her neck, and as far as I can tell, hasn't acknowledged Gretchen's presence, although I've seen her eyes surreptitiously find their way to us multiple times.

Gretchen has noticed this too. After we've been standing arm in arm for a while, she turns her face into my hair and asks, "Wanna kiss me?"

"Not a chance," I reply out of the side of my mouth, and she tweaks my ribcage. I yelp and twist away, which inadvertently draws attention our way. She pulls me back to her and laughs, like we've just shared a naughty joke. With her hand still in mine, I pinch the soft spot between her thumb and index finger, bearing down until she starts to wince. "Don't push your luck," I hiss, squeezing until she relaxes her hold around my waist.

"Okay, okay," she says, and I let go just as Adam reaches us.

"What are you two up to?" he asks. Unsmiling, he surveys me from head to and toe.

"She's all yours, brother. Delivered safe and sound as requested."

Shaking out the sting in her hand, Gretchen crosses the room, walking around the band and through an open door behind them. Jennifer follows two seconds later.

Meanwhile, Adam is giving me a look. I lift my hands, adopting an innocent expression.

"Mm-hm, right. I told her to take care of you, but I should've warned her instead."

"I don't need anyone to take care of me."

He takes my hand, lacing his fingers though mine. "Come on," he says, leading me rather aggressively through the same door at the back of the room. This opens to a second, smaller green room, with a piano in one corner and mirrors along the wall. We pass through another door, into a tight hallway with dressing rooms along both sides. The first door to the right is closed, a sign taped to the outside, with the name JENNIFER CARSON in big black letters.

He stops in front of the last room on the left, marked with his name, allowing me to enter first. The minute the door closes I turn and he's standing in place, arms crossed over his chest.

"What?" I ask, my heart beginning to flutter. Maybe he's angry about our little show.

The words his sister said to me begin to play in my mind like a needle stuck on a record, skipping to the same phrase again and again. *Already a goner. Already a goner.* I don't have to believe her, but my heart is now the golden snitch, winged and shiny, about to race up and out of my chest.

When he doesn't move, doesn't speak, eyes darkening as he scrutinizes me, I back a few steps farther into the room. "We were just having a little fun..."

"I don't care about that. I suspect it was your idea anyway."

Now I cross my arms. "Then what's your problem?"

"Look at you. How am I supposed to do my job when I'm not going to be able to think of anything else but you tonight?"

"Oh," I whisper.

"Oh," he nods.

"Do I look nice?"

"The phrase 'make a bulldog break his chain' comes to mind."

The room temperature shoots up twenty degrees. I drop my hands to my hips, arching my back so that my chest rises. His eyes flick there, and I feel bold, unable to stop the lascivious smile that lights up my face.

"Come here," I demand, a replay of our interaction a few hours ago.

"You come here."

We stare at one another, waiting to see who will move first. It absolutely will not be me. I slip off my jacket and toss it aside, letting my bare, glowing shoulders and the swell of my breasts do the work. I didn't squeeze myself into this getup for nothing. If I had a whip, I'd crack it.

"Come here before I tell you to crawl."

He chuckles, conceding defeat, taking step by deliberate step to me, the sound of his boot heels on the floor suddenly erotic. Eyes welded to mine, he connects us first at the hip, drawing us together with his hands snaking around my waist.

I lift my arms to circle his shoulders. "You think I look nice?"

He does a sort of slow lip-smacking thing, his eyes roaming

my face then down to take in the rest of me. "Baby, I hope someone around here knows how to do CPR." This makes me laugh. "You think that's funny, do you?"

"Inside joke," I say, bringing my face close to his, my lips at his ear. "Is that your way of saying yes?" I nip his earlobe.

In a flash he has his lips on mine, his tongue in my mouth, his hands up my skirt. In seconds, we're breathless, making out like teenagers ten minutes before curfew. His mouth goes to my neck, reciprocating with a nip of his own. "You look ravishing."

"You make me want to never stop kissing you," I breathe, thrusting my hands into his hair.

"Never stop," he repeats, his lips back to mine. We're in danger of undressing one another in this narrow little room when there's a sharp rap on the door.

"Mr. Sexton?"

Still in my arms, he calls out, "Yeah?"

The door opens and a young woman steps inside, stopping abruptly when she sees the state of us. Headset nestled atop her messy bun, she clears her throat and shifts her eyes to the wall and then the floor, looking anywhere but directly at us.

"Um, sorry, they told me to bring these to you." She has the gifts from the meet and greet.

"Sure, of course, thank you," Adam says, perfectly casual. Still in an embrace, one hand clamped to my ass under my skirt, when he feels me pull away his arms tighten, holding me in place.

She drops the gifts onto the narrow ledge of the counter so hastily that a container of cookies clatters to the floor. "Sorry, sorry," she stammers, picking it up. Her eyes meet mine in the mirror, and I smile sympathetically, which only makes her turn fully red in the face. She backs out of the room and closes the door.

"Now, where were we?" Adam says, slanting his mouth over mine.

"Making the young people uncomfortable," I reply against his lips. I really don't want to stop kissing him. "Don't you have some pre-show routine to do?"

Sighing melodramatically, he reaches into his pocket for his phone. Seeing the time, he plants his face into my cleavage. "You have to let me go because I don't think I can let you go."

I untangle us, arm by arm. "Are you sure I shouldn't leave you be for now? I don't mind, you are working."

"No, sweetheart. Stay."

I want to press his face right back into my boobs.

"Okay then, what would you be doing before a show if I wasn't here?"

He looks around. "Drink a cup of tea, do my exercises, change my shirt. Scroll through my phone. All the salacious stuff you've imagined."

I deserve that. "How about I get that tea for you? What kind do you prefer?"

"You don't need to do that."

I kiss his cheek. "It's just tea, and I'd like to, so let me."

After fetching the tea, I poke around the gifts from the meet and greet as Adam finishes his stretches. "Does this happen every time, people bringing things?" I ask.

"Pretty much," he says, unzipping the garment bag hanging from a hook on the wall.

"Do you mind if I look?"

"No, but you might not want to. I usually don't." He's taking off his t-shirt and I let myself appreciate the view. I want to nibble *him* like a cookie. In fact, I should be writing up a list of things I want to do to him.

Pulling a silky black shirt from a hanger, he slips it on, and I wave his hands away, stepping in close to button it up for him. His eyes roam my face as I go button by button, then reach for a sleeve, rolling it up past his elbows. My corset somehow feels tighter and I'm conscious of every breath now, and of his breathing, of his warm skin under my fingers.

"Why don't you?" I ask. He undoes two of the buttons, so the shirt is open part way down his chest. "Ah, okay, so that's how it is?"

"Got to put on a show."

Oh, that lethal grin.

Smirking, I do his second sleeve, then he steps beside me to inspect himself in the mirror and take a sip of tea.

"Why don't I what?" he asks, and I gesture to the gifts. "It's just not..." he hesitates, shifting me aside to get to his shoulder bag.

"Not what?"

He sets a black leather dop kit onto the counter and pulls out a small round container, unscrews the lid and scoops out a dab of hair wax. He rubs it between his palms before applying it to his hair, scraping it back from his face. I pick up the container and bring it to my nose.

"Not what?" I repeat.

He takes the container from my hand. Putting the lid back on, he swaps it out for a tube of lip balm, applying that while I watch. Rolling his lips together, he leans down for a quick kiss then applies a little more.

Finished with his kit, he swaps it out for a black leather pouch, taking out a few guitar picks and stuffing them into his front pocket. Then he roots around again in the shoulder bag until he locates a small velvet draw-string pouch. He loosens the strings and spills out a tangle of silver into his hand. Finally done with his bags within more bags business, he stops and leans back on the counter to look at me.

"Not healthy. Sometimes I'll look through the cards; most are fine but there are always, always ones that are problematic. Even if it's just one, that one will really get under my skin. I wish it wasn't like that; that I could enjoy the positive ones and ignore the rest, but that's not how it works for me. It's the other ones that'll hang on like a mosquito bite I can't stop scratching, and if I do that night after night, I get eaten up by things that really, I should never have let in. Things I don't want and didn't ask for, people I can't help or be what they want me to be for them. Gretchen usually sorts through it."

I look at it all again, the cards and gifts on the counter. "Why do they do it you think?"

"I stopped trying to figure it out a long time ago." He pulls a silver bracelet from the jewelry in his hand, holding it out to me. I look it over while he untangles the rest. The bracelet, chunky alternating links of skulls and roses, has real weight in my hand.

"Memento Mori," I say, more to myself than to him.

The tangle Adam is sorting turns out to be two long necklaces, one with a record spindle charm and the other a feather. He puts them on then holds out his left arm to me. "Memento Mori," he repeats, and I fasten the bracelet around his wrist.

A loud knock barely has time to register before the door swings open and I jump, startled. Gretchen steps inside, holding the door open with her shoulder. Carrying her jacket, to my eyes looking a little tousled, lips reddened.

"Holly, you ready?"

"Yep," I say, stepping around Adam and grabbing my jacket.

On our way out of the green room, she grabs two bottles of beer from a large bucket of ice. "One for you, one for me," she says, passing one to me and clinking her bottle to mine.

THE SAENGER THEATRE in Mobile is gorgeous, built in the 1920's to resemble a grand European opera house. Fitted out in red and gold, with carved mythic figures and glittering chandeliers, it's much larger than I expected. Our seats are in a box that juts out underneath intricately carved organ grilles, looking onto the stage from the left of the auditorium. Snapping photos, I watch as the seats fill up, the chatter and excitement of the audience contagious.

"I love these seats," I say to Gretchen, who is sipping her beer and scrolling through her phone. She might as well be waiting for a bus, she's so uninterested. I suppose she's seen this show, or some version of it, many, many times.

The house lights come down and a woman walks on stage to make a brief pitch about membership levels to support the theatre, then introduces the band to loud applause and cheers. Jennifer shakes her hand as they pass one another, coming to stand front and center. She's added an intricately embroidered black jacket to her outfit, and she beams at the audience while she gets her guitar in place. Her charisma is remarkable, flipped on like a light switch now, reaching all the way to the last row of seats in the balcony, and she hasn't even started singing.

When Adam walks out several seconds behind her, the crowd reacts with an extra burst of applause, which he acknowledges with a raise of his hand.

Gretchen leans forward, at last interested, her arms on the gold railing of our box, eyes dialed in to Jennifer.

What a show it is. Two hours, no break, and when it's over the crowd still wants more, stomping and clapping, hollering until the band comes back for an encore. I barely had eyes for anyone but Adam. In his element, prowling the stage, possibly the hottest low-key swagger I've ever seen.

The way he plays, I'm transported by his skill and soulful intensity. Gretchen gives me some side-eye a few times, outright laughing at me, ribbing me with her elbow when I start losing it, standing up and whooping over one particularly nasty groove he hits on an extended solo. I don't care. He's incredible.

Several times I found myself thinking, *what must it be like to be with a man that sexy?* Then I'd think, *wait a minute, I know because I did it! And I'm going to do it again, tonight. I'm going to fuck him until he has no idea what year it is.*

When we make our way backstage after the show, I've got nervous butterflies. I did know who Adam was, of course, but I haven't given it much thought really, not until this weekend. His status has been at a remove. He's just been another musician at the studio, that man in my pool house who's been flirting with me, the one I propositioned. The way we met, the isolation of my place, our easy chemistry, all of it allowed me to forget.

But seeing him work in front of an adoring crowd of several thousand people, I've been thoroughly reminded. His life is more complex, much larger in scale, than mine; and although this is Jennifer Carson's show tonight, he is the biggest star in the building.

CHAPTER TWENTY-EIGHT

HOLLY

ADAM HOLDS my hand on his thigh as we drive back to Point Clear. He's alert, drumming his fingers against the steering wheel with post-performance adrenaline, the electricity between us so charged I can't believe my hair isn't standing straight up from my head. My anticipation, my desire for him, is causing a throb between my legs so strong it's almost painful. I chatter to distract myself, describing my favorite moments of the show.

"Whose idea was it to do that duet of "Paying the Cost to Be the Boss"? It was brilliant."

"We started doing that years ago."

"It's so fun, the audience loved it. It's really sexy."

"Yeah?" he looks over to me, smiling.

"B.B. King is perfect for your style. I love that you don't over-play, you know what I mean? It's focused and potent, the way you play... it's sophisticated. That was incredible, all of it, what a beautiful way to see you be you." I don't care that I'm gushing.

"Thank you," he says, giving my hand a squeeze, and I stroke his thigh, letting my hand slide between his legs. "Easy there, baby," he lifts my hand, clamping it under the weight of his back on top of his thigh. "I gotta get you home."

"Drive faster."

His soft laugh tickles my skin all over and the car surges forward.

I need, *really need*, to get this man out of his clothes, and I'm more than ready to get out of mine, so as soon as we enter the hotel I take the lead, pulling him in the direction of the elevator, but he stops me, tugging on my hand.

"Feel like a drink?" He gestures with his head towards the faint sound of a piano.

I don't.

I want to be out of this corset. I want to be naked.

"I think you'll like it." He coaxes me along, his smile irresistible. We walk into the resort's late-night bar and a host greets us, not even having to ask for a name, I notice. He's made some sort of arrangements.

Before we're led into the bar, I point over my shoulder. "I'm going to pop into that ladies' room."

"What would you like to drink, and I'll order for you."

"Glass of champagne?"

"You got it," he says, and raises my hand, kissing the inside of my wrist, his lips lingering hot on my skin, before letting go and turning to follow the host.

I need to knock back this drink and get this man upstairs.

I pee and wash my hands, fluff my hair, lift my boobs again. I crunch on a peppermint I find in the bottom of my bag and touch up my lips with a swipe of gloss. There's some hand lotion because this is a fancy place, so I use that before looking myself over one last time and heading out to find Adam.

Find him I do.

Through the bar, out on the wide lawn dotted with a dozen or so fire pits. Each fire pit is surrounded by five chairs, and the chairs around Adam are all occupied. By women. He's sitting forward, hands clasped, forearms on his knees, listening to one of them speak. When I reach them, he stands immediately, taking my hands.

"Sweetheart, here, take my seat. I ordered a little food for us, it should be right out."

I don't sit. I square my shoulders and let my eyes travel chair by chair around the circle.

Three of the women, all at least ten years younger than me, stand to leave, but the one sitting to Adam's left, the one doing all the talking, stays put. She's, *of course* - it's how the world works –

a blonde with big boobs, boobs that are spilling out of her tight black exercise jacket, the zipper pulled down strategically low for maximum effect. I can't blame her there, since I'm over here with this corset working like a hydraulic lift, but still. Get the hell out of here, lady.

"It was a pleasure to meet you all, thanks for the kind words," he says. With my hands in his, it's polite code anyone would recognize for *please leave now*. The three on their feet get the message, making their way around the chairs, but their blonde friend isn't so easily dismissed.

"Don't I get a picture?" she croons.

"Not tonight, I'm with my girl here. But it was nice to meet you. Have a lovely evening."

"Well then," she pouts, holding out her hand. "Be a gentleman and help me up please."

Frustration and apology in his eyes, he turns to her, not bothering to hide his irritation. She clasps his hand when he offers it, hoisting herself up and straight into his body.

"You're so strong," she purrs, running her hands down his arms as he tries to set her away from him. "It must be all that strumming."

I don't like this at all. I'm right here and she doesn't care one bit. She's not that drunk.

"I bet you're a very good *strummer*, am I right?" she giggles, clinging to him.

"Alright, that's enough, off you go," he scowls, looking to her friends for help. They move to intervene, but she grabs at his shirt.

"If she's your type, then I'm doubly your type. We should have a party, honey."

"Get your hands off him, *honey*, or your friends are going to have to pull you out of this fire pit," I snap. I've had enough of this. Her and all the ones like her, from all the years and journals and secret humiliations.

She stumbles, and Adam manages to remove himself from her grasp. He side steps to me, arm lifted in front of my body protectively. Her friends take her in hand, but she shakes them off.

"What did you say to me?" she points her finger, her face scrunched into an ugly grimace. As much as one can scrunch with so much Botox.

"You heard me. You're embarrassing yourself. Touch him again and your head is going to be in that fire pit. Those cheap hair extensions will go off like a fucking roman candle."

"Rude," she huffs as her friends drag her away, apologizing as they go.

Adam draws me into his arms, and I can feel people watching us. It's been a bit of a scene. Great.

He kisses the top of my head. "Sorry about that."

"Not your fault. People are watching, I hope I didn't make it worse."

"Are you kidding me?" he laughs. "That was hot. You went all Loretta Lynn on her." He kisses my temple as a waiter arrives with a tray of food and drinks, and we sit. Adam passes my champagne to me and lifts his drink for a toast. "Cheers, killer. I don't know if I've ever had *my* honor defended before."

"You shouldn't encourage me," I sigh. My temper could cause real problems for someone like him, and I don't like the attention.

"I shouldn't encourage you to be all hot and possessive like that? I can't agree with you there, baby, 'cause I loved it." He pops a pistachio from the charcuterie board into his mouth. "That lady has no idea what you can do with a champagne bottle."

"I'm not possessive," I hiss.

He pulls a look that says, *whatever you say, dear, but you totally are.*

"I'm not," I press. "It was just so insulting." He makes that same dubious face again, this time a smile pulling up one side of his mouth as he puts salami onto a cracker. "And I imagine I'm not the first woman with you who's had to deal with something like that."

He chews thoughtfully. "No, I guess not."

I lift an upturned hand to him, my gesture silently saying *see there, of course I'm right.*

"But I believe you are the first woman I think would actually do something about it." He thinks this is very funny. "And the first woman who gave me a boner over it."

"I don't think this is funny."

"Really?"

"No."

He holds both hands up in surrender, but he's still smiling, going to town over the food.

"That made you *hard*?" I whisper.

He puffs out air through his lips, raising his thick eyebrows suggestively. "Oh yeah."

"Caveman." I shake my head but can't help myself. Those melted chocolate eyes with the firelight dancing in them, crinkling at the corners, make me heated all over. My nipples are standing at attention, like puppies up on their back legs begging for treats. "But thank you for this, I really like it."

"Caveman like fire," he grunts, waving his glass in front of himself. "And strong woman. Bring woman to cave, do... caveman things." He sinks back into his chair, sipping his whiskey, eyes flirting with mine.

"And cavewoman things."

His laughter, his ease, it calms me, even when he's turning me on. I let my head drop back onto my chair and take in a few deep breaths. The combined glow from all the fire pits stretched across the lawn creates a dome of light and warmth against the night, but I can still see stars blinking in the sky. Despite the muffled voices of people around us, it's soothing, as sitting around a fire usually is.

I look over to Adam. He's also staring into the sky, his glass in one hand on the arm of his chair. I watch the shadows cast by the fire dance across his features, waves of light and dark undulating over his skin. He's not just handsome. He's thoughtful. He's kind and affectionate, gifted and successful, smart and funny. He's a beloved little brother. A son worried about his mother.

He's also cocky, this caveman, and bossy; naughty, horny, and a fantastic lover with a beautiful dick.

Damn.

My heart does that slow thumping thing again, and I down the rest of my champagne. This might have been a miscalculation on my part, assuming he was perfect for my short-term, get revenge on Ronnie, see if my vagina still worked then cut him loose fling. I thought he was perfect for the job. A good time, uncomplicated bad boy.

But he's a different man altogether and how in the hell am I supposed to deal with that? What do I do? Because I can't pretend I don't see it anymore, that I don't get a jittery, bubbles percolating feeling in my chest around him. I like him, and that's precisely what I didn't want. Adam Sexton is turning out to be complicated.

He must sense my stare because he turns his head and meets my gaze. All he does is look into my eyes and smile, from three feet away, and I want to crawl onto his lap, kiss him until the sun comes up.

That's not exactly the flat ground I thought I'd reached in my life, the safe road I'd coast from here through the end of my days. Safely, quietly coasting along.

No.

He's a big warm ocean at the base of a cliff. When he looks at me the way he is right now, all I want to do is jump.

CHAPTER TWENTY-NINE

ADAM

HOLLY WENT QUIET, watching the fire. She was quiet in the elevator too, and in the long walk through the corridors to our room. I got a bad feeling she'd retreated into herself again. Pushed me back out to arm's length.

I should've followed her lead when we got out of the car. Taken her up to the room immediately, gotten her out of her clothes and my hands all over her instead of making a stupid detour for a drink under the stars. I had to fuck it up, trying to be romantic.

Those drunk women, what absolutely perfect fucking timing. I looked for a place to stay outside of Mobile, separate from the band, away from the attention the whole lot of us together would attract. I wanted to get her away from her house and the ghost there, show her a good time and maybe change how she sees me. But no, she has to find me surrounded by the goddamned junior league.

I have the sensation of being carried by an enormous wave, this day lifting me to a high where I caught a brief, euphoric view of the promised land, and now the wave is reversing course, grabbing me by the shoulders and pulling me back to where I started.

This day has been more than a day - the rules of time were changed, hours stretched and lengthened into much more than one ordinary day. This kind of day needs a new name.

When I came out of the shower this morning and she hadn't waited in bed for me, had gone out to the balcony, I again thought for sure this might already be over. That the exquisite fuck we had in the middle of the night was a goodbye. She got what she wanted, what she had been completely clear and up front about, and now she was done.

She didn't want to hurt me, that's what she said to me in the dark, but it was already too late for that.

Then she surprised me. Man, can this woman surprise me.

She started talking, cleaving her heart wide open to dissect her pain, with me as her witness. It knocked me back. When I took her in my arms, I prayed she couldn't feel me shaking. I wanted to comfort her, offer something beyond limp platitudes; I wanted to hold her tightly enough so that her pain poured through her skin into mine. She hadn't pushed me away or retreated; she had welcomed me to take a step closer, and hope sank a cleat into my heart. The delicious, painful hope of possibility.

There is possibility here. Maybe she could be mine.

As she talked, I looked across the marina in front of us and began to see the shape of my life in a way I've never considered before. A clear shape, a wide but shallow basin, extending as far as the horizon, in all directions, with a depth measured in feet, not fathoms. So much more experience, in terms of variety and distance, compared to hers, which I could see from her words was a singular, very deep well. I had set out in my life to go far, to see as much as I could see. She had picked a spot and gone deep.

I nearly became invisible to myself, a man made up of almost transparent, pulled apart filaments, so threadbare as to no longer support a purpose. Holly had drilled down so far, she plumbed depths that crush and drown a lot of people. Depths that nearly did crush her.

My mind went to that night I saw her all those years ago, sitting on another man's lap. Her love so palpable it damn well nearly had a color, wrapping them both in a glowing aura as lustrous as her eyes. I saw it and immediately wanted it, wanted her, but also knew it wasn't for me. Not then. I wasn't ready to dive deep. I wanted only to fly.

I believe I've been missing this woman, my heart in storage, for twenty years. We'd followed paths over wildly different terrains, taken different roads, to end up in the same place, literally crashing into one another, lost and lonely.

After our conversation, I felt high the rest of the day, and more fucking horny than I should ever be asked to handle. I was jittery to have her, couldn't think about much else. My cells were giggling like stoners, all systems set to pleasure. I thought I was getting a headache then realized it was just my face hurting because I'd been smiling all day. I was bathing in her closeness and pawing to get back into her pants.

There was the lunch with Gretchen. My few boundaries, shamelessly pussy-chasing sister told me to calm down over this woman, but then was practically drooling over her too, as I knew she would. Holly appeared to impress her, which has been nearly impossible for anyone I've ever dated in my whole life. Probably because she didn't try to impress her. Didn't wither under all that Gretchen-ness. Instead, they're breezing into the green room arm in arm like some leather gang, Holly looking so gorgeous I wanted to stand up on a chair to shout to everyone in the room that she's mine.

Her tits in that outfit, knowing full well she was making me feral. *Fucking hell.* I felt high and horny and energized. And *happy.* So fucking happy to have her there, watching me play, showing off for her. To have her on my arm, introducing her to the band. Happy to hear her insights and observations about the music. Rock hard fucking happy on the drive back here when she let me know again that she wanted me.

She fits in my world. She literally rolled up my sleeves like she'd been sending me off to work for years, eased right into a space beside me that seemed custom measured for her. Maybe I've been unconsciously marking time until we crossed paths again because there's this easy familiarity there, like she's made for me.

I don't know yet how to share this with her, how it could coexist with her grief or how to reconcile my feelings against the real love she still has for another man, will probably always have. I don't want his place. I want mine.

Yeah.

I had this extended day of deep, deep happiness and possibility. The possibility of partnership and contentment, a day where I've felt erotically charged, my skin like static electricity, snapping at any brush of contact with her. And she's been right in it with me, her desire matching my own. It makes me howl for the chase. Set a syringe of testosterone into my ass, this one has.

That's how I'm feeling. I'm savoring the best damn day I've had in years, stretching it out for as long as I can, until my dick can't take it anymore.

I'm going to fuck this woman until we're both demolished. I'm going to keep fucking her, pleasing her, talking to her, finding ways to impress her until every last one of her doubts and worries are gone and she can see the possibility right in front of us. Until my heart is one she can trust.

That's the wave I'm riding until these stupid, drunk fucking women, my ghosts of a past life, showed up.

Just perfect.

CHAPTER THIRTY

ADAM

HOLLY WALKS to the nightstand and begins to silently remove her jewelry. I hear each piece drop one by one and wish I had my stage jewelry because it would be funny if I could cross to my nightstand and let my pieces drop to my table, having a stare-off across the bed.

Could be a stare-off in a good way or a bad way. The I want nothing more to do with you, I'm now going to shoot you way, or I'm now going to tear all your clothes off with my teeth way.

Warily, I sit in one of the chairs to take off my boots. "I need a shower. Do you want the bathroom first, before I go in?" I look up to her for an answer and she's taking off an earring, hands lifted under her hair, head cocked to one shoulder.

"Did you notice how big that shower is?" Her voice is casual. I blink at her. "Sooo big, don't you think?"

My dick gets this before my brain does.

She lowers her arm, hand hovering over the nightstand, waiting a beat before she opens her fingers and lets the earring drop. She has my full attention.

"What a thoughtful way to conserve water," she says, bending to tug off her boots, eyes fixed on mine, using them for balance.

There she is.

"You feeling dirty, sweetheart?" I stand, unbuttoning my shirt and tossing it behind me.

She nods, lips pouty, pulling off her jacket, her breasts nearly lifting out the top of her corset as she does. "Been hot all day."

I close the space between us, close enough to see her take a sharp, short sip of air, her pupils expanding inside the warm blue sea of her eyes. Reaching for the back of her top, finding laces then a zipper, I rain kisses along the curve of her neck as my hands go to work. "I've wanted to rip this off you all night."

"Oh my god, thank you so much," she groans when I finally ease it up and over her head, rubbing at the red marks in her skin.

I lift her breasts, letting my face fall into them. "How did you get into that thing by yourself?"

"I called one of the desk guys to come up here to help me," she teases, voice ragged. She's unbuckling my belt and I'm fumbling with her skirt. Not fast enough, apparently, because she huffs and stands back from me, taking it off herself. She lets it drop to the floor, kicking it aside as I peel down my jeans and briefs.

She pulls off her tights and I grab for her panties, slipping my hands into the waistband and sliding them down her legs. She does a cute shimmy with her hips to help. I run my palm flat up over her mound, over her belly and chest, all the way up her silky skin until my fingers wrap around her throat, holding her in front of me. She shivers, eyes wide.

"I guess I owe someone a big tip then, don't I?" I bend my knees and shove my shoulder under her hip, straightening with a grunt, Holly thrown over my shoulder. She squeals and I slap her ass.

"What are you doing?" she cries as I grunt again, carrying her towards the bathroom.

"Caveman," I huff, giving her another smack. "Caveman tear up pussy."

"You're gonna hurt yourself caveman," she laughs, right as I stagger into the bathroom, banging her head on the doorframe. "Ow!"

"Of fuck, sorry baby. You alright?" I slide her down my body until her feet are on the floor. She nods, rubbing the side of her head. "Thank god that wasn't any farther," I hiss, hands to the small of my back.

"Okay, okay," she rolls her eyes, making to walk past me out of the bathroom.

"Ohhh nooo you don't," I say, hooking her waist and bringing her back to me, laughing. "Cavewoman light as feather." Her head cradled in the crook of my arm, she raises an eyebrow skeptically. "Light as *half* a feather, extra small feather. From smallest bird on planet. Caveman clumsy. Cavewoman perfect."

This earns me a goofy smile and a kiss, and my insides turn molten and gooey, but my dick is getting harder and harder. She makes me feel this way. A fucking feral fucking infatuated fool. After another deep kiss I step to the walk-in shower to turn on the water. As I do, she stands at the sink and begins to root around in her makeup bag on the counter.

Holding my hand under the spray to check the temperature, I watch as she pulls her curly blonde hair to the top of her head, appreciating the view of her ample backside. My dick does a little hop, shouting *fuck the shower, bend her over right there.*

Her eyes find mine in the mirror and she grins seductively and wiggles her ass. I'm behind her in one second, hands at her hips, my mouth at her neck, and she leans back, grinding herself into me.

"Fucking hell," I groan, my cock sliding between us, following the curve of her crack. She falls forward, hands on the counter, and I take myself in hand, rubbing my tip back and forth against her.

"Ahhh...how's the water?" she breathes, and some idea to make this last reaches its way into my caveman brain. Biting back a hungry *who cares about the fucking water* protest, I reluctantly let her go and step back to the shower, reaching in again with my hand.

"Just right."

"Okay, one second," she says, traipsing out of the bathroom.

"Where are you going?" My dick and I call after her.

"One second!" she trills, and I grab two wash cloths and step into the glass stall. The music reaches me before she does, the hand clapping and electric guitar instantly recognizable.

""Car Wash!"" She's boogieing up to the shower, phone in hand. "Get in here girl," I say, clapping with the song.

"It's five minutes eight seconds, can we do it?" She sets her phone on the counter and steps in, clapping with me. "It's for the environment."

"Let's go," I pass a washcloth to her, but she waves me off.

"No way," she wags her hands in front of me, dancing to the beat. "I'm gonna get in *everywhere*."

"Do it, baby."

There's a pump dispenser of shower gel on the wall and we fill our hands over and over for five minutes of making out, laughing, slipping and sliding around on each other. She pulls soapy hands up and down my dick and double teams my balls, giggling as she lifts them left, right, left, right, in time to the music. I spank her ass to the beat, thump the base line with my fingers onto her slit. She twerks against my cock as I wash my hair and dances with her arms in the air while I'm lathering her tits, a memory I'll be jerking off to forever.

Hands on my chest, she says, "We've got a situation here with you, don't we?"

"What?" I laugh.

"So hot, it's criminal." I reach to kiss her, and she pushes against me. "Turn around," she orders, spinning me to face the wall. "Hands up, spread those legs." She nudges my feet apart with her foot and I do as she says, letting my head drop as she works her hands in circles across my shoulders and down my back. "This is the fantasy I didn't know I needed."

I love, just love, letting her have her way with me like this.

She slaps my ass. "Look at you, cupcake. Fucking illegal."

I twist to look over my shoulder at her. "Cupcake?"

"Sweet and lickable." She's humming the song, working with the rhythm, soaping me up and down. I jump a little when she spreads my ass cheeks, fitting one slick hand up and down that channel. I jump again when her finger massages my butthole.

"Easy there, baby."

"Just doing my job, sir," she pushes me back to the wall. "Gotta make sure you don't have anything dangerous. You packing anything I should know about? Anything *big* to report?" Pressing herself close, I feel her hardened nipples against my back, sliding across me, slick and wet.

Christ almighty.

One soapy hand caressing my ass, she reaches around me with the other for my dick. "Answer the question," she nips at my shoulder and strokes my cock.

Clamping my fingers around her wrist, I spin her around so her back is against the wall, pinning her with my body. She shrieks, her eyes alight, lifting her mouth for a kiss.

"Let's get out of here," I say gruffly. I turn off the water just as the song ends.

"Look at us," she says, "We did it."

The room steamy and quiet after our disco shower, I wrap a towel around her, another one around my waist. Without saying anything, we both have the same instinct and step to the sink and grab our toothbrushes, watching each other brush in the foggy mirror, our hips touching. I sway us side to side a few times, and her eyes scan my body, unabashedly lingering at the tuck of my towel. She's beautiful, water droplets sparkling in her hair, creamy skin flushed from the heat of the shower.

She blots her mouth primly with a towel and passes it to me, as if this is our nightly routine. I mimic her dainty style, touching my lips three times just so, and she laughs.

Taking the hotel lotion from the counter, she shakes some into her hands, rubbing them together to warm it up. Silently working lotion into my arms and chest, her hands never leave my body as she moves around me, her touch soothing my muscles. She guides me to prop my feet, one at a time, on the edge of the bathtub, reaching under my towel to massage lotion into my thighs then all the way down my legs.

It feels so fucking good. Nurturing and sweet. I can't recall the last time a woman has tended to me like this.

When it's my turn, she drops her towel to the floor, a hand to her pursed lips in a cute "whoops" pantomime.

I feel her eyes on me as I go to work, intending to show her the same care as she did for me. I don't return her gaze, but find myself breathing in when she breathes in, out when she breathes out, my full attention on her skin under my hands, intently mapping all the details of her body. The soft curves, the scar on her knee, the birthmark on her side; two freckles on her right breast that I've not noticed until now, just above the nipple.

I kiss her there, softly, once, twice. *Mine. Mine.*

"You're gonna need more than that, it's a lot of real estate," she jokes as I rub more lotion between my hands, the first words either of us have uttered for several minutes. I pull her close into my chest, wrapping my arms around her, looking down over her back to plant my palms on her delicious real estate.

"Bodacious," I croon into her ear.

"Oh, that's a good word Mr. Sexton, I like it."

I keep rubbing, spinning us a half turn to walk us to the bathroom door. "Juicy, mouth-watering, bountiful. Bodacious."

"Good gracious." She's breathless, hanging onto my shoulders. Her tits jiggling against my chest are driving me mad. She grabs for my towel and tugs it free, and I'm done.

"We need to fuck. Right now," I growl, pulling her through the room to the bed, intending to tumble with her greased-up ass into the sheets, but she slips from my grasp.

"Sit down," she directs, leaning forward to rest her hands on the comforter. "And sit back, cupcake."

I do not need to be told twice. She did say lickable.

Reclining onto the bed, pillows behind my shoulders, I prop one arm behind my head to watch this show. I know I'm grinning like a fool, but damn, this day.

She brings one knee up between my feet and I widen my legs, running my free hand down my chest and stomach until I'm holding my dick. I stroke myself while she watches, my skin as tight as it can be, aching for relief. Anticipation animates my body - blood and bone, flesh and feelings - everything I am, everything she is, every single object in this room, until it's all one force, all flowing to one place, one concentrated beam of attention locked onto one central target.

My aching, rock hard cock.

What? What did you think it would be?

"You want this baby?"

Her answer is to crawl catlike between my legs, the swell of her ass in the air, tracing the inside of my calf with her tongue. Pushing my knees further apart, she licks up the length of my inner thigh until her nose is fitted right into the notch of my groin, pressing her lips into my skin. She draws herself away, staying low to drag her breasts teasingly along my leg, licking all the way back up my thigh again.

"That's a sweet girl," I murmur.

In no rush, she repeats this slow tease a few times, lavishing me with attention, licking and kissing, all the while her hands roaming up and down my legs, my hips, across my stomach. She's making me wait for it.

On one of her glides up my legs, when her face is snug into the crook of my inner thigh, she gives me a little nip and I twitch involuntarily. Her eyes flash to mine, a sly grin on her face.

"Not too sweet," she says, then sucks my balls fully into her mouth. I let out a long sigh, an exhale of breath that is pure bliss. She lets them fall wetly from her mouth then pulls them in again, rolling them against her tongue.

I've got both hands folded behind my head now, my knees open, Holly fitted between them. "Mmmm, that's so good baby," I murmur, encouraging her. "So good."

She finally touches my dick, wrapping her fingers around the base as she licks my balls, nudging them with her nose, drawing them in and out of her mouth. Tongue flat on the underside of my shaft, she licks all the way up, rubbing the head back and forth against her tongue before drawing the tip into her mouth. Her eyes stay on mine, and she does this again, slowly attending my length, following the vein and teasing my tip.

"You have a beautiful penis," she pronounces, her fingers, at last, moving to stroke me.

"I'm glad you like it."

She licks the underside again, then sucks in the head, a line of spit connecting it to her lips as she releases it. "I'd appraise it as…" studying my dick in her hand, she pulls her saliva up and down my shaft. "As…. late twentieth century…"

I lift an eyebrow at that.

"In excellent condition… generous proportions," she continues, voice dripping with agreeable flattery. I nod a thank you and she sucks the tip in and out of her mouth with a wet slurp, then interlocks her fingers around me, gliding them up and down.

"Aesthetically pleasing," I chuckle, lifting my hips to fuck this triangle she's made with her hands.

"Highly desirable," she coos, tightening her grip around me.

At this point, I'll confess, the degenerate reptile living in an exiled, depraved corner of my brain decides to make an appearance.

All this licking and talking, which is fucking fantastic, is because she really doesn't enjoy this. This is her hot work around instead of giving you a real blow job. A hand job plus.

No way, you saw what she did with my balls, I argue with the reptile. *Maybe it's so big it scares her.*

Of course. Absolutely. But man, just flip her over and fuck he, the reptile hisses.

I groan, closing my eyes, not wanting this voice in my head. I don't give a fuck, I'll let her take this wherever she wants. I focus on the friction, on the warm slickness of her hands. But then her hands stop, and I open my eyes, looking down my torso to the sight of her rising over me to swipe her tits across my dick, thrusting it up and down between them. *Now we're talkin'.*

"Do you like this?" she breathes, rubbing my cock against her taught nipples, watching my face.

"Fuck yes," I answer, reaching to fondle her breast. "Very much." She shifts herself into my hand, then sways side to side again, dragging herself across me.

Retreating down my body, letting my dick slide between us until her mouth captures the tip again, she fits her hips back between my thighs, swirling the head with her tongue.

"Mmmm," she purrs, "Or do you want this?" She takes me fully in one long plunge down my shaft and back, her eyes never leaving mine.

Thank fuck, that reptile in my head whispers. *Sweet and dirty.*

I inhale a few deep breaths to control myself, to not thrust into her, ramming my cock straight to the back of her throat. She takes me again, agonizingly slowly, sucking when she's back at the head, and I groan.

"Is that what you want, Adam?" Her voice has caressed my spine, digging a fist into the small of my back.

"Fuck yes, fuck me with that beautiful mouth, angel."

And she does. She opens her lips around me and gives me everything, like she was sucking my spinal cord out of my body.

I'll never say this to her; I've gotten a lot of blow jobs. A lot. We all know it, no one needs to talk about it. But my girl Holly here's got the mouth of a dirty little slut. Sloppily wet and firm, confident handling, impeccable tempo, enthusiasm, attention to the balls, not afraid of the taint - she has it all. I'm stunned. Her mouth is heaven. I'm stunned and tripping into another dimension, sighing and moaning and humming.

Where did she learn to do this?

Jesus, fuuuuck, I'm humming, maybe having a dopamine aneurism when she's taking me deep, her throat tightening around my crown, looking up my body into my eyes. She's ruining me.

I'm building up to shoot a load into another time zone, closing my eyes as I get right to the edge, when she stops to say my name, then takes me into her mouth again.

"Fuuucccckkkk... I'm there," I groan. "Suck that dick, baby."

She says my name again and I realize this must be her signal.

"Okay," I breathe, reaching down to pull out of her, but the second I open my eyes I see hers, waiting for my attention. She pushes me back with one hand before slowly, deliberately, scraping her teeth down then back up my shaft.

"Easy," I inhale sharply, grasping at the sheets with my fists. It's a complete knife's edge sensation. Thrilling, almost painful, erotic. The weeping head of my cock still in her teeth, she gives my tip a generous circle with her tongue before releasing me.

"Adam?"

"Yeah?" The word is almost a cough, my breathing ragged.

Eyes on mine, she strokes me firmly with one hand. "If I wasn't with you, would you have slept with that woman?"

"What?" I shake my head in the pillow. *Why are we talking about this? Why am I not coming in her mouth right now?*

But then it's her teeth down my length again, carefully calibrated, and I catch the glint in her eye, a flash like fire reflecting off a blade.

"If I wasn't here, would you have brought her up to your room?" She's gone still, a focused predator internal kind of still, holding my dick right below her hovering lips. Her breath on my exquisitely sensitive skin is like air on a burn.

This woman giving me some of the best head of my life, I should be buying her jewelry or a new car level head, the woman who asked me, *she* asked *me*, for this just sex thing and has made it clear - abundantly fucking clear - that she wants nothing more than that, so there's no reason on this whole goddamned earth why I can't fuck anyone I damn well want to, well, this woman, she would also bite my dick off.

God, she's special.

And she likes me. It turns me on so much my head might

explode, shit my balls are about to explode, and I really fucking *need to come.*

I rise up onto my elbows. "No. Not a chance."

She stares at me, scrutinizing my expression, until I see her accept what I'm saying. She dips her head, lips soft and wet, and I drop onto my back in relief, getting right back to it. So warm, so perfect.

Holly likes me.

She lets my dick slip out of her mouth and I'm back on my elbows again, eyes on hers again, willing my face to not show one hint of impatience. "Yeah, baby?"

"Would you have gone to her room?"

Fuck. She got me there.

I wait a beat, making a decision. It's too soon to say it, especially like this, and I know she's not ready to hear it. But I'm not playing games. Plus, there's the biting my dick off thing.

"Ten, fifteen years ago, I don't know, maybe. But no, I would not. Would *never*. Holly, I only care now if you want me. Because I only want you."

Time stops, our breathing stops, and I wait, praying for mercy. My words hang between us, I watch them walk through her eyes, her hand gripped tightly around my cock. She's totally surprised but I'm not taking it back. I meant every word.

The slightest of smiles ripples across her mouth and I'm bathed in heat. Something inside my chest blooms and burns, but I don't have time to think about it because she nods in her cheeky way, like *good to know, thanks*, and wraps her lips down over me and I'm curling my shoulders forward, taking her head in my hands, gasping and grunting myself in streams down her throat. She takes all of me.

Then it's my turn, destroying her, an hour or five, I don't know – like I said, time is working differently today. I've held her and kissed her, stroked and licked and bit and sucked her, my face interning in her pussy until she's detonating, squeezing my head between her thighs, moaning my name over and over.

Then I fucked her.

At some late hour, voices out in the hallway wake me and I get up to check the lock on the door. We had fallen asleep, exhausted, entangled, but I have to chuckle now. She's taken two small pillows from the sofa in the other room and created a barrier between us, sound asleep on her protected side of the bed, one foot peeking out from underneath the covers.

Even later, I hear her in the bathroom. Crying.

I want to go to her, tell her it's okay. Whatever helps her get through the pain, she doesn't have to hide it from me. But I don't believe that's what she'd want.

When she comes back to bed, she scoots all the way over to me, tugging the territory pillows out of the way and fitting herself to my back, her arm circling my waist. I don't bother to pretend I'm asleep. I scooch my hips back, fitting myself snugly in her lap, and take her hand, lacing my fingers through hers. We sleep this way until sunrise.

CHAPTER THIRTY-ONE

HOLLY

THE FIRST YEAR after Ronnie died, I jumped awake at every noise. Squirrel scampering across the roof, wind shaking tree branches against a window, the thrum and crack of the ice machine in the freezer. No longer needing to hold myself to the lightest top layers of sleep, listening for him to call for me, my psyche didn't so easily let that vigilance go, let me sink into the cool, darkened rooms of deep rest.

My psyche had its teeth clamped tightly onto this high-alert habit; it just shifted what I was listening for, shaking me awake night after night, heart racing, ears straining, convinced that someone was breaking in, that Luke and I were in danger. I'd walk to his door and check on him; I'd prowl the house, phone in hand, 9-1 already punched into the number pad. I'd sit at my dining table in the dark, waiting to see a shadow at the back door, wondering if I should get a gun.

It's remarkable, the work your brain will do, to stall and misdirect. Over here, over here, it shouts, waving hands at the imaginary burglars creeping into your house. Don't look at the empty side of the bed, don't replay Ronnie's last days in your head, don't think about your son's broken heart, his trauma, your trauma, don't sit in the kitchen with the bills and panic, failure about to suffocate you. That's not what you should be worried about, because did you hear that? That sound? That's what you really should be worried about. Get up! Right now! Get up, go see who's trying to get into your house.

I was exhausted in every way imaginable, the vulnerability of the situation all too real. It makes sense my mind would extrapolate those emotions into a terror that every part of our lives was in jeopardy. Of course there were murderers on the roof, danger at the door.

It took longer than I would've ever expected for this hypervigilance to subside but, over time, I inched my way back to some version of security and peace.

I downloaded a sleep app on my phone that played soothing rainstorm sounds and filled Ronnie's side of the bed with books and extra pillows. Occasionally I resorted to drugs.

I'd hear the noises, heart hammering, and I'd coach myself night after night. It's not real, it's not real, it's not real. You're safe. Luke is safe. You can sleep. You can figure this new life out.

So, it's ironic that Adam literally came into my life as a stranger creeping through my backyard, scaring the bejesus out of me. And he lectures me about gate locks and security lights, about locking my doors. Life sometimes does have a sense of humor.

After we screwed ourselves into satiated oblivion, I was too exhausted, my bones turned liquid, to lift my head from his chest. We fell asleep entwined together, I think he might have still been inside me. I woke sometime later and peeled myself from him limb by sticky limb, going to pee then making a pillow barrier down the middle of the bed, diving into deep sleep in the separate space I created.

When I wake again, terrified, thrashing at the sheets, I wouldn't call it ironic, but it's certainly not coincidental, that I'm with Adam. There are no scary noises or imagined threats. It's because of a dream.

Having lunch with friends, I saw someone who looked just like Ronnie. Same silver hair, same beard. In shock, I stood up at my chair, craning my neck. It couldn't be him. Then the tilt of all the heads across the restaurant aligned just so and our eyes met; it was him, and he ducked down to hide. My friends formed a wall with their bodies, blocking my view, helping him stay out of sight. They tried to hold me back, I had to shake them off, and I watched him making for a back door.

Ronnie was alive and everyone knew it, and now he was running away from me.

People got up from their tables, impeding my path, working to keep me from catching up with him. I pushed my way through, frantically calling his name. When I got to the door and stepped outside, he was down the sidewalk, turning the corner around the building. I called his name again, chasing him, getting to the corner only to see him already across the street. I screamed, running towards him. He looked my way just as a car struck me, the sound of tires screeching in my ears as I jolt awake, crying, gasping for air.

I went into the bathroom to keep from waking Adam. I rarely dream about Ronnie, ever, but of course my pathetic, guilty subconscious is poking me. I have this getaway with Adam, I confide in him about Ronnie and the journal, that whole tangled mess, and he's affectionate and sweet. I allow myself to enjoy him and my brain says, but wait, you're not supposed to enjoy this *too* much.

I only care now if you want me. Because I only want you.

That's what he said. It was in the middle of a blow job, he'd probably say anything, but it's the way he said it. The way he looks at me, touches me. He's drawing me in, I can't deny it.

I'm half crying, half laughing, trying to stay quiet so Adam can't hear me. This is a joke. Am I really this screwed up in the head? Ronnie's been gone five years, and I haven't worked this out already? It's like I'm back sitting in the dark, waiting for imaginary dangers.

I look at myself in the mirror. *What are you going to do?*

This gorgeous man crashes into your life and flirts with you, pursues you, for some unfathomable reason seems to like you, and you nearly kill him. You rebuff him, insult him, then you ask him to have sex with you. And he says yes. He makes all the plans, he takes time to get to know you, and fucks like a legend. While you spin sad weepy tales about your dead husband. Isn't he lucky?

Are you going to cry in the bathroom, or are you going to deal with your shit?

Grabbing tissues, I blow my nose, splash water on my face, and give myself another long look in the mirror.

Ronnie, sweetheart, you don't get to have an opinion here. I love you, even when I'm so mad I want to punch you, but we have to find a better way to do this next part. I don't know how, but I can't figure it out if you won't let me. If I won't let me. Get out of my head, darling. I have to do this next bit by myself.

I turn out the light before I open the bathroom door, finding my way in the dark to the bed. I know what I want, what I need right now.

Adam.

The comfort, the warm solid space that is Adam. I toss aside my stupid pillow barrier and he's there for me, waiting, taking my hand in his, bringing it to his heart.

CHAPTER THIRTY-TWO

HOLLY

Very early, Adam slips out of bed, and I pull his warm pillow into my chest. He moves quietly about the room then I hear the click of the door as he leaves. How did I manage to find an early rising rock star?

Columns of light from the curtains over the balcony doors cut across the bed, aiming straight for my eyes. Grumbling, I toss the blankets aside and go to my suitcase, pulling my silk sleep mask from the inside pocket. A text chimes on my phone.

ADAM

Gym. Won't be long. Wait in bed for me

"No problemo," I mutter, crawling back into bed and pulling the soft mask over my eyes, sighing contentedly into the darkness. I fall asleep immediately.

I don't know how long he's been gone, and I don't hear him come back into the room. I don't hear anything until he's wrapping himself around me in bed, his body warm and damp from the shower. I roll in his arms, pressing my face into his neck, inhaling dreamily. When was inhaling, the sound of breathing, ever so arousing?

"So warm," he whispers.

"Who is this?" I murmur, touching his face, feeling my way across his features, voice husky with sleep. His abs contract against my stomach with his chuckle and I hitch my thigh over his hip, fitting myself to him, my sex already yearning. "My boyfriend will be back any minute."

I lean away to pull the sleep mask off, but he stops me.

"Leave it," he says gruffly, lifting my hand above my head, holding it there against the pillow as his mouth finds mine. His kiss is slow and soft, his fingers threading through mine. "Mmm, boyfriend, is it?"

His lips are perfect, his taste familiar to me now. *I know his taste.* It's flooding my mouth, bitter and sweet all at once, like metal and whiskey, coffee and cream.

"I don't know," I whisper against his lips.

"Why don't you know?" He rolls himself on top of me, his weight pressing my hips open. He finds my other hand, sliding it up, so that both are now above my head, his body stretched heavily, possessively along mine. The rasp of the sheets as we move is sharp, the bed gasping and sighing with us.

"I don't know," I say again, my chest rising against his, my thighs squeezing his hips.

"This boyfriend, he left you all alone in his bed?" He lifts just enough for his cock to slip down between my legs. "Beautiful warm pussy all alone." I shift, trapped by his weight, pressing my heels into the bed. He's *right there* and I want it. He flexes and aligns deliciously with the cleft of my sex. "Left you here like this, needing to be fucked."

"He's so bad." His dick is inches from where I need it, where I'm already hot and throbbing. I arch into him, but he pins my hips in place with his.

"You need it?" The low timbre of his voice is sending very enjoyable vibrations down my neck and across my shoulders. He does this amazing roll of his hips, his hands driving mine into the bed.

"Yes... that... yes."

He rolls and grinds, plundering my mouth until I can't breathe. "Tell me."

"I need a big hard cock; know anyone who has one?" I try and pull my hands free, but he changes his grip, making a small clucking sound, a *no you don't tsk tsk tsk* of disapproval.

"You'll get what I give you."

"Is that right? 'Cause I want big and—"

I'm rewarded with a bite on my shoulder, his mouth lingering against my skin. When I protest with a squeal, squirming beneath him, he nips me again on my neck.

"Hush now," he drawls, trailing kisses along my jaw. "I'll give you what you need." The masculine gravel in his voice, his weight and hands pinning me... I'm turned on to the point of combustion. Without sight, I'm acutely aware of his skin, his body hair, every place we touch.

Levering himself over onto one elbow by my side, he lets go of my wrists, the air suddenly cool without him on top of me.

"Keep those arms over your head, open your legs for me." His tone is gruff and obviously hypnotic because I do as I'm told, letting my knees fall open. It's exquisite anticipation, wondering where he'll touch me next, his breath a feather that tickles before it reaches my skin.

He starts at the base of my throat, one finger in the divot there, and my heart rate accelerates from this single touch, my pulse calling to him. I swallow involuntarily, licking my lips. My nipples, already erect, tighten almost painfully imagining his gaze, his mouth. I shiver, my body fully surrendered to him, exposed and waiting.

His hand, warm and firm, explores slowly down my torso. Picturing the full roll of my stomach there, the rippled stretch marks, I want to stop, turn away and cover myself before he sees something he can't unsee, before he can study me this closely.

"No," I protest, and try to scooch away.

"Shhhh..." he whispers, pressing my hips down, tucking me back to his side. He rubs his hand back and forth across the scarred apron of my lower belly, caressing the place on my body I hate the most. Tears sting my eyes under the mask and I'm glad he can't see them. Despite all we've done together so far, this is more intimate than maybe I can bear.

"You don't have to—"

"Shhhh... stop, let me enjoy this," he says, bringing his fingers to my lips, skimming along the top lip, then the bottom, learning every ridge before leaning down to kiss me.

He kisses me for a long, unhurried time, until my senses have been scrambled in a shell game, all the pieces of my mind that might recognize up and down or left and right shuffled one over the other until I am only sensation. No thinking, only feeling.

Then, well... then he paints me with his touch. Languidly, adoringly, softly, slowly, tracing the curve of my shoulders and stomach and breasts. My thighs and hips, under my arms and down my sides. Long, gentle strokes, my skin so sensitive I can feel the guitar calluses on his fingertips. I'm untethered, floating beneath him, the reverence in his touch something I don't know if I've ever experienced.

When he finally takes one of my breasts in hand, cupping it so his thumb circles the nipple, his energy changes. It's the way he handles me, less devotional, more demanding. He works one breast, then the other, palming them firmly, tracing and tweaking until I'm sighing, arching my back, begging for more. When he gives his mouth to my nipple, I'm unprepared but oh so ready and suck in air sharply, crying out in pleasure.

I lift my knees, rubbing my legs together, and he pushes them apart, stroking the inside of my thigh. Reflexively I close them again, clutching his hand onto me.

"I said open." He nips at the skin just under my breast, his fingers sliding down my slit, and I let my legs fall. His command is lightening down my spine. He works his fingers through my folds and the wet, slick sounds of my need seem amplified, exaggerated, as he spreads me apart, mapping every centimeter of my pussy.

"Fuuuck, baby, the way you feel..." That lightening, it's now blazing white hot in my sex. He slips two fingers inside me and I pulse around them. "So greedy, this pussy. You haven't had enough, have you?"

"No," I whine shamelessly, bringing one of my arms down around him, cramming my face into his shoulder, begging him to thrash me. He pumps his fingers in and out, not so gently now, and I grunt, lifting my hips into his hand, claiming his fingers as far as they'll go. "More," I beg. "Harder, please... just... *more.*"

He lets me have it, a steady, relentless pace, his mouth crushing mine, until I gasp when he drags all the slick juices from my arousal to my clit, his fingers winding in wet, slurpy circles.

"Holy fuck, yes," I dig my nails into his shoulder. "Yes, just like that, that's perfect." And thank you Jesus for this man's rhythm, because I'm quickly close to climaxing. I squeeze my eyes shut tightly under my mask, seeing stars behind my eyelids. "Almost there," I pant.

With an "unh-uh," he rolls on top of me, entering me in one long thrust, not holding back a single inch of his cock. My head rocks back into the pillow as he buries himself.

"You fit so well," I moan. Already in third gear, he slips his hands down my sides until he's got full handfuls of my ass, lifting me into him with each sledgehammer thrust.

"Made for me," he growls into my neck.

Do I start crying with each stroke? Am I screaming? Because he is fucking me so relentlessly, I don't know if that's my voice or if it's in my head. Every thrust scrapes my clit until I'm clawing at him, wound so tightly I'm three deep breathes away from coming. With the first tremor he pulls himself out, dropping back down on one elbow at my side.

"What?" I cry, trying to keep him in place. His fingers are right back inside me though, plunging deep.

"You wanna come, baby?"

"Yes," I plead. He's back to my clit. It's practically sparking.

"Say it," he bites down a little too hard on my nipple, and I jerk with a yelp. He sucks it into his mouth, the wetness soothing the sting. I launch myself into his body, my hand hooked around his neck, feverishly pulling his hair.

"I want to come, please help me come."

Then he's on top of me, driving inside me, and I'm falling apart, my brain a power outage. He fits one hand between us, finding my swollen nub as he thrusts. "My name. I want to hear my name when you come on my cock."

"Adam," I cry out, "Oh God, yes, Adam that's perfect, please, just like that."

My hips jerk, my back curling in on itself in spasm after spasm. It's a surf pounding into the shore over and over, his name on my lips I don't know how many times until it's drowned out by his kisses then the groans and curses of his own launch over the edge.

CHAPTER THIRTY-THREE

HOLLY

I FELL BACK TO EARTH, back to sleep, with Adam on top of me, stretched out between my legs, head on my chest, my arms around his shoulders. His muffled, scratchy voice wakes me.

"Holly, sweetheart, we have to get up."

Ignore this, my brain says. *It'll go away.*

"Wake up baby." He speaks again, shifting his weight.

"Five more minutes," I protest, but he rolls us onto our sides and lifts my mask onto my forehead. He sweetly strokes my cheek and gives me a gentle kiss while I squint at him.

"Sorry, sound check at four, we need to be on the road."

"You should've thought of that before you did this to me," I yawn, stretching in his arms.

"If we don't get out of this bed, I'm gonna do it to you again." That lazy drawl, so low and sexy, along with his kisses down my neck, gives me full body shivers.

"Then yes," I pull my mask back down over my eyes. "I like that much better, please." When his mouth is on mine, drinking deeply, his hand stroking my back, I think I'm getting my wish. I try to pull him on top of me, but he gives my hip a squeeze then a light slap.

"Nope, get up," he laughs, letting me go and climbing out of bed. I fall back into the pillows, wanting to stay in this lovely Adam cocoon for as long as possible. It will be over soon enough, as it is.

Next thing I hear is a distinct, aggressively loud, stream of urine.

"Adam, you are not peeing with the door open!"

"Well, look at that, I believe I am sweetheart," his voice floats through the room.

Kicking free of the covers, I scramble out of bed. I get to the bathroom just in time to see him, dick in hand, feet spread apart, shaking the last few drops into the toilet.

"No, just...no," I huff, closing the door. I've pulled on panties and my black leggings when he comes back into the room, genuinely bemused.

"You'll put it in your mouth, you'll *swallow...*" I make a *don't be crude* face at him, rooting in my suitcase for a bra. "But peeing is too much for you?"

"Exactly, yes. It's not the same thing."

"Well, I don't care if you pee in front of me."

"I care!" Standing in front of his own suitcase, he's pulling on black boxer briefs. "There have to be some boundaries."

He slides his jeans up his hips, adjusting himself, a tug at his crotch then zipping up, the whole time closely watching me put on my bra. He's quite pleased with himself, and it would be extremely annoying if he wasn't so damn fuckable.

"Okay, okay noted. I'm sorry, I won't do it again," he says.

I walk to him, wrapping my arms around his waist. "Thank you."

"You can take a quick shower if you want."

"Is that your way of telling me I smell?" I sniff one of my armpits. It is a little ripe. "There's definitely a well-fucked sex stink about me."

He huffs, and I sniff myself again, then start sniffing him, my nose pressing into his armpit. "Mmm, you too." I touch my nose to his chest – *sniff* - up along his collar bone – *sniff* -stopping for a big inhale at his neck. "I smell myself all over you. It's gonna turn me on all day."

"Will it now?"

"Yes. Don't you like knowing I'm wearing you on my skin?" I murmur, kissing his jaw, rubbing the lace of my bra into his chest. My boobs are this man's undoing. That much I've figured out. "All that sweet cum, the scent of you in my pussy all day."

"Christ," he hisses, pushing me backwards onto the bed. I try rolling away, but he grabs me, turning me onto my back and sinking his face between my legs.

"You said we had to go!" I exclaim, laughing while he playfully roots like a dog at my crotch, sniffing and biting at me through my leggings.

"Don't worry, baby, I'm gonna make you come in about two minutes."

He is a man of his word.

IN THE CAR, flushed and disheveled, grinning like fools, Adam holds my hand on his lap.

"I didn't know I was trading away breakfast," I complain.

"It's your own fault," he lifts my hand to kiss the inside of my wrist, then my fingertips.

"I don't see how. You're the one who drags me out of bed then tosses me right back in."

"You knew exactly what you were doing."

I grumble, suppressing a laugh. "Not going hungry I didn't."

"Woman, you make me feel like I just got out of prison."

Yowza. He's like hormone therapy, the things he says to me sending all the pistons in my bloodstream hammering. I've become sexually deranged and all it took was forty-eight hours with Adam Sexton.

"Starving, you mean?"

It's his turn to laugh now. "Yes, starving." He nips at my fingers.

"Flirt all you want but trust me, you do not want to spend the next five hours with me in this car if I don't get some food and caffeine, *immediately*."

After a detour for a drive-thru breakfast and a lecture about spilling on his seats, I announce that I'm going to play DJ and connect my phone to the car's Bluetooth.

He sips a coffee. "This should be interesting."

"Was that sarcasm?"

"Nope, although you do seem to like everything."

"That's not true, there's plenty I don't like."

"Like what?"

"Um, I can't stand Dave Matthews."

"Thank fuck," he says, taking the biscuit I pass to him.

"You too?"

"God, that Kermit voice."

"I know! Thank you! But you tell people that and they look at you like you've bitten off their kid's ear or something."

"What else?" he asks.

"No Genesis, no CCR, no Yes or Rush. No Chicago. No Jefferson Airplane, Starship, whatever they are. God, I'm old. I don't care much for metal, or modern jazz, doo-wop, EDM, flag waving pick-up truck here's-my-dog auto-tuned new country, or jam bands."

"Um, okay..." he's chewing.

"What?"

"You had all that locked and loaded in your head, ready to go when asked?"

I shrug, taking a bite of my biscuit. "I bet you've got a longer list than that. Musicians are always snobs." He looks over right as part of my biscuit falls away, landing in my lap. I scoop it up and pop it in my mouth, wiping crumbs away and I swear, he winces.

"Do you include The Dead with your jam bands?" he asks, eyes back to the road.

"Ugh, yes."

"Ugh? What do you mean, ugh?"

"I do not like the Grateful Dead."

He rolls his head, his jaw literally hanging open. "I've finally found your big flaw. Besides your snoring."

I snort out a guffaw. "Um, A, I do not snore, sir, I'm a lady. You take that back. And B, don't tell me you're a Deadhead?"

"Um, A, yeah, you do. I'll admit it's more snuffling like one of those dogs with the smushed faces, but you absolutely do snore." Now I'm open jawed, my mouth frozen over the straw of my large Diet Coke. "Mm-hm, like a pug."

I'm about to protest but he holds up a finger to stop me. "And B, of course I like The Dead. I love The Dead. I've played with them when that twat John Mayer wasn't available. Didn't you Google me?"

"No, I haven't Googled you," I lie. Of course I Googled him, I just somehow missed this tidbit. "And The Dead? I can't believe it. It's the sound equivalent of a bunch of slow, stoned squirrels trapped in a maze, just going around and around aimlessly in circles."

"Come on."

"It's the sound of teenage boys or old men in ponytails at a circus, covered in crocheted blankets and patchouli."

"Stop it."

"I don't know if I'm attracted to you anymore," I shudder.

He scoffs, turning to give me a cocky grin. "We both know that's a lie."

I'm about to toss another quip his way when my phone rings, the sound filling the car so abruptly, so loudly, we both jump. I look at my phone and see the name. Adam uses a button on his steering wheel to turn the volume down.

"I should answer this, it's one of the GG's - the cleaners." Adam nods and I take the call.

"Hey, Teddy."

"Oh my God, Holly!" He sounds breathless, like he's running.

I snap to attention in my seat. "What's wrong?"

"I'm so sorry, oh my God!"

I look at Adam in alarm. "What is it? Are you at my place?"

"Hold on, let me take a breath—" I hear him rasping and

coughing. "Boo, I may have to pay you for today, because—" more gasping, he sounds hysterical.

"Tell me what's going on. You're freaking me out, are you okay?"

"Sorry, I ran to your house and Teddy don't run, so, whew! I nearly gave myself a heart attack, but what a way to go honey, let me tell you."

Then his voice is muffled, like he has his phone against his chest, speaking to someone.

"For fuck's sake, Teddy, what?!"

"*Sorry*," he says again. As if *he's* getting impatient with *me*. "I'll tell you what. Chip Walker, all the way butt naked, wearing just a cowboy hat like he's Brad Pitt in 'Thelma & Louise,' with little Cassie Touchet bent over the dining table in the studio, smacking her ass and giving it to her like he's sending her off to war. Lucky bitch."

Adam is shaking his head. And while I'm a little surprised, I'm not shocked. Young, good looking, I think both single. Why not?

"Good for them, and she's a doll, I hope he's nice to her."

Teddy hoots. "I wish someone was being that nice to me!"

"I hear that," I bulge my eyes at Adam. "What exactly happened?"

"I walked in, and there they were, and I just froze. That man has an ass that'll make you speak in tongues and worship the devil, I will testify to that..."

"That good?" I bite my lip in a smirk, watching Adam wrinkle his nose, pushing his sunglasses to the top of his head.

"I'm telling you."

"They saw you?"

"They heard me because I screamed."

"You screamed?"

"You think I was gonna shout 'eh, là-bas' like my grandmother? Of course I screamed! I panicked and ran but got the handle of my stupid Swiffer jammed in the door, ran it right through the screen, and then I heard little Cassie—"

"Stop calling her little. It's creepy - she's almost thirty."

"Yeah, but I know her mama. So, I heard her yell, and I turned back to look, and that's when it happened."

"When what happened, there's more?"

"When I turned back, there he was, he'd come right to the door, stark naked, sweaty..."

"I get the picture." I'm grinning, and Adam reaches over to pinch my thigh and I swat him away.

"I hope so, because it was some fucking picture. Not five feet away from me, hat up on his head. Bathed in sunlight, angels singing, *glistening* with sweat. *Still hard*! I swear to God, I've seen this exact thing in a porno."

"Did he say anything?"

"He said 'Hello, can I help you.'"

"That's it?"

"Uh-hm."

"And what did you say?"

"I said nice to meet you, I'm a big fan, and well... I *looked*."

"Looked?"

"I looked!" He laugh-screams, and I have an instant visual of him grabbing at the three tufts of silver hair he has left on his head.

Now I'm laughing, wiping tears from my eyes. "Oooohhhh, so you saw the toot toot!"

"Girl, yes, I saw the whole toot toot!"

Adam is tweaking my rib cage, and I twist away. "Hands on the wheel, buddy," I giggle.

"What?" Teddy asks. I give Adam a jab to the shoulder.

"Is it a real something special toot toot? Just how *nice* is he?"

"How should I say it... there's something going on there a judge oughta know, because honey, he might be injuring that young lady." And we both fall apart in peals of laughter. "Then I yanked open the door and ran up the road like my clothes were on fire."

"Oh my word."

"I know, can you believe? I wanted to tell you I'm sorry. I ripped a screen on the porch, I caught your big star *in flagrante*, and I think assaulted him with my eyeballs. And now I'm taking a bottle of wine from your frig. I'm done for the day. I've gotta go find a cowboy hat for Jim."

"Thanks for the report." He hangs up and I'm still laughing.

Adam scrubs a hand down the side of his face. "I could've gone all my days without hearing that."

"You mean about Chip's big, beautiful—"

"Stop," he cuts me off, stretching out his arm as if he's going to cover my mouth.

I dodge his hand. "How are you not going to think about it every time you're at the dining table there in the studio?"

"I'm buying you a new fucking table, and I don't as a general rule think about other men's dicks."

"Huge, glistening, *hard* dicks."

"I'm going to gouge my eyes out."

"Your mind already has the picture, so that won't help."

"Sounds like you're the one's going to be thinking about it."

Answering impulsively, I lean over to stroke my hand on his thigh. "Don't worry baby, your dick is the only one I'm thinking about."

"Obviously my much bigger, more beautiful, even harder dick."

I reach for my drink, biting down on my straw to keep from smiling, and give him a straight-faced, fluttering eyelashes, I only speak the truth look over my cup. "Mm-hm. Yep. Obviously."

"Good. Don't forget it." He winks, making a that's right, end of discussion, double click of his cheek. "And one more thing. You just called me baby."

CHAPTER THIRTY-FOUR

Baby?

Why can't I just be cool? But no. We have a few days of casual sex – okay, give the man his due, hot as hell, turn me inside out and call him daddy hot sex – and I short circuit. I don't know why I'm reacting this way, the inside of the car suddenly shrinking, but I'm like a startled rabbit who needs to run.

Fuck. I should open the door and jump out. I hate all these *feelings*. I can't stand myself when I get like this, it's so tedious. Which is why I try to avoid exactly all of this.

It's no big deal, calm down, I tell myself. It was just banter, one small flirtatious remark. It's not like you blurted out you loved him or anything.

But then a voice in my head, or, more likely, my vagina, whispers, *I only care now if you want me. Because I only want you.*

Adam breathed those words into me and now they're stuck in my chest. The way he just put it out there, removed a filter from his eyes and let me see all the way down into his soul. Those words make me want to fall into them. To fall into him. But I absolutely cannot, will not, let myself do that. No way.

I'm too old for sex to make me this neurotic.

"I don't think so," I say, keeping my voice light and teasing.

"You did," he nods, reaching over to adjust the temperature controls.

Dear God, am I sweating? Can he tell?

I busy myself with stuffing our empty food wrappers into the bag at my feet, smashing it all into a tight ball, putting on my sunglasses, and turning to look out my window. I need to say something witty but can't think of anything. I've gone blank. I knock my forehead against the glass a few times. I wish I had Xanax in my bag.

Quietly he says, "Are you that uncomfortable with one little off-hand endearment to me?"

"No," I scoff softly, still staring out the window.

"Have you been uncomfortable when I've said them to you?"

Surprised, I turn his way. He can be so kind it makes my chest hurt. And make me feel like a clumsy, lumbering bear. Look at him – after the morning we had, even disheveled and unshaven, he's self-possessed and gorgeous. I'm slobber and fangs and wet fur stink, making a mess. It's annoying, really, I should just get mad at him. That would be so much easier for me to deal with. Mad is more in my wheelhouse.

I exhale a long breath.

"You have?" a tinge of wounded disbelief in his question.

Oof, this man. Now I want to kiss him. See? Neurotic. Neurotic, flip-flopping mess.

He looks to the road, then back to me, the single groove between his brows deepening as he narrows his eyes earnestly. "Just talk to me."

I don't want to hurt him; that I'm clear about. I need to hitch up my ovaries and find some way to be honest. "No—" I say, voice strained. Clearing my throat, I repeat it more emphatically. "No. It seems more like just how you talk, your habit, than about me specifically, so no, it doesn't make me uncomfortable."

He flips his sunglasses down over his eyes. A muscle ticks in his jaw, like he's thrown a wad of gum in there, but I keep going. *Courage.*

"And… I like it." He glances briefly over to me then away, and I'm glad my eyes are also hidden. "I really like it; it makes me feel… I don't know how to describe it. When you talk to me like that, something inside me, I don't know, growls. Or purrs. Something like that. Growl-purrs. Because it's a touch of affection. I haven't had it, and I missed it."

He rolls his lips together into a firm line but doesn't speak.

"That might not make sense..." I trail off. Good lord. What am I doing?

He looks over his shoulder then steers the car into the left lane, passing a semi and several cars. When we're back in the right lane he says, "I make something inside you growl-purr, huh? I like the sound of that.... *baby*."

I let my head fall onto the head rest, blowing air in an exaggerated sigh, as if I'm praying for patience when I'm really trying not to laugh. I pivot my face to look at him and he's looking straight ahead, a grin on his face so shit-eating there should be feathers stuck to his lips.

"Do you think I walk around calling people baby? Sweetheart? That it's just the way I talk, like I'm some gum snapping truck stop waitress?"

It's my turn for a grin. "Yes?"

He dips his head to stare me down over his sunglasses. "It's definitely specific. To you."

"Don't make me feel punished for saying something nice to you."

"Punished? For talking to me? And I was saying something nice to you!" I lift my hands, then drop them back to my lap, frustrated, inarticulate. "No, I think—" he goes on.

"No? What do you mean, no?" I interrupt.

He rubs the back of his neck, as if what he's about to say is painful. "I mean, you're deflecting. You like me, and it scares you. You inch a little towards me, then you retreat."

I think he flexes his arm muscles to distract me, rubbing his neck like that. Bastard. Can't he wear a poncho or something?

"I wanted sex, you're good at sex..."

"Great at sex."

I shake my head, rolling my eyes, which he can't see behind my sunglasses, but I know he must hear it because I'm rolling them hard. So hard they surely are making a sound, my eyeballs knocking against my skull.

"It's confusing, okay. What do you want me to say? I haven't been with a man like this in a long time, you know that, and... it's..." I sigh heavily. *Dear universe, kill me, please just kill me now.*

How do I even explain this? That my attraction to him feels like flashes of a life sprinting across my heart, and I know I can't trust my heart. That this is all probably some weird sexual chemistry fog that will clear when the weekend is over, and the thought of this being over so soon already hurts. I know I'll miss him. And what if, by some highly improbable alignment of the stars, he is this miracle, delivered straight to my door, well then, that makes my blood run cold. The big terror that I know I'll do anything, anything to avoid because I'd not survive a second time. The big terror that makes me neurotic and inconsistent.

"It's too complicated. You don't have to worry about it," I say, dismissively. Apparently, my courage had about two seconds left on the clock.

"What does that mean?"

"Adam, you've been so kind to me when this could've been a humiliating disaster." *And maybe it still will be.* "Really, thank you. You've been wonderful."

"You sound like I just gave you a colonic." He scrapes a hand through his hair then down his face, frustrated.

"I do like you. Who wouldn't?" I swallow hard, running my palms down my thighs. "But can you see this from my perspective? I didn't expect..." I wave one hand in his direction. "You, to be so... *you*. You say things like you know me more than you do, like you've reached some spot on a map and think I should be there too. And I'm not, I'm not where you are. I wanted to feel something other than pain and anger, to feel alive for a minute. You were supposed to be easy."

I get a big time Adam scowl here, his face pinched like there's hot garbage in the car.

"Sorry, I mean uncomplicated. You were supposed to be uncomplicated. And of course, I fucked that up because I didn't count on you being—"

"Not a shithead stereotype. Handsome as hell. Big cock. Perfect for you."

"Oh my God, see there, you push."

"Is that how it feels to you?"

I nod. "I understand if I'm confusing you, I'm confusing myself."

After a long, weighted silence, Adam speaks.

"Why don't we—" he begins, then we're startled for the second time by my phone, still connected to the Bluetooth. It's lying on the console between the seats, my favorite face appearing on the screen. Grateful to be rescued, I accept the call.

"Hi Sugar Bee, how are you? I'm so happy to hear from you."

"Hi Mom," Luke says. "Are you in the car? It sounds weird."

"Um, yeah, I'm running some errands." I lean into my door, not looking at Adam.

"You want me to call you later?"

"No, this is good, I wanna keep you while I've got you. What's up?"

"Why didn't you tell me Adam Sexton's been in the studio? Adam fucking Sexton, mom. I could've been in the same room as him?!"

Adam coughs, and I whip around, grabbing for my phone, but he gets it first, swapping it over to his left hand and holding it out of reach, blocking me with his right elbow, all while trying to keep a grip on the steering wheel. We veer onto the shoulder and the rumble strips make the car vibrate loudly until he steers us back onto the road.

"What's making that noise? You okay?" Luke asks. I glare at Adam, one finger to my lips. He smirks back at me. I hope he realizes I'm perfectly capable of separating him from his testicles.

"I'm good! I just... I hit a bump and spilled my drink. How did you know he's been in?"

"Mike told me."

"You've talked to Mike, but you haven't called me in two weeks?"

"It was for a project. I had a Pro Tools question. So, have you met him?"

"Who?" I know playing dumb won't work but I do it anyway.

"Moooom, Adam Sexton. Have you met him?"

I shift onto my hip so that my back is turned to Adam. "Yep, I met him."

"What's he like? Mike said he's amazing which, for Mike, is like, gushing."

"I don't know. Just another guitar player." Adam pokes me in the butt, and I throw my elbow at him.

"Just another guitar player? He's already a legend, like, you know he's going to be in the Hall of Fame, right? He's so cool."

"Didn't seem all that cool to me."

Adam has a coughing fit, and I start coughing too, to cover his sounds. If I grab the steering wheel and make us crash, will it end this call?

"You alright?" Luke asks.

"Yep, there's a skunk." I'm glaring at Adam again.

"He's a good writer, too. Not Dad kind of good, but really good. You should pull those U47's for him, I bet he'd love those. That's what Dad would've done."

"Good idea, sugar." That's my smart boy. I'm beaming now and Adam, to his credit, smiles, dipping his head in a small acknowledgment.

"I wanna be the person who gets him to record music for a video game for the first time. We could do it at Riverside. It would slay so hard, it would be amazing. You know there's state tax credits for that."

Adam nods again appreciatively and my heart expands, then squeezes. I love this kid so much. To hear him talk about a dream like that, ambitions for the future, is true music to my ears. I have an immediate pang of missing him, of wanting to see his face and hug him tight.

"I love that. You should talk to Mike about it, and hey, I've been trying to reach you so I can buy your plane ticket home for Thanksgiving. I should've done it weeks ago."

There's a pause and all my mom alert senses stand at attention.

"About that," Luke says.

Oh no. No, no, no, no, no.

"About what?"

He blurts it out in one long run-on sentence. "Uh, well, there's this girl, I didn't think it was much of anything to tell, we went out a little bit last year, but now, well, her name is Amelia, and now it's more of a something, she's my girlfriend."

"Girlfriend?" my voice is a squeak.

"She's amazing, Mom, you'd love her. She's so smart and funny and gorgeous. She's from Charleston. Her family has this place on the water that is supposed to be amazing. She has a big family - they watch football, they do a bonfire on Thanksgiving night, and they have a boat."

"Oh."

He says the rest apologetically, like he's confessing to breaking a window with his soccer ball, like he did in fourth grade. "She invited me, and I'd kind of like to go."

I've slowly scooted forward in my seat, my hands clawing into the dashboard.

"Mom?"

I clear my throat and force myself to sound cheerful. "That does sound pretty... amazing. This girl..."

"Amelia."

"She's your girlfriend?"

"She is. I'll send you a picture."

So I can use it for target practice.

"You're okay with this?" he asks, voice hopeful.

There's this girl. He's more excited to spend the holiday with her than with me. It's inevitable. It's natural. It also sucks big hairy donkey balls. Of course I'm not okay with this. It should happen when he's thirty-five. Or forty.

Hoping he can't hear the tears in my voice, I say, "Sure, yes, it's okay. You'll be home in a few weeks anyway."

"Thanks Mom, I love you." He exhales, clearly relieved to have this conversation over.

"I love you too. And Luke?"

"Yeah?"

"Do you still have condoms? You can use my credit card for something like that."

"Mom! Jesus Christ, what the fuck do you think I'm doing out here?"

"Watch your tone, son." I can picture him, pacing his room. But he's not the gawky boy in my mind and I shake my head, changing the image until I see him as the twenty-year-old young man that he is.

"Yes ma'am, sorry." He starts again. "You sent me here with, like, four thousand condoms. Even I'm not that popular. I'll be okay for a while. At least until Christmas."

I can't help it; I let out a little laugh and Luke laughs too.

"I'm not stupid," he grumbles.

"Oh, honey, we're all stupid."

"I know, Mom. I hear you."

"Bring her mother some flowers. And help with the dishes."

"Of course, who do you think raised me?"

I'm still leaning forward onto the dashboard, my forehead on my folded arms, when we end the call. Adam reaches over and places his big warm hand in the middle of my back, consoling me wordlessly while I absorb the news and reset myself.

Sitting back in my seat, I dig through my purse for a tissue, then wipe at my eyes and blow my nose. I put my hand over my heart, the place where I'm hurting.

"We've never been apart for a holiday before. It might seem silly, but..."

"It's not silly." I smile at him, grateful he said that. "And he impressed me already. I hope I get to meet him sometime."

"You do?" The thought makes me nervous. Introducing Luke

to someone that I'm what... hooking up with? A man with me that's not his dad. We've never even talked about it. "I didn't think you liked kids."

"I never said that. I said I didn't want kids. I have three nieces; I love being an uncle."

"Oh, I bet you're a big softy, fun Uncle, aren't you?"

He grins. "Drives my sister nuts."

"Sorry about the songwriting thing he said, he'd be mortified to know you heard that."

"Eh, can't knock him for having his dad's back. And he might not be wrong."

"Thank you," I say, holding out my hand. He takes it, bringing it to his lips for a kiss.

A few miles pass, both of us lost in our thoughts. I don't know where Adam's have led him but mine, although I might look like I've calmed down, haven't really gone all that far.

I blurt out, "One thing I will say is I already don't like this little tramp, Amelia."

"Holly!"

"What?"

"Maybe we don't call young women tramps."

"Och," I cough out. "Maybe *we* don't but I do. And what the hell was all this about a house on the water, bonfires, football... we have a house on the water, we build bonfires, we watch fucking football."

"He just sounded excited." I give him a death stare, so he throws up a hand in surrender.

"We all know what he's excited about, and it isn't the boat," I mutter under my breath. Adam leans his head in my direction, about to speak, but I cut him off. "Nope. Whatever it is, don't say it."

"Alright," he concedes, the surrender hand raised again.

"Can we stop somewhere, please? I need to pee, and I need chocolate."

"Right now?" he frowns, which tells me, without telling me,

that this is a grown man who, even though he has those sisters, those nieces, he's never been married. He's spent a lot of time on the road alone, and he thinks of himself as the one in charge.

Bless his heart.

"Adam, *baby*," he grins at my use of the word, as I knew he would. My voice sugary sweet, I give him the gospel. "I said please. I said I had to pee. I said I needed chocolate. Have you been with any woman, ever in your life, when she said those words or any words like those words, and meant in an hour? Or just, you know, whenever you felt like it? Or do you think she meant right goddamned now?"

He does take it on the chin, though. I can tell he wants to laugh, but he bites his lip and keeps it to himself.

"Next exit it is."

AFTER THE STOP, when he's opening my door, he reaches for my wrist before I can climb in.

"I wanted to finish the conversation we were having."

"Okay," I look at him expectantly, not loving the sound of that.

"Why don't we agree that I'll try to stop pushing..." I raise a skeptical eyebrow and he kisses me once, soft and quick. "I'll *try*, and you agree to keep an open mind and, well, talk to me. There's something special here. You might decide you don't want it, I get that, but don't pretend you don't feel it, that it's just me. Don't treat me that way please. Don't lie."

Heat flushes my skin from my chest to the top of my forehead, and I look down, speaking to the faded fabric of his black tee shirt. "That sounds like more work for me than for you."

"I don't think so," he says, lifting my chin. He presses another soft kiss to my lips, then hovers just above my mouth. "Because I'll have to make myself wait for weeks now before I can ask you to marry me."

"Adam!" I smack his chest, shoving him away.

"What?" he laughs, grabbing at my waist to hold me close. "I said I'd try. And that's gonna be a long time for me to wait."

"Let me go - you're ridiculous."

"Alright, I hear you," he says, releasing me and walking around the car. "You drive a hard bargain there, killer. I'll wait six months, how's that? Better?"

"No! Get in the car!" Inside, I keep going. "What about that is not pushing? Can you even hear yourself?"

"I said I'd try; this is me trying. Six months is a long time for, um, mature adults like us."

"The only thing mature about you right now is your breath."

"I'll get a really big, huge ring."

I scoff, reaching for my seat belt. "You're forty-five years old and never been married, so I know you're full of shit, but seriously, cut it out."

"I've never asked anyone before, never wanted to ask anyone before, until you."

His sincerity lands in the car like one of those rubber life rafts, slowly inflating between us, loud and squeaky, awkwardly filling the space. Adam, who's been all teasing and bravado, looks shocked himself that he said it. I have to get us out of this ludicrous conversation.

I lunge over and pinch one of his nipples, hard. He yelps and grabs at his chest, twisting away from me. "I know! I'm sorry! I go too far!"

"You're not sorry." I bite him on his shoulder.

"Ow!" he yelps again, wiping at his eyes. "I don't even know why I'm doing it; you're making me nuts."

"It's not me, it's you!"

I settle back into my seat. He shakes his head with such a bewildered expression on his face that I can't help but soften. At least he's behaving like an emotional lunatic now, too.

He takes a ragged, deep breath. "I feel better now though, don't you?"

I flash a snarky grin. "I do."
We both double over in howls of laughter.

CHAPTER THIRTY-FIVE

ADAM

There's this girl.

It's the basic story of every straight man's life from age fifteen until his last breath on this earth. I knew where Luke was coming from even before he went on to gush about his girl, how smart she was, how funny, how gorgeous. I'm sitting there with his mother, watching her face as she talks to him, thinking *I know just what you mean, buddy.*

I'm not much different from this twenty-year-old kid. Hell, I probably sounded just like him yesterday when I was telling Gretchen about her. No wonder she told me to calm the fuck down. And that's exactly what I need to do. I need to calm down or I'm going to scare her off.

She told me to stop pushing so what did I do? I shoved.

Spectacularly, I shoved. I don't even know what came over me. I meant to be funny, cajole her out of her mood after Luke's call. And then I guess I had a stroke. What else could explain whatever the hell that was coming out of my mouth? I'm having to work my ass off to impress her, and I'm usually automatically impressive to the women I meet. It's a cliché, but it's true. Even her son said it, I'm Adam fucking Sexton.

Holly fucking Theriot doesn't seem to care.

I do love that we can talk about music. She cued up her playlist, and we spent the rest of the ride talking about songs. Hers were all over the place. Miranda Lambert then George Michael; Waylon Jennings, Irma Thomas, Sturgill Simpson; Mary J. Blige to Lucinda Williams to Susan Tedeschi to some local Cajun music. The Pointer Sisters came up in her shuffle, and she nearly lost her mind, singing full blast. The woman is possibly the worst singer I've ever heard in my life.

"I know," she said, when she caught me wincing. "If I had one wish, it would be to put on tight leather pants and really belt it out to a crowd. I used to beg Ronnie to let me be in his band, to set me up with a dead mic and let me pretend to be a backup singer, just one time. He'd never let me do it."

I sure as hell wouldn't but I don't think I'm going to volunteer that information.

"Cover Me Up," the Jason Isbell song, played, and she clasped both hands to her chest, pressing every word into her body, like she was hearing it for the first time, absolutely wrecked. Part of her left the car for four minutes, enthralled, off somewhere watching a movie playing in her head. I got this pang of jealousy, wanted to text him right then, tell him I'm going to punch him in the face the next time I see him, the bastard.

None of my songs came up in her shuffle for her to swoon over, no deep dives into the craft of them. How did she put it about "Wichita Lineman"? Oh yeah, there's been no 'perfect poem of loneliness' reverent critiques coming my way. What's a man gotta do to impress this woman? Just top fucking Jimmy Webb. Stevie Nicks. Bruce Springsteen.

Oh, and her husband. The songs he wrote for her. That's all.

And yeah, I know how fragile male ego that sounds, so go fuck yourself. I'm already putting together a playlist in my head of songs I want to share with her, like I'm back in time making a mixtape because, you guessed it, *there's this girl*.

It's incredibly stupid to let myself fall for the possibility of us, for all this chemistry - a fantasy of what life could be like with someone who fits into my world, who understands my world, like Holly does. But we get each other on so many levels, it's like we're naturally tuned to the same frequency. She's a note so clear I could tune my guitar to it.

I know I need to pay attention to how easily spooked she gets, to what she says, not this fantasy in my head. I know that. I know

I need to set a limit on how much I'll invest, on how much rope I'll give these giddy hopes I have for us before they strangle me. If she's always going to pull away, then what'll be the point?

This has got to be some sort of karma. I've always been the withholding one, the one with one foot out the door. My freedom, my career. If getting a taste of my own medicine were a zip code, someone should kiss my ass and put a stamp on it because Holly is shipping me straight there.

Pretty amusing, really, if it were happening to someone else.

CHAPTER THIRTY-SIX

THE ALABAMA THEATRE IS GORGEOUS; another gilded age beauty miraculously saved from the bulldozers of progress and parking lots. It's impressive, with similar red plush seats to the Saenger, but more ornate, with two tiered balconies instead of one. Just like in Mobile, Adam has his own dressing room, which is where I'm delivered when I arrive after sound check. He's just beginning his routine, and I offer to help.

Sitting on the countertop, my back to the mirror, I take one of his hands between mine, massaging his fingers one by one, circling the veins on top of his hand with my thumb before inching my way up to his wrist. Increasing the pressure, I knead the muscles in his forearm with both hands, then his elbows, moving slowly up his biceps to his shoulders. Eyes closed, he exhales a few soft grunts of pleasure. I repeat the whole process for his other arm.

"You're an angel," he murmurs as I pull him to stand between my legs, facing away, and massage his back. His head drops forward, and I keep one arm wrapped around his chest to hold him close, using the heel of my hand to work under his shoulder blades, feeling him relax under my touch like a candle in front of a fireplace. He confessed he's fighting off some early signs of arthritis, which isn't uncommon for musicians, especially guitar players. You get older and the hotels, the cars, lots of things get a bit nicer but oh those aching joints sure do not.

He turns to face me, his features disarmingly soft. "You're hired. Come with me everywhere." I brush his hair from his forehead, and he dips his head into my hand, like a cat soliciting affection. Holding my gaze, he whispers thank you before kissing me. And kissing me and kissing me. I believe we made the lights flicker.

He reluctantly pulls away to get on with his preparations. A few minutes on the hair, check. Lip balm, kiss me again, check. Guitar picks, jewelry from their special pouches, check and check.

"Where's this from?" I ask, holding up one of the long silver necklaces, the one with the record spindle, the chain smooth and flexible, almost serpentine.

"It was a gift." I lift it over his head, settling it around his neck and down onto his chest. I lift the spindle and study it, rubbing my thumb along the cool, small shape. "A birthday gift from Gina," he adds, his hands resting on my knees.

"I like it, it suits you." I look him in the eye so that he knows I mean it. It gives me comfort to be reminded I'm not alone in navigating love lost in some way or another. Of course I'm not. How could anyone get to our age and not have these sorts of memories and tokens? People do move forward. Can I figure out how to do that?

He gives my thighs a squeeze, and I hold up the second necklace. "And this one?"

Adam takes it from my hand and settles it into his palm, tracing the ridge that runs down the middle of the feather and the defined, almost sharp edges. "This was Heather's, my oldest sister. Mom gave it to her when she turned eighteen. Leaving the nest, that sort of thing."

"That's sweet. How'd you end up with it?"

He puts it around his neck. "I claimed it from her things when she died."

Taken aback, I touch his shoulder. "Oh no, Adam, I'm so sorry, I didn't know."

"It was a long time ago." He looks down at his chest, lifting the feather to his lips. "She was twelve years older than me, acted like another mother, like I was her baby. Well, they all did I guess," he quietly chuckles. "But Heather was...we were very close."

"What happened?"

"Car accident, black ice, New Year's Eve." He steps away, grabbing his kit bag from the counter and turning to stuff it back into his shoulder bag, rooting around, arranging things inside. "We were supposed to be together. I lived with her. We had just played a gig, The Pub of Love, but I went home with someone I met at the show."

"She was a musician?"

He pulls his iPad from his bag and sits down in a chair, finally looking at me. "She was a middle school English teacher who could've been a super star if she wanted to be. She got all the looks, all the talent in the family. The rest of us just had the leftovers." I must look skeptical because he huffs. "I'm serious, she was such a beauty, with this really warm charisma, and maybe not a great guitar player, that's true, but her voice, it was special. Singular, powerful, moving."

"But she was a teacher?"

"That's what she loved. Kids and books, being at home. She didn't like being out on the road, and she didn't like all the attention, either, fronting a band. Every label on music row tried to sign her but she just wanted to live her life."

"You said you lived with her?"

"I moved in with her when I graduated from high school. It's how I was able to go to Nashville. She really did take care of me. She liked doing shows with me, showing up and letting everyone fall in love with her, then slipping back into her cozy life like a bandit. And I loved singing with her... my God, she could sing anything."

He taps the iPad on his thigh, staring at a spot somewhere on the wall to my right. "My dad blamed me, said if I'd been a man and taken her home like I should have..." he lets his voice trail off.

"How old were you?" I ask quietly.

"Twenty-two." I shake my head and he sighs, "I know, he was an asshole. But he wasn't completely wrong, either. That's what I believed back then, anyway, and I went off the rails for a while, I was so..." he hesitates, searching for the right word.

"Angry."

He lifts his hand in acknowledgment. "Lost without her. It was so painful, I just couldn't... well, you know, I don't have to explain it to you." He sighs heavily again. "I became even more committed to living how I wanted. That's what she did, and I think... I think part of me had to prove that I deserved to be here, when she wasn't."

"Heather sounds like she was someone special. Thank you for telling me," I stand, sensing he's shared all he's going to for now. "Let me go get you some tea."

"You don't have to do that. I can get it myself."

"I know; that's why I like to do it." I put a hand on his shoulder and lean over, kissing the top of his head affectionately.

"Watch the hair," he grumbles. Then he puts his hand over mine, taking it into his, pressing his lips into my knuckles.

My seat for the show turns out to be a prime spot in the wings, perched on one of the big cases used to transport guitar amps. And whether by coincidence or design, but something tells me it's all a certain someone's specific direction, I'm on the same side of the stage as Adam, so I get a close-up view of him throughout the night.

Considering how many musicians I've been around, I should be more jaded, but it's fun to watch from this vantage point, to see how he interacts with the band and the crowd. Plus, I love the moments when he smiles at me, stalking his territory, watching me have a good time, which seems to make him very happy. I think he's loose and free because he's not the headliner, not carrying the full load.

After the last song, when Jennifer has offered her thank you's and farewells, the band exits together on the opposite side of the stage from me, waving to the audience. Last night they had an encore, and tonight the crowd is loud, on their feet, so I stay in place, expecting there will be one here too.

A crew member walks on stage with a music stand and an iPad, while in the wings, I see Adam and Jennifer with their heads together conspiratorially. Then the whole band comes back out to more applause, and Jennifer, without her guitar, walks to the center mic while Adam goes to the mic beside hers and starts tapping away on the iPad set up between them. He has his Martin hanging from his shoulder. This is not how the encore went last night.

"Thank you for a great night, Birmingham! We're pulling one out of the hat for y'all tonight... it's sort of our version of karaoke. You don't mind if it's a little rough and ready, do you?" she asks the boisterous crowd. "See, Adam here has this woman he wants to impress..."

The audience loves it, responding with whistles and cheering. He milks it, holding out his hands as if to say, *what's a guy to do*? Meanwhile, I've scrambled off my box, my hands on my cheeks. He looks over his shoulder to where I'm standing and flashes me a smile.

"I knew you'd be cool. We worked this up today in sound check, let's see how we do. Y'all ready?" Jennifer checks with the band then leans back and gives me a huge smile too. I'm wondering what in the world is about to happen. So is the crowd, restless now, their collective buzz of anticipation driving the pulse now roaring in my ears. "Adam, are you ready?"

He drawls into his microphone, "Let's do it."

Jennifer holds out her hands for quiet. When the auditorium is hushed, Adam hits the opening staccato chords. I know it instantly. He plays only the first few measures then stops, letting the crowd clamor for more, teasing out his control of the moment. I can't help myself; I let out a yell, and he throws his head back in laughter.

Launching into "Fire," the Pointer Sisters song I love - well, technically it's a Springsteen song, but to me it will always be a

Pointer Sisters song - Adam takes the first two verses. They do a sultry, flirty duet, and I'm losing my mind, laughing and singing, dancing like I'm alone in my bathroom. In a theatre full of several thousand people, he's talking to me, might as well be whispering right into my ear, of a desire that is undeniable.

When I get to the green room afterwards, my eyes find him the minute I walk in the door. I'm across the room in a few steps, throwing my arms around his neck. I stay in his arms, teary face buried in his chest, until he takes my hand, pulling me towards his dressing room. I look back at the band and wave, choking out a garbled, "That was unbelievable, thank you. I'll never forget it."

When the dressing room door is closed behind us, I fall into him, laughing. He takes my face in his hands. "Too much?" he asks.

I run my fingers under my eyes to clear the mascara I'm sure is smeared there. "Of course it was too much, and I loved it, you big romantic fool. You know I did. Look at me! What are you doing to me?"

"A man's gotta work to impress you," he says gruffly, smoothing my cheeks with his thumbs.

I lay my hands over his. "Adam, you are impressive. Just you. You know that right? You don't have to try to do anything to impress me."

For a millisecond I'd swear he's shocked, all the cool confidence falling from his features, his deep brown eyes glowing with emotion. "But you don't know how good it feels when I do."

How could anyone not combust under that gaze? It's a joke, I know it now, that I ever thought I'd be able to keep this man at arm's length. He was never going to let that happen. He was a freight train on a single track from the minute he stepped out of the dark by my pool.

Fire, indeed. I thought maybe I was playing with matches but really, I've been juggling blow torches and dynamite.

Realizing how thoroughly and quickly I've been run over, I hear words come out of my mouth as if I'm perfectly calm and normal, but I'm staring at him as if I've been unconscious and have just opened my eyes, dazed and bewildered to be in an unfamiliar world. "Thank you. I meant what I said. I'll never forget that."

That's what I say to him.

In my mind, I'm shouting, *what in the ever-loving fuck have you done to me?!*

Sliding one hand down my back, the other behind my neck, he holds me where he wants me, his mouth closing on mine. He kisses me until I'm dizzy, barely able to stand, my hands twisted in his jacket. I'm helpless, his mouth taking everything he wants. His kiss is all swagger - I didn't even know that was possible. Lips firm and possessive, this man knows he's gone for it and won and I'm the prize.

If I had any sense about me, I'd be furious he pushed me again, but God help me, it is burning me to the ground.

WE END the night at the hotel, in an area reserved for the band in the rooftop bar, a sparkling view of the city spread out around us. I hear about how Adam walked into the sound check and suggested the encore, apparently "suggesting" being a euphemism for announcing it was going to happen, according to Jennifer. I keep my hand in his all night, reclining into his side, his arm around me.

There's a lot of insider shop talk around the table but Adam is thoughtful about keeping me in the conversation, bringing up songs we listened to today, which launches several lively debates. The fall evening here in the Appalachian foothills is much cooler than at home and his body is warm and solid, comforting, against mine. I feel sheltered by him. It's the kind of night you want to last forever. I'm a version of myself I haven't felt for a long time.

There is one thing that happens.

"I knew your husband," Jennifer's drummer, Brian, tells me. As it goes in this business, they had a friend in common. "He hired me for a few demo sessions in Nashville, long time ago. What a great writer, great guy too." He rattles off a few of Ronnie's songs, the ones covered by well-known artists. That's usually something I would do.

"He wrote that?" someone at the table says, and I nod, the words *your husband* carving themselves into my skin. I stare at the candle on the table in front of me, my vision blurring into a kaleidoscope of orange and red as the discussion about Ronnie's songs plays out around me.

Adam, silent during all the talk of Ronnie, gives my arm a squeeze.

Cocktails keep appearing in front of me, not ordered by me, just magically showing up, and I keep drinking them. I want to blur out everything but candle flames, city lights, and the feel of Adam's body next to mine. The conversation around me, Adam's deep voice vibrating against my back, it all begins to sound further and further away. Like the party is going on while I'm sitting at the bottom of the pool.

I curl myself into him and whisper in his ear, "I think I accidentally had forty cocktails."

Because it seems like a good idea, I let my head fall to his shoulder and close my eyes. I just need to rest them for a second.

CHAPTER THIRTY-SEVEN

ADAM

HOLLY FLOPS down onto the bed, sprawled on her back, lifting one foot in the air with a silent request for me to pull off her boot.

"Where did all those drinks come from?" she asks, fumbling with the button on her jeans.

"The bar," I chuckle, dropping her boot to the floor. She flings her arms to her sides melodramatically.

"I know, the bar" she grunts, frustrated. She's in this flustered sort of huff, which is adorable. "They just kept coming and coming," she waves her arms, "And I kept drinking them. Like an amateur. In front of all the cool people. Did I embarrass you in front of your friends?"

"No, baby, you were a sweetheart."

"You're always so nice," she yawns, throwing one arm over her forehead. Her eyes close, she goes silent, her booted foot propped up on my thigh. Did she just fall asleep?

"Thank you," she murmurs. Not asleep.

I pull off this boot and let it fall, standing between her knees. I study her splayed out below me and a powerful sense of possessiveness floods me. It's an ache in the pit of my stomach and a fist squeezing my heart.

She opens her eyes, lids heavy as she gazes up at me, reflecting my desire, turning it up. The lust is undiluted and unabashed, a come fuck me look that will make a man commit crimes, thanking whatever god he worships for making him a man.

"I don't know if anyone has ever looked at me the way you are right now."

"How am I looking at you?"

"Like you're about to devour me. Or demand the severed heads of your enemies be delivered at your feet." *Because you know I'll do anything for you.*

"I don't have enemies. I have ghosts," she whispers, desire shifting to something more like a challenge, or a warning, as she continues to stare into me.

She laughs, shaking the thought out of her head and out of my reach, squelching the moment in a quicksilver mood back to frisky. "And I don't believe you. So fucking sexy. There were literally a thousand women tonight who wanted to take you home."

"It's true. Only you."

"Maybe they haven't walked the proberbial...broferbial..." she stammers on the word.

"Almost got it."

She smirks, waving a hand in the air to shush me. "The pro-ver-bi-al sexual desert... starving, thirsty, stumbling into this... damn, I wanna lick you."

I can't think of anything better. "Anywhere you want, baby, but—"

"Like where? Where's your favorite spot to be licked?"

I cock my head at that one, giving her the textbook *you even have to ask?* expression.

"Elbow?" She thinks this is hilarious, cracking herself up with snorts of laughter.

"That's my second favorite spot."

"Ahhh, right, because you have two of them." More snorting. "You know, there are romance novels where aliens have two—"

"Alllllright now, time for you to go to sleep."

"But my vagina has a lot more to say to you, and I really wanna lick your elbow."

I lean over, planting my hands on either side of her on the bed. I want to kiss her, roll around and rub myself all over her. But what I'm going to do is tuck her into bed and take a cold shower.

"I can't wait to hear what that is but come on, let's get you under these covers." I tug at the comforter, but she stops me.

"No, wait. Take your shirt off," she commands, rubbing her thighs against my hips.

"How drunk are you?"

"Perfectly the right amount. Now take your shirt off." She tucks her arms behind her head, waiting to be obeyed. I stand upright, pull my shirt over my head, and toss it onto the bed.

"Stay right there," she says softly, greedily inspecting my torso. Hounds start baying in my bloodstream. "You are so beautiful. God, I wish I had The General."

"The what?"

"My favorite vibrator."

That's a new one on me.

"Baby, I'm right here." I fit myself against her, resting my hands on her thighs. "Texas born and bred, red-blooded American rock star dick, and you want your vibrator?"

"Yes." Her smile is wicked. Must be some fucking vibrator.

She licks her lips, nailing me with a salacious stare. "I want you just like this. I'd make myself come while you watched. Then I'd get on my knees and fuck you with my mouth, worship that gorgeous lone star cock until you're begging to lick your cum off my tits, until you're falling apart and you don't know where you are or who you are, just that I'm the only one who can give you what you're desperate for, my name the only word you can remember."

Goddamn.

I'm staring at her mouth now, that's a given. Her beautiful, pink, wet, filthy, filthy mouth.

"Something like that," she says, enjoying having stunned me. "Maybe I need to say please?"

"Maybe you do."

She stretches, arching her back and yawning. "I think you'll let me do whatever I want."

She figured that out fast. "Now you'll definitely need to say please."

"Gonna play hard to get, are you?" Eyes drowsy, she dares me.

"I could flip you over, sweetheart, back that fine as hell ass up. We'll see who'd say please."

She likes the idea so much, her face the very essence of indecent mischief, that I know I've fucked up, because, Christ, if she makes a move to twist beneath me right now, I don't think I can take it.

My breathing matches the rise and fall of hers, the banter settling between us into something quiet and concentrated. How does the weight of air change between two people with only a look?

She holds out her hands to me. "Come here," she whispers.

"You need to go to sleep."

"Please."

I hesitate, gaging the danger level here, but I'm helpless to resist her outstretched arms and imploring blue eyes. I settle at her side on the bed, pulling her body into mine. Our arms and legs intertwine automatically, already knowing how to fit together.

She nuzzles her face into my neck. "Thank you for today, for the song. Thank you for the whole weekend. You're so kind, you really are, you gave me all these colors. I thought they were lost, that I didn't... have them... in me anymore." She shifts into me, sighing, her words growing thick with sleep. "Sorry, I'm not making sense, but, you know, everything goes dim and gray, and you get used to it. After a while you don't even remember. You're not even that unhappy. Gray is normal. And then you - you opened windows and turned on lights and... I remember. I remember what color feels like. I remember... myself and, thank you."

Close to tears, I can't speak, my heart doing such a shudder and throb against my ribs she must be able to feel it. I'm glad I can't speak because the only thing I can think to say, the words shouting and stomping in my heart, are I love you.

I know she doesn't want to hear it, and fuck, I don't even want to say it because it will bury this tender gift under the weight of the word. But I do. I love this woman. I've known her only a few weeks, I *know* it's crazy, but I also know it's irrefutably, irreversibly true.

I love her. I'd be crazy *not* to love her.

Maybe I've loved her since I saw her twenty years ago, this love hiding itself away inside me, taking up space so I haven't had a full heart to offer anyone else. It's awake now and vibrating through my body like the low toll of a bell sounding the moment, marking the finality of my fall, an echo expanding to fill every nook and cranny of my soul.

I love her.

It might not be a love meant to last. She might not ever love me back. She might crush me under her heel and leave me in a pile of dust. This might be impossible. All the terrible heartbreak could happen, but it won't change this fact.

I love her.

WHEN HOLLY'S breathing is deep and even, I ease my arms from around her, kick off my own boots, and strip away the rest of my clothes.

"Will you help me get these jeans off?" she mumbles, rolling over onto her back.

"Here, stand up for me, sweetheart." I help her to her feet, reaching for the top button of her blouse. "Let's get this first." Holding on to my upper arms, hair tousled and sleepy, her cheeks are flushed pink from the alcohol.

"A kiss for every button," she smiles, and my stupid, stupid heart contracts in my chest. "One," she presses her lips softly to mine. "Two," she kisses me again as I reach for the next button. How in the hell is she making my fingers shake as if I've never undressed a woman before?

She watches me, her patience endearing, like we've been here a million times before, taking care of each other, touching each other. The words *my wife* play through my mind like a scrap of familiar melody. She should be my wife. The last woman I undress like this. Pain shocks my heart with the thought. I've never wanted that before. I don't know if Holly would want that.

I make my way lower, my fingers stroking the skin right above the button of her jeans. I undo the button and pull down the zipper, tugging the hem of her blouse free.

"Wait, I forgot what number," she says with a small, breathless laugh.

"I got it," I pull the blouse open and slide it from her shoulders.

"Nooo, you owe me kisses," she pouts.

"I know I do, baby." I give her three small, slow kisses.

"Mmmm, whiskey on your lips, I love that," she reaches back to unhook her bra, pulling it free with an exhale of relief.

"What did you say?" I ask, hoping like hell this heart attack I'm having takes me out quickly because Jesus mother fucking Christ, I'm trying not to ravish this woman, not tell her I love her and beg her to marry me. She's had too much to drink. *And now* she's quoted the song I wrote about her, standing in front of me with those lush breasts right in my face?

I do not have the fortitude for this. She is gonna end me.

"I *said*," she licks her lips and I say a prayer in my head for strength. "I could taste the whiskey on your lips. I *said* I love it."

She's massaging her breasts, holding the weight of them in her hands, and my cock just can't take it. It twitches, like a jump offsides, lunging for her. Which of course she sees.

"Whoa..." she giggles, reaching for it with greedy fingers wiggling. "You're so naked."

"Nope," I grab her hands. "Not for you killer, not right now. You are going to bed."

"But Adam, it's soooo pretty, I want it."

"No. And don't call my dick pretty."

"Alright," she sighs, then whispers down to it, "I'll see you later. Macho penis."

I get her jeans off, leaving her panties on because I'm at the end of my fucking rope here, and grab my t-shirt from the bed and pull it over her head. In the bathroom, she does a quick wash up, leaning against the sink, leering at me in the mirror. She's incorrigible and it would be hilarious if it wasn't torturing me.

"Such a great ass," she says when I reach in the shower to turn on the water.

"I know, baby."

Apparently glad we're in agreement on something, she claps her hands together, which makes her wobble a bit off balance, and pronounces, "Okay, you need to get out so I can pee."

That's it. I have found my limit.

"Nope. It's late, I'm tired. I'm not leaving. From now on everybody pees in front of everybody."

"But... I don't—" she stammers, and I cut her off.

"Holly, you are going to sit your sweet ass down and pee, right now, and then you are going to bed. Understood?"

We have a stare-down until the corner of her mouth quirks with the effort not to laugh. Or sass me. Maintaining eye contact, she steps to the toilet with all the exaggerated, dignified but put upon drama she can muster, pulls down her panties, and plops down.

I nod my head, once, and yeah, I'm gloating a little, waiting to hear her pee before stepping into the shower stall. She doesn't revenge flush, which is classy of her.

When I slip into bed, she's finally asleep. She's on her side, facing me, and I lie in the dark watching her, learning the time signature of her deep breathing. I ache to touch her, pull her body into mine.

I slide my hand, palm flat against the mattress, under the pillow clutched against her stomach until my fingertips reach the warm skin of her arm. That's what I allow myself.

CHAPTER THIRTY-EIGHT

ADAM

"Adam."

The voice calling my name is husky, soft, and low. Awareness comes to me in pieces. Hotel room, warmth at my back, an arm around my waist, legs tangled with mine. I crack open one eye and make out a hint of pale light around the curtains. Hours to sleep and Holly snuggled against me. Sunday. Fuck the gym. I pat her hand at my stomach, falling back into sleep.

"Adam," the voice again. I love that voice.

"Hmmm?"

She shifts against my back, trailing kisses against my shoulder.

"I need you," she whispers, pressing her hips into my ass. Her hand moves down my stomach and inside my thigh until she's found my balls. She cups me gently, her lips nudging featherlight touches to my back.

Eyes closed, enjoying the heaviness of sleep, pleasure begins to wake up the rest of my body cell by electric cell. I lift her hand to my dick, and she wraps her fingers around the base, my hand with hers as she starts to slowly tug at my relaxed shaft. Settling onto my back, I tuck her into my side, our hands working together languorously in the dark.

Showing her what I like, the pace perfect, I'm nearly all the way hard when she pulls her hand away to reach between us. I only recognize what she's doing when her fingers come back to my cock. She has mined her pussy for her own arousal, bathing my erection in her wetness.

"Fuuuck," I hiss through an inhale, rolling towards her,

flexing my hips into her hand. "Baby... baby, I love how that feels," I groan into her neck as she slides her slick hand around me.

"I need you, Adam. I need you to touch me. Touch me, be on top of me, inside me."

She pulls me on top of her, opening her thighs wide. Sliding my hands around her waist, her plush body fleshy and yielding beneath me, I take her in one strong thrust. Her cry of relief is so satisfying I rock my hips from side to side, fitting myself as deeply into her as I can go.

The way this woman makes me feel.

Holding myself still, I inhale her desire, her stare like hot rocks pressed into my chest. It shoots straight through me, little climbers sinking cleats and threading ropes into the summit that is my undefended heart. Every sigh and whimper another turn of my bindings. Looking into my eyes, she lifts her hands to caress my forearms, then grips my wrists and tilts her pelvis in invitation.

It's a slow fuck.

Not desperate to catch a fast ride up to an orgasm, it's an I'll feel every single inch of you, you'll feel every single inch of me, breathe together, moan together, slow down time, turn off our brains and *feel* each other slow fuck. Goddam this is heaven. This is a what it means to be alive and making love slow fuck. A mother fucking *making love* slow fuck.

Her pussy is a jelly roll cushion of warmth hugging my shaft. Each stroke deliberate, the wet hasp of flesh slipping through silky flesh, I see how slowly I can go, her pussy swallowing me exactly as I'm giving it, sucking me in up to the hilt, barely releasing me to withdraw. Her tits bounce like ocean swells and my cock hardens so much it feels like the skin will unzip itself. I am tethered by the want in her eyes, a satellite held within her orbit.

No one else could ever be her, none of them ever had a chance. She etched an impossible code into my heart and disappeared with the key before I even knew her name. She was the idea of something. A fantasy. A glimpse of a future I didn't know how to get, didn't think I'd ever deserve. It could only be her, which was impossible, yet here she is.

She's lit up with pleasure; lost to it, surrendered to it, to me. And that makes me harder still. She's letting me give. Not just do to her. Not take from her. Not carry out a have mercy on me and lend me your cock situation between almost strangers. Her eyes pin me with a need that surpasses want. The woman who always gives. Who's angry about how much she's given. She told me she needed me. And she's letting me give.

I stop thrusting, pausing to cradle her head in my hands. I want to tell her everything. She, this, us, it's all a miracle. Staring into my eyes, waiting to be kissed, her pussy clenches around my cock, and I move again inside her, the slow roll of her hips matching mine. Her hands sweep through my hair then fall to the bed above her head where I take them in mine, lacing my fingers into hers. I want to fold myself into her until she can feel every single word I want to say but that she isn't ready to hear.

I barely lift my body from hers to fuck her. Our tongues twist and caress with so much heat we could set these sheets on fire while every one of her gorgeous small gasps sends ripples of cool air down my spine. Not much fits between us but sweat.

Whispering I don't even know what words of worship into her skin, I kiss down her body until I've pushed myself onto my haunches between her legs. I work my dick in tandem with my thumb, stroking and rubbing until she arches her back, her hands pressing into the headboard. I could come just from the sound of her heavy breathing.

Her orgasm rolls through her body and spasms around my cock, shuddering up through her stomach and torso. Bucking under me, she goes quiet, her breath suspended as she lets it take her. I don't let up with my thumb until she falls back into the mattress, until the last flutter has subsided. Then I crawl forward, settling my weight fully on top of her.

"It's heaven to be inside you," I groan into her neck, reaching an arm underneath her to pull her tightly into me, urgency building with each thrust. I'm right at my own release, the relief of it gathering throughout my body. The smell of her, the little cries every time I pull out and drive back in, her nipples moving against my chest, it's all perfect. Her legs wrap around my waist, her arms around my neck, holding on as I bear down with the speed I need.

"Yes, angel, yes, there it is," I exhale as I begin to spill inside her. "Oohhh... Goddamn... Goddamn, you're heaven baby. You're everything."

CHAPTER THIRTY-NINE

HOLLY

Lingering in bed with a lover. I forgot what it could be like.

Adam gives me his full, undivided, meticulously unhurried attention. I admit, it could be addictive. There's not a soundcheck or show to get to, no gym, no gentlemanly tucking the over-served woman into bed. No checking our phones. Falling in and out of sleep, we spent hours touching each other. Cheeks, ears, hips and bellies, fingers and hands, skin and limbs all charted with a slow, sensual curiosity.

And talking. That's really what I love. The hushed conversation, the low laughter. Tangled in the sheets, bathing in his scent.

Slow screwing until finally checking out of our room, spine melted, limbs wobbly, my blood turned to warm honey in my veins. You'd think my vagina would be ready to tap out, cry uncle, and put the closed sign on the door after a weekend like this. But no. I simply look at this man's face, he takes my hand or touches the small of my back, smiles at me and those wrinkles deepen at the corners of his eyes, hell, he flexes his forearm as he steers the car, and my vagina starts panting. Banging all the pots and pans in the house, shouting here! Down here please!

Because I, and my vagina, we now know thoroughly, very totally and quite completely thoroughly, exactly what he can do.

We can't un-know his cock. His mouth. His hands. We can't unknow his moans, the words he whispers into my skin, the way he calls me baby, or angel when he's losing his mind and getting all kinds of dirty. We, my vagina and I, are literally and figuratively, expertly, fucked.

I asked him for one small favor, and he opened himself up and gave me everything.

We go for barbecue, all the while touching and talking - music, his family, my family, my work, the studio - and afterwards stop to rummage through a pawn shop before leaving Birmingham. He seeks them out, he told me, looking for guitars or vintage gear. And records, always records. Unnecessarily, of course, because I'm fully aware that musicians like pawn shops. I get the feeling he was compelled to explain so I wouldn't be impatient while he nosed around, but I love this sort of thing. I wave my hand to dismiss his concern, and he sets off to explore the small shop.

Soon, he's back by my side where I'm casually looking through the glass cases of watches and jewelry near the front door.

"See anything you like?" he asks, and I shake my head.

"No fifty-four Stratocaster lying around back there?"

"Not today." He leans over to look where I'm looking, his hand going to my hip so naturally, so possessively, that yep, there goes my vagina. And my nipples too. The gangs all here, fawning over him like he's big rock candy mountain. Which he is.

The man behind the counter, very thin and very wrinkled, sweet faced, in blue Sansabelt slacks and a short sleeved polyester shirt, shiny silver pompadour combed high off his head, does not miss the vibe. His finely tuned radar for a sale pinging loudly, he slides off his stool to stand across from us.

"Your pretty lady here ain't got no ring on her finger. You oughta fix that, son. Take a look, we got new rings, just came in. I can give you a real good price." He pulls a tray from the case with all the diamond ones that look like wedding rings.

"Thanks, man, but not today." Adam backs away from the case like it's radioactive. I bite back a laugh, making a small snort with the effort. I know he must be cringing inside, after how well his ring comment went down yesterday.

"Ready, baby?" his hand grips my elbow to steer me to the door.

"Wait." I point to a ring in another tray. "May I see that one please? The blue one there. " It's one large, oval stone, probably from the sixties, with a simple border of crimped gold. It slips right onto the ring finger of my right hand.

"Look at that, perfect fit," the man says. He's right, it is perfect. Gorgeous, in fact. "Beautiful like your lady here, same color as her eyes."

Adam moves closer and takes my hand. "What's that carved on top?"

"I can't tell, a crane maybe?"

"Cranes mate for life, you know, kinda like them swans do, so it's meant to be a love ring. You know, loyalty. People say lapis does all kinds of things. Wisdom, clarity; they say God wrote the Ten Commandments on lapis." This guy suddenly full of information.

"Loyalty and clarity in love," Adam murmurs, touching the ring. "How much to get some of that?"

"Um, no," I blurt, pulling my hand from his and removing the ring, passing it to the man behind the counter. But he hands it right over to Adam.

"Nine hundred, but today I'll let you have it for eight."

Adam weighs it in his hand and looks down into my eyes when I tug on his sleeve.

"It just caught my eye, that's all, but no, leave it. I can't afford it, and I don't want you to buy it for me. It's too much. Please. I only wanted to look at it."

He scowls, and I imagine he's chewing up the inside of his cheek, battling with himself. Listen to me or do what he wants. I can see it all over his face. It would make him incredibly happy to give this to me if I'd let him, and the stupid truth is I picked out a perfect ring and I do want it. Part of me now wants him to get it for me. That part of me is wrong, and I'm embarrassed.

"Men like to get their ladies gifts, you know? Pretty things." The man nudges, feeling his sale hang in the balance.

"It would be a nice memento from the weekend," Adam says,

looking back at the ring in his hand, a sincere and genuine sweetness in his voice that does something painful to my heart.

I kiss his cheek, whispering in his ear. "I don't need anything to help me remember this weekend. You're enough." I take the ring from his hand and pass it back to the man behind the counter. He shrugs, looking at Adam with a very man to man *women, what can you do?* resigned expression.

In the parking lot, when he opens the passenger door for me, I take him in my arms. "Have I thanked you for this perfect weekend?"

He grins and I'm flooded with relief to see the smile reach his eyes, like what just happened didn't happen. "You have."

"Not enough," I say, kissing him fervently. "Thank you, thank you, thank you," I repeat between kisses until he's laughing, pulling my arms from around his neck, telling me to get in the car before he hauls me into the back seat and gives me something to really be thankful for.

That bit of effervescent playfulness takes us down the highway for a while, but as the miles roll by our conversation slows until eventually, we're riding in silence. It's a companionable but noticeable shift. I ask if he wants me to play some music or find a podcast to listen to, but he says if I didn't mind the quiet, he'd prefer it for a while. And that's what we do, we ride with the quiet, each lost to our own thoughts. I stare out my window as Alabama becomes Mississippi, a blur of one green field and farm blending into another.

The weather follows a predictable script, adding a *this is where the story takes a melancholy turn* vibe to our drive. It begins to rain, the soothing sound and darkening sky turning the inside of the car into a cocoon. Normally this would put me right to sleep, but I can't sleep, sadness gnawing at me as we get closer to New Orleans. Closer to the end of the weekend.

Because that's what I'm thinking. This is probably it. The end of our time together, the end of this arrangement. Tomorrow, it's back to Lafayette, back to work for both of us. Back to real life.

I don't want this to be over, but I also don't know what I'd want it to be. I have so many conflicting feelings, so many fears, I wish I could call Madeline right now and talk it through with her. I wish I knew what he was thinking. I could ask him what he wants but I don't know if I'm ready to hear his answer.

I study his profile and take inventory of what I know about him. Aside from his dick - because I've done enough waxing poetic over that national treasure - in no particular order:

I know about his body; from the sounds he makes to the texture and temperature and smell of his skin. I know he's not ticklish. He doesn't like his ears to be kissed but loves kisses on the inside of his thighs, his stomach, and any attention to his nipples. I know the length and shape of his fingers, the feel of his palms, the expressiveness of his hands when he speaks. I know he has gray in his hair that's hard to see until you're up close, until you run your fingers through it. His beard is growing in gray too, when he doesn't shave.

I know he prefers things to be neat and tidy, an orderliness to his life, not so much a fly by the seat of his pants kind of man. He's a bit particular about his looks – imagine that, a male musician, vain?? – but I wouldn't call him fussy, either. Just... particular.

I know how he takes his coffee. How he likes his steak and what he prefers to drink.

I know he loves to laugh. He's a great kisser.

I know that everyone I've met so far in his world respects and admires him, nearly all defer to him as the man in charge – he's the star - so he walks through his life with an unusual ease and confidence, as someone who is by default listened to. Catered to. Adored. He's cocky as hell at times, yes, but not gross about it, abusive or entitled. He doesn't seek attention because he doesn't have to; it comes to him. I know I'm attracted to this way he takes charge, his quiet swagger, but I'm also perversely compelled to resist it because I've been in my own singular, small world where I'm the boss. And I know he likes it.

I know that despite all the adoration, he's lonely.

I know his talent is spectacular, and I understand and admire his devotion to his music, his ambition. I know I'm attracted to this as well. A lot. But he's on a very specific train with no plans to get off. Sacrifices have been made. Hearts have been broken. If you want to be with him, you will have to get on that train.

I know he's kind and generous. Openly affectionate. Romantic. Maybe not all that patient. He's close to his mother and sisters and nieces. Refer to note above about being catered to and adored. I know I prejudged him as a stereotype with every bad boy musician trope in the book. The joke's on me because, out of the two of us, he's the more emotionally stable and available. I'm the flailing one, the one most likely to cause harm.

I know he makes me feel a sort of hunger some might describe as hope. It's shocking, really, like finding a field of tulips on the moon.

I know that despite the short time we've known each other, if I needed anything, if I asked him for anything, he would help me, would give me anything that was possible for him to give. I know that if I reached out to him right now, he would take my hand and bring it to his lips and my heart would to a thump-thump two-step in my chest.

These are some of the things I know about Adam Sexton.

I don't know what sort of list he'd make about me. Grumpy. Frequently hungry. Overly dramatic. Overly caffeinated. Neurotic. Cries easily. Potty mouth. Starting to see more wrinkles. Cellulite. Leans toward being a loner. Heart impaired.

Would he have anything nice to say? Dedicated sleeper. Big boobs. Travels with snacks. Lust in high gear. Great shower fore-play song choices. Would he call me sweet? Kind? Loyal?

Here's one thing else I know. I'm tired. Really fucking tired of this emotional pendulum, all the back and forth of these feelings. I need to find a way through or retreat to some safer, stable ground.

My sigh is loud, the first sound from either of us in over an hour. He glances my way, and I can tell he's been deep in his own head too, his flat expression showing how far away his thoughts have been. He rubs his eyes.

"You good? Do you need to stop for anything?"

"No, I'm good, thanks." I say, and he nods, looking back to the road. "You're really good company Adam."

"Ah, sorry, I'm working out some lyrics in my head."

"I didn't mean it like that. I wasn't being sarcastic. You're good company."

"Well then, I like that you think so. You're wonderful company yourself."

"Want me to drive a while?" I ask.

"Nah, I got it. It's all..." he motions to his forehead, "Coming through."

"Ronnie wrote a lot of songs on long drives. We had this running joke where he'd just say, out of the blue - *Holly, tablet* - and I'd take out a notebook and write down whatever he had. Usually only a line or two, but one time it was a whole song. Just spilled out the whole thing for me to transcribe, like he was channeling it over a crystal ball. It was unbelievable. If you want me to write anything down for you let me know." I bend to dig my Kindle out of my bag at my feet. "Oh, look, I still have Twizzlers! Want one?" I hold up the package, but he shakes his head with a nose wrinkle that I ignore.

I've read one page when I become aware of Adam's gaze on me. I offer one of the red strands to him, but he shakes his head again. "Then what is it?" I ask, tapping the Twizzler on his arm.

"Nothing," he clears his throat and grabs the candy from me, taking a bite.

"Uh-huh," I mutter, but can't shake this tension picking at the back of my neck. I stare at my screen, not seeing the words, until the thought slowly dawns on me.

"Is it uncomfortable for you when I talk about Ronnie like that?"

He doesn't answer.

"It's too much, isn't it? It's weird. It just came out, I'm sorry."

"No, don't apologize," he looks over to me then back to the road, twisting his hands on the steering wheel. "I've been thinking about how easy it's been to have you with me this weekend, to share this with someone who understands it all, who just fits. You make it look easy but it's probably taking a lot of effort, and pain. And I don't have a clue what it's like for you to process this, much less ride beside me basically living out the life you had with someone else for twenty years and wonder if you should talk about it or not."

He rubs at his chest, the place with the fresh scar, exhaling out a long breath. I don't know what to say. He's gone right to the point, and I wasn't expecting it.

"I'm sorry I've been insensitive about it, showing off, pushing you with all my feelings for... well, anyway, I'm sorry. You can talk about it, about him, whenever you need to. We don't have to let it be weird."

There's such an enormous lump in my throat I couldn't speak even if I had words to say.

We ride for several more miles in silence. I'm focused so intently on the scrape of the wipers across the windshield, the white noise *whack, whack, whack* as they move back and forth, I'm startled when he speaks.

"Tell me something about him."

"What? What do you mean?"

"Tell me something you loved about Ronnie."

I wasn't expecting that either. "We don't have to do this. It's okay, I'm okay."

He reaches over and squeezes my knee. "Come on, just one thing."

I think it over for a minute.

"Ronnie really *felt* things. He laughed out loud, he had this big chest shaking laugh, and he cried at sad movies, sentimental movies, anytime the underdog won the game. He loved righteous anger, to get really into a debate. He had all the feelings, and it made him a wonderful father, and it made people around him feel free to do the same. I loved that about him."

Adam nods appreciatively.

"Will you tell me about Gina?"

His rolls his lips together, turning his face to glance out his window. The rain has slowed; he adjusts the wipers. Unsure if he'll answer, I shift so I'm angled in his direction, watching him and waiting. He flicks his eyes over to me then back to the road. Is he nervous?

"Gina dated my best friend Owen for eight years. O was my bass player, we met early on in Nashville. They were already dating. We all were friends back then. I started touring, he moved to Austin when I moved to Austin, her career was growing..." he shrugs. "They broke up."

"What's her career?" I ask.

"She works in finance. After they broke up, she took a job in London."

This surprises me. It's not what I'd expect for him, to date someone so far outside of a creative field, but I don't have any good reasons why I'd think so.

"And O married someone else, like six months later. Had two kids straight away."

"Wow."

He shakes his head grimly, acknowledging the sentiment. "Yeah, I should've seen it..." the sentence evaporates as he scratches at his neck. "She moved back to the states about five years later, for a job with a tech company in San Francisco. Invited me out to dinner when she was in L.A. for one of her races."

"Races?"

He nods. "She does triathlons."

Fuck me. I shove my bag with my feet, getting those Twizzlers out of sight.

"I thought it was probably her way to check up on Owen. And maybe it was, but we already had this history as friends, we were both single... we fell straight into each other."

The bile of jealousy rises in my stomach, but I push it away. He doesn't deserve that from me. Adam has listened to me talk about Ronnie, cry for him, seen the shadows my marriage casts over my life even now. I can do this for him.

"What did you love about her?" I ask. He sends a quick look my way. I offer a smile, letting him know it's okay to keep talking.

"She was independent, super driven. With everything she did. We were in our late thirties and it felt... adult, like I should be with a woman like her. Serious, accomplished, and she had a career that was important to her, as important to her as mine was to me. I believed I was finally with someone who got it." His expression is bitter.

"How did Owen feel about it?"

He huffs ruefully. "Oh, we royally fucked that up. We planned to tell him, but some friend of Jenny, his wife, saw us at a restaurant and snapped a photo, sent it to her before we had the chance. We didn't know this, of course, and he stormed into the studio where I was producing a record and tried to tear my head off. We had a horrible fight, damaged the shit out of the place; I broke my hand breaking his nose... it was a shit show. The studio was wrecked, thousands of dollars in damage... it was so God-awful embarrassing, and he quit the band. Best friends for fifteen years and that was the last day we ever spoke to one another."

"But why would he care so much? He was married, with kids."

"I should've told him the minute she first contacted me. I'll regret that for the rest of my life. It was so fucking stupid, and selfish to think he was beyond caring."

"Is this what broke you up?"

"No," he sighs heavily, taking a long pull from his water bottle. "She moved to L.A., moved in with me, and I thought... I thought we were happy. We were both working like crazy, but it seemed good, you know, solid." He runs a hand down his thigh, flexing and unflexing his fist. I wait. And wait, but he doesn't go on.

"What happened?" I ask carefully. Whether I need to or not, whether he should tell me or not, I want to know. He swallows hard.

"We'd been together almost three years, and she got pregnant." I inhale sharply before I can stop myself and he glances my way. "She had her IUD removed without telling me, without even one conversation about it. Just made the decision unilaterally, decided that's what she wanted and did what she had to, to achieve her goal."

"You've got to be kidding me, Adam, I can't imagine. It's so—"

"Wrong? Fucked up, disgraceful, deceitful?" His rage shows up in the grip of his hands on the steering wheel, in his face, the lines growing more pronounced with tension.

I'm at a loss. I try to think of her with empathy, imagining she panicked as her window of opportunity for having a baby was closing. That I can understand. Wanting to have a baby with the man she loved, that I can also understand. But going about it the way she did? I'm shocked.

"How does someone... how do you..." I struggle. Is he about to tell me he has a kid out in the world somewhere, a child he abandoned? "What did you do?"

"Lost my shit. She thought I'd change my mind about children if she forced the issue, that I'd just come around, and we'd get married. She broke this elemental trust I thought we had, broke my heart with her manipulation, and acted like I was the asshole. She was furious when I didn't immediately get on board. I didn't know how to get past it, could hardly look at her, but she knew, she *fucking knew* I wouldn't walk away from my own child."

"What did you do?" I ask again.

"Called my lawyer, moved into the guest room, then left for six weeks of dates in Europe. I was playing in Stockholm when she miscarried. When I got home, she had moved out."

I sit with that, stunned.

"Adam, I'm so sorry. That's truly awful."

I understand so much about him now. Why talking things through is so important to him, why he was so sensitive to how I judged him, the vasectomy. All of it.

"It did have sort of a happy ending, in the end," he says.

"How so?" I ask, incredulous.

"Owen left Jenny shortly thereafter, left his kids, and married Gina. They have a little girl, so I'm told."

"Whoa," I mumble, looking at his profile.

"Whoa," he repeats, staring through the windshield, the storm outside playing across his features.

His story, my story, we've both navigated loss and betrayal. How have we shared so much in one road trip? I reach over to him and, as I knew he would, he takes my hand, lifting it to his lips.

Yep, there it goes. That thump-thump of my heart.

CHAPTER FORTY

HOLLY

It's still raining when we get to Adam's place in New Orleans. He offers to take me out to dinner, but I suggest we order in. My treat.

"Relax, you've been driving for hours. Why don't you turn on the TV?"

He picks up the remote from the coffee table and tunes into a football game. When our food is delivered, you'd think I made an eight-course gourmet feast, he's so delighted when I transfer our salads to plates and bring them over to the sofa, along with a cold beer for him that I've tucked under my arm.

"Usually, it would be just me here with a can of soup."

Leaning over to bump his shoulder with mine, I watch him dig in, his eyes on the game. I get how I'd be the one eating alone on Sunday nights, but him? It's still hard for me to believe. The man just received standing ovations from thousands of people.

Pointing to the game, I say, "If you tell me you're a Chargers fan I'm taking your plate away."

"Course not," he huffs around a mouthful. "Cowboys fan, obviously."

"Oh, God, no, that's worse."

"Texas always, baby."

"You're lucky you're so handsome, and my ride home tomorrow."

"Awww, come on," he takes a long drink of beer. "You get to have REO Speedwagon. I can't have the Cowboys?"

"I'd say they are not at all equivalent."

"I'd say you are correct, but not in the way you think." He

gives me a wink. "Some might say you're also lucky I'm so handsome."

I grin, shaking my head at his cockiness.

"See, we can work all these little things out, sweetheart," he says, pleased with himself.

After we've finished eating, he stretches out full length on the sofa. Holding out an arm, he says, "Alright, back it on in here girl," and I do, fitting myself into his body. "Perfect," he breathes into my ear as he draws me close. "This is good, having you here," he sighs, squeezing me tightly to him.

And here we are, Sunday night, crashed on the sofa watching football, the picture of middle-aged domestic contentment. In no time, Adam is asleep, his breathing deep and regular against my back.

Couldn't I want this? Couldn't I want more? More Adam. More of how he makes me feel. Couldn't that desire be strong enough to beat back my terror of changing the life I've managed to piece back together? My peaceful life alone.

He doesn't stir when I pull myself from his arms. I grab a throw from a nearby chair and cover him, then walk down the hallway to his bedroom. Soon, I'm blissfully soaking in his enormous bathtub, room full of steam, hair piled on top of my head. I found a bottle of Castile soap in one of the vanity drawers and brought the candle from Adam's dresser in here, lighting it and the one on the bathroom counter.

I begin sifting through a cascade of thought folders, from how I'm going to tell Madeline about this weekend – that's going to be an epic phone call; to Luke's call – he has a girlfriend! - to the workload I have to catch up on and the chores waiting for me on the property, to how do I have this conversation with Adam. Do I even need to have a conversation with Adam? Maybe we just wake up tomorrow and keep hanging out, and no one has to say anything, nothing has to be defined. It just is. We let it happen.

Adam walks in, sleepy-eyed, hair mussed from the sofa.

"You're the first person to use this tub. You make it look very inviting."

"Well, it is big enough for two. Get in before my Tinder date gets here."

Watching him undress in the candlelight is thrilling. He takes his time, eyes on mine as I study his body. He's lean and agile and it all excites me, even after these past few days together; the dark hair across his chest, the way it sneaks down his stomach, the sound of his zipper causing an erotic ripple between my thighs.

When he pushes down his jeans and briefs, freeing his cock, I can't help but greet it with a smile. *Hello friend.*

"Careful, it's hot," I warn as he grabs the side of the tub, swinging one foot over.

"I'm sure it's... holy hell, woman, fuck me!" he gasps when he has both feet in. He's not sitting, but leaning forward over me, water up to his knees, hands braced on the edges of the tub. "Are you trying to cook yourself in here?"

"It feels so good."

"When you've lost all sensation in your skin?"

"I can add some cold. Lift the thingy behind you there for the drain, let some water out."

He shakes his head with a sheepish laugh. "No, no, hold on, give me a second. If you can sit in this, so can I."

I raise my hands to his chest as if I might have to catch him. "Take your time."

He stands above me, blowing air through pursed lips, shifting his weight from foot to foot. "This is gonna melt my goddamn dick off."

"You're being dramatic. I wouldn't let that happen."

"Okay, here we go," he says, moving one hand to his balls, lifting them protectively. He lowers himself into the water, gasping and groaning as he settles himself opposite me. His legs are on the outside of mine, knees bent, and I settle my feet on either side of his torso.

"You okay?" I ask, watching his head fall onto his shoulders, eyes closed.

"Need a minute," he says tightly.

I sit back, bringing my hands to his calves. I massage the muscles with long strokes, candlelight flickering on the walls, the lap of water echoing in the room, and the tension slowly leaves his body. The hair on his skin glistens, darker now that it's wet, a very masculine contrast to my fair skin, flushed pink from the hot water. My nipples harden simply from the picture of testosterone he presents.

"What happens now?" he asks quietly.

"Umm, soap?" He opens his eyes, tilting his head to the side meaningfully. I guess we are having this conversation.

I rub my lips together, nervous, waiting for words to come, looking into his eyes to remind myself of how much I enjoyed the past few days with him. To let him know I'm not avoiding his question, just thinking about my answer.

"Would it help if I tell you what I want?" He takes my foot and brings it to his chest, resting his hand on top of it, creating a solid point of attachment between us. I nod, wishing my heart would stop racing. "I want more of this. Being with you, getting to know you. I don't want it to end." He squeezes my foot. "Would you want that?"

I realize I've got a death grip on his calves and relax my hands. "Yes, I could... want that too." There. I've said it out loud.

He breaks out into a smile.

"Stop," I plead.

"Stop what, smiling?"

"Yes."

"You're smiling. I can't smile?"

"I can't help it; you're making that goofy face."

He moves my foot, shifting forward in the tub to reach for me, splashing water over the sides. "Give me a kiss so you remember that you like me." He tugs at my legs until I scoot closer, then frames my face in his hands. His kiss is gentle, filled with so much affection, that my heart doesn't race. It slows, like an elevator gliding to a stop at the right floor.

"I do like you," I say when he pulls his face a few inches away.

"But?" His deep brown eyes search mine, candlelight shining in them. "We've scalded through several layers of skin to get in here, my nut sack has shriveled up like a wool sweater—"

I laugh. "But now that you're in here you love it."

"Now that I'm in here I love it," he agrees, voice dropping down into his smooth low drawl. He pulls a damp curl away from my forehead, eyes scanning my face. "And now that you're here, talk to me."

I trace the lines framing his mouth with my finger, then through the stubble shading his jawline. When Adam looks at me the way he is right now, he *really looks*. He searches, he observes, he waits. It's unnerving for someone to see into you like this, for them to ask you to reveal yourself. Unnerving and at the same time, undeniably, seductively magnetic.

"You're safe to say whatever you need to. Tell me two things you're afraid of." He presses his lips into my hand.

My list of fears is long but maybe sharing two won't kill me. We drift back to our corners. He lifts his arms out of the water, resting them along the sides of the tub, and I feel myself cross over some invisible low wall.

"I'm afraid if I step towards you, you'll want to jump twenty steps ahead. It's too much pressure. I feel like you're ready for more than I'm ready for, that you're not seeing me for who I am right now."

"Pushing you."

"Yes."

"I didn't want you to write me off as just your weekend revenge fuck."

"I'm not."

"You were."

"Yes, okay, but look where we are now."

"Look where my pushing got me?" He makes a face.

"Adam..."

He lifts his hands off the tub in what I take to be a *I did what I had to do*, unapologetic gesture. I nudge his armpit lightly with my toes, but then remember he's not ticklish, so I give it a little twist. He squeezes his arm down onto my foot to fend me off.

"I'm done with casual. That's what I want to be clear about. I'm looking for someone to build something with, I want a partner. I told you that. And I see—" he holds up a hand to ask me to wait when I move to speak. "There's so much potential here. I get excited about it, about you. I don't know how much of that I want to apologize for. Holly, you are a treasure."

His words reach through my chest, caressing my heart. I want to make my point before he melts me away. I speak carefully. "I'm not asking for an apology. I need to know you're hearing me. Can we spend time together without it feeling like the stakes are so high?"

"Okay."

"Yeah?" That seemed a little too easy. I dip my head skeptically.

"Yes." He reaches into the water and rubs my thigh. "Don't be so cocky, woman. I'm looking, but you might not be the one, I hardly know you." I splash water at him. He's maddening. "What's number two?" he asks.

This one is harder, and I let my head fall back, watching the shadow flames dance across the ceiling, taking a few steadying breaths. "In the car today, when I mentioned Ronnie..."

He rubs my thigh again. "I told you; you can talk about him whenever you need to. I don't want you to worry about that."

"It's more than that," I say, dropping my chin so I'm looking at him again. "It's... I told you how mad I am at him, but there are times when I miss him..." Pain twists my vocal cords, my voice airless, climbing in pitch. I don't want them, but tears fill my eyes. "When I miss him so much. I drive around talking to him, you know?" I bark out a tearful chuckle. "I love him. I'm mad at him, but I love him. I loved him so much, and things come up - memories, songs, something with Luke, and I'm knocked over with how much I miss him."

He looks to be holding his breath, his eyes glued to mine, but I can't stop now. "When that happens, what do I do? How do you see it in my eyes and want to be with me? How can you see this love I have for another man and not hold it against me? Who could? I don't think I can stop it, it's just..." I hold one hand to my chest. "It's there, he's in there. I don't know how to hide it. I haven't figured out where to put it all, and I don't want it to hurt you."

Adam dips his hands into the water and brings them up to his hair, scraping it back from his forehead, sighing heavily. And I know I've blown it. It's too much.

I cross my arms over my chest, sinking lower into the tub. Why did I say this out loud? I got suckered in by those eyes.

The immediacy of my reaction to his reaction, the stab of regret in my chest, should be a clue about my feelings for him. This instant sadness when I see that I've lost him. The bathwater feels about ten degrees cooler than it was five seconds ago and I want to get out.

"Please don't let this freak you out," he pinches the bridge of his nose. "I've been wondering if I should even tell you."

"Tell me what?" I stiffen, bracing for whatever he's about to say.

"I know very clearly how much you loved your husband. I saw it with my own eyes. I wrote a song about it. About you."

He's not making any sense. "What?"

He shakes his head.

"I, um... you what?"

"Twenty years ago, at this show in Shreveport, I saw you together. I didn't meet you; I never knew your name until a few weeks ago." He rubs a hand across his eyes. "Something about you... the sight of you made the hair on my arms stand on end. It was magnetic. You were so beautiful; you had this little skirt on. I was so fucking full of myself, I was sure I'd be taking you home with me. But you took a seat on Ronnie's lap and only had eyes for him. You were pure solar energy, this glowing force field of love wrapping around him. Your light - it filled the whole room."

He sighs. "It sure put me in my place." His eyes drift to the side, losing focus as he goes inward to the memory. "I wasn't ready to meet someone like you back then, but you became my... my one day I'll deserve that, I'll have that kind of love, I'll meet a woman like that... woman."

Shocked, I struggle for what to say. "I did remember you were on that show, but—"

"But I didn't become your unattainable ideal of the love you'll chase for years?"

I shake my head apologetically.

"Don't worry about it," he smirks. "I did a lot of searching for a runner up, so there was that to keep me occupied." When I grimace, he says, "Hey, don't put a lot of stock in this. It just seemed like the time to tell you."

I smile weakly, trying to conjure up the picture he described of what Ronnie and I looked like to an observer. We had just found out I was pregnant; we were over the moon in love with each other. One of the happiest years of my life. I don't need to share this part with Adam, but it's good to be reminded of those days.

"What's the song?" I ask.

He waits a beat. "Whiskey On Your Breath."

My mouth falls open. "You wrote *that* about *me*? That's your... that song is..."

"One of my biggest hits? Yep. About a version of you, inspired by an idea of you, yes. So, thank you for never noticing I existed and being totally in love with someone else."

"Do I get half of it?"

He barks out a sharp laugh. "Absolutely not."

Still stunned, I look at him in wonder.

"Talk about him whenever you need to; you don't ever have to hide anything from me. Why would it hurt me if you have love for him? Of course we come to each other with pasts. How many people in your life do you have love for right now? Luke, Ronnie, your family, your friends. Are you all full up, is that what you're saying? There will never, ever be space for anyone else? I would never want you to have less love in your life or take anyone's love away from you. Would you want that for me?"

"Of course not," I say.

"Because you can show me kindness, and I can do the same for you. That's what I want." He shifts in the tub, pressing his legs into mine. "And one more thing. The way you loved, with all of yourself, the devotion," his voice turns ragged, surprising me with its emotion. "I hate the pain of that for you, what it cost you, but don't apologize for it. The way you love is only... it is *only* beautiful."

His arms go back to rest on the edges of the tub, signaling the question has been asked and answered. In all the scenarios I imagined when I voiced this fear to myself, I never pictured this. I pull my arms out of the water, lowering them on top of his.

"Thank you," I say, knowing it's criminally inadequate. My heart has pins and needles, like it was numb with sleep and has been shaken awake. "Tell me something you're afraid of."

"Mmm," he demurs, dipping his chin to his chest.

"Please."

"Aside from what my dick looks like when we get out of here?"

"Come on," I shake his wrists. "One thing. I told you two."

He grimaces, as if forced to make a confession. "This anxiety, your fear - that scares me. I worry that when something big spooks you, you won't talk to me about it. You'll just cut and run. You won't turn to me, you'll turn away. That's how you'll hurt me."

Oh. He really went for it.

"Couldn't you have just said spiders?"

We laugh, but his face shows me his worry, like he's looking ahead to the moment when this happens, anticipating the pain.

"I don't want to do that," I say, meaning it. Part of me wants to apologize in advance.

"I know." He gives me a look of almost pity. Not for himself, I don't think, but for me. Before I can say anything else he pushes himself to his feet. "Come on little bathtub raisin, let's get out of here." He helps me out and wraps me in a towel.

"You have more of that lotion?" he asks. I retrieve it from my suitcase in the bedroom. When I walk back into the bathroom, he has his phone in hand. "My turn to pick the music," he says, pressing play. It's Jimmy Reed, "Caress Me Baby," the volume low.

If I thought I was going to have a minute to think over what we just talked about, or if there was going to be some sort of awkward energy between us or maybe even extra gentleness, I would be wrong. Because with the opening notes, gone is the sensitive, understanding man from the bathtub. Sweet Adam. Joking around Adam. That was not holy water in the tub because this man looks anything but sweet.

This is a wolf licking his lips before he feasts Adam. Focused, undisguised lust Adam. Eyes blazing, candles flickering, he is a gorgeous, virile devil with a filthy smile, a carnal energy most accurately described as (this is from a transcription provided later by my pussy) *I'm about to fucking tear you up and it's going to be the best damn thing that ever happened to you. Baby.*

I have the urge to run, adrenaline and desire spiking my pulse, a shiver down my back at the thrill of running just so he can catch me, but I'm frozen in place in the doorway. He crooks his finger, beckoning me to him, and relieves me of my towel straight away.

Singing in my ear, pulling my body into his and dancing slowly, rolling our hips with the undulating, insinuating rhythm of the music, he eventually backs me up against the sink. He works lotion over my shoulders and arms, his knee rocking slowly to the beat between my thighs, then squeezes and licks and sucks my breasts until I'm panting, before slathering them with lotion, leaving me shiny and slick.

"Turn around." His voice silken, promising delightful reward for obedience, I turn in his arms to face the fogged-up mirror. He holds me against the counter with his hips and gives one of my cheeks a slap. I yelp, the throb between my legs immediate. "You love it," he says, palming my bottom.

Good God, do I.

I swipe a hand across the mirror to clear away some of the condensation and meet his eyes in the reflection. They're hungry and amused.

"Tell me," he says.

"Do it again, cupcake, and I'll let you know." His low chuckle is sinful, and I reach back to grab his hips, locking myself into him. Rewarded with another smack, then another, I grind myself into him.

"Sweet Little Angel" begins, and he squirts more lotion into his hands, working it up and down my back, over my ass, my hips, my legs, pressing the song into my skin note by note. Hypnotized by all the sensations, from the absolute focus of his attention, I lift my hands to clasp them around his neck, arching my back and swaying my hips. I don't know if I've ever felt sexier in my life.

We watch together in the mirror as he slides his hands all the way down my arms, down the curves of my waist and hips, wrapping them around me to caress my breasts. Humming, he moves a hand to my stomach, pressing me into him so that our bodies circle and roll as one with the music.

"My sweet angel," he purrs into my neck.

Opening one of the vanity drawers, he lifts my leg to rest my foot on the edge, holding me across my chest, his hand at the base of my throat. I grip his forearm, leaning into him. When his other hand slides along the inside of my raised thigh and dips between my legs, I let my head fall back onto his shoulder, closing my eyes, lost to my body, to how we're moving together, thrumming with anticipation.

"Eyes on us, baby," he growls.

The sight of us in the mirror is a picture I won't soon forget.

Damp hair, slick skin, the glow of our bodies in the candlelight. "Ohhh..." I breathe raggedly, groaning from the small relief when he dips two fingers inside me.

"Silky warm," he sighs, his cheekbone at my temple.

He's working me slowly, working with the music, one hand back to my breast, teasing the nipple, the other sliding through my folds, all while keeping up a relentless easy roll with his hips into mine. His erection is rock hard against me, prodding, reminding me of more pleasure to come. *Don't forget, you get this too.*

"I need your... aaaahhh—" I rasp, cut off mid-sentence, distracted when he trails kisses down my neck, mouth open, his tongue licking my skin.

"Here?" He pushes his fingers inside me again, pulsing in and out, his eyes locked on mine. Biting at my lip, an involuntary clench of my pussy squeezing his fingers, I reach down with one hand and place it over his, lifting his fingers to my clit.

"Look at us," he whispers to our reflection.

What I see is beautiful. In this moment, we are beautiful. Naked to one another in every possible way, exposed and completely present. Just the two of us. No yesterday or tomorrow, no questions to be asked and answered, no fears. Raw, primal, hard and soft, the essence of him and the essence of me conjoined.

The music changes, more B.B. King, "Three O'Clock Blues," and it makes me feel drunk. I disappear into the song, into my body, into him.

He's all but holding me upright when I come, my spasms jerking through our hands, through my body into his, the walls of the room collapsing around us. The way he feels around me, the strength in his arms, like he'll never let me go, the unintelligible words of praise he moans in my ear, makes my orgasm feel like his. Like my gift to him.

My legs are shaking as he turns me in his arms to kiss me. I'm ready to be led to the bed, collapse onto my back and enjoy a slow fuck like the one this morning. He carries one of the candles to his nightstand and crawls in beside me, but straight away it's clear this devil isn't done with me yet.

He fits himself on top of me, arms around my back, lifting me into an embrace to kiss me deeply, so passionately I'm swooning, which I didn't really think one did lying down. I'm seeing stars, maybe from lack of oxygen, and when he begins to kiss down my body, I'm slow to realize what's happening. He gets to my stomach, lifting himself up and away from me to settle lower down the bed, between my legs, and I understand his intentions. I rise onto my elbows as he kisses the inside of my thigh.

"Adam, honey, I don't think I can come again tonight." I sound like I've run a mile. He chuckles roughly, licking his lips, smiling at me wickedly. He palms my thighs, pressing my legs apart. Just the air, the *air,* touching my flesh makes me shiver. "It's not a challenge; I'm telling you I want your big hard dick."

"Oh, don't worry, *honey,*" he promises, and damn, he doesn't miss a thing, this one. Lowering his head, he looks up my body, eyes avid. "But I'm getting my face in here. And it was absolutely a challenge."

Using both hands, he spreads apart my folds, eyes trained on mine as he takes one long, purposeful lick. I press my lips together, holding his stare, determined to keep my expression neutral. He arches one fiendish eyebrow and licks again, giving my clit a flick, and I bite the inside of my cheek. His fingers holding me open, his pressure increasing with each slow stroke of his tongue, I ball my hands into fists, breathing heavily through my nose.

I'm done for when he burrows his tongue into my pussy. A whimper makes it past my lips, then another one.

"I know, baby," he drawls in a low, soothing purr.

"I think..." My pant is my white flag, my head rolling back on my shoulders.

"Mmm...hmmm."

"I think... oh, God..." I *can't* think with his tongue doing what it's doing. "... ohhh... God... I think you... you convinced me."

When he begins sucking my clit, his lips sealed around it, I fall onto my back, moaning, grabbing for his hair. I come like a creature possessed, some unholy animal rolling through my spine, howling to be set free. Bucking against his face, huffing out sounds that are not human.

He lingers between my trembling thighs, kissing me tenderly all along my delicate bits before helping me over onto my stomach and hitching my hips up off the bed. He runs his hands down my back, around my hips, across my ass. Every nerve ending extra sensitive, I shiver and twitch like he's spreading static electricity across my skin with his touch.

He folds over me, his dick hard and hot against the seam of my bottom. My pussy is throbbing, begging to be filled. "So beautiful," he whispers, kissing along my spine.

I spread my knees further apart, ass lifted in invitation.

"One second, sweetheart" he says, and the bed dips as he leans over to the nightstand. I shift my head to see what he's doing – a millisecond of mildly alarmed curiosity at what he might be reaching for – but he just pulls out a bottle of lube. Straightening himself behind me, he climbs forward, his thighs lining up to mine.

"I'm gonna fuck you hard," he slides a hand, slick with lube, through my folds. "You still with me, baby?"

"Yes," I plead, clutching the sheets. "Please, please fuck me. Fuck me hard."

"Yes ma'am."

He gives it to me in deep, powerful thrusts, all domination, bearing down with his hands clutching my hips, grunting and hissing as he takes me exactly how he wants. "So... God... damned... perfect... baby." He bottoms out with every word, a cry of pleasure from me each time the crown of his cock reaches as far as it can go.

When he starts to really let me have it, the pace relentless, skin slapping skin, I don't know if I can take it, thank God for the lube, and I'm holding on for dear life. But the friction feels amazing, my sex swollen and sensitive, the rasp of skin across skin taking me right up to the edge again. Soon, unbelievably, I'm pushing back against him, begging for more.

"Fuck, don't stop, I'm going to come," I cry.

He slides a hand down my back, between my shoulder blades, pressing me deeper into the bed as he thrusts. I'm at his mercy and the angle is exquisite. I can feel every inch of his shaft sliding through me and I work a hand between my legs to get to that last place I need.

"Give it to me," he growls, driving into me, hard.

"Adam," I cry his name as I fly off the edge. "Oh my God, Adam." My climax rips from my belly up though my back, pulsing around his cock, turning me inside out and knocking any breath I had left out of my body.

"Fuck yes, fuck yes, baby" he moans, "That feels so good." He pulls me into him for more long, hard thrusts. "Yessss... Jesus, fuuuuuck yes." He's growling curses, fingers digging into me when I take the hot streams of his orgasm.

Sinking into an exhausted stupor, it comes to me as I fade out - a thought, a word, something floating across the last flickers of light behind my eyes before the darkness falls. Something I've read about in books maybe? I reach for it.

Ravished. Plundered. Ruined. Fucked to within an inch of my life.

I catch it, hold it in my hands like a lightening bug. The word.

I believe I have just been *claimed*.

I don't know how long it's been when his voice reaches me, dragging me close to the surface of this blissful, deep blue pool of orgasm nirvana.

"Holly."

I'm exactly as I last was, face down, naked. He's draped over me; hairy thigh nestled between mine, breath warm against my back.

"Let's get under the covers."

"Not moving," I mutter, the sound muffled by the duvet under my cheek.

His inhale is heavy, a sound I find so sexy, and he runs a hand sensuously down my back, over the curve of my hip, cupping one side of my bottom. His mouth grazes my shoulder.

Is this affectionate, satisfied afterglow or, *no, is that... surely not...??*

If I was capable of more brain activity I'd be laughing, thinking this man is trying to kill me. I'm going to die impaled on his cock. I'd laugh, wiggle my ass, and go for round three, or ten, or forty – whatever it is. But dear lord, I'm on empty.

With my last ounce of strength, I manage a string of incoherent words something along the lines of, "Sex... coma... no more... fight... another... cowboy." And I slip back into blessed unconsciousness, his throaty chuckle in my ear.

I do feel when he leaves the bed, when something soft and warm drapes over my body. I hear the click of the bathroom door. And from far away I swear I hear whistling.

Sinful, victorious whistling.

CHAPTER FORTY-ONE

HOLLY

"SEXY TEXAS FALLS into your pool, you go away for a weekend road trip, and come back with a boyfriend," Madeline laughs.

It's Monday night. I'm walking through the house with my phone tucked under my chin, arm full of clothes, headed for the laundry room. When Adam and I got here this morning, he went straight out to the studio, and I went right to my laptop. Aside from all the work to catch up on, I needed the time to myself; the weekend has given me a lot to process. There might also have been an ice pack for my hoo-ha.

"He's not my boyfriend."

"You said you agreed to keep seeing each other."

"Yes, but I wouldn't call him my *boyfriend*." The word sounds so strange. "Do you say boyfriend and girlfriend at our age?"

"Why not? Why wouldn't you? I love having boyfriends."

"Well, I'm not his girlfriend." As the words leave my mouth, I wonder what Adam would say, imagining a cocky *wanna bet* look on his face, and there's a little squeal at the back of my head. I swat the girlish reaction away, annoyed with myself.

"Sounds to me like you had a wonderful time."

"I did."

"Maybe too good?" she says gently. "All this armor, it helped you survive, you *needed* it, but you've carried it for so long now I imagine it's very scary to put down. Like taking a cast off and your arm feels super weird at first."

"Your therapy really pays off for me."

"You're welcome."

"He's not what I expected, that's for sure." I concede.

"In what way?"

Walking back down the hall and into my bedroom, I consider how to phrase it.

"I thought he'd be good in bed but, I don't know, maybe bored with it all. Just cool and fun, detached. That's what I wanted," I sigh. "But he's the opposite of detached. He made effort. Lots and lots of effort. Introduced me to his sister, his friends. Talked to me, listened to me, looked out for me. And he's caring. Really caring. Seriously, the man gave me more orgasms in four days than I thought was physically possible. Calls me baby and angel and tells me I'm beautiful. When I was a sure thing! He could've bent me over my kitchen island and been done with me in ten minutes. And I would've been thrilled."

Ooh, I like that idea though. I need to make that happen.

I leave out the 'wrote a song about me twenty years ago' part. Another story for another day.

"The nerve," she says.

"I know, I know, but it's seriously freaking me out."

"Yeah but listen to your bestie. Adam is a gardener, and that is exactly what you need."

"A gardener?"

"In relationships there are flowers and there are gardeners. Ronnie, bless him, he was a flower. You took care of him. You nurtured him. He got to be the artist he wanted to be, a father, build his own little playground out there in the middle of nowhere. You found this beautiful soul and... you gave him a place to bloom." Emotion chokes her voice. "One of the last times we talked, he told me how grateful he was for you, for the life you gave him. He said you saved him. And he told me to look after you, so right now I need to say something that you need to hear. You've been dangerously close to wallowing. I'm sorry—" she senses me about to interrupt. "Let me finish, this is a monologue."

We're both sniffling.

"I'm not saying that getting through this grief isn't hard. It fucking sucks, but that's just it, you need to *keep moving through it*. Not get halfway and stop, say that's it, I'm done. It's too hard, too scary, I'm just letting my life end right here."

"You don't know..." I interject.

"Look at the strength you have! You can do anything. You were *beloved*. You made a family, you were the last thought and last sight on this earth for someone you loved." She takes a deep breath. "Don't look back and forget that; you're this woman now because of it. And you're strong enough to move on."

"Because you said so," I laugh, tearfully.

"Because you know what I'm saying is true. I know you do."

"Thank you, I love you." My heart aches for my friend. She should be someone's beloved; he would be the luckiest man alive.

"Love you too," she says. "Now—"

"That wasn't it?" I snort, wiping at my nose.

"No. Now, see, it's your time to be the flower. Let someone tend to you. And Adam, he's already the center of attention everywhere he goes, so for him, he's looking at the back half of his life and saying, oh shit, I made all these sacrifices for my career and now I'm alone. He's ready to be selfless for someone." I hear her blankets shuffle as she shifts in bed, her voice changing gears. "Don't be cavalier about how rare this is. Maybe he's not the end game, I don't know. Maybe he just gets you through this next part, but I hope you're not afraid to let yourself enjoy this, to enjoy your life. You can handle being a little scared. You had a good time this weekend with him, didn't you?"

It takes me a second to realize I'm allowed to speak. "I had an incredible time, but—"

"But what? I bet you've been running through a long list of 'but what if's' for everything that could go wrong and none for what could go right."

"Now you've made me feel bad."

"Just uncomfortable. Look, live any way you want to - big,

small, alone, in a foursome, that's not the point. The point is to *live*, to make choices. Opting out of life won't protect you from bad things happening. And I can't think of a better way to feel alive than amazing sex with someone you connect with. And *love*, having love in our lives. Otherwise, there's no point to any of this."

CHAPTER FORTY-TWO

ADAM

Friday.

2:20pm

I'm totally not counting that it's been more than one hundred hours since you kissed me. Not me. 😟

2:41pm

Why is this door unlocked? Where are you?

Post office. Are you at my house? You're finished for the day?

Hello???

2:57pm

Studio. Totally didn't rush up to your house to "get guitar strings"

LOCK THE DAMN DOOR

Then how will you get in? 😏

6:19pm

If you were in my bed waiting for me tonight I wouldn't have to worry about it

. . .

I KNOW she's here when my hand touches the doorknob. I can feel her energy, as if her proximity heated the metal, her breathing a hum in the wood of the door.

I take a minute before I go in. Something in my gut settles into place, a deeply satisfying missing piece found, this low-level ache for her I've had all week simultaneously stoked and soothed. She didn't answer my text, but I let it be, enjoying the anticipation, the uncertainty.

This is what I hoped for, that she would miss me. Damn hard, too, giving her the chance to get rattled and cut me loose. But I had to do it. Better to grit it out now. It's been distracting but damn if I don't like the edge - a little worried, a little pissed off, a little horny.

Some fucking brilliant records have been made this way.

Think about it. I bet you can hear it; you know exactly what I'm talking about. *Let me tear some shit up and wail, bang it out on this guitar until I can bang this person I love or I hate or who's driving me crazy/broke my heart/doesn't know I exist/finally told me they loved me.*

You've heard that power. The sex and rage and longing - that pain, that *love*, coming through your speakers. You want to feel it too. Live through it. You wanna fuck to it, dance to it, drive down the highway with the windows down and sing at the top of your lungs to it until the music invades you, possesses you body and soul for those perfect three and a half minutes.

She's here, and I want to throw my head back and shout. Fuck, it's the best feeling.

The room is freezing, which makes crawling under the blankets and taking her warm, pliant curves into my arms an absolute heaven. She sighs, snuggling into me, letting her head fall onto my bicep. I settle myself around her, pressing my nose into her neck. Fig and coconut, earthy and sweet. *My angel*. Made for each other. I'm asleep in minutes.

CHAPTER FORTY-THREE

HOLLY

Adam texted about a quarter to five, asking me to come down to the studio at six. I'm in the kitchen area now, waiting to be invited in.

I'm nervous. I'm telling myself it's excitement - *call it excitement* - but this is truly Ronnie's inner sanctum, and I'm about to be in there repeating another familiar scene from my life with a different man, as if I've simply re-cast the role.

Adam and I slept together in the pool house last night. We haven't had a conversation about it, but I'm aware of how it must feel to him, my house full of mementos and photos. How many photos does one keep on display of their dead spouse? How do I explain his shirts in my closet, his mud boots in the garage? And what would Luke want? I've never asked him.

How does someone new fit it? How do I do this?

On top of this, I keep thinking about Teddy's breathless shrieks when he called to spill the gossip about Chip and Cassie. It makes me wonder if the guys know anything about me and Adam. I'd like to say I don't care, but I loathe the idea they might be gossiping about us. About another studio fling, Adam's bonus piece of ass - although technically, one could argue *he* was *my* bonus piece of ass. I'm not judging anyone; I simply don't want to be in the conversation. I don't want their eyes on us, speculating, trying to figure us out. *We're* still trying to figure us out.

To distract myself I've been relentlessly texting Adam a barrage of song titles from my playlist. I've been particularly good at it this afternoon. He hasn't responded.

Dear Mr. Fantasy. If I Said You Had A Beautiful Body Would You Hold It Against Me

Ain't Too Proud To Beg

Do You Wanna Touch Me. Touch My Body. Get Ur Freak On

Use Me

I Touch Myself. One Hundred Ways

Baby Did A Bad Bad Thing

Moanin'. Levitating

Help Me

Sex On Fire. You Don't Know How It Feels. Feels Like the First Time

WAP. Sweet and Dandy. Honey Molasses. Slippery When Wet

Just Like A Woman

Come And Get Your Love. Lover. The Door Is Always Open

Lover Man

Let's Get It On

Baby, Come To Me. Call On Me

Get A Leg Up

I'm No Angel

Your Good Girl's Gonna Go Bad

I'm Into You. I'll Take Care Of You. I Want To Do Everything For You

Kiss You All Over. Ride Your Pony. Faster & Faster

Mike walks into the kitchen alone, opening the refrigerator, holding his water bottle to the filtered water dispenser.

"What's this surprise?" I ask.

"You'll see."

"Just tell me."

He shakes his head, looking to the door that leads to the studio, then back to me. "He's a great guy," he says confidentially. "I think Ronnie would approve, even if he is a guitar player."

So much for no one knowing about Adam and me.

"How did you... I mean, I don't know what you're talking about," I stammer, dropping my voice to a whisper.

"Right," he coughs. "Guitar strings." He backs away, shoulders up to his ears in an unapologetic shrug, right as Adam barges in.

"You!" Adam barks, striding straight to me. Mike, as if he's just slipped from the grasp of the school principal, shoots me a *you are soooo in trouble* look before he's out of sight.

I let out a yelp, making like I'm gonna run for it.

"Not so fast," Adam snatches my phone. I try to take it back, but he uses his body to push me into the counter, tucking my phone into his back pocket. "Where—" he bats away my hands as I reach around him to grab for it. "Do you—"

"Give it back!" I'm laughing.

"—find the time?" he manages to clamp onto my wrists and lift my hands between us, holding them to his chest. I huff, shaking my head like I'm tossing hair away from my face, which isn't the case. I just needed to huff.

"Hello, sweetheart," he smiles down at me.

"You shouldn't have your phone on while you're working."

"It was on silent. I check it in case you need me." That gets an eye roll. He quirks his mouth and leans in close. "You know I'm going to have to punish you for all that distraction, don't you?"

My heart thumps, my vagina thumps. "I should hope so. I went to a lot of trouble."

"Trouble," he murmurs, kissing me softly. "You are beautiful trouble."

"I like this beard." He hasn't shaved all week.

"I believe you'll like this surprise. Ready?" I hesitate, pulling our hands from his chest to mine. "What?" he asks, squeezing my fingers.

"I think they all know about us."

"Just try to keep your hands off me, and it'll be fine." So smug. He pulls me away from the counter, leading me to the door. "Come on, keeping them waiting while we're alone out here isn't helping. Besides, we're the least interesting gossip out here right now anyway."

Telling myself to be cool, shoulders back, I walk in ahead of him, into the seating area. There are four rolling office chairs lined up at a counter overlooking the recording console, a glass partition dividing us from the band. Mike is in his usual spot at the board.

In the open recording area on the other side of the glass, the floor is layered with rugs, the left side of the room subdivided into four vocal booths. The drummer and base player, I can't remember their names, along with Rob, the guitar player, are clustered in the big open space, all wearing headphones. Chip is in one of the vocal booths and to my surprise I see Cassie in the one beside him, her fiddle held upright against her chest.

Adam hops down the three steps to join Mike at the board, and I take a seat at the counter. He pushes a button to talk to the band. "Say hello to Holly." Their voices come through the speakers in greeting, and I wave my hands in return.

Grabbing his guitar from a nearby stand, he sits with it across one knee, turning his head to look up at me, grinning. He doesn't wear headphones, which isn't unusual. He wants to hear the full sound through the big speakers in here, not the mix the band has in their headphones.

He turns back to Mike. "All set?"

Mike nods and presses the talk button. "We're rolling, count us in Chip."

Cassie brings her fiddle to her chin as Chip's smooth voice fills the room. "Alright y'all... a one, two... one, two, three, four."

I know it within four measures, hands to my mouth, aghast. Adam and Mike are smiling broadly, knowing they've pulled off this epic surprise, but neither of them is looking at me. Mike makes small adjustments to the board, scribbles in the notebook at his elbow. Adam is curved over his guitar, bending notes to dance above the rhythm section, his head going up and down with the beat, eyes moving between his hands and through the window to the band.

It's "Cry, Cry, Cry," the song I suggested to him weeks ago. Something I'd forgotten about, something we never discussed again. They're playing it now, recording it in front of me. The arrangement is wonderful, beginning with a slow, swaying groove, Cassie's fiddle wailing, weaving around Adam's riffs and Chip's voice.

And Chip's voice, it's more than I imagined. His range and control, the swagger and pain. He's incredible. I know my smile is splitting my face in half, I'm delirious. When the band makes a tempo change halfway through the song, shifting into some Hendrix at Woodstock crossed with country rock magic, I stand, banging my fists on the counter. Chip digs in, singing through the glass right at Cassie. She returns his stare, daggers and defiance, before closing her eyes to saw at her fiddle. It's intense and private. I look away, back to Adam below me.

Everyone's making their way through something.

The song is a wish for romantic justice. *I want to see you suffer because you made me suffer.* And here I am in Ronnie's most sacred space, his smiling face watching from dozens of photos on the walls, my new lover presenting this gift at my feet. I'm standing at the highest point in the room, observing this musical cooperation between complex, individual talents, the moment of creation of one small work of art, and I'm suddenly filled with compassion for him. Moments like this are what he lived for. When the musicians and the song, all the parts, the stars, aligned to become something more. Something magic. I close my eyes and listen.

I sing the words in my head, but I don't feel them, not for Ronnie, not in this moment. I feel love, not retaliation. I open my eyes and look at one of the photos on the wall. That face I will always love. I smile back at him, tears glistening, half expecting him to give me a wink like he loved to do.

Joy. It finds me. Pours through me with every note, fills me with an immediate hunger for more like a drug. *More, more, more*, it thrums. *More joy, don't wait.*

At the last note I raise my arms in the air, celebrating, my cheeks burning. They all know how great it sounds; they don't need me to tell them.

"You guys, unbelievable!" I exclaim, rushing down the steps to the board. Adam stands, shifting his guitar right before I throw my arms around him, planting a big wet smack of a kiss on his lips. I don't care one bit right now who knows about us. Shocked, he recovers quickly, wrapping an arm around my waist. His face is fierce, full of pride. When he kisses me back the band all cheers.

Well, in my head they cheer, like in a movie, but really, they don't care all that much. That's the truth of these things. They're focused on another take of the song, what's for dinner, and whatever person is rattling the chains of their own hearts.

I retreat to my perch at the counter, settling in for the night. I wish I had my phone back, because I need to text Madeline. I want to let her know that yes, I believe I do have a boyfriend.

. . .

ADAM and I walk through the dark up to my house, hand in hand, well after midnight.

After we come through the gate, he leads us towards the pool house. I tug at his hand, pulling him to a stop. "Let's go to my room tonight."

A grimace crosses his face like headlights from a car, there and gone in a flash.

"Please. My back's a little tweaked from yard work this morning." He puts his hand in the small of my back. "It's fine. It's just been a long day. I'm tired and I want to sleep in my own bed. With you."

"Come into mine. I'll give you a massage," he offers.

I place a hand on his chest and study his face, the lines of fatigue around his mouth, around his eyes. He's exhausted, and I speak gently. "My house is not haunted. I replaced the mattress, the sheets, pillows, years ago. I'm the only person who's ever slept in that bed, it's all mine. I want you to be the first man to share it with me." I kiss him, holding my lips to his for several seconds. "Please."

His exhale is long before he nods, once. "Let me take a quick shower and I'll come over."

I kiss him again. "Let yourself in and lock up, then come on back to my room."

When I'm inside, I take the photo of Ronnie from my dresser and stuff it in my sock drawer then do a hasty wash up in the bathroom, slipping into a short slip of a nightgown and spritzing on perfume. I'm closing the curtains when Adam comes in, hair wet, in jeans and a clean tee, his kit bag tucked under one arm.

"Hi," he says, looking around the room. He looks nervous, which makes me nervous. "This is nice."

"Thank you," I reply, giving an odd little laugh.

Crossing to me, he caresses my hip through the silk of my nightgown. "So is this," he murmurs. "This is very nice."

These silly nerves make me laugh again, a gurgled sort of choking sound. Very sexy. I don't need to be this nervous.

This is perfectly normal. This is all normal, normal, normal. My house, my room, my bed.

"Bathroom's right there if you want to put your bag in there." When he leaves the room I have a moment of panic, unsure of what to do with myself. Stand here, and what, pose? Get in the bed? Run to the kitchen and make a tray of snacks?

"Is this what I think it is? Or should I say *who* it is?" Adam's voice calls, walking back into the bedroom holding my favorite purple, curved in the shape of a question mark, vibrator. "Could this be the infamous General?"

It was charging on the counter, and I hadn't thought about it. At least that annoyingly delighted smirk on his face is better than nerves, I guess. The tension has been broken.

"Whoops. I'll take that." I reach for it, but he steps away.

"No way. I seem to recall you wished to have this," he runs one finger along the curved edge, a fully indecent gleam in his eye. "Make you come while I watched."

Does he have no shame? "I don't recall any such thing."

"It's not the kind of thing a man easily forgets. And I think you absolutely do recall."

I level him with a glare, trying not to smile. I will not smile. "That's not very gentlemanly."

"Oh, pardon me... you want a gentleman in your bed now, do you?" And dammit, I do smile. "Didn't think so."

He fiddles with it until it starts to vibrate, then presses a finger onto the open bit, feeling the suction. His eyebrows raise in unison. "Whoa, that must feel amazing."

My pulse is fluttering, rapid wings knocking inside my chest.

"You know, something does come back to me now that you mention it. What was it?" I light the candle on my bedside table and blow out the match. "Oh yeah, your 'red-blooded Texas rockstar dick.' That's certainly a mouthful." I lift my eyes to his, grinning at the accidental double entendre. The exchange of humor and desire, the combination of the two, this energy between us sparks and snaps. "I'm much more interested in that tonight."

"What was that?" he asks, raising his voice like he's trying to talk to me in a noisy bar. "You'll have to speak up!" He presses a button and the buzzing changes from a steady one speed to a series of short, staccato bursts. "Oh, I see," he pushes the button again and the buzzing changes to a different pattern. "Which is your favorite?"

"Alright," I laugh, walking to him, "You've seen plenty of vibrators before."

"Not one that looks like it's from a space movie."

He manages to turn it off and I hold out my hand, which he ignores, so I open and close my fingers, gesturing for him to give it to me.

"Show me," he says, his voice a rough timbre that cuts right through me.

"What? No, that's... I can't do that." I wave him off and retreat a step away.

"Have you ever let any other man watch you before?" he closes the gap between us. I shake my head. Ronnie was no prude, but it's just something that we never did. We used a vibrator together sometimes, sure, but he never just *watched*.

"Holly. *Show me.* I want to know everything that gives you pleasure, all the ways you like it."

"I don't think you want a competition with The General," I tease, my mouth dry but my good time girl pussy ready to go.

"He and I are on the same team." He pulls me into his arms, kissing me deeply, kissing me again and again until my body is one live wire of need from head to toe. If my boobs are his undoing, his kisses are mine.

He whispers in my ear, "This was your fantasy. I'm here, so show me."

I step out of his embrace, reaching for the glass of water on my nightstand, taking my time with a few long drinks. I take my lube out of the drawer. Looking over my shoulder I fix my eyes to his. His expression is avid, every part of his body alert to mine, and I feel suddenly powerful.

He asked for it.

Keeping my eyes on his, I climb onto the bed, settling myself against the pillows. I hold out my hand, and he lifts one knee onto the mattress, leaning over to give me the vibrator. While I dot it with lube, he lets his hand linger over my breast, circling my nipple through my nightgown as it grows taught and defined under his touch. I slide lower and spread my legs, lightly stroking myself, rubbing the flexible, flared end along my folds. My hands know what to do, my body knows what to do, and I sink into all the familiar sensations.

"Have you ever done this and thought about me?" Adam caresses the inside of my thigh, his fingers warm against my skin.

"Yes," I whisper, dragging the wand back and forth across my clit with every up and down stroke, taking my time as he watches.

When I'm ready, I slide the longer end inside, exhaling a soft hum of pleasure. I move it in and out, gently at first, then harder, going deeper to press the tip of the curved shaft into just the spot I want. It's a marvel how unselfconscious I am, how quickly I've been able to trust him like this.

"Your pussy is perfect, angel, so perfect," he praises me softly, the scruff of his beard grazing my neck. I shiver as he kisses my throat, my jaw, his greedy lips seeking mine.

He moves his hand to where the hem of my nightgown is gathered on my stomach, feeling his way underneath the fabric until he's cupping one breast. His mouth, his hand, his clothing against my bare skin – every touch turning up high voltage wires connected to my center. I press the button of the vibrator until it buzzes to life and gasp into his mouth, my hips rocking into the suction. I do exactly what I'd do if I were alone, grinding myself into The General, sighing and moaning as I enjoy the ride.

He lifts himself away from me to stand at the foot of the bed, hands clenched into fists at his sides, brown eyes burning. His desire makes me feel beautiful and uninhibited. Throbbing tension building between my legs, I pull my knees further apart.

"Do you get hard for me, Adam? Do you want to fuck me?"

"Got news for you baby; I *am* gonna fuck you."

"Let me look at you." I'm breathing harder now, voice husky. Moving the suction of the vibrator side to side across the swollen nub of my clit, the contact is intermittent, holding me back from the point of no return.

He grabs his tee shirt at the back of his neck, pulling it over his head, dropping it to the floor. Off go his jeans and briefs, the lean and darkly handsome devil before me once again, feet planted apart, erection in hand. Every time I see him naked it's the same whole-body reaction of pulse and heat and vibration. It's coded on a cellular level. *Gimme. Gimme. Gimme.*

Spitting in his hand, he begins to slowly stroke himself. Watching him work his cock, staring at my body hungrily, sets a match to the very short fuse inside me. I close my eyes, giving over to the exquisite, rising tension in my body.

"Fuck yes, baby, get after it." His voice is fierce, strained.

"I'm there..." I cry, spasms taking me in waves of release. I press my face into a pillow and ride it out.

When I've come down enough to look at him his eyes are on my sex, his hand sliding up and down his length aggressively. I'm lying there, legs wide open for him, and something almost wild crosses his features. I watch him fuck his fist until he lets out a sharp grunt, shoulders hunching forward. I toss the vibrator aside and hold out my hand to him.

His name is all I say. He's on the bed in a flash, crawling up my body.

"Can I have you, Holly?" he rasps.

"Yes." I dig my hands into his hair. His hips settle between my thighs, and gripping himself, he lines up the head of his cock. That thrilling code thrums inside me again, that greedy *gimme, gimme, gimme.* I lift my legs around him.

"Are you mine?" he's nearly growling.

"Yes." The word is barely past my lips and he's inside me, panting, groaning words of praise over and over, but they're lost to my own sounds of pleasure as he completely, *reverently* rails me.

There is one word I can make out in his breathless declarations, one word that lifts high above all the other unintelligible ones to sing to me in a single clear note before settling itself onto the ceiling. The ceiling I stared at for hours while Adam slept soundly at my side.

Love.

He said the word love.

CHAPTER FORTY-FOUR

HOLLY

THE NEXT WEEKS pass in a wonderful, heady blur, until the guys in the band peeled away, leaving Chip alone to finish recording. Well, Chip and Cassie, because she's adding backing vocals to several tracks. I asked Adam about it late one night when he came in to find me awake, reading in his bed. "What's the deal there, you think?"

"No one's fucking business is the deal there," he grumbled, stripping off his t-shirt and tossing it onto the dresser.

"I was just curious. I know her mom," I offered by way of explanation. It's sort of true. I know someone who knows her mom.

Pulling off his jeans and briefs, sliding into bed naked, he said, "That's a heartache head-on collision, those two."

"Ooohh, what a good song title - 'heartache head-on collision.'"

"Baby, they just keep on comin'," he drawled, wrapping himself around me with a yawn, falling asleep in seconds with his head on my chest.

We fell into an easy, affectionate rhythm; he did his work, I did my work. I went to yoga, saw my friends, ran my errands; one weekend he went to Shreveport to check on his mom. And all the while, almost every minute with the man is foreplay. Scrambling eggs, washing dishes, driving to a restaurant, picking out a movie, brushing our teeth. A caress, a laugh, a look, a sexy text. All foreplay.

We slept together most nights, but not all, finding excuses to be apart, like it was something we should do. Like eating more vegetables and checking our blood pressure. He was supposed to leave for Los Angeles for mixing, but decided to book for two more weeks and do the job with Mike since we didn't have anyone else coming in until mid-December.

Now here we are, all his work for the record that can be done at Riverside complete.

I'm flying out Wednesday to spend Thanksgiving with my parents in North Carolina. He leaves for Dallas the same day. We haven't talked about anything that happens between us after the holiday. Or, more significantly, that other little thing.

What was it? That other thing?

Oh yeah. The night he said he loved me.

This past weekend was basically a repeat of our first weekend together, fucking each other senseless, lingering in bed for hours, soaking in my bathtub. It's been a spell in some ways, these weeks, conjuring the idea of what a life together might be like. It's tempting and dreamy. And terrifying. Feelings of contentment pushing against ones of anxiety.

Nine weeks ago I was alone. Now here I am with this meteor of a man who crashed into my world. It feels that out of the blue. Random and rare and ground shifting.

I'm at my kitchen island Monday morning, laptop in front of me but unable to focus, when Adam comes into the house, freshly showered after his workout, carrying his iPad.

"You smell delectable," I grin up at him as he leans down for a soft, lingering kiss.

Hand on my shoulder, taking a seat beside me, he says, "Are you working, or can we talk?" *Oh, God, here we go.*

Closing my laptop, I nod my head, unable to speak because I'm trying to take deep breaths through my nose without it being obvious, like I'm diffusing a bomb and don't dare to even blink.

He squeezes my shoulder. "You alright?"

"Um-hum." I'm thinking of suggesting we go for a run, but, like Teddy, I don't run. Maybe clean the oven? Play cards?

One hand still resting on my shoulder, he looks to his iPad on the counter and covers it with his other hand, gathering his thoughts. "I think we have to talk about the big thing we've been ignoring." I feel every one of his fingers as if I'm all soft clay, his touch sinking deeply into my flesh. This is it. *The talk.*

Reflexively, I flinch against him. Frowning, he looks first at the place where I tried to shrug him off, then to my eyes.

"We don't have to..." I stammer. "I know you didn't mean to, and I don't know if I'm..." I trail off, withering under his intense expression.

"I didn't mean to *what*, exactly?" His eyes remain leveled on me, a crease pinched between them. "You don't what? What are you talking about?"

"What are *you* talking about?"

He drums his fingers on his iPad, and I feel like a suspect about to be interrogated. Withdrawing his hand from my shoulder, he rubs the back of his neck, staring across the kitchen.

As unnerving as the prospect of having this conversation with him is, when I've no idea how to handle it yet, I do know I don't want to hurt him. Even if we're not on the same page. Even if it's going to make me throw up. I reach over and take his hand. "Let's talk about whatever you want to talk about."

He sighs, bringing my hand to his mouth for a kiss. Then, rapping once on the counter, like he's calling a meeting to order, he jumps in.

"We haven't talked about what it looks like to keep seeing each other now that Chip's record is done, when I don't have a job keeping me in Lafayette."

"Oh." We're not talking about the L word.

"Could you see yourself spending some time in New Orleans with me?"

This does make me smile, despite my guardedness. Tension melts a little off his body, his shoulders dropping a fraction. "I would like that, yes. Maybe on the weekends."

"I'd want to see you more than that. And I have gigs on a few upcoming weekends."

"You can still come to Lafayette, can't you?"

"I can." He says it like he's agreeing to a root canal.

"Oh my God, you're still freaked out in my house, aren't you?" And I know, I hear it. I'm a total hypocrite, calling him out like this.

"I'm working on it," he mutters. I arch one eyebrow, crossing my arms over my chest, ready to wait him out, but his face softens into a broad, sweet smile. "I'll do better," he kisses my forehead. "But it's more than that. After the holidays I'll go back into my usual touring schedule, which means a lot of weeks away, so when I'm home, I'd like to be in *my* home. With you. I don't want another situation where it's the same old slow, resentful drift apart. Not this time."

"Adam, I'm not those other women. I know this business, I know what it demands, and I don't need from you what they did. I don't need a baby or a ring. I have a full life that I love, a place that keeps me busy, so I don't have to be pining for you while you're out of town."

He twists his mouth to one side. "A little pining wouldn't kill you."

"I can do that. I can pine." I run my hand up his thigh until my fingers reach the zipper of his jeans. "You like your house; I like my house. We're both going to have to give a little."

He moves my hand from his crotch back down to his knee, laughing when I reach for his zipper with my other hand. He moves this one too, pulling both my hands up to the countertop, then grabs his iPad, tapping away until his calendar fills the screen.

"Would you ever want to come with me? We've got Scottsdale and Tucson this weekend," he points to the first weekend in December. "Then the Franklin the following Saturday. We could make that a road trip, spend the weekend in Nashville if you wanted."

"You'd want me to come?" I ask, looking at his screen.

"Yes, I do."

"I can't in December, sorry. I have too much work to finish to make Luke's tuition payment, and he'll be coming home, but thank you."

He frowns, swiping at the screen, shifting the calendar view to next year. "Okay, let's start looking at these dates. Plus there's Australia and New Zealand in the spring."

"Australia? How would I... how would that work? I'd have to figure out flights, and I don't even know if my passport is still valid."

He waves his hand as if this is nothing, reaching in his pocket for his phone. "My guy will take care of it."

"Your guy?"

"Benny," he says, texting away. "Road manager. The cuddly little pit bull that makes everything in the Adam Sexton world function. Him and Gretchen, I should say. You'll love him, and he'll be available to you now too."

"Did you just refer to yourself in the third person?" I hear my phone ding and pick it up. He has shared Benny's number with me.

He looks up, blankly, in full checklist mode. "What?"

"Never mind. What does that mean, *available to me*?"

He types a few more seconds then puts his phone down on the counter. "It means not worrying about my girlfriend when I'm halfway across the country or on the other side of the world. It gives me some peace of mind and maybe it will for you too, that you can get in touch with me, or those closest to me, whenever you want. You have full access. Anything you need, if you can't reach me for some reason, you call Benny. Or Gretchen."

I frown, chewing the inside of my cheek. Some soft-focus filter is slipping away, reality becoming visible.

"I know," he says, tugging me from the stool until I'm standing between his legs. "My life is scheduled out far in advance, but it would be wonderful to have you with me."

"I'll think about it, thank you. But..." I hesitate.

"But what?"

"You want me to come with you when you're out of town,

and when you're here, you want to be at your place in New Orleans. How is that not the same old situation you just said you don't want anymore? Because it sounds like me being manhandled straight into your life while you stay exactly the same."

His hands smooth over my hips, down to my backside. "Is this because I called you my girlfriend?" His voice is teasing but I see the wariness in his eyes.

I look down at the feather tattoo on his forearm, tracing it with my finger, one of my new favorite pastimes. I find it soothing. The intricate design, the warmth of his skin, this small intimacy akin to walking a familiar meditation path. "What's that mean to you, aside from the already agreed to pining?"

"It means we don't see other people. I give you my word," he squeezes my butt and I look back to his face. "I'm yours, Holly, and I want you to be mine. I want to build something with you, to work through whatever it takes to have you in my life. You make me so damn happy; I'm getting more wrinkled every day from all the smiling."

I bring one hand to his face, cupping his cheek. "You sure that's not from scowling?"

My evasive answer hangs between us. He watches me for several long seconds, and I feel every one of them in my pulse.

"Have you been happy?" he asks.

"Yes." He leans in to kiss me, but I shake my head. "Wait—" His eyebrows scrunch together in confusion as he pulls his face away from mine. I take a breath. "I want to make sure—" I begin, then falter. "I want to make sure this is still a conversation, not a list of directives to me. That you don't see this as just me coming around, of *me* changing. What are you willing to change, to meet me where I am? To fit into my life?"

He goes tense in my arms, defensive, and a quick shot of dread pierces my heart. I can practically hear his teeth grinding. I study his tattoo again, and he rests his forehead against mine as I trace the design.

"Baby," he sighs. "It is a conversation. But my schedule is my schedule."

"I get that. But you do have a say in it, when you work, when you don't work. And where you are when you're off, correct? Because I have—" My phone rings, and I see the screen out of the corner of my eye. "It's Luke," I say, glad to step out of his arms, pause this new tension before it escalates.

He nods his understanding and rises, walking over to the sink to look out the window. I press the button to take the call, my eyes on his back.

"Luke, honey, how are you?" I say cheerfully.

"Mom..." Luke's voice is strained and hoarse.

"You okay? You sound a little rough."

"No," he groans. "Something's wrong, mom, it's really bad. My stomach..."

"You've been sick? Is it something you ate, you think?" He doesn't answer; I only hear his heavy breathing, the rustle of fabric, then the sound of retching. "Luke?" Adam has turned to face me, and we exchange a grimace.

"Mom..." I think he's crying. My son is *crying*. Immediately my body shifts into high alert. "It hurts so much. Like I've been stabbed or something... I don't know what's happening..." I put the call on speaker and begin to pace back and forth across the kitchen, staring into my phone, willing myself to see straight through the connection to him.

"Honey, where are your roommates? Is Julien around, or—" I draw a blank on the other boy's name. "The other one," I blurt out. "Can you get one of them to the phone?" Luke groans and a sickly panic invades my chest. "What about Amelia? Does she live nearby?" I'm tapping my forehead, trying to remember any of his other friends.

"No one's here." Pain muffles his voice. "What do I do? Something's really wrong."

I stop in front of the sink, next to Adam, gripping the edge of the counter to tether myself to something solid, willing myself to breathe, my brain to function. He puts a firm hand on my arm. "We should call 9-1-1. Send me his address. Can he get to the door?"

I drop my eyes to his hand, where his skin meets mine, feel the counter under my palms. *That's an odd feeling, the warm and cool.* I stare at his hand, swallowing hard, waiting for the room to stop spinning. Luke makes another sound, a garbled sort of sob, and my gut twists painfully. *No, no, no, no. This cannot be happening.*

"Holly." Adam's voice again. "Give me Luke's address, love. Stay on the line with him, and I'll call for an ambulance." I drag my attention to his face, searching his eyes for anything I can anchor myself to.

"Mom?" Luke's weak voice, that word, hauls me into action. I shake my head to reset myself and pull up Luke's apartment details in my notes app. Adam takes a screen shot of it and stands aside to make the emergency call. He's on his phone giving information to the operator while I talk with Luke, sending soothing words down the line, trying to wrap my arms around him across the miles and make the minutes go by faster.

"Did you take any pills, honey? Drugs from someone? You have to tell me." The idea he could be poisoned is absolute terror.

"No... nothing."

"Alright. If this is just one too many burritos, kiddo," I attempt to joke, not fully disguising the quiver in my voice.

"One huge poop, that what you're saying? This is gas?" The fact he's joking back gives me a small measure of comfort, but I can tell he's struggling, in pain, speaking through gritted teeth. It makes me start to cry. I swipe at the tears; I don't want him to hear them.

"Guess not. No one farts more than you."

"I'm gifted."

"That you are," I say, keeping my tone light. I look to Adam, silently pleading to know if the ambulance is almost there. He nods. "Can you get to the front door? Help is almost there."

"I'll try," Luke says, grunting, breathing heavily. Fabric rustles, presumably he's walking. "I... I don't think..." there's a loud crash, a tumbling cascade of items clattering to the floor, a muffled mix of sounds, then silence.

"Luke!" I call his name urgently. "Luke, are you okay?" Through the phone I hear banging on his door. They're there, help is right there. An image of my son flies into my head, his body crumpled on the floor, helpless. "Luke, honey, can you hear me? Get to the door."

I'm frantic. The banging continues, I can hear voices, far away voices, shouting, and I'm feeling it all inside my head. *Bang, bang, bang.* And in my chest. *Bang, bang, bang.* Adam is barking into his phone. He reaches for me, and I dodge away as if his touch will sever my connection with Luke.

I'm pleading now. "Get up, Luke. Get to the door honey. Can you hear me? It's mom. Get up baby. Luke... Luke!"

He doesn't answer.

CHAPTER FORTY-FIVE

ADAM

For several excruciating minutes it's escalating chaos, with Holly shouting into her phone while the paramedics bang on Luke's door. Her fear rips at my chest, her face ashen as she cries out for her son. She shrugs me off every time I reach for her.

The paramedics finally get inside. We hear their clipped exchange, the static and beep of radio communication, the shuffling sounds of movement. It's hard to make out details. She's grimacing, a deep furrow between her watering eyes, the heel of one hand pressed to her forehead. At last, thank God, we hear him weakly answering questions. This kid is so polite, though I know he's in pain and must be scared. He says thank you again and again, answering with yes ma'am, no ma'am, yes sir, no sir.

"Luke? What's going on?" Holly cries into the phone. "Someone talk to me!"

"Are you mom?" a man's voice comes on the line.

"Yes! I'm Luke's mother. What's happening, please, is he okay?"

"He's conscious and talking, got a cut on his head from the fall. Might have appendicitis here, but we've got him now, we're gonna take real good care of him." Holly looks up at the ceiling and wipes at her eyes as the paramedic tells her the name of the hospital they're bringing Luke to. "I'll give the phone to him for a sec, then we need to get going, alright?"

"Thank you so much," she replies, a small sob choking her voice.

"For what it's worth, he's doing some charm job on my colleague here."

Then it's Luke's voice. "Mom?"

"Luke!" She breathes out his name, and I swear, she would jump through the phone if she could. "Call me when you see a doctor, I don't care what time it is. I'll be there as soon as I can. And I'll call your grandparents - they can get there before I can."

"Okay, I will. They want me to hang up now. I love you."

"I love you too, sugar. Everything's going to be okay."

She stares at her phone, absolutely shell-shocked, her face drained of all color. It's fucking killing me to see her like this. Her panic went off the charts and I feel helpless.

"Let me get you a glass of water," I say.

She looks at me as if she's confused to see me standing in her kitchen. Her eyes are glassy, a sheen of sweat across her top lip. Then she begins to heave, rushing to the sink just in time, her body convulsing. She throws up again and again, enormous sobs causing her to gulp for air.

"Shhh, shhh, shhh…they've got him, it's all okay." I scoop her hair back, running a hand along her back. "Shhh, sweetheart, he's going to be alright."

When she's got nothing left, she runs water from the faucet into her mouth and around the sink, then drops her head onto her arm, slumping over the counter. With my hand on her back, I feel her efforts to slow her breathing. She stands and I try to pull her into my body for a hug, but she resists, swiping one hand across her mouth.

"I need to see how soon I can get to Savannah. If Luke has appendicitis, he's going to need surgery. I have to be there."

I grab her shoulders, bending my knees so we're eye level. "Let's take a minute. Come sit down, drink some water. Luke's going to be fine, you know that right? He's going to be fine."

"Stop," she pushes against my arms, grabbing her phone from the counter. "I need to call my parents. If you want to be helpful, find me a plane ticket please. Or should I call Benny?"

She's not even looking at me. She's already walked away,

punching up a number on her phone. The abruptness of her demeanor is a shock, like I've dropped myself into a cold plunge.

She paces in a circle around the dining table, talking to her parents, and when she does look at me, she holds one hand up in a questioning, impatient gesture. *What are you waiting for?* I take a seat at the island and begin a search for flights.

"What did you find?" she asks when she walks back into the kitchen. No preamble, no filling me in on the conversation with her parents.

"Are they able to go to Savannah?" I ask, choosing to ignore her current state, keeping my voice light.

"Yes, they're driving over now."

"That's good. Some peace of mind for you."

"Flights?" she presses.

I grind my teeth but answer as calmly as I can. "Um, yeah, there's a flight out of Lafayette this afternoon that connects through Atlanta, gets us to Savannah around ten-thirty. That's the earliest possible arrival I could find. I booked a hotel room for the week, close to the hospital."

"Us? Why would you be going?"

I sigh heavily, suddenly tired as fuck. "Because you're worried sick and you shouldn't be traveling alone. I thought you might appreciate the support. I would."

"You think the first time Luke meets you should be in his hospital room? That I'll waltz in and announce, by the way, here's the guy I'm seeing. No."

Now I'm mad. "I'm a little more than 'some guy' you're seeing."

"This isn't about you, Adam. This is about my son, and I just need to get there."

"Jesus, Holly, I know it's not about me." My voice is hard, louder than I intended, and she blinks, jerking her head back. I start again. "I'm only asking to help you. Don't shut me out. I know you've been carrying everything on your shoulders for a long time, but I'm right here. You can lean on me, let me be here for you."

"I need to stop what I'm doing, *right now*..." her voice is rising, her eyes shining coldly. "When I just heard my son, my only child, lose consciousness, with no idea what was happening, if he was even *alive*... while I can do nothing, *nothing*, and now he's in a hospital, hundreds of miles from home, alone, and I need to stop and check in with *your* feelings? Give you some recognition for being my boyfriend? Are you telling me to calm down and make you feel better about us?"

What the fuck is she talking about? "You know that's not what I'm saying."

"Can't you see how this would feel to me?" She's crying again, and I'm stabbed in the heart. I don't understand what's happening, I don't know why we're fighting. Her phone rings. "Please," she pleads, raising it to her ear.

"Yep, got it."

The phone keeps ringing while she looks at me, really looks at me for the first time since this whole thing started. I think she'll say more but after a few heavy heartbeats she begins backing away from me.

"I'm going to take a quick shower and pack a bag. You should head on home." She accepts the call, turning and walking down the hallway.

The worst part of me reacts first, a voice in my head saying *fuck this, fuck all of this.* I feel like an ass, not even sure why, and yeah, I'm stung, but I'm not leaving, not letting her push me away. I'm sitting in the kitchen when she comes back into the room an hour later.

"Adam," she says, surprised to see me. Her eyes are red and swollen.

"I'm driving you to the airport," I declare firmly, no room for discussion in my tone. She doesn't object when I reach for her suitcase. "Is this everything?"

"I just need to pack my laptop and some work things."

"I'll wait for you outside. Take your time."

She's on the phone during the drive with the hospital admitting desk and again with Luke. He does have appendicitis, but it hasn't ruptured so he'll have surgery first thing tomorrow, and she'll be there.

At the curbside drop off, I get out to retrieve her bag and she kisses my cheek. "Thank you," she says, looking at my face but not really into my eyes. "I mean it, thank you."

I wish I knew what was going on. Should I be apologizing for something?

"Please let me know when you get there, and keep me updated, okay?" That's all I say.

"I will," she nods.

I watch her walk into the airport, pulling her suitcase behind her. There's no last look over her shoulder, no turning back to wave. When the double doors close behind her, I climb back into my car, a cold lead weight sinking into the pit of my stomach.

CHAPTER FORTY-SIX

HOLLY

I hate hospitals.

The smells, the lighting, the slow elevators. The squeak of my shoes as I rush-walk through the endless maze of corridors. The accidental encroachment into the heartache of strangers, arms around one another waiting for news, or the agony of a lone soul sobbing outside a doorway while someone else rushes by with flowers and balloons, their loved ones safe and celebrated. The random cruelty of this life, of who lives and who dies.

When I finally get eyes on Luke, my arms around him, this terrified animal that's had my heart clenched in its jaws relaxes just a little. He has an ugly cut above his eye that's been stitched up, but he's comfortable and sleepy. My mom tells me they've given him something for his pain.

Where can I sign up for that?

Despite some sparse patches of stubble along his jaw line, to me he looks about twelve years old, and I'm flooded with tenderness. I kiss his cheek, stroking his forehead while he falls asleep, silently thanking every known entity in the universe for him. After speaking to his nurse and then a short catch up with my parents, they head for their hotel, and I settle onto the small, hard sofa under the window.

This, I could've done without, I say silently to Ronnie. *I know you're watching out for him, but don't get distracted on me now, please; please keep him safe.* A tear escapes the corner of my eye, rolling down my cheek, into my ear. *He'll be fine. I know, you're right. He's going to be fine.*

I hug myself under the thin hospital blanket and when I do,

it's Adam that comes to me. Not his voice, but his touch, my body seemingly imprinted with him now.

"Sorry," I whisper to the ceiling, not sure if the apology is for Ronnie or for Adam.

That didn't go so well today. I know I did the right thing by not bringing him here, but I also know I didn't handle it kindly. I can hardly even remember what I said. I was out of my body, something in me split apart, terror shaking me like a rag doll. I let my guard down, and Luke's call was a mean right hook to the head, a nasty wakeup call. With the adrenaline of the day fading, I feel the damage, the shrapnel of my reaction floating in my veins.

The more Adam tried to help the more it hurt. His concern was painful, and it made me angry. I just wanted to get away from it. I feel it, the disconnect, and it's so fucked up, I'm ashamed of myself. What the hell is wrong with me?

Yet, here I am, my body now calling to him for comfort. My head is saying *slow down, is this really what you want? You really want to walk right out into the open again like that? This scare is a reminder about life, how fast it will take from you, crush you. You won't survive.* But my body wants him to hold me. Take me into his solid, strong arms until I feel solid and strong.

My heart? Well, I don't know about my heart.

My phone rings and when I look at the screen, of course, it's Adam. I slip out of the room to take his call before I can talk myself out of it.

"Hey," he says softly. "How's Luke?"

"Good, sleeping. He was floating on a cloud of drugs when I got here." I slump against the wall, my chest churning as if I'm fighting off a rush of acid reflux. I push the fingers of one hand into my sternum, hard.

"Good." His breath is heavy. It sounds like he's rolling over, and I wonder if he's in bed. I picture white sheets tangled across his torso, sleepy eyes, messy hair.

I have no idea how to sort through all this tonight, much less what to say to him.

We speak at the same time. "I should—" I blurt out, while he says, "Holly, are you—"

Then there's silence between us, a silence heavy with nerves and questions, with unease and vulnerability. The threads of our connection delicate and untested.

"Will you let me know when he's back from surgery, and if you need anything?" he finally says.

"I will."

"You promise?"

And I can't. For some reason, those words just won't come out of my mouth. My head is taking charge of my frightened, indecisive heart.

"Thank you again. For everything. You're a..." my voice breaks and I rap the heel of my hand onto my forehead. I don't know what to do. Every option seems painful. "You're a really special person, Adam Sexton. A good man. I'm glad I met you."

CHAPTER FORTY-SEVEN

WHAT THE FUCK WAS THAT?

You're a special person? I'm glad I met you?

I knew this emergency with Luke freaked her out, but I thought when she saw him, saw that he was okay, she would be okay, too.

I knew, *I knew,* Holly's instinct would be to pull away when something scared her, but I hoped she had let me in enough to trust me. That she would want to reach for me. It's all I want, to reach for her. A real partnership, where we reach for each other.

But that - that wasn't it. That's what you say to someone right before you say *it's me, not you.*

Fuck.

CHAPTER FORTY-EIGHT

HOLLY

"THAT'S NOT what I'm saying," I whisper into my phone, closing the bathroom door behind me. Luke fell asleep on the sofa while we were watching a movie, and I came into my bedroom to call Adam. I've moved into the bathroom to put as many doors between us as possible.

"I hear exactly what you're saying," Adam's voice is low and hard. I've been slow to answer his texts over the past few weeks. We've barely been able to talk on the phone, and I understand he's frustrated. I've kept him at a distance while I tended to Luke in the hospital and since I've brought him home.

"I don't think you do." I drop onto the closed lid of the toilet. We've had a version of this conversation for days. It's four days before Christmas, and he's on his way to Dallas. He asked to stop here on the way, but I said no. This he did not like.

The hum of the road is the only reply I get. I wait for him to speak, imagining the luxurious all black interior of his car, the glow of the dashboard, his hands on the steering wheel. I take a deep breath, knowing just what he'd smell like. Knowing that if I was in the seat beside him, he'd reach for me.

This is miserable, these competing instincts I'm wrestling with - to push him away while at the same time craving, absolutely craving his touch.

"Hello?" I say when he doesn't talk, thinking the connection has been lost.

"I'm here."

"I'm asking you to give me a minute. This—" I wave a hand in the air as if he's in front of me. "This, *you*, happened so fast, and then this thing with Luke... can't you hear what I'm telling you? I'm overwhelmed. I just need a minute."

"To figure out how you feel about me."

I school my words into a measured, patient reply. "I need to figure out what I'm feeling, and how those feelings work with my life. And right now, Luke is my priority. He just is." My voice begins to tremble, dammit. I can't hold onto any control with him. "I wish I could ask for this without hurting you, I really do. Hurting you is the last thing I want to do. But I'm asking you anyway. Please, please hear me. Can you give me a little bit of room to sort this all out for myself? Please, Adam. We've known each other, what, three months? I don't think I'm being unreasonable; I'm... trying..." my words catch on a sob.

"Shhh, baby, don't cry," he says. "Please don't cry."

I stand to grab a tissue from the box on the counter, wiping at my nose. My reflection in the mirror is ghastly. There's no trace of the flushed, wanton woman who fucks her boyfriend in his bathroom. This woman in the mirror is the middle-aged mom who hasn't washed her hair in days, wearing a stained sweatshirt over flannel pajamas.

"I understand if it's too hard for you to wait. If you want to end this right now, I'll understand." I squeeze my eyes shut at the thought.

"That's not what I want. You know that."

"It's not what I want, either, but I have to do this at my pace, not yours. I'm sorry, but I don't know what else to do. We keep going round and round and... it doesn't feel like you're really hearing me." I grab another tissue and dab at my eyes.

"Okay." His response is clipped, resigned.

"Okay?"

He sighs a heavy exhale. "I understand what you're saying. I hear you." I clamp my lips shut before I blurt out something stupid. "And you don't need to apologize. You've got to do this your way, I know."

"I know you don't like it but thank you."

"No, but I like you, so... no more tears, okay sweetheart?" We stay on the line, not knowing what else to say, not wanting to let go. "Holly, I'll do whatever you want. Just don't shut me out completely, please."

"I wish it didn't feel like that to you. I'm just asking to catch my breath."

"Yep, I got it." He's affectionate as we say our goodbyes, but that last exchange leaves me unsettled. Because I know, deep down, what he knows, what he's trying to pin me down to admit. I'm very close to cutting him loose.

A text comes through a little before three in the morning.

ADAM:

You awake?

I don't answer, weary of more back and forth, more trying to explain something I don't fully understand myself, but also afraid he might have decided to move first and break this off.

Another text comes through, a song, "The Shape of a Storm" by Damien Jurado.

I listen to it over and over. Searching for a message, for meaning in the words, for our fate, until it's Adam's voice I hear, singing straight into my heart. By the time I fall asleep, I haven't worked out if I should feel caressed and seen, reassured, or utterly, bitterly defeated.

AFTER CHRISTMAS, Luke is feeling good. Anxious to get back to his life at school. As for me, let's just say I'm a little rough.

We watch movies, and I cook. He naps, and I clean up or work at the dining table. But I'm not sleeping. At night, alone in my room, Adam is all I think about. I try to read, but I find myself just staring at the page. I've tried soaking in the tub. I think of him, in his huge tub. With me. Or worse, with someone new. That made me angry, and we had a fight about it in my head.

I've refolded all the t-shirts in my closet, cleaned out the drawers in my bathroom. I've ordered lip gloss and pretty bras from ads on Instagram. I've looked up more songs with love in the title for my book. *That* feels fantastic, let me tell you.

One thing I haven't done? I've not turned to The General. Shocker… I'm not in the mood. I finally had to put him under the sink because he just kept glaring.

Another thing I haven't done is talk to Adam. He's been true to his word and given me space. I texted him Christmas morning, and we had a quick, sweet exchange.

All this to say that Luke and I were more than ready to get out of the house, and we found ourselves at Mike and Jackie's for some Sunday gumbo and football. Poppy, the oldest at five, offers Luke her special Paw Patrol Band-Aids, and Grace, three, drags her favorite unicorn fleece blanket from her room for him. He oohs and aahhs over their Christmas presents while I head to the kitchen to deposit the bags I'm juggling.

"Potato salad," I announce. "And what's left of two pies."

"Good Christmas?" Mike asks over his shoulder, stirring his gumbo in an enormous old Magnalite turkey roaster.

"Yeah, not bad," I say, reaching to hug Jackie where she sits on one of the stools at the island. She's all baby belly now, a month until her due date. Still glowing, still smiling. "Don't get up, how are you?"

"Ready to not be pregnant," she laughs. "This one's a drummer, I think."

"Kicker for the Saints," Mike corrects her. He turns from the stove, wiping his hands on his apron, and walks to stand behind his wife, wrapping his arms around her until he has her belly cradled in his hands. "Definitely a boy."

Jackie laughs, hands resting over his. "If not, there's always the next one. Four is a nice, even number."

"Nope, stop it," he groans, shaking his head. "If it's a girl she'll be the best kicker in the NFL."

"How's Luke doing?" Jackie asks, patting Mike's hands. "We heard it got scary there for a minute. You must've been going out of your mind."

I note that bit of information. Of course I let them know about Luke's surgery, but not how the whole event started. But Adam, he knew. *Great.* I guess he talks to Mike now. This thing between us sure got.... entangled quickly. The friends and family are all up in this.

"Restless from having to take it easy, but he's pretty much recovered."

"Youth," Mike snorts and the three of us nod to this universal truth.

"There he is," Jackie says as Luke joins us. His eyes go wide at the sight of her, not having seen her since August. "Give me a hug, darlin'. We were so worried about you."

"Please don't have that baby today. I really want this gumbo," he jokes.

Before long we're all settled in. Jackie, Mike, and Luke on the large u-shaped sofa in front of the game, Jackie's feet elevated with a pillow, tray balanced precariously on her belly. Poppy is nearby at a toddler sized plastic table and chair, happily slurping up her dinner, dipping saltines into her bowl. I'm at the kitchen island, Grace on my lap, watching the game over their heads while I take turns feeding myself and blowing on her small spoon to cool off her gumbo before she takes a bite.

The doorbell interrupts this cozy scene, and Grace does a startled hop in my lap. Mike stands, setting his bowl down on the coffee table. "I'll get it," he says, giving Jackie a look. The sort of look married people have that contains an entire conversation. Her eyes dart to me then quickly away. He pats her foot as he passes.

Poppy jumps from her chair. "I'll get it, Daddy!" she cries, scrambling to get ahead of him.

"Wait, wait, wait," he calls, reaching for her as they head down the hall. "What did we say? No answering the door without Mommy or Daddy, right Poppy? Poppy?"

"Come on!" she commands.

There's commotion at the door. A deep, unmistakable voice separates itself from Poppy's giggles and Mike's greeting, a cruise missile aimed right for me, locking in on my pounding heart like in those movie-style red crosshairs. I snap my attention to Jackie, who gives me a weak, guilty smile, then Adam is in the kitchen, Poppy chattering in his arms, packages hanging from his hands. His expression tells me he's as surprised to see me as I am to see him.

Wearing a loose gray sweater that I'm guessing is cashmere, faded jeans, black boots, and a good two weeks' worth of scruff on his face, he's as sexy as ever. I, on the other hand, am in an over-sized bright green hoodie that I like to wear for the holidays, and old saggy leggings. Big wool socks. Half my dirty hair haphazardly scraped back from my face with a clip. I look like a big green M & M. With gumbo stains.

"Hi." I mouth the word more than say it. *Is anyone else feeling short of breath*? I wonder.

"Hi," he says back, a small, cautious smile lifting the corners of his mouth.

That's all we get before Poppy puts one small hand to his cheek, pulling his attention to her. "Who are the presents for?" she demands.

He gives her an exaggeratedly confused look. "Presents? What presents?"

"Adddaaam," she draws his name out. "I can see them!"

"Ohhh, you mean *these* presents," he laughs, lifting the bags in his hands as if seeing them for the first time. He sets her on her feet, holding out the two large gift bags.

"Go on, honey" I say to Grace, helping her slide from my lap. She toddles over to Adam shyly.

"What do you say, girls?" Mike says.

"Thank you, Adam," they chime in unison in that adorable

little girl sing-song way, dragging the bags over to the Christmas tree.

Adam steps to Jackie at the sofa. "Merry Christmas pretty mama. How you feeling?"

"A teeny, tiny bit pregnant, you know?"

"Hardly noticeable." He holds out a plastic Buc-ee's grocery bag to her. "Excuse the wrapping."

"Oh, you shouldn't have." She digs in the bag as the girls start squealing, jumping up and down, having unwrapped their gifts. Cute fuzzy animal sleeping bags. "Is this? Oh Lord yes, yes you should have. Thank you! Fudge *and* Beaver Nuggets." She grabs his arm, declaring with mock earnestness. "You really get me, Adam. I feel so seen. How do you do it?"

He laughs. "House full of sisters. Merry Christmas."

"Thank you," she says again, looking pointedly at me. "You're a special, special man."

Good grief.

I look away, but then hear Luke's voice and snap my eyes back in their direction just as he's standing. He stretches his tall frame with an arch of his back, bringing himself up to his full height, shoulders back. I've seen him do this sort of greeting before with other men, literally measuring himself up to them. He's an inch or so taller than Adam. He extends his hand, looking Adam right in the eyes, just like his father taught him. My heart does a weird squishy thing, like a sponge twisting then springing open to wring pride throughout my whole being.

"Hey, I'm Luke. Luke Theriot."

Adam shakes his hand. "Luke, good to meet you. I'm Adam."

It's a small thing, a handshake. This handshake. But I know it for what it is, two worlds colliding. I stand abruptly. I'm not even aware I do until I feel eyes upon me. Adam and Luke are looking at me. Jackie is looking at me. I feel Mike looking at the back of my head.

"Mom, you okay?" Luke asks, breaking the silence.

"Um, yeah, honey. I just... um..." I'm at a complete loss.

Everyone is still staring, Luke the only one in the dark. He looks at me expectantly, innocently.

"Sweetie, will you take this tray for me please?" Jackie asks him, coming to my rescue.

"I got it," Adam says, bending to grab the tray. "Luke, you getting seconds?"

"More like thirds," Luke grins. "You better get in there."

"There's plenty!" Mike calls from his place at the stove.

And there they are, my son and my... my what? My was for ten seconds but I don't know about now boyfriend? Walking together into the kitchen, chatting away, Luke smiling like he's meeting a celebrity, which I guess he is.

I avoid eye contact with Adam and move to the sofa to sit beside Jackie. "Thanks a lot," I hiss.

"I'm sorry. Mike invited him. He told me not to say anything." She holds out the open box of fudge. I pick a piece then she pops one into her mouth. "He's a romantic."

"With Luke here?"

"You didn't want them to meet?"

"I don't know. I've been trying to figure that out." I glance over to the guys, and her eyes follow mine. It's a gaggle of male-ness, the three men taking over the kitchen island.

Luke looks really happy. It's easy to forget how he missed this with his dad, bonding as a man, not a boy. How he must be hungry for it. It's partly why he gravitates to Mike - I need to remember that I'm grateful to Mike for that. It's a reason I love him and should not murder him.

Jackie catches my frown. "They seem to be hitting it off." She's right but I stubbornly don't want to agree with her because my hand was forced, the decision pushed upon me. "You had some sort of fight?" she ventures.

"I don't know what you'd call it," I sigh. "I don't know if we're going to keep seeing each other."

"You what?!" she says a little too loudly, causing the guys to look in our direction. "Yay! She brought pie... I love pie." she calls out to them in a cheer, improvising.

Mike stands, ready to fulfill her every wish. "You want some sweetheart?"

"Later, yes I do, so don't y'all eat it all, okay?" All three men nod in unison, then go back to their conversation.

Satisfied we no longer have their attention, Jackie shifts to her side, stuffing a pillow between her knees. She whispers, "What in the f-u-c-k are you talking about? He seems head over heels for you. Did he do something horrible?"

I shake my head.

"He doesn't want a relationship, is that it? He's moving back to L.A?" I shake my head again. "Oh my God, what? Because unless that man has a harem of groupies locked up in his apartment or owns ten thousand ceramic clowns I can't think of a reason why you wouldn't bag that buck my friend. He's perfect for you."

"It's not him. It's me. I—"

Grace climbs onto the sofa, dragging her new sleeping bag, wedging herself between Jackie's legs and the back cushions. "Mama," she murmurs.

"Hi, pumpkin," Jackie coos, reaching to stroke Grace's hair.

Half-time over, the guys move to the sofa, carrying their food. Mike squeezes in between me and Jackie. I give him the stink eye, but he pretends not to notice. Luke sits on my other side, and I tuck my legs under my body, angling myself in his direction. Adam gets the left side of the sofa to himself, with Poppy sprawled out on the floor. Occasionally I feel his eyes on me. When we do make eye contact, he smiles, his expression neutral.

I don't feel neutral. I feel high tension, amazed that everyone around us can't feel it too, or hear it like bees buzzing in a jar. But everyone is into the game, until it gets boring in the fourth quarter, and one by one they all drift off to sleep.

I pick up the dishes scattered around the coffee table and bring them into the kitchen. Standing at the sink, my back to the living room, I know when Adam rises from the sofa. My body tracks his body, awareness fizzing under my skin. I turn my head, intending to tell him *not here, this is not the time or place,* but he's not walking my way. He's heading into the hallway.

Is he leaving? Was he going to just leave?

He holds up his vibrating phone, the screen lit up. He motions to the door, whispering, "I'm taking this outside. Can we talk?"

CHAPTER FORTY-NINE

ADAM

I END my call just as Holly walks onto the porch and sees me sitting in my car down the driveway. As she trots down the steps, I climb out and lean against the door to wait for her.

A month without seeing her. We're yards apart, and I can count the rhythm of her breathing, see the rise and fall of her shoulders, my chest and hips mapping from memory every curve and swell of her body. My eyes go to the skin of her neck, just below her ear, and the wispy blonde strands that have fallen from her clip. I want my lips there. I badly want to hold her, yet I'm certain I can't touch her. Not here.

But she walks right into my arms, burying her cheek into my chest, and I hug her tightly. We stand like this until the energy changes, as it always does with us. She burrows in closer, her hands at my back, pressing her body into mine. Relieved, I lean down to kiss her, but she pulls out of my arms, looking over to the house. With a small shake of her head, she takes another step back from me.

Fucking hell.

She clears her throat. "Everything okay... with the phone call?"

"My mom. She had an episode when I brought her back to her place this morning. She got confused about where she was, really agitated. They were calling to give me an update."

"I'm sorry, that's got to be wrenching. Is she alright?"

"For tonight, seems to be."

"And you? How are you?"

I look past her to the house. "Luke seems to have recovered

well. I like him. I'm glad I got to meet him, although I don't think you are."

"Adam..."

I shift my gaze back to her. She looks tired. She's been tense since I walked into Mike's.

"I didn't orchestrate this. I didn't know you were going to be here. Mike conveniently forgot to mention it."

"I know."

"But what I can't understand is why it would be such a bad thing. Why is this suddenly so... off? Why wouldn't you be happy to see me?"

"I am happy to see you. I've missed you."

I wave an arm at the distance between us. "I can tell."

"This is not the way for me to have this conversation with Luke."

"All these weeks, you've not said anything to him about me? Nothing?" Her silence is her answer.

I might as well have been blasted with a shotgun to the chest. The hurt is instant, and it makes me furious. I bang a fist on the car door. "What the fuck is happening? Baby, can you talk to me? Tell me how in the hell we got here, please, because I thought we were making plans together. And then, one phone call... I understand being careful with your son, but he's fine now. And he's not a kid; he's old enough, smart enough to know his mother would eventually have another man in her life."

"This isn't about Luke."

"Then what is it about?" I shout in frustration. "Can you explain this to me? How something wonderful went straight off a goddamned cliff?"

"Keep your voice down," she hisses, looking over her shoulder again.

"You said you wouldn't shut me out, so start talking, or I'm going to lay on the horn until the entire parish hears us."

"I can't un-know what I know!" she snaps, throwing her hands up.

"What does that mean?"

She starts pacing, gesticulating, tearing at her hoodie. "Adam, I've tried to tell you. I don't know if I can do this again. These feelings... they're terrifying. My life was burned to the ground, I barely survived, and it's been so hard to get back up, to reclaim a little bit of peace and stability. I've gone to hell and back for... for caring for someone, and I'm sorry. I can't un-know what I know, what I've lived.

"I wish I was stronger, but I don't know if I'm ready to go where you want to go. I don't know if I'd survive again. My heart is damaged, I wouldn't recover. That's the truth. Another loss could kill me. I wish, more than anything, God how I wish I could have amnesia, take a pill and forget all of it. Give you everything you deserve. But I don't know if I can. I don't know if what I can give you will ever be enough for you."

"I'm a risk for you? We're back to this again? I'm not a cheater. *I'm not him.*" I push off the car, squaring off.

"That's what you just heard? What I'm saying is you want everything right now, on your timetable, on your terms. In your house, on your tour—"

"I can't change the music business for you, Holly. I have to tour. I've been honest with you about that, what *that* cost *me.*"

"And I heard you. Your life is what it is. You have no plans to change. I get it. That's your right, to be clear about what you want." She points a finger at me, she's pissed. "My right is the same. To decide if and when I want to change my life. That's all I'm saying. This is about me. My life. Because when I'm in, I'm all in, and I'm not willing to make such a gamble, after all I've been through, on anyone's timetable but my own. I will not be pushed."

We're staring each other down now, eyes flaming with anger.

"You said you were mine, and I believed you. Do you remember? When I asked if I could have you. Did you mean it? Do you have any feelings for me at all, or was this really only ever about sex?"

She makes a face like she's swallowed something vile. I've hurt her. I see it cross her features. The shock crumples her. Her hands come to her chest, over her heart, her eyes filling with tears. I hate seeing it so much I wish she'd hit me. I wish we could find a different way through this conversation. If she would just let me hold her.

I reach for her, but she takes another step away from me.

"How can you think…?" she cries out hoarsely, the sentence dying in the air. She shakes her head. "If you listened to me, you'd know… you'd be patient. I am trying…"

"I am listening to you. I've been patient. I just don't see why we can't work through this together. Why do you have to push me away?"

"Mom?" We snap our heads in the direction of Luke's voice. He's standing on the porch. "Are you okay?"

"Yeah, honey, we're just finishing up a little studio business." Her voice is falsely cheerful, transparently so. He eyes us curiously, uneasily. "Go on inside, I'll be right there."

After a long moment of hesitation, he reluctantly goes back into the house. Holly's eyes stay on the closed door, her breathing ragged. When she turns to me, her expression is haunted, all her defenses down. She's done. She's given up. It nearly brings me to my knees.

"You said you loved me. Did you mean that, or was that just about sex?"

Fuck. I wasn't sure if that actually happened. If I said it out loud that night or if it was just in my head, but she makes it sound like an ultimatum. I still don't understand how this is happening.

I reach for her. I have to, and this time she doesn't resist. I take her face in my hands. "I did mean it. You know I did. I'm in love with you." I kiss her. "I love you. Sweetheart, please don't give up. This is right; *we're right*. You know it. I know you're afraid, but I'm here. We can walk through this together. I love you."

I kiss her again, hoping to show her everything in my heart, everything we could be. She wraps her arms around my neck, melting into me, and I deepen the kiss, my heartbeat pounding loudly in my ears.

Hold on. That urgent message screams in my head. *Hold on. Don't let go.*

That's what I'm thinking when she sobs into my mouth, tearing herself away from my embrace. She wipes a hand across her lips, her face scrunched in pain.

"I'm sorry," she chokes out on another sob. "I'm so sorry."

And she walks away.

CHAPTER FIFTY

No regrets.

Who are those people? Because I've never managed it. I can look back over my life and go right to lots of mine. I've revisited and replayed them so many times they are dog-eared for quick and easy reference. The things I should or shouldn't have said or done.

I think most of the no regrets crowd simply don't look back. That's what they really mean. It's not that they've never royally fucked up, tumbled down a metaphorical staircase, because they have. They just don't bookmark it and return to it time and again like a favorite vacation destination or a movie they're compelled to watch every time it appears on the big screen of their memory. They find new places. They change the channel.

Perhaps it's admirable, these non-ruminators. I've managed it a few times. It feels good to toss regret over your shoulder and leave it there. However, although it likely says something unflattering about my character, I find this mostly a highly irritating trait. These are not my people. My people hang on. We absolutely ruminate.

It's been more than two months since Adam and I last talked. Since he told me he loved me and I knew I had to let him go. And, plot twist, it's also been more than two months since I last cried. Those tears I found so tedious, so beyond my control? Gone. All dried up.

Now, to be real, I cried from the minute I walked away from him until the sun came up the next morning. Sobbed. Snot nosed, eyes swollen crying.

I waved off an alarmed Jackie as she asked what happened

while Mike rushed outside as if he'd just been left. Thankfully, the girls were asleep, so I didn't have to make up an excuse for them, but no such luck with Luke. After I sent him inside, he watched through the window. Saw us kissing. Saw me pull myself from Adam's embrace and race up the driveway. Saw the look on my face when we got into the car and I found the ring box on my dashboard, tied with a gold ribbon, and hastily stuffed it into my purse without explanation.

I told him we'd gone on a few dates, but it wasn't meant to be. Nothing more than that. No big deal.

"Then why are you so upset?" he asked.

"Ah, well, this?" I motioned to my tear-streaked face. "This is... he's a nice man, he just wants more than I can give right now, and I'm sad. But I'll be okay, honey."

"He wants to be your boyfriend, or something? He wants to wife you up?"

Wife? Adam wouldn't give me that kind of ring right now. Would he? What a colossal mess I made of something that was supposed to be simple.

"I wish you'd marry someone like him. He's awesome. Why wouldn't you like him?"

"I do like him, he's wonderful." I sniffled, swiping at my nose with my sleeve.

"Then what's the problem? You're going to meet another Adam Sexton? On your next trip to Costco?"

"Forgive me, but I'm not having this conversation with you, Luke."

"I don't see why not. Dad and I talked about it."

This was news to me. "You and Dad? You talked about what?"

"He said you'd fall in love with someone one day, and it shouldn't scare me, or make me sad, because you were very picky. He said you only went for the best of the best."

We both laughed, me through tears and Luke's eyes gone misty. "Dad said this to you?"

He nodded, and I reached over and rubbed his shoulder. It's beautiful and strange to see him like this, in the body of a man, big and strong, protective of his mother, moving into adulthood yet still with some innocent sweetness of a boy.

"He said when you found someone, he hoped I'd be happy for you because it was what he wanted. For you to be happy. That you deserved it, and it would be good for both of us. And he hoped I'd marry a girl one day who was as good to me as you were to him."

Well done, Ronnie.

I had to pull the car over and hug him. Then we mutually decided the only thing to do was get chocolate milkshakes from Borden's, his dad's favorite.

And that was it. After that first long night of crying, the tears disappeared.

It was a relief at first. A sign I'd done the right thing, setting Adam free. Luke went back to school and I dived into work, into my routines. *See.* I told myself. *Back to normal. Isn't this much better, in the long run? I can be happy like this. Peaceful, calm, and happy.*

After about a month, the comfort of my routines began to feel less peaceful and more... empty. Boring. I found myself staring into space, chin on hand and work abandoned, thoughts lost to absolute nothingness. No crying, no wailing, just a big old empty internal warehouse. The old me who loved those routines, she seemed like someone I didn't know anymore. The old me didn't fit.

This is when it became nearly impossible to keep thoughts of Adam at bay.

I picked up my phone to text him. Stared at it constantly, wondering if he missed me, if he was ever tempted to call. I would get mad he hadn't called, hadn't texted, then remind myself that I broke up with him. I hurt him, and I was trying to keep from hurting him more. I told myself this would pass. I'd feel better. I hadn't let it go too far, after all. It was for the best. I knew it. Or

I'd eventually know it. This was a recoverable, survivable situation for both of us. That was my whole point of ending things, after all.

I tried to stay busy. I called friends and had lunches, went to plays and estate sales and exercise classes. I went to the dentist – I *hate* the dentist – but thought an hour of laughing gas might do me good. I started my taxes. I took the racks out of the oven and scrubbed them in the driveway. I cleaned out the refrigerator in the studio. Exhausting myself daily, all so I might fall into a dead, dreamless sleep at night. Waiting to wake up and be over him.

But he'd creep back in.

Well, more like I hunted and gathered him back in.

His songs popped up more frequently on my playlist, my algorithm reading my mind. Or my search history, because I took to watching videos of him on *YouTube.* Psychotically, I ordered the hair wax he uses, dipping my fingers in it, smelling it, placing it on my bathroom counter as if he'd have to come back for it. A shadow would pass outside the kitchen window and my heart would leap, expecting him to walk through the door. I longed for him during the night. And in the morning.

That ring box, though, that I never opened. I couldn't deal with that.

I was sure Mike was in touch with him. One day I broke down and asked, "Have you talked to Adam? How's he doing?" Still mad at me about it, the traitor, he wouldn't answer. Just mutely shook his head and shrugged.

We had a temporary thaw when Jackie had the baby, another healthy baby girl, and I sided with him when he wanted to name her Bonham, after the drummer. "You could call her Bonnie," I suggested. Jackie was unconvinced. Little Maria Belle is already adored by her big sisters.

Here's what else I did.

I burned that journal. Page by page, tossed it into the fire pit. And I spent the better part of two weeks cleaning out the office. Repainted it and ordered a new desk and shelves from Ikea. I kept a few photos and things, but most everything of Ronnie's went to Luke's room, down to the studio, or was boxed away and shifted to the attic.

None of it worked.

If anything, the low hum of Adam's presence in my head grew to a hammering, relentless ache. My head hurt, my stomach hurt, my whole body was rebelling. My vagina was mad at me too, shouting slogans into a bullhorn and waving flags of protest. I was miserable. No amount of distraction could cover up this truth.

Adam confessed to me his fear, that night in his bathtub, and it's exactly what I did to him. The anguish on his face the last time I saw him haunts me.

But didn't I do the right thing? He said he loved me. How could I keep him if I wasn't ready to say it back? Didn't know when I'd ever be ready. Didn't I tell him I was scared, warn him about my brokenness?

I just need time. Time to shake this off. Shake *him* off. Right? Time heals, as the saying goes.

But as the song says, sometimes so does sex.

Fucking hell. What have I done? What do I do?

I don't know. I don't know. I don't know.

I miss him so much by the time Mardi Gras rolls around that he's become a taste in my mouth, metal and whiskey at the back of my throat making me crazy. I can't get away from it. From him.

I finally break when I find myself scrolling online for local rescue dogs to adopt. I do not need a pet. If I was going to get a pet, I might as well get a man.

I book a hotel room in Orange Beach, throw random clothes and wine into a bag, and hit the road. I cannot sit here, staring at the walls. I'll try what those no regrets people do and change my scene, turn the page. I'll figure out what to do.

I'll find some sort of sign.

CHAPTER FIFTY-ONE

HOLLY

THE RAIN STARTS before I reach Baton Rouge. It's torrential by the time I'm in New Orleans. I wonder if he's there but then remember he's got a show in Boston. I saw that on his website. Because, yes, I've checked his website.

When I pass through Mobile, I fight the impulse to head straight for The Grand, see if our room is available, but know that even if it was, aside from the fact I probably don't have that much room on my credit card, I don't need to do that to myself.

After I check into my hotel, thunderstorms keep me inside for the afternoon. I sit on the balcony, watching the waves lunge against the shore until a dramatic bolt of lightning flashes across the sky, sending me scurrying inside with the hair on my arms standing on end.

Rooting around in my purse for a hair tie, at the very bottom I find the ring box from Adam, the gold ribbon a little squished. Unopened, after all this time. That surely hurt him, not to hear from me about it, no thank you or offer to return it. Or has he moved on? Has it even crossed his mind? This, all of it, pains me.

I place the box on the desk and stare at it. I don't know how I've been able to resist for all this time. I wish I could ignore ice cream with this much iron will. But I know when I do open it, I'll be unable to resist reaching out, and I don't want to do that until I know what I want to say, until I'm prepared for whatever his response will be.

When that will be, who knows? It's been this long, and I haven't found the courage. This ring is the last thing keeping the door between us open, one final opportunity before it's likely slammed shut for good.

I need some clarity, some sort of sign from the universe.

There's less than an hour of daylight left when it stops raining, and I look up from my laptop. I've been searching for love songs and drinking – yay for mental health! I bundle up, heading outside to the beach.

Inky blue storm clouds move fast and low over the waves, the surf crashing loudly, the wind blowing in gusts that rip at my scarf. The wildness matches my mood perfectly and there are few other walkers out this evening, a rarity on such a popular beach even this time of year.

Head down against the wind, nose and ears stinging, the cold sand moving under my feet, I root myself in these elements. The roar of the ocean pans through my inner monologues, sifting and sorting until one by one they are swept away.

What do I want?

For this next part of my life, what do I want? That's the question left for me to answer when all else is brushed aside.

That, and one other obvious question I've not considered before.

When it occurs to me on this walk, I'm surprised it wasn't one of the first things I asked myself when I found that stupid journal. But it comes to me now with an emphatic *thwack*, landing in my mind with the force of an arrow pinning a note to a tree.

What would I have done if I'd found the journal when Ronnie was alive? Would I have divorced him, or would I have stayed?

The surf catches me off guard, and I leap away, skittering back from the incoming tide. I pull my sweatpants, wet now at the ankles, up to my knees.

What would I have done?

Would I really have left him? Regardless of how long ago things happened or any of the details, would I have been angry enough, foolish enough, brave enough – whatever enough – to walk away?

In the middle of this tumult, literally on shifting sands, I admit to myself that it's possible. Unlikely, but possible.

And if I entertain this possibility, then I must ask, as a divorced woman, would I have dated again? Would I have looked for love? Would the pain of that betrayal, when I had agency to do something about it, been any different from this grief that has left me bereft and hollow, and - don't tell Jackie or Madeline - languishing?

The answer flashes in my head with a *ding ding ding* of a game show win.

Yes. I can imagine that yes, under those circumstances, a person with half their life left to live might not want to do that alone. A person might take that terrifying leap of faith and fall in love again, risk getting hurt again, if they met someone special. Someone wonderful.

I double over, hands on my knees, the insight clanging in my chest. Oh my God. I wrote this script. All the things I did to get through the years after Ronnie died, to coach and console myself, when it got down to the last, worst part, detaching the final bits of sinew binding me to him, it had been too painful to let go. Too scary. I clung to this illusion of predictability, of stability, even when I was craving connection.

I threw myself at Dr. Narula. Threw myself at Adam. My body, my spirit, was a flower fighting its way through my grief, searching for a crack in the sidewalk. Yearning to feel alive.

In this world of billions of people, I met someone kind and caring, sexy and fun. Someone perfectly wonderful, and I let him go in the name of safety and self-preservation because I was hurt and scared, my emotions supposedly protecting me but in reality, blinding me.

I walked away from the wrong man.

Raindrops begin to fall, then a tremendous clap of thunder booms overhead. I look up into the raging, darkening sky. Was that my sign? A rebuke of sound and fury for my foolishness?

"Was that my sign?!" I yell into the air, laughing at the horrible absurdity of it all.

I walked right by it at first, the universe's answer to my question.

With my head covered to ward off the rain, convinced I'm going to be struck by lightning at any minute, it's a wonder I saw it at all. But some shout of exclamation went off in my head and I whipped around and there it was, carved in twenty-four-inch block letters in the sand, as clear as any sign could be:

CUNT

I screamed with laughter, shouting deep from my belly into the night. It was the kind of joke Ronnie loved. The one word he knew would get my attention.

I stood watch over my sign, ridiculously filled with joy and tears at the madness of it all, waiting for the encroaching tide to carry it away. Watching the letters erode, waves excising the message from the sand, it was a cleansing, a last rites to reset my perspective.

Take the hint. Lay your burden down, cunt.

Maybe it's too late but I know what I want.

Adam. I want Adam.

I make a run for it. For about twenty yards, until my lungs feel like they're going to explode. I walked way farther than I realized. By the time I've staggered back to my hotel, I'm soaked through. And filled with a giddy serving of hope.

CHAPTER FIFTY-TWO

ADAM

"That's a sixty-eight Fender, not a fucking cigar box," I bark at this new guitar tech when I leave the stage. "If you don't know how to handle it, don't fucking touch it."

Benny appears and taps the tech on the shoulder, wisely keeping his mouth shut, and I pass the guitar to him. He knows to leave me alone. I don't stop for anyone, just put my head down and go straight to my dressing room.

"Why are you still here?" I huff to Gretchen, slamming my door. She's sitting with her feet propped up on a coffee table, playing solitaire on her phone.

Eyes on her screen, she says dryly. "Good show."

"Fuck all the way off." I walk into the bathroom.

"I'm here so you don't blow off another meet and greet like you did last weekend when I went back to the hotel instead of babysitting you."

Ignoring her, I lift the lid of the toilet. It takes only seconds for her to yell.

"Jesus, Adam, close the door!"

This makes me smile, bitterly, at the memory. Another memory of *her*. "How about you get the fuck out and close the door behind you."

"You don't have to be such an asshole, you know. Just call her, please. I'm begging you. We're all begging you. Call her and work this mess out."

Ignoring this for the millionth time, I wash my hands and go back into the room, grabbing my bag. "I'm not doing the meet and greet. Tell 'em I need vocal rest or whatever. We'll refund the money, and I'll cover it. Cut a check to the charity." I root around for my phone. "I'll text Benny. He'll cancel the damn thing. I think he still remembers who he works for."

She stands, wearily. "If you want to be miserable, fine; be a dick to everyone, fine. But it's in your contract, so you are going to march your sorry ass out there and do it."

I don't answer. The air has left my body, my heart imploding.

"Let's go," she says, walking to the door. "Adam!" she turns back when I don't move. "Adam, brother, I swear, I will kick your —" She stops when she sees my face. I'm staring at my phone. "What's wrong? Is it mom?"

"It's her." I hold out my phone to show her. Six missed calls, one voicemail, a string of texts. Blindly shuffling to a chair, I begin scrolling through the messages.

HOLLY

I'm so sorry will you ever forgive me? Can we talk? Please

She's sent me two songs. "Reconsider Me" by Margaret Lewis. "True Devotion" by Kristin Diable.

Please. I'm sorry. So very sorry.

I miss you. Adam, I love you

Please call me

The screen goes blurry, and I swipe at my eyes.
She loves me.
"What does she say? Is it good or bad?" Gretchen asks, her hand on my shoulder.

I'm laughing, chest shaking, hand over my heart. I press play on the voicemail, putting it on speakerphone. Her voice, the voice I love, the voice I've longed to hear for months, the voice that walks through my dreams, the voice of the woman who *loves me,* is breathless and a little slurred, speaking in broken sentences:

"Adam, I... um... I wanna be a flower - your flower. I've been so scared... and stupid... you might not want to talk to me... the beach called me a cunt tonight if that makes you feel any better... I shouldn't have said I love you in a text... shit... but I do. I love you. I love you. You deserve to hear it. Maybe you don't want to hear it? From me? I... I opened the present tonight, the ring..."

"What?" Gretchen gasps, and I shush her.

"Not that kind of ring."

"I can't believe you did that, well, I can, that's who you are... I love it. I'm wearing it now, remembering our first weekend. Really fabulous... sex weekend... I'm gonna wear it forever... unless you want it back, maybe you want it back? I'll understand if you do... remember what that sweet old guy said, the thing about clarity? Love and clarity... right? Our swans..."

She sighs and stops talking. Gretchen and I exchange looks. Is she finished?

Holly sighs heavily again, tears choking her voice. *"I thought it would be better this way... I really did, please know that... do the right thing... let you go... I just... I can't do it. Adam, I can't do it anymore. I love you more than I'm afraid... so much more. If there's a chance you could still love me, please, call me. I'm here, I'm in love with you... and if you don't want me... if you never... oh God, please, don't let that be... please... but I wanted you to know. I love you. I'm yours, if you'll have me. I... I love you."*

"About time," Gretchen beams at me, flicking my head.

"Are you crying?"

"No," she laughs, wiping her face on her shoulder. "I'm just allergic to all this drama. What was that about a flower? Some weird hetero sex thing?"

I stand and hug her, both of us sniffling. "You gotta get me home tonight. Figure out where she is and get me there."

CHAPTER FIFTY-THREE

HOLLY

AFTER A SHOWER, I hang my sweatpants up to dry because, turns out, I packed two bottles of wine and no other pants. I pull a sweater on over a t-shirt and climb into bed. Turning to the back of my love song notebook, I begin writing.

I tell Ronnie all the things I loved about him and everything I'm angry about. I forgive him and ask him to forgive me for all the ways I fell short. I get a little weepy at times and crack myself up at times. In a bittersweet way, it's almost fun - a deep conversation with a long-lost dear friend. He's in the room with me. I can feel him, hear his voice. Tonight, all these years after his passing, we know this is goodbye.

Letting him go - I'd been trying to do that for so long. Dreading it, angry about it, afraid to do it, but finally, I know it's time to let him rest. Not to forget him or cut him out of my heart – I'll always love him, always check in with him - but it's time to let him have his peace. And find mine. Give myself permission to not be in a relationship with him any longer.

I'm deep into the second bottle of wine by about eight. Bolstered by rosé, I pick up my phone and, ordering my pride to jump out the window, I begin texting. Then it occurs to me Adam's still on stage. If I called, he wouldn't have the opportunity to decline. I could leave a message. Which I do.

I think I rambled, maybe I begged? But I put my heart out there for him.

I keep checking my phone, calculating when his show should be over, when he'd be back in his dressing room. I even carry my phone with me when I go to the bathroom. Half an hour, then an hour clicks by. There was a meet and greet, I tell myself, when he hasn't responded.

Madeline texts me a little after eleven. Which for her, in her time zone, is after midnight. And she's an early to bed, early to rise woman.

MADELINE
Where are you right now?

Orange Beach, why?

Just checking in. Everything okay?

Yes and no – You okay? You're up late

Yes and no

Maybe I'll join you – hotel and room number?

This is strange and random, but I know she's been worried. I send her the details.

🩶 Here til Sunday if you can make it. Would love it.

You might just get a surprise visitor

Another hour passes. I'm in knots, sure he's seen my messages by now, all the reasons why he hasn't responded racing through my mind. Maybe he's thinking about what to say. Maybe it's too late, and he doesn't care anymore. I went too far. I sounded too desperate. I'm too damaged and neurotic for him.

Maybe he's already moved on, has someone new with him in his dressing room. Like I'd been with him not long ago. That one killed me.

By two a.m. I know it's over. My heart doesn't want to believe it, but I feel it breaking. Sliding the balcony door open, I lie in bed listening to the rhythmic low hum and crash of the ocean, a metronome of sorrow, sorrow I caused myself. I weep, truly weep, at the idea of never seeing Adam again, never holding him again.

If only...

I stop that line of thought. I'm not going to punish myself for my grief, for my stumbles as I navigated my way. Not for any of it. And I'm not going to tell myself I'll never get over this, never recover. No more of that script. That's done. I screwed up, and Adam will be a difficult regret to get over, another wound to my heart, but I'll own it and I'll endure. I know that now, without a doubt. That's something I can take away from this, and it's not a small something.

But still, I'm wrecked at what I've done. Absolutely shattered. My sleep is shallow and restless, every part of me aching, anxious dreams tossing and turning me until sunrise, when exhaustion finally pulls me under.

Knock. Knock. Knock.

I pull a pillow over my head because I also forgot to pack my sleep mask.

Knock. Knock. Knock. Who would be knocking? I have the do not disturb sign out for housekeeping.

Oh! Madeline! She wasn't joking. But she would've called me, right? I reach for my phone, squinting at the screen. Eleven fifty. No call.

Knock. Knock. Knock.

As I untangle from the bedding I hear it. Tom Petty, "The Waiting." A stadium of lights fires on in my body all at once. It could only be one person. The person.

Please, please, please, please, please.

I yank open the door. It's him. In all his black t-shirted, scowling, come fuck me glory. He taps his phone to stop the music.

"How did you... how are you here? Did you get my messages?"

"Say it," he demands.

"What?" I'm shaking, my heart pounding so fast I might faint.

"I want to hear you say it." His eyes burn into mine, and I step back from the force of it. He pushes into my room, slamming the door shut with his foot. "Holly, say it to me right now."

"I'm sorry, I'm so sorry..." I stammer, "Please..."

He pulls me into his arms. "Not that, baby. I need you to tell me. Look at me and tell me." His *baby* sings through my soul.

I take his face in my hands. This is it. I'm running to the edge and leaping off that cliff. I want him to leap with me, defying gravity with three elemental, sacred words.

"I love you."

With a deep sigh, his shoulders rise and fall. He studies my face, scanning every centimeter. And I'm able to see the fatigue in his. He's almost... haggard. Has he been as miserable as me? I wait for him to say something.

"Okay," he nods, and turns me loose, heading for the door.

"Adam!" I grab for him, panicked. "That's it? Adam, please, wait, talk to me," I plead, tugging at his shirt. He would come all this way for *that*?

His back to me, he snaps the lock into place. The sound, the rightness of that bolt sliding home, I'll always remember.

He turns to me, that cocky grin I've missed with all my heart, lighting up his face. "We're gonna be here a while, I don't want to be disturbed." He leads me to the foot of the bed, sitting us side by side, taking my hands in his.

"I love you," I say again, lifting our joined hands to kiss his knuckles. "I'm sorry I hurt you... while I figured things out... I can't believe you're here." I'm simultaneously beaming from ear to ear and crying.

"Shhh..." he pulls a hand away to caress my face. "Shhh, no more of that, sweetheart. I'm sorry for letting my own insecurity shit scare you away. I told you I understood how you were feeling, I told you I could take it, could give you time, and I fucked it up. And you were right - I went on autopilot, about my schedule, my place in New Orleans. Same old mistakes. I've been so mad at myself. God, I'm sorry baby. I swear to you, I really, truly swear to you, I want to be yours when you're ready to be mine. Whenever, wherever, however you want that to be. I'm in love with you. I'll do whatever it takes to earn your forgiveness."

Shaking, sniffling, I say, "Thank you, but before you say anything else..."

"What?" He leans forward and kisses me softly.

Shoot. This is a hard one.

"Tell me," He says, stroking a thumb along my cheek, wiping away a tear. I rest my hand on top of his.

"I don't know if I ever want to get married again. Maybe I'll change my mind one day, I have no idea, but I need you to know that. I want to be with you, Adam, I love you. Does your happily ever after have to be marriage?"

Leaning back, he spots the ring he gave me. He tugs at my hand, rubbing his thumb across the carved blue stone. "I love it," I say quietly.

He stares at it, moving it back and forth on my finger as he thinks. "I would like to marry you. I'd marry you today if I could."

"Oh." I'm about to hit the ground at a thousand miles an hour.

"But," he shifts his gaze to me, eyes shimmering with unshed tears, a parachute flinging out from his heart to offer a soft landing. I choke back a relieved sob. He's got me. He will never let me fall. "If you're telling me you're committed, you're in this, that I'm yours and you're mine, I can accept that. I'd consider myself the luckiest man in the world."

"Really? Are you sure?"

You hear that sound? It's Beethoven, or Bach, or Bohemian Rhapsody, every choir singing every ode to boundless, euphoric joy ever written.

"Yes, I'm sure. I just need to ask for something in return." He swipes away another tear from my cheek, then holds my chin firmly. "No more running. Tell me you'll turn to me, talk to me. I need to feel secure about that."

"I give you my word. This has been horrible; I've missed you so much. I never want to feel that way again. I never want to put you - put us - through anything like this again. You're stuck with me now."

With a nod, he seals our pact with a kiss then pins me with those melted chocolate eyes, a mischievous, bemused expression making them sparkle. "And I want to ask you to marry me one day each year. It's fine if you say no, but I want to ask."

"I won't hate that," I laugh. "What day is it today?"

"March seventh."

"Ask me every March seventh."

He slips down onto one knee at my feet, my hands in his. "Holly Theriot, I love you. I will love you and cherish you for the rest of my life. Will you marry me?"

"Adam Sexton, no, I will not." I giggle, leaning forward to kiss him. "But I love you madly."

"Now that that's out of the way," he drawls, getting to his feet. "Let's get to the make-up sex." In one swift motion, he lifts my sweater and t-shirt up and over my head, leaving me in just my panties. Which he removes with the bravado and efficiency of a Las Vegas magician.

"Hotel sex *and* make-up sex," I say, falling onto my back, stretching my arms over my head, displaying myself for him. "I'd say that makes me the luckiest woman in the world."

He pulls his shirt over his head, his eyes raking hungrily over my body. "You're damn sure about to be, sweetheart."

Ah, there's my man. I shudder with anticipation, right before spotting the new tattoo sitting over his heart.

"Adam! Is that—?" I scramble to my knees. "That's my name!"

He looks down at his chest. The swan, in black and white, neck elegantly arched, with intricately shaded feathers, rests in holly leaves, my name written across its body in cursive script. I touch it carefully. "It's beautiful. You can hardly see the scar."

"Gave me something to do while I waited." He tugs off his

boots and socks, then unzips his jeans, dragging them off with his briefs. He's already hard, his cock jutting forward, veined and glistening. He's also clearly done talking.

He eases me onto the bed, and I scooch backwards on my elbows as he crawls forward, hovering over me. Sweeping my leg aside with his knee, staring into my eyes, he claims me in one hard thrust. We both groan at the joining, and I pull his mouth to mine, kissing him deeply.

"I've missed you so much," he kisses down my neck, holding himself still inside me.

"Wait," I push at his chest. "You got my name permanently inked on your body. What would you have done if we never got back together?"

"Wouldn't change the fact that you own my heart. Might as well have your name on it."

"Oh, Adam…" I lift his face, tenderly caressing his cheek. We stare at one another in shared, silent awe that we're here. No vows could ever say more than what we promise in that moment.

Then he grins slyly, lowering his mouth to my breast. "Plus, I knew you'd come back. I mean, look at me."

Laughing, I run my hands through his hair. My cocky, sexy Texas. All mine.

"I guess you could've changed it. Golly. Jolly. Folly—" I stop, gasping as he sucks my nipple and thrusts his hips simultaneously. "Molly… Polly…" he drives into me again, and I lose my breath.

"Just kiss me, baby," he growls. "Tell me you love me."

"Every day," I murmur into his lips. "I love you. You can't see it, but you're written on my heart, too."

EPILOGUE
ADAM

Six weeks later.

Holly in a white sundress is perfection.

We're both sun and sleep and sex drunk from the four days we spent at the resort in Byron Bay. I flew us in early for the Bluesfest, and now we're in the festival's artist catering tent with my band. It's mellow back here, with crew, security, and other musicians quietly settled in, eating at tables or, like us, lounging around the area set up with sofas and chairs. I go on in about an hour. I'm melted, in the best way, more relaxed than I can ever remember.

But fuck, it's a problem, because I'd almost rather be back in one of those poolside cabanas than about to go onstage. She's my new favorite activity.

I've got another week of shows here in Australia, two shows in New Zealand, then we're headed home. I had planned on recording my next record after this, but I gave the time to Jennifer Carson, so when we get back, I'll be in the studio at Riverside with her. I'm in no rush.

I was thrilled when Holly agreed to come with me for this trip. I love having her with me. She's opted out of coming with me to other gigs so far, which gives her the alone time she needs, and me the pleasant anticipation of coming home to a warm and affectionate welcome. I don't dread it like I have so many years before; in fact, I race home now. Sometimes home is my place in New Orleans, sometimes it's her place outside Lafayette. I'm well aware that we're building a new dynamic between us, building a life on terms that work for both of us.

This is the last year of this festival. Another great one closing its doors. Another sign of the changes happening in this business, and I'm reevaluating the next part of my career. And my life. Maybe I'd be anxious - but that gorgeous woman across the room, because of her I'm excited. Excited for something new, excited for change.

I didn't expect that, that all these parts of my life I felt were locked in and settled, nonnegotiable, how I'm now actively seeking ways to shake it all up. It's partly my age, I know, reevaluating priorities in the middle years, but still, it's shocking how fast it happened. From that day we reunited, we've been in sync, life easing into place with a natural flow. She's put fresh batteries into my soul and now the clarity, the energy in my life, is remarkable.

Here's some breaking news: I've been thinking about something Holly said to me, that I needed to do a few things differently if I wanted a different outcome. She's right. And I'm ready. I've told Gretchen to keep my calendar open next year. I'm taking a break.

I knew Gretchen would read me the riot act, come at me with a list of reasons why it was an impossible, stupid idea. She was dead silent on the phone when I told her. I thought maybe she was waiting for me to say "just kidding" or possibly shredding her phone with her teeth, but after a minute all she said, calm as could be, was, "Good idea, bro. Let's make that happen."

Stupefied at the lack of resistance, I had to ask if she heard what I said. Her reply was classic. "Not fucking deaf, Adam."

"Supportive, thanks."

"Just taking a moment of silence to mourn the cranky old bastard my brother used to be. Holly's ready for you to be around that much?"

"I'll still be working, just not traveling. And yes, thanks for that, we'll be fine. She's excited."

"Okay then, give your girl a big, tight hug for me. And bro?"

"Uh-huh?"

"Good job. Seriously, I'm really happy for you. You deserve this."

So, yeah. Taking a year off. And everyone's on board. My family, my band, Benny, Holly. No resistance. Maybe I've been more of a cranky old bastard than I realized.

I haven't had an extended period of time off from touring in about twenty years. Haven't wanted one. But now I have new priorities, and, in truth, my body could use the rest. Hell, if I could, I'd start my year off now and see how many hours a day I can keep Holly naked.

I watch her cross the room, radiant and smiling, oblivious to the admiring glances directed her way. I don't mind. Who wouldn't want her? When her eyes find mine, a smile only I recognize for the dirty promises behind it is lifting the corners of her mouth into a smirk. I sit back and feel like a goddamned sultan. We eye fuck each other as she walks.

Until she reaches into her cleavage and pulls out a cookie, taking a bite with a big goofy wink. I throw back my head and laugh.

I reach for her before she can sit in the chair next to me, pulling her down onto my lap. A small "oof" escapes me as she settles herself across my thighs and I snatch the rest of the cookie from her hand with my teeth. I can't exactly put my hands down her dress here, but I slip a finger under one of the thin straps and kiss the faint tan line on her shoulder.

"Hush," she whispers, squirming in my lap when I nip at her throat. "You love it."

"I do," I murmur into her golden honey hair, drinking in her smell. I can't believe this is my life, that's she's really mine. Every time I hold her like this, I get a shudder down my spine, my past self in awe of my future self.

I've never been one for religion, but when Holly and I were apart, on one of the many sleepless nights when I stared at the ceiling, wondering how in the hell this could be happening, in my misery I started talking to Ronnie. I'm fucking serious. Some would call it a prayer. I'd call it a man-to-man conversation.

Despite that damn journal, the man had life by the tail. I know he'd never have left her. I know he loved her.

I told him she was struggling, she was hurting, and I asked if he could find a way to help her. We both wanted her to be happy, and if she did find her way to me, if she chose me, I promised him I'd give her and Luke everything I had in my power to give. I'd protect them and love them and spend the rest of my time on earth trying to make them happy.

I heard from her two nights later.

Coincidence or manifestation or divine intervention - doesn't matter to me what you call it. I'm grateful, and me and Ronnie, we're good.

I nuzzle my lips under her ear, holding her close. This woman is my dream that came true. Every love song I'll ever write.

Speaking of songs. I have a surprise for her in tonight's show. Gonna play a new one, one I only recently finished. Can't wait to hear what she thinks, see her face. That'll be fun.

She's recently suggested I write a song called "Growl-Purr." Yep. Been spouting out the filthiest lyrics imaginable, non-stop. I think I've managed to do a little better than that. We'll keep the other one just between us.

"Can I get you anything, honey?" she asks, slipping her arms around my neck.

"Mmm, angel, I have everything I need. Absolutely everything."

STEAL AWAY GIRL

STEAL AWAY GIRL…

WE LAY STILL BUT I FEEL MOTION
LEAVING ME SO FAR BEHIND
ONCE THOSE MAGIC DOORS OPEN
I'LL RIDE THAT RAINBOW IN YOUR MIND

(CHORUS)
SO STEAL AWAY GIRL TO YOUR OWN SECRET WORLD
WHERE CLOUDS ARE YOUR PILLOWS
TEARS TURN TO PEARLS
WILL YOU ALWAYS SEE YOUR WAY BACK TO ME
AND REMEMBER YOU WILL ALWAYS BE MY STEAL AWAY GIRL

ARE THOSE HEAVEN'S WHEELS TURNIN'
SOMEWHERE DEEP BEHIND YOUR EYES
SOMEWHERE THERE'S A FIRE BURNIN'
SETS YOU FREE TO SEARCH THE SKIES

(CHORUS)
STEAL AWAY GIRL…

CLOSE ENOUGH TO FEEL YOU BREATHIN'
WE LAY GALAXIES APART
LOVE SWEET SHEETS OR SEVEN SEAS
I SWEAR I'M WITH YOU NEAR OR FAR…

(CHORUS)
STEAL AWAY GIRL…

ACKNOWLEDGMENTS

Dear reader, I'm so delighted you're here! I've wanted to meet you for a long, long time. Thank you for taking a chance on my book - you are making a dream come true. I hope I've delivered an experience worthy of your time and that we meet again soon. If you feel like it, please leave a review where you can or recommend this book to your friends. I'd be forever grateful for your help.

Joe, thank you for the open door to ask all the music questions I wanted. I knew you'd be kind to me, but you were more than kind – which was a level of respect and friendship I deeply appreciate.

Thank you, Denise, for the patient copy editing, even when I stubbornly ignored your corrections or suggestions. Sometimes I choose my own way instead of the right way and you are very sweet about it. Why are commas so damn difficult?! I'll learn. Reader – any errors you find are totally on me. Denise is awesome.

Annabelle, thank you for the wonderful cover! Your design is just the vibe I hoped for and makes me ridiculously happy. I love it. You helped my book feel real, helped it become something I could finally hold in my hands and call *mine* and be proud to share with readers.

I'm a woman blessed to have incredible female friendships – women who have loved me, supported me, advised me, shown up for me, inspired me, laughed and cried with me, and been gentle about my flaws. An over-serving of talented, soulful, smart, fucking hilarious girlfriends. Johanna, Maura, Melissa, Sally. My life is immeasurably richer because of you. I love you all.

Bernadette. My beautiful and kind triple Aries bestie. The one who says YES! GO FOR IT! Creator of beautiful spaces that are my happy places. And now, just when I needed it, professor of all things romance. I thought we'd talked about every single thing two women could ever talk about over decades of friendship, then you went and read everything you could get your hands on and opened doors to new conversations that we likely would otherwise never have opened. I've lost count of all the times you told me to keep going and I could do this and I was good at it, bolstering my confidence, courage, and commitment when I was flagging. Thank you. Positive feedback, *helpful* feedback, endless plot conversations, encouragement when it all seemed to be an overwhelming, out of reach pipe dream. Thank you. You've been there every step of the way. You always are. Thank you. I can't say it enough. Thank you from the bottom of my heart. I love you.

Mom, I'm a reader because of you. Books are my constant companions. My solace, my escape, and my education - what a gift that truly is. I can't recall a day when you didn't have a book in your hand. Ever. Still do. Specifically, always a romance novel. And yes, might as well now confess that over the years I have stolen a few. Even when I pretended to turn my nose up at them. What a beautiful mother-daughter moment when I told you I was writing one and your first and only comment was, "Better have a lot of sex or no one will read it." Umm... thank you? I love you.

Dad, stop asking if you get to read my book. Go read one of mom's books. Thank you for passing along your passion for music, a love that nourishes my life to this day. It's no accident I was voted "Most Likely to Marry a Musician" in college. Thank you for always telling me you're proud of me and for being there when I need you. I love you.

Reuben, darling son. This could have been really awkward. So, you doubled down to make it extra awkward, which is your thing and was totally the right move. Because you made it fun, which is also your thing, and a delicious part of who you are. Thank you for cheering me on, helping me laugh at each rejection, reminding me to stay in the struggle. You have so much more courage than I did when I was your age, and seeing you chase your dreams with such fire in your belly inspires me more than you can know. I love being your mother. I love you.

David, it would be another book to try and say what I'd want to say to you, and even attempting it here has my eyes blurred over in tears. And maybe it doesn't need to be said. We know already. And just as we agreed that you could write about whatever you wanted and I decided only the sweet songs were about me, I've taken my own artistic liberties here. I hope you're laughing, appreciating the fair play. We can talk all about it when we meet again. I miss you. I love you.

ABOUT THE AUTHOR

R. S. Egan is an author of sharp and sexy contemporary romance for modern, mid-life women. A West Virginia native, after a stint working in fashion in New York City, she is now based in South Louisiana, with a career in art sales. She divides her free time between complaining about how other people drive and buying makeup from Instagram reels. It is possible - at the time this is written - she is being held hostage by two ungrateful cats. *They're Playing Our Song* is her debut novel.

Connect with R. S. Egan
www.rsegan.com
@rseganauthor

www.ingramcontent.com/pod-product-compliance
Lightning Source LLC
Chambersburg PA
CBHW031110160726
47991CB00004B/1317